BACKPACKERS

BOOK 2 IN
THE FIREBIRD SERIES

IAN DOLBY

DISCLAIMER:

This is a work of fiction. While names, characters, businesses, events and incidents are the products of the author's warped imagination, places and locales are as correct as possible, but are used in an entirely fictitious manner. Some characters are a composite of several personalities the author has encountered in his travels across Australia as such richness of true-life character could not be ignored. However, any resemblance to actual persons, living or dead, or actual events is unintended, accidental and purely coincidental.

The opinions expressed by the various characters in this story are deemed appropriate for their role and should not be assumed to be those of the author. I ride bikes and embrace the right to freedom of the open road on two wheels for everybody.

Published in Australia by Sid Harta Publishers Pty Ltd,
ABN: 46 119 415 842
23 Stirling Crescent, Glen Waverley, Victoria 3150 Australia
Telephone: +61 3 9560 9920, Facsimile: +61 3 9545 1742
E-mail: author@sidharta.com.au

First published in Australia 2019
This edition published 2019
Copyright © Ian Dolby 2019
Cover design, typesetting: WorkingType (www.workingtype.com.au)

Dolby, Ian
Backpackers
ISBN: 978-1-925230-65-9
pp450

ABOUT THE AUTHOR

I was born and raised on the Gold Coast, Queensland and my love of boats was instilled by the family before I could walk, as indicated by an early photo that shows me crawling around the deck of the family boat in nappies. The love of sailing developed through a series of ever-larger racing catamarans and led to the purchase, at the age of 21, of an old 47-foot wooden, engineless, monohull cutter-rigged yacht that had been built in Ireland in 1905 and taken part in the WWII Dunkirk evacuation. I lived on this boat at a marina in Rushcutters Bay, Sydney Harbour for several years and my engine-free adventures on this wonderful old boat may one day appear in writing.

The love of flying dragged me away from the boating scene, commencing with gliding, which in turn led to the establishment of a commercial gliding school at Narromine, NSW. After six years of gaining valuable flight experience in this successful enterprise, I sold out and undertook the necessary study and flight training to gain both Aeroplane and Helicopter Commercial Licences. After some 38 years and 16,000 hours of mixed Aeroplane and Helicopter flying, I have retired to a country town in New South Wales with my partner and two young cats where I am now relishing the new challenge of full-time writing.

I read that writing becomes a compulsion and as a completely novice writer having finished three manuscripts, I can so totally appreciate that. Two years ago, there was no way I'd have left my comfortable bed at Zero Dark Thirty, especially in the dead of winter, to sit in front of a screen, pecking at a keyboard. Now when the words want to flow, there's no stopping them. Jenny has well and truly given up on trying to feed me at designated times and also just goes with the flow.

*To Jenny for your endless support, love,
more plot suggestions and mugs of tea.*

To my loyal beta-readers who kept pushing me for the next Part because you wanted to know what happens next. You provided the greatest encouragement.

Thank you, Mark. Your character lives on. Again.

Smokey and The Bandit — my early morning companions.

CONTENTS

PROLOGUE

The neat, white-painted cement block building was set back from the access road with a small carpark out front and a larger one out the back. The back one was mostly filled with large, black, expensive motorcycles of American origin. In one corner of the carpark, a three-bay carport sheltered a sidecar outfit consisting of a Harley-Davidson with a highly polished, full-size wood coffin mounted as the chair.

The outfit shared space with a plain white Toyota Camry and a late-model HSV GTS Commodore.

In a conference room inside, 32 men sat around a very large, beautifully polished wood table. Their dress varied from bikie typical grunge to very elegant.

There was no doubt as to who was in charge, a 6' 7" tall, very thin man wearing his trademark black Armani suit, highly-polished black shoes and tie with a crisp white shirt, occupied the head seat at the table.

Without raising his voice over the general conversation, his first words brought instant quiet to the generally unruly group. The tall man looked at his Lieutenant, 'Mr Draper. Please report on the status of the delivery and payment handover of the next shipment.'

A burly man with the looks of a bikie and the brain of a super-computer, looked up from a sheaf of papers. 'Tomorrow afternoon our courier is scheduled to arrive at the Surfers Paradise coach terminal at 14:00. To maintain cover, he has instructions to make his way to, then check-in at the Mariners

Cove YHA before meeting with our Bagman, Mr Wells, for the exchange at 16:00 in the Boathouse Tavern on the wharf nearby.'

'Thank you, Mr Draper. Mr Chen. What have you arranged for security at the meeting, seeing as there will be quite a lot of cash and particularly valuable merchandise in a very public area?'

'We'll have four Enforcers roaming the carpark and another two in the bar area with two female associates for cover. The inside ones will be in street clothes and all will be heavily armed.'

'Thank you Mr Chen, that sounds adequate. However, please consider that we have heard that our erstwhile rivals are aware of the incoming shipment, although they should not know the timing. There's a great deal at stake with this shipment, quite apart from its monetary value, so all Enforcers must be on the lookout for any sign of the Zombies.'

He looked slowly around the room, meeting each set of eyes in turn with his startling, penetrating bright blue ones. 'This is the first time the timing has been mentioned outside of the Executive Committee, so to remove temptation, the Club is in lockdown from now until the delivery is complete tomorrow afternoon.'

Despite his intimidating presence, a muted grumble of discontent ran around the room, until the tall man raised his hand and the talk slowly subsided.

'We've done this before, although it's been when there was a rumble on, but this shipment is too important to our income to take any chances. A supply of cots and inflatable beds are being delivered this afternoon, all meals will be fully catered from an a-la-carte menu and I'm sure there is a plentiful supply of alcohol at hand.'

That raised a few chuckles as the sense of what he had said sank in.

'Thank you for your patience gentlemen. The very large sum of money we've committed to paying for this shipment of experimental, highly concentrated MDMA, could easily be increased 30 times over due to its increased effectiveness and, as I've been led to believe, some side effects that are very attractive to the user. Those side effects should create an expanded market that will in turn increase demand so I anticipate that our business unit will be kept very busy. If there is no further comment or additional business, I declare this meeting closed.'

CHAPTER 1

The humid Gold Coast air, scented with a unique blend of salt mist and pollution, was so dense that one could almost feel it, and seemed a perfect compliment for the soft, purple-tinted dusk that was quietly descending over the dimly-lit marina. For a short time, only a few bird cries disturbed the peace, and certainly nothing so crass as the sound of an engine. At least, that's how it would have been, if it weren't for the droning rattle of Ray's antiquated diesel-fuel pump that always seemed to be about to expire, but still managed to deliver fuel. Although the figures on the counter rarely agreed with the tally on Ray's invoice!

I'm Harry Stevens, an ex-SAS Major and fortunate inheritor of a sizeable fortune courtesy of a wealthy, highly eccentric and delightfully gay uncle who for some inexplicable reason, thought I was a person worthy of his largess. Personally, I always thought Uncle Jack was a wonderfully, wacky old guy, a very talented painter, and very outspoken on all and every subject! He was always marvellously entertaining and totally irreverent, so I missed him terribly when he died in somewhat mysterious circumstances.

As he had lived very modestly in a small, three-bedroom cottage, I'd never had cause to consider his financial state, so it was a shock to be told that not only was he ridiculously wealthy, but that he'd left me everything, his house, investments, bank accounts and the key to a safe deposit box.

At 34 years old, still fit from the Service and moderately attractive to females, after my discharge I'd been just bumming around seeing the country that I'd been away from for too long. I'd also had no clear direction for my new civilian life, living fairly frugally on savings and a rather lean Military pension, until Uncle Jack's will lobbed like a mortar round into my somewhat aimless life. When he finally tracked me down, a smart-arse young Gold Coast lawyer with gelled hair sticking up like a cocky's crest, delivered the details in dry legalese, then immediately after the signing process, wanted me to commit large chunks of my new fortune in a range of wild, money-losing schemes on behalf of his crooked clients.

After telling Larry the sleazebag lawyer to piss off, I'd dug the yellow pages out of the drawer in the tacky 3-star Gold Coast motel I happened to be staying in at the time and called the first accountant listed who looked like he was a sole practitioner. For the second time in a week I'd got lucky in finding Mike Adams, a very switched-on young dude who worked out of the front section of an old house. He and his lovely girlfriend, Eva who was the receptionist, lived in the back half. He impressed the hell out of me at our first meeting by wandering out into reception dressed in shorts, a garish yellow, orange and blue Jimmy Buffet parrot shirt and sandals, looking like an eccentric client rather than the main man.

He had also seemed to treat me the same as any other client despite the crazy numbers the whole estate added up to. Although the old house in a stunning, double frontage beach-front position at Mermaid Beach was worth nearly $4M and the blue-chip bank and mining shares added just over $3M to the pot, it was the safe deposit boxes, hidden from official view that held the greatest surprise.

While the 300 Krugerrands and 74.4 kgs of gold bars fattened the total very nicely, the surprise was in a small, chamois leather bag that contained 20 emeralds of a glorious, deep blue-green hue and as round as my index finger nail. They were round-cut, faceted and to my untutored eye, were flawless.

Amazingly, that was also the opinion of the gemmologist I visited in Brisbane, although I learned that there were always some slight flaws in emeralds, but the inclusions in my stones were very small and almost impossible to see with the naked eye. The colour and clarity was classed as exceptional, while their weights were between 5 to 6 carats each.

The gemmologist got very excited by the collection of virtually perfect emeralds and valued them at about $260,000 each. Which meant that the little bag that hardly bulged my shirt pocket was worth $5.2 million!

Mike officially ignored the contents of the safe deposit boxes and after discussing what I wanted to do with my life, recommended selling the house but to keep the shares for their income, which was steady and quite substantial.

He had additionally endeared himself to me by presenting me with a very modest bill, payable on the spot, which I happily did!

Mike had explained about the delay with Probate, but in hindsight the waiting period gave me time to consider what to do with my life. I cashed in a few Krugerrands and two gold bars to fatten my bank account and rented a small, but neat townhouse on a short-term lease.

After a few months of contemplation and putting on weight, I decided that when I had the house money, I would indulge in something I'd always lusted after, a decent-size catamaran that I could live on and travel with! I thought I knew what I wanted, but until I had sat down with the designer, I realised that I had a lot to learn. Nevertheless, he'd listened to me as well, so in the end, we'd struck a very good compromise. I had wanted a fast boat, but with plenty of room so we had to go big. But to be able to handle a 60ft cat single-handed, required careful planning and took a lot of money to get the best and most suitable gear, although in the end we were both happy and the final result became a benchmark design for the Australian company for single-handed or small crew.

The comfort for myself was taken care of by allocating the

entire starboard hull to me alone! A large, walk-through bathroom and laundry were right aft with my queen sleeping cabin forward with a separate dressing and wardrobe cabin forward of that again. The port hull was the same as my setup forward, but had a double cabin aft with minimal storage space. A compact shower and toilet compartment that serviced the guest side of the boat, sat at the foot of the port companionway, while the saloon held the galley, a nav station and a comfortable, extendable dining area.

The cockpit had the main steering station with a double seat set to port with an overhead hatch for improved visibility in tight quarters, along with a decent table, a sink and 'fridge, thickly-padded bench seats and a few folding chairs that could go inside if needed.

With twin diesels for propulsion, a gen-set, solar panels covering every horizontal surface except for the forward deck, quiet wind-generators and triple water makers, it made me fairly independent, except for fuel and food. The sail setup had a roller furling screecher right forward, a boomed roller-furling inner staysail and a boom-furling main that was electric or manual operation, and meant that I could sail just about anywhere I wanted, saving the engines for bad weather, tight harbours or calms. Twin dagger-boards, raised or lowered from the cockpit, made sailing much more efficient and reduced the boat's draft to just 22 inches and let me sneak into places no other boat could go.

On this lovely evening, I was thinking more of the present, as in, filling the fuel tanks then filling my rumbling belly with a lovely steak, salad and chips at the pub located just a 100 meters away at the head of the wharf. To stretch my aching back, I locked the filling lever and carefully stood, looking around. The only visible portion of any other human was Ray's head as he sat in his little fuel shack above me on the wharf, talking incessantly on the phone.

I knew he was alive on account of the way he talked with both hands at once. No mean feat with the phone jammed between his shoulder and his ear! I took the opportunity to reach over to the instrument panel and switched on the spreader LED down-lights that threw a large pool of pure white light across my boat's very wide decks.

Finally, a rising gurgle, sounding remarkably similar to my stomach, announced that the twin tanks were almost full. When done, I shut the nozzle down and after catching the last few drips, fastened the fuel cap and climbed over the rail to reunite the nozzle with the pump. That had the other advantage of shutting down the unholy racket the pump made.

Right on cue, Ray's aging, snowy curls showed above the wharf edge.

'All done, Harry?' he asked.

'Yeah, thanks Ray. I'll come up and square the account.'

At the mention of money, he disappeared back into his office like someone pulled a chain, so I wandered up the ramp that joined the floating fuel pontoon to the wharf, digging my Platinum Visa card out of my pocket. I was just about to step into his office, when I heard a choked, asthmatic growl and felt something wet gumming my ankle.

Looking down, I saw it was just Ray's ancient, dysfunctional Chihuahua called Fang, possessed of foul breath, the worst farts, no teeth and near-zero eyesight. The bloody thing walks off the wharf so often that Ray had to tie an empty milk-bottle to its collar as a float and keeps a long-handled landing net propped up outside his fuel shack. A sideways kick soon dislodged the bad-tempered little shit, as Ray shoved the fuel docket at me.

'There you go, Harry! 155 litres of the best diesel, although if I had to rely on you for my living, I'd be broke a long time ago!'

'Bullshit, Ray! At the rate you charge for that crap you call diesel, it's a wonder you haven't moved to a condo on Hamilton Island with all the chicky-babes!'

'Oh, come on Harry. That's very unkind! With the special

discount I give you, it costs me every time you fill up. And that's not very bloody often!'

'Well, you should be grateful I use my sails so much, in that case,' I grinned at him.

We sling off at each other all the time, but a stranger might think otherwise.

'You going up the pub tonight, Harry?' Ray asked seriously, 'you can leave the old girl there if you want. It's only the coppers who might need a fill in the middle of the night if they have to chase after some wombat!'

'Yeah, I was actually. I fancy a beer or two and a good feed. And a perve at the girls won't hurt, either!'

He laughed, 'I'm buggered if I know why you don't latch onto that beaut barmaid, Ellie. She'll do anything for you.'

'Yeah. She's a nice lady all right, but you know that Sandy's only away for a little while on relieving duties. Promotion to Inspector has some disadvantages, but she'll be back in five days or so when the dude she's relieving comes back.'

'Yeah! I know,' he grumped, 'but you might at least take a few of the bar staff out sailing occasionally! Lovely big boat like that and hardly ever a bare tit in sight, let alone a fully naked lady! What's the point in living down here if you don't let me look at your naked ladies?'

I laughed at him. 'Funnily enough, Ray, I'm just thinking about your heart. Seeing too many naked ladies can fairly put your blood pressure up where it doesn't belong!'

'Crap! Don't you worry about me! Just get your nice lady back on that boat and get her pants off. Do both of you good!'

'That'll happen, Ray. Don't you worry about that! And maybe I will ask a few of the girls out sailing. That should keep you happy.'

'Good on you, mate,' he grinned, 'it'll beat having to go look for them myself!'

The fact is that Ray lives on the only three-story houseboat ever built and has it wedged into a berth only twenty paces from his office. It has about fifty ropes tying it to the mooring piles on three sides, so the fool thing won't fall over, and it's never moved from there since a tug dragged it into place 5 years ago.

Over the years, barnacles and weed growing down from its bottom, has met up with the small mountain of party-generated glass bottles that has grown up, to firmly anchor the whole thing to the bottom of the berth and creating its own little weird eco-system.

And despite his carry-on about my temporary lack of sex life and naked girls, he has a party almost every weekend that seems to last for several days, with just a couple of days break before it starts all over again. There are guys and girls dropping in at all times of the day or night, and there are always several girls who seem to live there for a week or two then move on. One way or the other, Ray never lacks for female company!

'Anyway, I might take you up on your offer, thanks Ray.'

'Yep. No problem! Maybe you can move its fat arse back to the channel end of the dock to leave room for the coppers.'

'OK, thanks mate, I'll go do that now. Cheers.'

'Goodo, Harry. Cheers mate,' he muttered, as he locked the office and wandered a slightly unsteady course toward his condo-like houseboat. After trying to piss on my foot, the repulsive Fang waddled after him, its short little legs working overtime to try to keep up, the milk-bottle float scraping along the concrete beside it, and a steady stream of noisy, smelly farts helping shove the thing along.

'Come on Fang,' he muttered, 'you smelly little prick! Jeeze you stink worse than I do and that's really saying something! Gotta get you a cork for your arse one day! I'd trade you in for a real dog like a Rottie, but who the hell would want you!'

I watched until both somehow negotiated the gangplank without falling in, marvelling to myself the way that alcoholics and water don't mix, but seem to survive anyway.

CHAPTER 2

A SMALL FACTORY BUILDING IN MOLENDINAR, SOUTHPORT, WEDNESDAY PM

...'*Ah...Hello?*'

'Good evening Mr Wells, this is The Undertaker. As the time is now 17:00 and I haven't heard from you, I am getting just a little bit concerned about the results of the transaction you are supposed to be conducting. Please reassure me that all is well.'

'*Umm...I was about to call you, sir, but the fact is, the courier hasn't shown. I've been in the agreed place since 15:30, and I can see that Mr Abrams and Mr Truss are still in place with their companions, but there's no sign of the delivery.*'

'That's very upsetting, Mr Wells. I do hope for your sake that the problem lies only with the courier.'

'*I can assure you sir, that I've done everything you've asked of me, exactly as you said. I don't know why he hasn't shown.*'

'Call me the moment he does, Mr Wells, as in instantly. Do you understand?'

'*Oh, yes sir. I certainly will do just that. Thank you, sir.*'

Barely five minutes later, the phone in The Undertaker's ornate office attracted his attention with it's muted purr. Trying not to rush, the tall man waited for the second series of rings, before picking up the receiver.

'Yes?'

A cheerful, nasal voice with an American accent, trying to sound like a true blue ocker, said, '*Gidday, cobber. How're they hangin'?*'

'I'm not in the mood for your childish games this evening, Mr Edwards, thank you very much. In fact, I'm waiting for a colleague to call on this phone, so please do something useful like go play in the traffic.'

'*Ah, that's my boy. I love it when you talk dirty to me. Fairly gives me a bulge in my panties! But what I was really calling about was to suggest that since it looks like your delivery isn't going to turn up, perhaps you should pull all your heavies back to base. You might need them if we decide to go for a ride.*'

'That's a very dangerous thing to suggest, Mr Edwards. I could even take exception to that remark, although I will ask how it is that you think you are privy to our club's business?'

'*Ask all you want, cobber, but in the spirit of rivalry and just between you and I, perhaps I might suggest that a little dickey bird sang a lucrative song and I happened to be listening.*'

'You're fishing, Mr Edwards, just fishing, but this fish isn't going to bite. Good night.'

'*Maybe I am, and maybe I ain't. But time will reveal all, now won't it? See ya when I'm looking at ya!*'

A NEATLY MAINTAINED, FIVE-ACRE, RURAL PROPERTY WEST OF SOUTHPORT – WEDNESDAY PM

Brad Edwards, the laid-back, charismatic President of the Zombie Eaters OMC, hung up the phone with a gleeful expression on his face and turned to his 2IC, Tony Bradford.

'That stirred up that long, skinny streak of shag-shit! I'd say that whisper you picked up was right on the money, sport. Well done!'

'No problem, boss. I wasn't sure how good the info was, but it sounds like that mob might be onto something really good. Pity we can't grab it for ourselves.'

Brad thought a moment then looked at the clock. 'Yeah, it'd be good alright, but might cause a bit too much fuss if we tried that now. But maybe we could stir the pot just a little bit, which after all, is our job. How many of the boys are here at the moment?'

'Might be fifteen or so. I'm not sure.'

'Okay, that's enough to make a bit of noise. Let's kick Road Captain Terry into action and go do a formation ride-by of Mariners Cove. We won't stop to engage in any way, just the ride-by. Tell the boys — no action unless they do something stupid first.'

'Sounds good, boss. Did you want to do that now?'

'Of course I want to do it now, ya dill! Like immediately! From what we were told, the dickheads are standing around, cocks in hand, waiting for a delivery as we speak. If we get there first, it'll send a message that maybe we've caused the delayed delivery. What a hoot this'll be! Let's go, daddy-oh! Haul arse and all that rev-up shit!'

There was a quick flurry of activity as the group dropped what and who they were doing at the time and mounted up. The riders hastily pulled on the club's trademark ice-hockey facemasks in a variety of horrific designs that terrified any old ladies or small children they came across, before they roared out of the rural property and formed up into a two-by-two formation and headed for Mariners Cove, disregarding most traffic rules in the rush to get on the scene.

CHAPTER 3

After checking that Ray and Fang had at least survived the gang-plank leading up to his floating condo, I returned to *Firebird* and since the night was calm, was easily able to slacken some lines, tighten others and drag her bulk back a few meters to clear space.

On board, I quickly cleaned up, fed Jasper, my overgrown Chausie-cross cat and his new companion Krazy, a tiny short-haired kitten with a jet-black coat speckled with tiny silver tufts of hair. She was a present from a pair of lovely talented ladies, Hilary and Debbie, whom I'd worked with on a previous job.

She'd earned her name by having almost manic energy levels that caused her to make the most incredible leaps from and to everything, including twice in the cockpit where she missed her landing and sailed cleanly overboard. That was on the first day! Jasper watched over her like a doting big brother should and jumped in the water both times to retrieve the tiny bundle of hissing, spitting black fur by letting her perch on his head, apparently her favourite vantage spot. Since then, she'd moderated her leaps enough to avoid any more wet retrieves.

With the crew fed, I whacked on some anti-stink, changed my shirt, locked the doors and headed for the pub.

The Boathouse Tavern was a very popular pub, being built out over the water, and was part of a small group of shops, take-away food outlets and a YHA hostel.

Through many nights and a lot of beer and food purchased there, I'd become a real regular and got on well with the staff, especially the girls who were a happy crew and had been sailing with me several times before. Prior to hooking up with my lovely Sandy, I had become very keen on Ellie, the bar supervisor and a single Mum who worked hard to raise her two kids the right way. I'd taken them out sailing and her 8-year-old son Pete, was very enthusiastic to learn more. I hadn't told Ellie yet, but I planned to put Pete through a Sail Training Course then get him a sailing dinghy of his own.

Ellie was on duty tonight so I sat at the bar and chatted for a while as I drank a beer.

'When's Sandy due back from Cunnamulla?' She asked

'Not for another two weeks,' I replied, 'but she says she's enjoying herself and staying out of trouble.'

Ellie grinned, 'Good thing you have been too!'

'Yeah. She'd have my nuts if I messed around, but there's not too much happening at the moment, although the whole Coast seems to be really jumping with this new horse racing carnival firing up on Friday.'

She groaned, 'Tell me about it. We're on extended shifts from tomorrow, so if you want a quiet drink and feed, you might have to stay aboard your lovely boat.'

I shook my head, 'Nah! Then I wouldn't get to chat up the best-looking sort on the Coast.'

She laughed at my clumsy flattery. 'Yeah right, good one Harry. Now I presume you're eating in tonight? I'll take your order if you're ready.'

'Yeah, I will, thanks Ellie. Ray let me leave the old girl at the fuelling pontoon overnight, so there's no dinghy work for me.'

'That's handy. He can be nice sometimes.'

'Yeah, but not too often. He's got a reputation to live down to. Anyway, I'd like some of that thick-cut rib-eye fillet that Jeff's been hiding away, pepper sauce and with the usual chips and salad with Italian dressing. He knows how I like it.'

She smiled, 'No problem, I'll fix that. Do you want to eat in the end lounge?'

'Yeah, that'll be great, thanks Ellie, and I'll have another schooner when you're ready.'

She flashed a grin as she tapped the order onto the computer screen, quickly served another thirsty customer then pulled me another sparkling beer.

'There you are, mate. I'll bring the food in shortly.'

'Thanks, Ellie.'

Beer in hand, I wandered around the end of the semi-circular bar and headed to a small annex room at the carpark end of the building. While meals were served anywhere in the huge room, this did duty as a slightly more secluded eating-place, and held only 5 other persons this evening. Two couples sat at separate small tables, while a strange-looking fella in his early 30's sat on a padded bench seat set against one wall, a beer on the small table in front of him.

I sat myself at a table at the other end of the small area and because he seemed very nervous, surreptitiously checked him out.

He had long, lank hair, a thin, weasel-shaped face, narrow-set eyes and a worried expression. What struck me as odd was that he had a schooner of beer in front of him that was barely touched and had gone totally flat. This was a dude who was waiting for someone who was seriously late. Somehow, I doubted it was his girlfriend.

I also spotted a large, black carry-on bag that looked bulky, tucked back under the bench seat behind his feet.

As I nearly finished my delightful steak, cooked to perfection as usual, I heard the distant, soft thunder of a large group of two-cylinder motorcycles that slowly grew in volume as they came closer, until the walls were vibrating as they stopped close-by. Abruptly, the thunder quit as though chopped by a knife, instantly suspending all conversation in the whole bar.

Weasel-features looked like he was going to have a heart attack and broke out into a major sweat. He tried to lift his glass of beer, but his hand was shaking so much some of it slopped over the table.

Less than a minute later, the doors closest to the carpark crashed open in dramatic fashion, admitting two very large, heavily tattooed bikies, complete with the obligatory greasy vest with the club colours on the back.

Like all good bodyguards do, they folded their arms and stood immobile either side of the entrance, only their eyes moving as they scanned the room for any sign of trouble from the happy, half-pissed bunch of drinkers. After an initial glance at the pair, most patrons lowered their eyes and suddenly became very interested in the contents of their glasses or the wood-grain pattern of the tabletop.

Following another drama-building pause, a very tall, very thin gentleman stepped quietly into the room. He was impeccably dressed in a beautifully tailored black suit with white shirt, a narrow black tie and gleaming black shoes. His mane of jet-black hair was slicked back and accented his stark white face that carried a faintly quizzical expression as he calmly scanned the faces in the room, supremely unconcerned about the disturbance his appearance had created.

His gaze lingered on me a bit longer than the rest, but then moved on to weasel-features, whereupon a happy smile lit up his excessively severe features.

'Roger, my dear fellow,' he said in a soft, beautifully modulated voice, 'how good to see you still here. Please come and talk to me.'

As he shuffled sideways to clear the table, I saw that he contrived to push the black carry-on bag further sideways so that despite it's bulk, it was tucked into the corner formed by the wall and the bench seat and was reasonably out of sight.

Pasting a dopey grin on his face, he walked slowly up to the tall man who reached out and grasped him by the shoulders in what appeared to be a very companionable gesture. Unfortunately for Roger, I could see that the tall man had the biggest hands I've ever seen on a human, where even his finger muscles stood out like jungle vines, so that Roger gasped with the pain as his shoulders were squeezed almost beyond what human tissue was designed to withstand.

Tall man's enigmatic smile grew wider as Roger squirmed beneath his grasp.

'There, there! Dear boy, there's no need to worry — provided that you've been doing the right thing by us, that is.'

He squeezed a bit more, drawing squeaks of pain and fright from dear Roger.

'Unfortunately, I'm told that you may not have been doing the right thing. Now, tell me where the goods are.'

'I don't know boss!' Roger bleated, 'Truly I don't. I've been here since before four o'clock and there's been no sign of the bloke. Check with your Enforcers, they'll tell you I've been here all the time.'

Tall Man looked at him appraisingly, like a tiger eyeing off a very succulent rodent.

'Actually, dear boy, I'm inclined to believe that part of the story, but dare I ask if the money is somewhere very safe? I mean, you wouldn't be stupid enough to have it with you here and now, would you?'

Roger shook his weasely head and said, 'No way, boss. It's tucked away safely in my car just outside.'

The predatory smile increased in intensity, 'Oh, excellent! What a cunning place to hide it. I'm sure that nobody would think to break into a car looking for valuables!'

Roger didn't dare turn his head, remaining fixed on Tall Man's hypnotic blue eyes.

'I've been hearing nasty whispers about you, Roger. How long have you been our bagman? One year?'

'Ah, actually, boss, it's two years and I've always done the right thing.'

'Yes, indeed. You *have* always done the right thing, but have you done so *now*? That's the question. Let's take a little walk out to the carpark to see what's what, shall we?'

Just as the Tall Man transferred one massive hand to the hapless Roger's neck, I heard another distant, deep rumbling sound that rapidly grew until the walls were shaking again, starting dust filtering down from the ceiling like a fine rain.

Tall Man cocked his head like an inquisitive bird, listening as the thunderous roar peaked, held steady then slowly diminished as the bikes slowly went past. He then squeezed his massive hand and lifted slightly, easily holding half his weight and forcing Roger to walk on tiptoes. 'My, my,' he said, 'could that be your new friends come to help you out, or maybe they think they can collect our property directly? Let's go and see, shall we?'

With a strangled squeak from Roger, the pair swivelled about and left the building, while the two goons manning the doorway waited a few moments as if daring anybody to move or speak, before stepping backwards out the doors and disappearing after their boss. The thunder of the other group of bikes built again as they rode back past the other way, after turning at the first roundabout up the dead-end road.

Talk slowly resumed in the bar, the noise level building as everybody wanted to recount to each other, what everybody else had just seen. The two couples at the other tables in the dining alcove decided that the lovely selection of desserts on offer weren't worth staying around for and hurriedly paid at the bar and left via the water-front door, while two other couples at the far end of the room abandoned their drinks and hurriedly left the room. While the staff were busy behind the bar talking excitedly between themselves, and before someone came to clear away my dishes, I acted purely on impulse, and strolled over to the corner just vacated by dear Roger and after making sure I was still unobserved retrieved his bag, grunting as I lifted it.

It was far heavier than even its bulk suggested and would have weighed a good 20 kilos. In moments, I had regained my seat just in time to ask Ellie for a plate of pecan pie and ice cream. She looked a bit worried as she said, 'On behalf of management, I'd like to apologise for the invasion. That could have been nasty and you were a bit too close to the action. Are you OK with it?'

I waved airily, 'Da Nada. I'm cool with it, thanks Ellie and no harm done. But who were they?'

'It's a new mob that call themselves the Undertakers for obvious reasons. They've apparently moved to the Coast from Victoria and have been creating a lot of waves, excuse the pun, with the other local groups, but primarily the Zombie Eaters. There's a lot of bad blood between the two groups due to a few defections of high-ranking members both ways.'

'How bad is the level of disagreement?'

'It's been pretty bad,' she grimaced, 'and because they seem to like coming out here to the Spit, we seem to be in the middle of things more often than not. But in this case, I think that this argument was internal, which should be a bit more benign, although I didn't like the sound of that ride-by. I reckon that was the Zombies, so there might be some action later. I just hope it's somewhere else and not back here.'

Which just showed how wrong one could be!

Underscoring her words, the pack of Zombies, if that's who they were, roared past yet again, as if to provoke a confrontation with the Undertakers.

With further reassurances that I wasn't traumatised, Ellie departed to fetch my dessert, now 'on the house.'

She'd just disappeared into the kitchen, when over the sub-dued wash of talk in the bar I heard two sharp 'snap' sounds from outside. Automatically, my mind catalogued it as; 'small calibre, and probably low-power .22 rounds with a well-used silencer.' Since pistol silencers only muffle the sound of a shot at best, it certainly wasn't a centre-fire round and nothing of any size. Two snap sounds like that wouldn't attract attention, particularly if they weren't repeated, as these weren't.

Seconds later, all the Undertaker's bikes fired up as one with a shattering bellow of gut-wrenching sound, before roaring out of the carpark, down to the roundabout then back past us again. We could hear the roar slowly fading into the distance as peace and quiet slowly and hesitantly crept back, allowing the normal chatter in the pub to resume.

I casually scanned the bar for anyone who may have recognised the gunshots, but everyone was still talking animatedly about the Undertaker's visit. Ellie returned with my dessert, but as the bar trade had become particularly brisk, she didn't stay to chat, so I ate in solitude and enjoyed every mouthful. When I'd finished, I took my empty plate and my purloined bag to the bar and asked Ellie for a new garbage bag. It disguised the carry-on bag very effectively and instantly turned me into just another boatie with perhaps his load of very heavy washing. Wishing Ellie a good night, I headed back down the wharf to *Firebird* and the patiently waiting Jasper and Krazy.

Once aboard, I tucked the bag away in a locker well hidden under my dressing cabin flooring, but not before having a quick peek inside. As I suspected, it contained cash. Lots and lots of cash and all of it in tightly bound bricks of hundreds. I did a quick set of calculations in my head, remembering that one $100 note weighed about 1 gram. That made 1,000 notes to the kilogram or $100,000, so if there was 20 kilos of notes in the bag, that added up to $2 million in a carry-on bag that little weasel Roger had been wandering the streets of the Coast with, clutched in his grubby, sweaty little paws!

I pondered my level of involvement, voluntary and otherwise in this business, as I fed the pussies again before they gnawed my foot off then poured a generous measure of a particularly pleasant Grandfather Port for myself, before taking it out to the cockpit where I sat a spell in the comforting, quiet darkness with my beautiful big cat rumbling contentedly beside me, his diminutive fuzzy sidekick perched on his shoulders.

CHAPTER 4

I was still contemplating the current state of affairs with the help of my second glass of Mr Penfold's best, when I noticed there were two figures at the far end of the wharf, slowly working their way down toward my position at the end of the arm. They were almost the same height, but had strange humps on their backs. Some boats had live-aboards, but most were closed up tight. The two strangers seemed to be checking the closed boats for something and it wasn't until they were much closer that I realised that their odd shape was due to the large backpacks they had on.

They finally arrived at the refuelling facility where *Firebird* and I were floating, but as Jasper, Krazy and I stayed in the shadows and kept quiet, we were nearly invisible. They briefly tried the door to Ray's office, but quickly turned away when they noticed movement back up at the end of the wharf where two large figures were walking slowly toward us, heads turning to check each boat as they passed.

A muffled, 'Oh, shit!' drifted softly across from the pair, silhouetted against the wharf lights, before they moved quickly to the head of the pontoon ramp and scurried down, ducking behind the fuel bowsers that resided under the ramp. With them out of sight, I waited to see what the other two figures were up to. They were finally revealed as two very large bikies who were scanning every possible hiding place very carefully, although not boarding any boats.

They stopped up on the wharf, looking down at *Firebird* for a few minutes and conversing in low tones before one made his way down the ramp and over to *Firebird's* side. By now, I'd quietly opened the concealed locker cover under the helm seat where a Grizzly.44 Magnum had been hiding and now held its comforting bulk down by my side as the burly bikie reached up to grasp *Firebird's* safety rail.

After pressing gently down on Jasper's head in the sign to 'stay', I stepped forward and said quietly, 'May I help you?'

There came a muffled oath and the figure stumbled back in fright, but quickly recovered to step forward to grasp the rail again.

I didn't speak again, just racked the slide of the Grizzly, letting the ominous metallic sound speak for me. It would seem that he was familiar with firearms as he immediately stepped back, and half raised his hands.

'There's no need for any misunderstandings here boss,' the one up on the wharf said in a deep almost cultured voice, 'we're just looking for a couple of people.'

'I'm afraid you're the only ones with the misunderstandings,' I said, raising the Grizzly into plain view, 'attempting to search boats without permission is a rather serious breach of etiquette.'

'I apologise for the rash actions of my partner,' the guy on the wharf said reasonably, 'but perhaps you can help us. We're looking for a tall, blonde-headed fella, probably with a big backpack on. He may have a girl with him. Have you seen anyone like that down here?'

I thought a moment, but realised that I had already chosen sides in this affair.

'Nah. It's been dead quiet down here tonight mate. Just the way I like it. I was about to turn in for the night.'

The bikie on the wharf considered my words for a few moments before saying, 'Thank you sir. I'm sorry we disturbed your evening. We'll be off then. Good night.'

'Yeah, good night. I hope you find who you're looking for.'

Even in the dim light of Ray's weak security light, I could see the bikie wearing a rather feral grin. 'Oh we will, sir. You can count on that.'

On that ominous note, they walked slowly back up the wharf and out of sight.

I waited a few more minutes, taking a few more sips of my port, before I called out quietly, 'I think you had better come out now.'

There was a soft girlish sound, a scraping of fabric on metal, then the two persons I'd seen earlier stepped out from behind the rusting fuel bowsers, the long, heavy backpacks now carried rather than worn.

They walked to *Firebird* and looked up, firstly at the large metal mass of the Grizzly still in my hand, then up at me.

'Umm... Ah...Thanks for covering for us,' the tall, blonde-headed guy said.

'Yeah, thanks,' his companion offered. She was a tall, slim and pretty girl who, in the dim light, looked very young.

'OK. What's the story?' I asked, in no hurry to let these characters on board, the evening already having produced enough odd happenings.

'Ah...I'm sure it's a case of mistaken identity, but some of those bikies have been chasing us since we arrived. And, umm...Is there any chance we could come aboard where we can't be seen? I'd, ah... be happy to tell you all about us.'

Certain that I wouldn't hear the truth and with the thought that he was really going to have to clear up that speech defect, I waved my hand toward the stern where the boarding platform was at pontoon height and offered a safe way aboard. Their worried looks reminded me that perhaps I shouldn't have waved the hand holding the Grizzly .44, but they braved my menacing demeanour and made it aboard, with packs and without mishap.

Jasper had soundlessly retreated into the saloon doorway, but as there still weren't any lights on, his all-over black fur made him next-to invisible.

They parked their bulky packs and sat nervously, although I noted that the girl immediately sat well away from the guy who looked like an aging surfie. As he started on his story, I was immediately annoyed by his ingratiating manner.

'Ahhh…Thanks for letting us aboard, Skipper. I'm Gary and this is Lisa. We're from Sydney and were heading for Cairns, but I've got some friends here and thought it'd be fun to stay a few days and catch up. We were supposed to be here at three o'clock this afternoon, but the bus broke down just out of Coffs Harbour and it took a mechanic three hours to fix it. Then we came here since I'd made a booking for a room at the YHA Hostel out front, but there'd been some sort of cock-up and they were full. So we thought we'd walk down the wharf to see if there was somewhere safe to kip for the night, where those bloody bikies couldn't find us. We weren't going to break-in or anything like that.'

I didn't answer straight away, just looking at him in the dim wash of light from up on the wharf. As planned, that seemed to un-nerve him more than the gun that I still held or the bikies had!

'Ahh…So can we stay here? Maybe just sleep on the floor right here if you'd prefer and we'll be gone in the morning?'

I still didn't answer straightaway, but finally the girl spoke, her voice a low, husky contralto, totally at odds with her very youthful appearance.

'You need to understand something — I'm actually not with him. I mean we're not a unit or anything like that. I only stuck around because he said we'd both have beds tonight and those bikies did seem to be chasing us.'

'Okay,' I said, 'I'm not happy with your story about mistaken identity and find it very strange that some bikies are trying so hard to find you for no apparent reason. There's some heavy stuff you're not telling me, but I'll sort that out with you in the morning. For now, you can kip on the floor out here, but don't try to come inside, even though the door will be open. I have a cat here who'll make sure that you don't go roaming and the bikies still looking for you shoreside should keep you quiet.'

'Oh, great. Thanks man, you're a lifesaver.'

I grunted, 'Maybe, let's wait and see.'

'Can I use the toilet?' the girl asked.

I shook my head, 'Fraid not, since I don't trust your story, so I'm not letting either of you inside the boat. But you're welcome to hang over the stern provided you don't make a mess. If you do, then clean it up or I'll use your face for a scrubbing brush. There's a good handrail to hang onto, plus being a backpacker, I'm sure you're used to ducking behind bushes.'

She gave me a dirty look, but didn't say more.

'Now, I've already said I don't believe your lame story, although because of the girl and the bikies I'm letting you sleep in the cockpit tonight. To keep you in line, I mentioned that I have a cat that will guarantee your good behaviour. I strongly advise that you don't test his resolve or ability to protect the boat and myself.'

Gary and Lisa looked around, but in the dimness, didn't spot Jasper.

I grinned mirthlessly, 'Believe me, he's watching you right now. Anyway, I'm off to bed, so you can sort yourselves out and we'll talk in the morning if you still want a refuge from the bikies. If not, then piss off and don't try anything clever on the way out or you'll regret it.'

Gary shook his dopey head. 'No man. We'll be cool. We just want to keep our heads down for the night. I'll chase up my mates tomorrow and we can leave you alone.'

Lisa spoke up again, 'Speak for yourself dickhead!' She looked at me, 'I'll talk to you in the morning without this arsehole around, if you'll listen. I've got nowhere else to go and no money. This prick bludged the last of it on the way up to feed his face.'

Gary looked like he was going to burr up, but subsided when Lisa delivered him a withering glare.

I stepped inside and slid the heavy door three quarter closed, stopping to talk softly to Jasper for a moment, after which he planted himself behind the closed part of the door and mewled softly at me in his uncanny way of showing that he understood. Krazy had wisely parked herself on the chart table out of the way. Leaving the lights off, I used the toilet and retired to my spacious queen bed in the right forward cabin, but didn't try to go to sleep straight away since I was certain that Gary-shit-for-brains would try to be clever.

Sure enough, after about 30 minutes or so and a round of fierce muttering between them, I heard the sliding door make it's usual soft rumble as it was slid further back. There was a faint creak from the flooring just inside the door as weight came on it, then an unearthly howl of sheer terror erupted from the saloon, rising in pitch and overlaid with a deep growling. Finally, he stopped screaming and yelled out:

'Holy shit! Get him off me! Fuck! He's ripping my fucking arm off! Help, somebody do something!'

I flicked the switch for the red night lighting as I headed for the saloon, hoping that the bikie foot patrols were somewhere else at that moment. As expected, Gary was laying on the floor on his back, with Jasper's two front paws planted firmly on his chest. Gary's left arm was clamped between Jasper's jaws, but I could see that even though there was some blood showing, my big cat wasn't trying very hard, since he had previously proved that he was quite capable of chewing right through an arm.

Despite appearances, there was no real danger of Gary losing his arm unless he kept on struggling, so I stood looking down at the idiot, wrinkling my nose as I smelt the stench of urine as he pissed himself. Lisa was out in the cockpit, backed up against the far bench seat, whimpering, with a horrified look on her face.

Gary started a pathetic round of pleading when he saw me, but I just looked for a few moments, before touching Jasper lightly on the head.

'Thanks boy, release but stay.'

Jasper released Gary's arm, but remained planted on his

heaving chest, as he started crying with a combination of pain, shock and possibly relief.

'I suppose that you're going to tell me that you lost your way in the dark and instead of going to the stern to piss, you mistakenly slid open the saloon door?'

'Oh, shit man. I didn't know!'

'Just what part of 'stay in the cockpit' didn't you understand? Or for that matter, how about my warning that I have a cat and not to test his ability and resolve?'

'Yeah, but! Like, I didn't know.'

'You're an idiot. You just didn't listen so don't give me any more crap! Now Jasper's going to let you up and this will be your last chance to behave, so either fuck off right now or clean yourself up then settle down. You're hardly scratched so stop carrying on like a big girl's blouse!'

Still whimpering, Gary dragged himself up off the floor, only to slip in the puddle of his piss, fall back down and bang his head. The second time around, he made it to vertical and hobbled out to the cockpit and down the stern steps to wash off. I cleaned up his piss, waiting until he painfully climbed back up the stern steps, a handkerchief wrapped around his arm.

With a shaking hand, he pointed at Jasper, sitting glaring at him from the saloon doorway, 'You can't keep a wild animal like that just running around loose. He should be in a cage!'

'I'm afraid not sunshine. He's a legal domestic animal and hasn't done any more than a big dog would do to protect it's home, so belt up or I'll point him at you again.'

That statement caused an immediate stop to the stream of complaints, and even Lisa sat down at the table, while keeping a wary eye on Jasper.

'Okay dickhead. Let's start again. Stay in the cockpit or fuck off right now and run the gauntlet of the bikies. I don't care either way, but Jasper's got a taste for you now, so he won't hold back next time.'

Gary's shoulders slumped and he held his hands up.

'It's okay, man. I'll behave, I didn't know. Just keep that thing away from me.'

'If you behave, he will too. Trust me on that. And now I'm going to bed, but Jasper will be right here all night.'

There was no more discussion and the rest of the night passed peacefully.

CHAPTER 5

FIREBIRD, MARINERS COVE, THURSDAY AM

It's my favourite time of day, when the soft explosion of golden fire spreading from the eastern horizon slowly pushes the shroud of night westwards, so I was up just before dawn as usual. I wandered into the galley to make a mug of tea and while the kettle was coming to the boil, I eyeballed the cockpit to see that only one body was visible, wrapped in a sleeping bag and stretched out on the bench seating closest to the saloon. Jasper and Krazy greeted me with their usual enthusiasm to make sure they got fed promptly, so I took care of that important job before I quietly checked the cockpit for damage or mess and on impulse, looked in all the lockers to see if anything was missing.

Nothing was missing, but there was an addition. It was Gary's sleeping bag, still neatly rolled up in its waterproof cover and tucked deep down into one of many lockers in the cockpit. Out of curiosity, I poked at it and was surprised to feel it was quite hard, not the soft feel of a normal bag.

Therefore, with hot tea in hand I parked myself across from Lisa's slumbering form, studied her relaxed features for a while then poked her somewhere around one thigh with my foot. It took several tries to even get a grunt out of her, but suddenly she sat up, a look of fright on her face.

'Settle down, princess. It's only me. Where's your boyfriend?'

She blinked a few times, looked around then held out her hand for my tea. Shrugging, I passed it across and watched while she took a few sips.

'That's better. Buggered if I know where he is, and I tried to tell you last night he's not my boyfriend, so I don't give a shit where he is.'

'OK. Time to tell all,' I said.

'Gladly, but I'd really like a mug of tea first and I badly need to pee. Can I use your toilet?'

I shook my head. 'Nope. Not yet. You're very much on probation, especially now the boyfriend's shot through. There's no one around to see you use the stern, so do that while I get you a tea.'

'Bastard!' she cursed, struggling out of her sleeping bag, revealing her very nice shape clad in a T-shirt and a pair of bikini panties.

'Now, now. Be nice or no hot tea and you get to take the walk of extreme peril!' I admonished. 'Just remember that this bastard kept you out of the clutches of an Outlaw Motorcycle gang. They wouldn't have fed you mugs of tea!'

Still grumbling, she headed down the stern, starting to pull down her panties on the way, while I fired up the kettle again and set out a mug. Walking to the top of the steps, I asked, 'Milk and sugar?'

She looked up from her squat, still peeing, 'Milk and two, thanks.'

'Coming up.' I didn't tell her that Ray was sitting in his over-stuffed armchair on his upper balcony, watching the proceedings with the avid interest of a professional pervert. He kept quiet as well.

Back in the cockpit, she washed hands and face in the sink in the corner then gratefully accepted the steaming mug. 'I'm sorry for not thanking you for last night and the bikie thing. I guess I was a bit upset by that fucking prick Gary and the bikies chasing him, but thanks for rescuing me.'

'Alright Blossom, you're welcome. Now, how about I hear your story and please make it the real one. Your boyfriend fed me a pack of bullshit last night and I don't want to cop another load from you as well!'

'There's not that much to tell, really. I got on the bus at the Sydney terminal, with an open ticket to Cairns. I had a job lined up as a waitress in a restaurant and that was going to build up my finances again. Anyway, this guy gets on and parks himself across the aisle and starts chatting me up. Then he comes up with this story how we should travel together so he can protect me and that we should stop at the Gold Coast for a while and have some fun.

He went on about his mates and how there were plenty of beds at their flat, so I ended up agreeing to at least travel with him and he did stop other blokes trying to pester me.

The downside was that from that point on he assumed he owned me and I spent the day being groped. So that's the story, I don't know him — I've never seen him before and never want to see him again. And I am broke.'

I considered her story and concluded that she was probably being truthful.

'Did he say anything about bikies during the trip?'

She shook her head. 'No. He mostly talked about himself, as these dickheads always seem to do. There were a few things he said that seemed odd, but I can't remember exactly what they were, but he's way too old for the backpacking circuit. I mean, he tries to look young, but after spending the day beside him, I reckon he's closer to 40 than 30.'

'Did he talk about drugs? As in, having them, using them or did he offer you anything?'

She thought a moment, 'Yeah. Just the usual offer of a joint when we stopped for lunch, but I didn't want to do that. I don't really do drugs at all — whatever swinging dick supplies them, he always seems to want me to have sex with a bunch of his mates as payback. So I don't do that.' She shrugged in resignation, 'However, when you're female and broke, sometimes you've only got one thing that's tradeable.'

I looked at her, 'You're not the first to realise that and won't be the last, but it was your choice to go backpacking and that's always going to expose you to sleazy guys.'

'Yeah. I suppose so, but I didn't have a lot of choice. My boss at work was always trying to get into my pants and my step-dad was the same, so I gave that whole scene the flick and got out of town.'

She suddenly looked very depressed and several tears slid down her cheeks, 'And this trip seems to be headed the same way. An ex-surfie type with octopus hands, a killer cat, bikies, a boatie-dude with a fuckin' cannon for a handgun and I don't know where this is going to end up, but I know it's not going to be good!'

I tried not to be swayed by her tears, as I usually am, so resorted to more questions.

'How old are you, really. 'Cause you look about fourteen.'

'Yeah. I get that a lot too. I'm twenty, with a Driver's Licence and a Responsible Service of Alcohol Training certificate to prove it.'

I considered that then asked, 'So what are you going to do now?'

That brought on a fresh flood of tears, so I waited stoically until she went and washed her face again in the sink. 'I don't know. I've got about $10 tucked away and that's it for the finances — I don't know anybody in this place and the only work I had lined up is a couple of thousand kilometres away! Got any suggestions?'

I studied her face for a few moments. 'OK. I'll let you stay here for now in case the bikies are still looking for your mate, but I reckon there's some shit about to go down this morning, so I really suggest you don't go walkabout alone or anytime soon.'

She looked worried, 'Thanks for letting me stay, at least. But what's the trouble you mentioned?'

'There was a bit of aggro in the pub last night with a bunch of bikies that might blow up very soon. I can't say more for now, but I need to go ashore and check a few things out.'

'Well, please don't leave me here alone,' she said, panicking, 'that beast of yours will kill me. I saw what it did to Gary.'

'Gary tried to come into our home without permission and my cat defended it. It's really that simple. Jasper doesn't hate anybody unless they try to harm the boat or me. Anyway, you'll be safer here.'

'Bullshit! I want to come 'cause I need you to buy me something to eat. My last meal was lunch yesterday.'

I relented, but said, 'Okay. Come along and we'll have a feed.'

'Can I leave my pack here? Will it be safe?'

By way of answer, I pointed to Jasper's black form sitting in the doorway behind her. She gave a start but got the point.

'Oh, yeah. But does he always bite people he doesn't like?'

'Yeah. Pretty much,' I replied casually, 'so you want to behave yourself around him but it's usually much easier just to make friends with him.'

She shuddered, 'Maybe later. Let me think about it.'

So we left Jasper in charge and wandered up the wharf. I called out to Ray that I'd be back after breakfast to shift *Firebird* back out to the mooring, and got a wave in return. I noticed Lisa checking the boat out in the morning light.

'That's a pretty nice boat you've got there, but do I get to call you by your name, or will 'Sir' have to do?'

I laughed, glad to see her spirit bouncing back. 'My name is Harry, you know Jasper and my boat is a 60ft catamaran called *Firebird*. I usually park it out on a mooring over near the Yacht Club, but I came in yesterday evening to refuel and stayed over.'

'Cool. I love boats. Are you retired or something?' She asked.

'Sort of,' I replied, 'I'm ex-Army. I like boats and life on the water.'

She nodded approvingly, 'Good choice.'

We walked the rest of the way in silence as I led the way around the pub, all doors securely locked at this hour, and headed for a small cafe at the front of the complex where I often go for a newspaper and breakfast. The staff are happy and friendly, and I always get a warm welcome. This morning, I led a meandering path through the carpark that butted up against the sprawling bulk of the upscale Marina Mirage, drawing a comment from Lisa.

'What are you looking for?'

'Maybe something, hopefully nothing,' I replied cryptically, but in fact, I did find what I half expected. I didn't pay obvious attention to it and stayed clear of where an old, rusty Holden Commodore was parked, with some bloke behind the wheel, leaning against the side pillar, apparently sleeping off a big night on the booze. Unfortunately, I recognised the clothing and the greasy mass of tangled hair as belonging to dear Roger, now very ex-bagman to the Undertakers.

Lisa noticed my glance and commented without knowing how ironic it was, 'He must have had a hard night.'

'Very hard!' I agreed, as I took another long look, but all that was visible was what seemed to be a nosebleed. At least his eyes seemed to be closed so he looked to be more or less asleep. I noted the car's rego number and we continued to the cafe where I treated Lisa to one of their famous Big Breakfast's that had enough food to keep a truckie going for a week.

When she'd finished and washed it all down with two mugs of tea, I asked, 'Are you easily upset by seeing injuries or dead bodies?'

She looked at me strangely. 'What an odd question, but no, that sort of thing doesn't bother me. Why?'

I thought a moment, but said, 'Because that guy sleeping it off in the car out there was involved in the bikie business last night and he's permanently asleep with two gunshots to the head!'

Lisa paled a little, but otherwise kept her cool. 'How do you know all that?'

'Because I was in the pub last night and saw and heard everything. But now I'm going to have to call a friend I have in the local Police to let him know about all this.

The reason I telling you this is that you need to understand that you'll be questioned, since your mate Gary is up to his nuts in this and the coppers will want to wring every drop of information out of you as well. I'll do what I can to make them go easy, but I'll only help if you're sure you've told me everything! It'll be a lot harder on you later if they find out that you've lied or held stuff back.'

Lisa looked solemn and shook her head. 'No Harry. That's it. I've told you all I know about Gary and his business.'

'Okay. In that case I'll call Greg.'

I let my mobile dial his number and he picked up quickly.

'Hi Harry. How's things with you?'

'I'm fine mate — are you working or off duty?'

'Working. I'm off at 08:00, in around 35 minutes. Are we still on for a few beers tonight?'

'Maybe. We'll see how busy you still are tonight, on account of I've got some work for you.'

'Ahh shit Harry! I should've known. Things have been way too quiet lately and that's not natural with you around! What've you got?'

'You might have heard that there was a bit of a fuss last night at the Mariners Cove Boathouse with the Undertakers Bikie mob and their mates the Zombies?'

'Yeah. Heard about it, but no complaints were made so there's nothing official.'

'OK. But you might like to send a few General Duties uniforms to the Mariners Cove carpark ASAP, along with an ambulance. About halfway down the Marina Mirage side of the carpark, there's a white VB Commodore, rego 728-BGF. There's a bloke in it with a matching pair of .22 rounds in his head. Might be good to isolate the area before some tourist trips over him.'

'Bloody hell, Harry. You don't fuck around! May I presume that you weren't responsible for this bloke's condition?'

'You may correctly presume that, Inspector. I was a mere spectator, but there are other considerations that are for your and maybe Bob Casey's ears only. You'll find me in Rosie's cafe with a young lady, finishing breakfast. Chop, chop old mate.

People are stirring over here and the Council won't like a tourist finding a dead body in the carpark. Very bad for the Coast's sleazy image.'

'Yeah, yeah. Jeeze Harry, you really know how to cock up a bloke's day! Don't move and I'll see you in 5.'

Lisa was looking a bit stunned after hearing all that, and commented, 'Who are you really? You seem to know that Police Inspector pretty well.'

'Let's just say that we've worked together in the past. That's all you need to know for now, except that so long as you tell the truth, you'll be looked after by the good guys.'

'I guess you were right when you told me on the boat that there was some heavy shit going on, but I didn't know about all this. How are Gary and I involved in all of this?'

I smiled to try to settle her down. 'You need to know, so I'll tell you now before the coppers arrive and lock the place down. As I said before, Gary's up to his nuts in it and is probably the main cause of all this, or to be more accurate, I reckon that the bus breakdown and the three hour delay was the real reason. I suspect that Gary was carrying drugs to be handed over to the dead guy who was the bagman, in exchange for a great deal of cash. When you guys didn't turn up on time, the Undertakers got suspicious and when they found the bagman, but couldn't find the money, they put two and two together, came up with seventeen and topped the bagman as revenge.

Unfortunately for the bagman, I think he was telling the truth and it was your bus breakdown that stuffed up the deal.'

Lisa looked really stunned, 'Do you mean that numbnuts was carrying drugs all the times I was with him? Shit!'

I grinned at her anger, 'Yes he was. I found his sleeping bag stuffed in a stern locker this morning while you were sleeping. He must be planning to come back to retrieve it after he does whatever business he's gone off to do. He obviously didn't want to have it with him when he meets his friends.'

'Yeah. I saw him unstrap it last night, but he didn't unroll it. He just sat there looking at it and cursing you and your cat, but I was stuffed, so I got comfortable and went to sleep.'

CHAPTER 6

Right on the five minute mark, a plain white FG Falcon braked hard for the driveway turn-in then accelerated again down the carpark, sliding to a stop in Hollywood style approved fashion, several car lengths short of the rusty white Commodore parked against the concrete dividing wall. Three uniformed coppers jumped out, followed a lot more slowly by a medium height, brown-haired man in a grey suit who moved as though his muscles and joints were very stiff and sore. There was no doubt that he was in charge, however, as he directed the three uniforms to carefully check the car before directing the placement and tasks of all the other uniforms who arrived en-masse to flood the carpark with a sea of blue. The locals were disgusted when barriers were erected at all entrances and exits to the carpark, manned by Police who asked pointed questions of everyone who approached. The entry barrier was hastily removed to admit an ambulance that trundled quietly into the area, then parked out of the way, its crew sitting inside drinking coffee until the uniforms had finished investigating the little they could find to investigate.

Once all the uniforms were busy searching the carpark for clues, like cartridge cases, the grey-suited man limped slowly up to the cafe and pushed inside. A tired smile of welcome briefly crossed his face as he stepped up to our table and sat heavily with a sigh.

'Gidday, Harry. What a clusterfuck! Who's this young lady?'

'This is Lisa. Lisa, say hi to Inspector James. You can trust him to do the right thing, so answer all of his questions very truthfully.'

That statement raised Greg's eyebrows.

'There's a lot to this event,' I said to him, before turning to Lisa. 'Would you mind sitting over the other side for a few moments? There are a few things I need to tell the Inspector that it would be best if you didn't know for now.'

Obviously intimidated by Greg and the flock of uniforms all around, she happily grabbed her coffee and moved over to a far table. All other patrons had bailed out long ago and uniforms were starting to drift in one at a time to get a coffee — take-away only once they saw the Inspector had commandeered two tables to set up an on-site office.

Rosie initially looked upset that all her regulars had left in a hurry, but was mollified when the uniforms started coming in for coffees and stuff to eat.

I started to spell out the whole story to Greg, but before I got too far he stopped me to call for a note-taker. Who turned out to be an attractive female Senior Constable, whereupon I had to start again, but at least she was competent in shorthand so I could speak at normal speed.

'Your eyes and ears only for now, Senior Burke,' Greg warned, 'anybody wants to know what you're doing, refer them to me.'

'Yes, sir. Thank you.' She said without lifting her eyes from her notebook.

Fifteen minutes and a coffee and pee break for Greg saw my story finished.

Both he and the Senior Constable gave me very strange looks, before he said, 'So if I understand this right, you're sitting on about 10 kilos of some unknown drug, as well as the payment for it which totals about $2 million in cash? Is that about it?'

'Yeah, mate. That's about it. But don't forget that the girl is a material witness and the Undertakers are still looking for her as well, since she knows a lot about Gary shit-for-brains, so she'll need some protection. She's also broke, has nowhere to stay and I'm not offering since I want to keep low profile — plus Sandy would rip my nuts off if I put her up. The bikies don't know of my involvement, and I'd like it to stay that way for now.'

'Yeah, got that, Harry. I'll think of something, but we'll probably have to put her into short-term Witness Protection. As I said before, what a clusterfuck!'

'Fair enough, but get that one rolling ASAP if you can please mate. I think she really is innocent and has no resources to fall back on, so you'll find probably that she's willing to enter a program. And good luck taking the money and drugs into evidence, they'll be a huge target.'

'Yeah, Grandma. Copy that. We've certainly had enough problems with stuff going walkabout from the Evidence Locker lately. There's an internal investigation going on at the moment.'

He looked at Senior Burke, 'And keep that one very close to your chest, Senior,' his eyes dropping only briefly to her generous and very shapely chest. 'You seem to be gaining access to all sorts of confidential information today.'

She grinned cheekily, 'Yes, sir. No problem for me. It beats filling out traffic accident reports, but I just hope that you and this gentleman with the unknown, but apparently highly influential background don't have to kill me once I've typed this statement!'

Greg smiled for the first time that morning. 'I think that you're safe Senior, but you may end up being far more involved in this mess than you'd like. We need to keep this information in a very close circle.'

'Again, no problem for me, sir. Bring it on. As I say, it sure beats General Duties and I might add that I've completed all my modules for the Detective Training Program.'

Greg frowned, 'That's a rather a big step Senior, but I'll take it under consideration.'

'Thank you sir. Any hands-on experience I can get with this case will be very useful.'

'OK, we'll see. So in that case, you might as well sit in on the rest of this discussion, but I'll need that transcript by tonight.'

'No problem, sir. I have a laptop and printer in the squad car and can do it immediately.'

With his usual flair for the dramatic, Greg tossed his hands in the air and appealed to me. 'Spare me from the enthusiasm of the younger generation.'

I grinned, 'Yeah, you poor old bastard. I really feel sorry for you. However, I might have to call this one in myself seeing as Interstate travel is involved. Do you want to inform Bob about that?'

That earned me a bright, inquisitive look from Senior Burke that I met with an impassive look.

'Yeah, thanks for reminding me. I'll do that shortly, once I've worked out what to do with the hard evidence. There must be some very angry bikies in town tonight if they're missing so much money and all those drugs.'

It was my turn to chuckle, 'I think that's a fair understatement, but think carefully. After all this trouble, I'd hate it to go walkabout.'

He looked pensive, 'Have you still got that bloody cat with you?'

'Yep. He's bigger and meaner than ever. For your ears only, he ripped a bloke to pieces a couple of months back. Of course, the dude was trying to shoot me at the time, so Jasper had a good excuse.'

By now, Amanda Burke's baby greens were very wide as Greg replied, 'Oh, yeah...I forgot about that. I wished I'd been there, but you were lucky, it could have turned really nasty.'

'It wasn't too bad,' I demurred, 'his mate was lucky. He just got his head blown off by a combination of Sandy's .40 Glock and my Remington TAC 14!'

Amanda Burke's eyes were almost bugging out as he laughed, 'Yeah. That'll do it every time. Anyway, getting back to the evidence in your possession, how do you feel about leaving it where it is for now?'

I thought for a moment, before replying, 'I don't mind, but Bob's going to have a pink fit, isn't he?'

'Yeah, he will, but I think I can cover that for a while. The only other way is to pack it up and stow it in another station's locker. But that just raises different questions and people get suspicious.'

I thought carefully then shrugged. 'Yeah, okay. Leave it there for now, but if anybody starts getting too close while looking for it, that means that Gary the dickhead has shot his fool mouth off. At that point, you'll need to come and take it away.'

Greg nodded in appreciation. 'No problem, Harry.' He looked at Amanda, still scribbling busily, 'No need to write that down, Senior. And definitely no pillow talk!'

She grinned, 'No chance of that, Sir. But I'll make sure I don't even think about drugs, cash and boats!'

Greg looked at her speculatively, then at me. 'Just a passing thought, Harry. But who's looking after your boat and the cargo at the moment?'

'Jasper, of course,' I replied. 'As usual. He has a little companion now, but I don't think she'll improve security much. Anyway, I wasn't about to cart 30 kilos of cash and drugs back up here with me while I had breakfast. Don't worry, it'll be fine with Jasper on the job.'

Greg got a bit red in the face. 'Aww fuck it, Harry. You can't just leave $2 million in cash and who knows how many millions of what must be some very special drugs on your boat with just your cat guarding it! Christ on a broomstick, my arse will be toast when Bob hears about that! He'll have me reporting to Senior Burke here within minutes as a Probationary Constable!'

I chuckled irreverently and said mildly, 'You'd look nice in uniform again Greg, very smart and blue suits you. But seriously, Jasper's pretty good at defending home and property.'

Senior Burke made a sound that she adroitly turned into a cough, but quickly stifled it as Greg went red in the face again. 'Yeah, sure. But a fucking cat for Christ's sake! We both know how good Jasper is, but Bob's going to go off his tits! And if something goes wrong, how the bloody hell would he explain it to the Commissioner! I gotta think of something better than that.'

So we let him think quietly for a few moments while I went to get us more tea and coffee. I was pleased to see that Senior Burke was a tea drinker. There needs to be more tea drinkers in this world that's slowly drowning itself in rotgut coffee.

Rosie, knowing my taste for sweet things, winked at me and passed over a plate of hot cinnamon doughnuts.

Back at the table, I noticed that thinking didn't stop Greg from scoffing several doughnuts, but maybe it did some good, since he suddenly sat back and smiled at Senior Burke.

'OK. Here's your chance Senior, to step up to the big time. Where do you live?'

She looked puzzled, but replied, 'Just up the road from here in Main Beach, sir. I share a flat with another female Constable and a Court Reporter.'

Greg beamed, 'Excellent! I'd like you to go home, change into civvies and pack enough casual clothes for a couple of weeks. Minimum luggage. You're going on a sort-of holiday deployment, so don't worry about a uniform, but I want you to throw in all your Service equipment, especially your weapon. Before you leave, see Sergeant Smith outside and tell him that I want him to round up a bunch of spare ammunition for you, including extra magazines and have them ready by the time you get back. Which means that I want to see you back here in about 15 minutes or sooner.' She looked confused for a moment until he barked. 'Go on. Move it, Senior. There's no time to waste.'

She grabbed her notebook, stabbed herself in her left tit with her pen while trying to get it back in her breast pocket and headed for the door. Greg called at her back, 'And don't forget to pass that message to Sergeant Smith on the way.'

She half-turned, flapped her hand in acknowledgment and pushed out the door, a bemused look still on her face.

Then turned to me, 'Harry, you're going to have Senior Burke as a backup guard, I'm afraid. It's the only way I can justify leaving that stuff aboard, even though it's the best place for it, for now.'

'Yeah. I knew what you were thinking, and I'll go along with it, but you get to officially square it with Sandy that I've got a very attractive female houseguest and it's strictly on business. OK?'

He chuckled, 'Yeah. OK. That's fair enough. I'll call her later, if only to let her know that you've stepped into the shit yet again.'

'I thought it was more like, 'right place, wrong time' but that's cool. As for Sandy, she'll be back in about 5 days I hope, so I'd better call her as well. You're bound to cock things up.'

Greg ignored that and looked across the room at Lisa. 'I'll need to get a full statement from your witness, and then organise short-term Witness Protection straight away. Can you tell her what the plan is so we don't have any aggro?'

I nodded. 'Yeah, OK. I'll do that now, then I'll have to call my people.'

'Goodo. I'll get all these other balls rolling, but don't forget that we'll need a statement off you as well before long. It's going to be a fucking long day, just like you suggested.'

CHAPTER 7

So several balls were set rolling.

I went over and sat with Lisa and told her about the required statement and the Witness Protection program.

She shook her head, 'I don't want to be locked up somewhere.'

I gave her a stern look, 'You aren't going to be locked up! But do consider your choices. Walk out of here after giving a statement and see how far $10 is going to take you before, to put it crudely, you end up hawking your fork just to survive. That's assuming you've managed to avoid the bikies who, incidentally, run most of the prostitution on the Coast!

Or you can co-operate with the Police, give then all the information you have on Gary then go along with the Program that will get you paid, fed, housed, clothed and safe from the bikies in a nice flat somewhere with an Officer to look after you 24/7. You will have to testify at trial, but you'll still be protected. I can assure you that you'll be better off than waitressing in Cairns or hanging out in the streets of sleazy Surfers Paradise.'

Lisa glared at him, 'Yeah, sure. But in Cairns I'd at least be free to do as I want.'

'Yes, that's right. But you chose to hook up with Gary so right or wrong, from that point on, the stage was set for this turn in your life. You'll have full freedom back once the trials are over and you are relocated. Anyway, it's your choice, because nobody can force you to enter the Protection Program. That part is entirely voluntary, but I urge you to carefully consider it as an alternative to hitting the streets.'

She looked sad and thoughtful. 'Yeah. I know, and thanks for helping me, Harry. I guess I'll have to go with the Program and try to be a good girl.'

'Excellent choice. The streets of Surfers Paradise are already full of young girls selling what they believe is their only asset and they don't need any more.'

She smiled weakly at that.

'Stay here and I'll tell the Inspector your decision. I'll go and get your bag from the boat, since Jasper won't let anybody else touch it. Then they'll probably take you to Southport Police Station for the interviews and reports. Please remember that you aren't being arrested!

After that, you'll be looked after properly. I'll try to see you if I can, or call me on this number anytime.' I scribbled my mobile number on a serviette, dropped $20 on the table for more food or drinks and returned to Greg.

'Is she going to co-operate?' He asked after answering some questions from a Forensics woman who didn't look old enough to even have left school!

'Yep. All good. Program and all interviews as well.'

'Great! I'll get one of the female Constables to take her back to the Station shortly and we'll get all that organised. She'll be looked after, I promise.'

'I'm sure she will be,' I said, 'but I've got to go fetch her bag from the boat. Jasper won't let anyone aboard if I'm not there.'

'Why don't you wait until Senior Burke is back, then you can take her down and get her settled in? I want that stuff under guard ASAP. There's not that much rush to send her to the Station now she's going to co-operate.'

'Good thinking, dude. I'll do that.'

So I sat back and had another tea, watching Greg direct operations and not mentioning that Senior Burke was taking longer than 15 minutes, but it was a big ask for her pack on the fly without knowing what it was all about. Finally, she did arrive and the transformation was very effective. As much as I liked ladies in uniform, tight jeans, a tight T-shirt and a denim jacket is a very good look on a well-built young woman.

And Senior Burke was a very well built young woman of above average height, well above average pretty, and with a trim athletic shape topped with shortish fine blonde hair.

To her credit, she only had a medium size soft carry bag and a small leather handbag slung over her shoulder that I presumed held her gun and other hardware, as there was absolutely nowhere for her to conceal it on her person, unless the gun was shoved in the waistband in the small of her back.

She dumped her bags on the floor and stood at the table, waiting until Greg finished barking a series of orders into his phone.

'Reporting for duty as ordered, sir,' she stated crisply, her tone at odds with her outfit.

Greg looked up and smiled, 'Ah, excellent Senior. Now, I'm giving you a plain-clothes assignment to provide an additional guard for the very valuable evidence currently held on Mr Stevens' boat, commencing immediately. Between you and Mr Stevens, and ah... his cat, you are to maintain constant watch over the items, regardless of future events, until relieved of duty. I'll let Mr Stevens provide the inductions and work out an effective roster, but I'd like you to consider yourself under his authority for the duration.

In case you might have issues with that, I can tell you in the very strictest of confidence that he's associated with the ACP and holds a rank superior to myself.'

That little statement opened her very expressive eyes wide. 'Yes sir, that won't be any problem at all. And thank you for the opportunity to become further involved with this case.'

Greg chuckled, 'To quote an old Chinese saying, 'Be careful what you wish for.' You also may not thank me if you suffer from seasickness. I do and it wasn't pleasant the last time I was on the rotten thing.'

'I know that won't be a problem, sir. I come from a boating family.'

'Oh, good. Now Harry. She's yours for the duration, so take

her with you and put her to work. I'll send a Constable down to the boat with you to bring our witness's bag back.'

'Goodo, Greg. Just have him or her put a plain coat on over the uniform. I don't want any association with uniformed Police down at the boat right now if we can avoid it. I'll also be moving *Firebird* back out to the mooring as soon as we're aboard, so when you want my statement, call my mobile.'

He considered a moment, 'No problem. But Senior Burke can take your statement and if I remember rightly, you've got all sorts of fancy communications devices on that thing, so sign it and send it. Or we can call by and pick it up.'

'That's a good idea. In fact, as people are used to the Water coppers dropping around, that would be a good way to pass paperwork and anything else.'

He smiled, 'Thanks Harry. I know you didn't go looking for it, but it's another big pile of shit that you've walked into. I suppose that life was a bit quiet at the moment — and thank you, Senior for your co-operation. I hope you won't find the assignment too boring.'

She smiled, 'I'm sure I won't, sir.'

'Very well, carry on and good luck.'

I waved at Lisa, sitting forlornly at her table across the room and left the diner, Senior Burke trailing obediently behind.

FIREBIRD

Outside, I paused and said to Amanda. 'Now. Since you're going to be living on my boat, which is my home as well, for an indefinite period, I'm calling you Amanda and you're calling me Harry, 'cause they're our names. No farting about with rank and other bullshit! Are you right with that?'

She grinned, 'Yes, sir...That is, yes Harry. Definitely no problem with that.'

We found a young female Constable waiting for us, a plain Forensic team dustcoat draped over her uniform, who introduced herself as Tracy Edwards. I led the two ladies through the Police Crime scene tape and past the pub that was just opening its doors to a team of uniforms waiting to start the lengthy round of staff interviews on the night's happenings.

'Busy morning Tracy,' I commented.

She grinned, 'Yes, sir. But I probably feel the same as Senior, in that it's a great break away from typing up reports or attending traffic accidents.'

Amanda grinned back, 'Yep. Absolutely!'

We walked on in silence until we reached the end, whereupon Ray popped out of his office like a puppet, a lecherous grin on his face.

'Now that's what I was talking about, Harry, and two at once. Good lad!'

'Yeah, good on ya Ray. Thanks for that, but I'll be moving back out to the mooring shortly, so you can have your pontoon back.'

He waved a hand vaguely, 'No rush, m'boy, no rush. Do some entertaining first. Break out the drinks and get the ladies comfortable and used to being on the water.'

'Thanks for the offer, Ray, but we've got to keep moving. This is business.'

His face fell. 'Oh dear. Now I see that one lady does look rather official. You're not in strife again are you? We don't want any more of those bikies hanging around like last night.'

'No Dad. All's well. Anyway I'm not the one in trouble, the bikies are.'

He gave a twisted grin and disappeared back into his cave, leaving the dysfunctional Fang outside to peer myopically at the source of his disturbed sleep.

Amanda giggled and said, 'That thing's got a milk bottle tied around its neck.'

'Yeah. It can hardly see, so it keeps walking off the wharf. That keeps it afloat until Ray can fish it out with that long handled landing net propped up against the wall.'

Both ladies shook their heads, before turning their attention to *Firebird* as I led them down the ramp to the fuelling pontoon.

'This is a very impressive boat, Harry,' Amanda said, eyeing off *Firebird's* lines and rigging.

'Thanks. It's a good boat and very comfortable as you'll see. I'll give you the full tour shortly.'

I turned to Tracy, 'Come on down and I'll get Lisa's backpack for you.'

She nodded, so I led them aboard via the stern steps and fetched Lisa's pack from the cockpit seat and handed it over. Tracy grunted at the weight, but hoisted it onto her back and trudged back up to the wharf, not looking much like a backpacker.

'Okay. That's one thing out of the way. But while I think of it and in case you missed me telling Inspector James, my lady friend is returning from relieving duties in about 5 days. Her name is Sandy Thomson and she's an Inspector as well.'

Amanda smiled, 'Oh, yes. I've met her. She's a really nice lady. But she was on some really heavy undercover operation down south not long ago. She's a bit of a legend around the Station.'

'I'm glad you know her. This is the boat that was involved in that operation, but I can't tell you too much about it yet. There's still some cleaning up going on as an aftermath.'

It must have been a bit of a party trick, but her eyes widened disconcertingly. 'Wow! I didn't realise. There've been some wild stories going around about the operation. Like a whole bunch of high level people were arrested for being paedophiles.'

I grimaced, 'Yeah. I'll tell you what I can sometime later, but for now let's get you settled in, after you meet the resident guard cat, Jasper and his killer sidekick Krazy.'

She grinned, 'It sounds weird the way you call him a guard cat and trust him to look after the boat and the evidence.'

'You'll see, but he has to meet you properly so there's no problems later. Once he knows you, he'll protect you as well.'

Amanda had a quizzical expression on her face as I unlocked the saloon doors and Krazy the kitten, looking like a small ball of bristling black fur, fangs and claws, belted out and attacked my leg in greeting.

Amanda cracked up laughing as she bent down and with one hand, scooped the feisty little bundle off my leg, then with two strokes of her hand had her purring loudly and kneading Amanda's chest with her tiny paws, something I wouldn't have minded doing myself. 'I'm sorry to laugh, but I can see why Inspector James was concerned about security. She doesn't look like much of a guard cat to me.'

I smiled at the way she settled the kitten so quickly. 'No, you're right. She hasn't quite learned the routine yet, but that's Krazy the understudy. This is Jasper!'

On cue, my beautiful, sleek black 25-kilo Chausie-cross cat stepped into the cockpit, his head and shoulders as high as Amanda's waist, before sitting down in front of her, staring intently into her eyes.

To her credit, Amanda didn't shriek or carry on like most females do when they meet Jasper for the first time, but she did gently hand the kitten to me, not taking her eyes off him.

'Goodness me, Harry. He *is* a big boy. You'd better make those introductions before he decides I'm breakfast.'

I approved of her reaction and Jasper seemed to as well as I squatted down beside him. 'Jasper. This is Amanda. She's our friend and will be staying with us for a while. Please look after her for me.'

Amanda gave me an odd look, but stood still as Jasper stepped forward, sniffed at her several times, then firmly nuzzled her crutch. She staggered back slightly with the push, but stood fast as he circled her, still sniffing. He sat down again in front of her, then lifted his right paw and held it out to her.

With a look of pure delight, she took it and squeezed gently, feeling the strength in his muscles and the sharpness of his claws. The sides of Jasper's mouth moved in what passed for a grin, before he took his paw back.

'Wow!' Amanda breathed quietly, 'that's amazing. I've never seen a cat as big as that outside a zoo and never knew of any sort that shook hands.'

'Yeah. He's pretty special all right. He's supposed to be a Chausie, but a vet told me that the domestic part of his cross was probably replaced illegally by another hybrid jungle cat, which would account for his size, but he's normally very docile and behaves just like a domestic cat, so it's simplest if you treat him like that.'

'Can I touch him?' she asked.

'Of course,' I laughed, 'but be careful. He may not let you stop if you scratch him in all the places a normal cat likes.'

So she did, hesitantly at first, then more boldly when he didn't take her hand off, but purred loudly and rubbed against her legs, almost making me envious, but I controlled my urges and thought of Sandy coming home soon.

'Okay. I hate to break up Jasper's scratching session, but I'd better show you around and get you settled.'

CHAPTER 8

I had started to explain the shower and toilet procedure, but Amanda looked up from scratching Jasper's head. 'I know this bit. I've spent a lot of time on boats and know that I can't waste water and not to put anything in the toilet that hasn't been through me first. Apart from toilet paper, of course.'

'Goodo. The other thing is that everything in the galley is electric with only the gas Weber BBQ safely out in the cockpit for doing roasts and grills on. I don't suppose you happen to like cooking?'

She smiled, 'Yes, I do. If you want, I'll be happy to take over cooking duties.'

I grinned, 'That's great. I can if I have to, but prefer not to if I have a choice. Therefore, when the shore is close, I eat at the pub, which is where I was last night when the bikie stuff started. Which reminds me, I'd better do the tour, let you unpack, then we'll get that statement done for Greg.'

She nodded, so I took her around the rest of *Firebird*, showing her where everything was, explained that I had the whole of the right hull, and ending up in the portside aft double cabin. 'Will this suit you? It's more private than the for'rard cabin, but there's not as much storage space. Still, it looks like you travel lightly so that shouldn't be a problem. There's more storage for'rard in this hull if you need it.'

She was delighted with the whole setup and very happy with her cabin. 'This is absolutely terrific, thanks Harry. It's an amazing boat and I can't wait until we go for a sail, if we can.'

'Oh, yes. We'll go sailing all right. I just don't know when. It'll depend on how this investigation develops. Now when you're ready, I'd like to move back out to my mooring before we do anything else. I'll be happier away from this wharf.'

In answer, Amanda stripped off her denim jacket, leaving her in the delightfully tight T-shirt, tight jeans and runners, dug a cap out of her duffle and grinned, 'Ready now, Skipper. I'll do the lines if you like, when you say the word.'

I grinned back, 'Excellent! I'll just kick the engines into life first. The mooring lines are looped, so they stay with us and you don't have to go onto the pontoon, just untie one on-board end and pull them in. There are no spring lines as the pontoon is floating.'

She appeared to understand all I said, which boded well for future help with boat handling but I'd watch her carefully until I was sure. I started the twin Yanmar 85 horsepower diesels and let them warm up for a few minutes while I checked oil pressures and charge rates.

Amanda was standing beside the cockpit when I said, 'Drop the stern line first please, so I can drive forward against the bow line and swing the stern out.'

She nodded and moved aft with easy grace, particularly with an unfamiliar deck layout, dropping one end of the line carefully then pulling the free end aboard. While she untied the line and neatly coiled it, I nudged the right engine ahead, which, since the bow was held fast, pushed the stern out from the pontoon. With it well clear, I pulled the engine to neutral, had Amanda drop the for'rard line then backed out of the berth into the main channel. One engine forward and the other in reverse rotated us quietly 180° and we headed for the mooring, just a few hundred metres away on the outside of the moored array of boats off the Yacht Club.

Without needing to be told, Amanda untied the lashings on the long boathook and stood ready.

As conditions were fairly calm, it was a simple task to ease up to the small floating buoy, that she snagged on the first try, before I went for'rard to help haul in the chain and secure it to the mooring bridle that kept us from sheering side to side in a wind.

'Nice work,' I complimented her, receiving a broad grin in reply.

'I'd forgotten how good it is being on the water! This is great!'

I went to shut down the engines, leaving Amanda to wander around, checking things out, then I dug out the evidence from the hidey-holes and carried them into the saloon — one sleeping bag roll look-a-like, and a carry-on bag full of cash. When Amanda joined me a couple of minutes later, she whistled when she saw the cash.

'I haven't counted it yet,' I said, 'so I guess we'd better do that and record it officially.'

'OK.'

So we emptied out the bag and checked the note count in each of the bundles, leaving the paper bands in place. I dug out the very accurate galley scales so we could weigh the notes, and there was a consistent $10,000 per bundle, or 100 x $100 notes, that in turn were rubber-banded into bricks of ten bundles each making a brick worth $100,000.

Out of interest, I fetched a ruler from the chart table and measured a $10K bundle to find that it was just 10mm thick.

After counting every note, we ended up with the dining table covered in money. But after stacking the re-assembled bricks in orderly rows gave us 20 bricks for a neat $2 million.

'Holy crap!' Amanda eloquently said, 'it's one thing to read and talk about that much money, but to see it in the flesh, so to speak, is stunning.'

'You're right there,' I said, 'now, let's take a few photos for the record and try to stuff it all back in that bag which looks way too small.'

So we photographed, then after several attempts, managed to get the right alignment of the bricks so they all fitted back in the bag.

'Right,' I said briskly, 'that was the fun part. Now let's see what this shit is that all that cash is buying.'

THE UNDERTAKERS HQ,
MOLENDINAR SOUTHPORT, THURSDAY MIDDAY

'Undertaker'...

    'Davies, sir. I have news of the shipment.'

    'Good afternoon, Mr Davies. What is the news?'

    'The courier, a fellow called Gary Williams, was sighted entering a flat in Main Beach this morning, rented by a friend of his. It looked like he may have stayed there the night before as he only had a bag of groceries and fast food with him. There was no sign of his large backpack.'

    'Excellent news, Mr Davies. Are you able to gain entry to the premises?'

    'Not without alerting the subject and maybe other occupants, sir. I intended to wait and see if the subject and any others in there leave before I made a search, but I can do a forced entry if you want.'

    'No, you are correct. We should try to keep this low profile if possible. Are there any signs that the opposition is watching as well?'

    'No sir. No watchers and there hadn't been any ride or drive-by's either.'

    'Very well, Mr Davies. Please keep the place under close watch. Do you have back-up with you?'

    'Not yet. But Mr Jones and Mr Strahan should be on their way soon.'

    'Good. If the subject leaves, please pick him up, then search the house for the goods. After that, bring Mr Williams to me.'

    'Yes, sir. We'll do that.'...

ZOMBIE EATERS HQ, WEST OF SOUTHPORT, THURSDAY – MIDDAY

President Brad Edwards and his 2IC Tony Bradford, were seated in the comfortable lounge area of the modest rural property, sipping large mugs of coffee.

'I just got a call from a friend who says that those fuck-witted clowns really made a balls-up of their shipment over at Mariners Cove last night,' Brad said.

'Oh, yeah. What was new?'

'They've not only lost the delivery of this super-MDMA shit, but managed to misplace the payment as well!'

'Oh, bloody hell! That'll make the Sydney boys happy.'

'Yeah. They won't sit still for that. Not $2 mill in cash.'

Brad rubbed his hands together gleefully. 'I love to see that walking corpse step on his dick! I'm trying to think of a way we can profit from all this.'

Just then the phone rang again.

'Andy! Speak to me, O wise one. What news?'

'*Yeah. Gidday Brad. Wise one to you too mate. Listen — Pete just heard from his source that the Undertakers have a line on the Sydney courier. He's gone to ground in a flat in Main Beach. Some mate of the courier rents it, and they think he's still got the merchandise with him.*'

'Good one, dude. Are they doing anything about it?'

'*Yeah. The boss has told them to snatch him if he comes out, then bust in and search the place.*'

'Ooh. The neighbours won't like that! How many of their guys are on it?'

'*Just one at the moment, but two more should be on the way soon in a car.*'

'Okay. I see an opportunity for some fun and games. Get around there and wait 'till we show up. I reckon they'll all sit in one car for the watch, so I'll bring four of the boys in the

Suburban and we'll immobilise them. Then we'll bust in, yell out loudly we're the Undertakers so the neighbours can hear, grab the dude and his gear and bugger off. How's that sound?'

'Sounds a bit wobbly to me mate. But you never know. They won't be expecting a move like that.'

'That's what I figured, so we'll get rolling now. See ya there!'

Five minutes later, an immaculate, black Chevy Suburban, the size and weight of a medium truck, rolled quietly out the drive-way, and obeying all traffic rules, headed for Main Beach. Five big men, armed with a variety of weapons, including Mace canisters, occupied the seats with room for several more in comfort.

CHAPTER 9

Amanda untied the cords holding the sleeping bag cover in place and with some difficulty, we slid it off a cylinder wrapped tightly with black plastic and secured with packaging tape. Unwrapping it was an exercise in caution, but after just one layer was off, we were left with a cylinder made of some thin plastic that I guessed was about 12 litres in capacity and had a very basic, push-on lid with tape sealing it closed.

The contents looked like a very fine, white powder, packed very densely so we had to un-tape the lid to get at it. I found a small, new, zip-lock bag and using the tip of a knife, carefully transferred a small quantity.

'Been a drug-test dummy before?' I asked Amanda with a grin.

She regarded me seriously, 'Yeah, I have. It was MDMA that I tried a small sample of, although the so-called normal dose is supposed to be 100mg to 125mg. But we don't know exactly what this stuff is. I mean, it's a lot of money for 10 kilos of any wholesale drug. I don't know how much uncut MDMA goes for, but I'm sure it's nowhere near $2 million.'

'True. Paying that much for 10 kilos of this stuff would suggest that it's a new form of the drug, perhaps highly concentrated or highly potent, or worse, maybe both of the above! We need to get this sample tested in a lab ASAP, but it might help if we knew how powerful it is.'

She shrugged, 'Yeah, okay. I'll sacrifice my mind for the cause.'

With the tip of the kitchen knife I'd used, she dug into the container and scooped up a tiny amount that looked like it would just cover my little fingernail when spread out.

'That's about 10mg, so I'm going to divide that in half. Normal MDMA would have little or no effect at that dosage level, so even if this is a very powerful form, I shouldn't be affected too much.'

Shaking about half of the tiny pile back into the container, she moistened the tip of her little finger, dabbed it into the fine powder that was left and touched it to her tongue. Nothing happened for a few moments as she handed the knife back, then she suddenly gave a wide beaming smile and gave a chortling laugh.

'Holy shit! That hits like a train wreck! It's beautiful and I'm tingling all over, feel high as a kite and happy as all hell!'

'I take it that means it's different to MDMA?' I asked, slightly amused by her reaction and unused to sitting in on druggies taking hits of their favourite lollies.

'Christ! This is nothing like the 'normal' MDMA. It's a 100-times more potent and apart from the strong feeling of euphoria, there's a very powerful sexual rush! Apart from making you happy, MDMA tends to make you just feel like getting very friendly with people, but this stuff makes me want to rip all my clothes off!'

While I wouldn't have minded that at all, I realised that she was describing exactly how she felt and was trembling with the effort to stay under control and be objective for me. As it was, one hand was pressed firmly across the front of her jeans, well below her belt, while the other was gently kneading one breast, a happy look on her face.

'Will you be alright?' I asked, aware that taking her clothes off in front of a virtual stranger would be classed as slightly unusual for a policewoman on duty.

She smiled happily at me, 'Oh, sure. It's just got to run it's course and we don't know how long that'll be, so kick back and keep an eye on me in case there are any unexpected side effects.'

Shortly after, she slumped back in the seat, breaking out in a heavy sweat, so I quickly fetched some water and she took a big drink. She stayed slumped back, grinning happily, twitching and squirming slowly and sinuously in the seat, but not saying much that made any sense for another twenty minutes, when she sat forward with a groan and said, in a fairly normal tone, 'Shit! That still feels good, but I think it's nearly over. I still want sex, but not so badly, so that's easing too.'

Her shirt was quite wet in patches, as were her jeans, but I didn't point that out, guessing that all her Christmas's had come many times over rather than just the proverbial once.

Another five minutes and she seemed almost back to normal, so after helping her to her feet, I sent her to have a wash. While she was gone, I made sure that the sample was secure in its zip-lock bag, before carefully taping up the container. I didn't bother with the black plastic wrapping, but managed to work the outer cover back into place and drew the tie-cords up tight.

Not long after, Amanda appeared looking much better, her short, blonde hair still damp and wearing loose shorts instead of jeans, that showed a pair of long and nicely tanned legs.

'How do you feel now?' I asked, holding her head steady so I could examine her eyes, but apart from some dilation, she seemed to be over the worst of it.

Amanda sat down and blew out a big breath. 'Not bad, thanks. But that was pretty incredible! It's far more intense than the normal MDMA and much faster acting as well. The sexual side is very different too — very specific and much more intense. I hate to think what a stronger dose would do.'

I nodded, 'I think that if what you took was considered a normal dose and these guys cut it accordingly, they could have increased their investment by a factor of 10, at least. But we'd better get you to a doctor for a check-up and testing for any after effects or addiction.'

'No way,' She protested violently, 'I have no compulsion to try any more, and I'm feeling almost back to normal, apart from feeling a bit jumpy and still....'

She paused briefly, closed her eyes and gave a shudder that

seemed to go on for a while, before leaning back while letting out a big breath. She had a silly grin on her face for a few moments more while she seemed to go off with the fairies or somebody but pulled herself back with a visible effort.

She struggled to pick up on where she'd been, but then appeared to remember and said, 'Sorry about that! It hit a bit quickly but was very lovely! Much more intense than usual and I'm still very...extremely stimulated! I'll just hang about here on this lovely boat doing what I'm supposed to be doing and you can make sure I don't appear to be doing anything too weird.'

I realised what she'd been objectively describing and was trying to think of a suitable response, when a saviour in the shape of little Krazy jumped up on her lap, purring and kneading her legs with needle-sharp claws. 'Hi little girl, settle down please,' Amanda spoke softly and the tiny kitten responded, curling up happily in her lap, while Jasper watched impassively from the cockpit doorway.

Leaving Amanda to her little pussy, I went up to the bows, dug out my mobile phone and dialled Greg.

'*Yeah, Harry.*'

'Hi. I suppose you're up to your arse in crocodiles by now?'

'*Did you call just to tell me that? I've just had the bloody Commissioner on the horn telling me to settle this thing down before it blows up into bikie gang warfare on the streets of his beloved Gold Coast, before a cast of half a million Racing Carnival tourists.*'

I chuckled, 'No, actually. I called to say that we took a look at the items I'm babysitting. The money is all cash in new hundreds and it adds up to a neat two million.'

'*Bloody hell, Harry. I thought you were just bullshitting before when you dropped that number. So it really is all there?*'

'Yep. Senior Burke and I counted it twice, photographed the lot and with great difficulty stuffed it back into the bag. In regard to the merchandise, Senior Burke put her well-being on the line and tried a small sample....'

'*Ah, shit! Is she all right? I didn't want anybody messing with that stuff, Harry. It's totally unknown and we don't know what it'll do.*'

'Settle down big dog! She's okay and thanks to her, now we do know what we're facing. I've got to tell you mate, even though she tried the smallest bit, it's incredibly potent. She got bombed really hard, almost immediately with just a tiny taste, like a bit on the tip of her finger, probably less than 5 mg! If this stuff is on the streets, it'd better be cut heaps, or there are going to be some weird things happening.'

'*Like what?*' He demanded.

'Like it's the ultimate happy pill and the ultimate aphrodisiac all rolled into one. You'd have people laughing their heads off while they fucked each other senseless in the main street in broad daylight if they got even a normal dose of this stuff.'

'*Oh, shit! That's all we need. It'll be too much to hope for that there's no more coming in.*'

'Amen to that, brother, but we both know that's not the case. This stuff is way too good. Anyway, we reckon that it could easily be cut by up to 90% or so and still be stunningly potent, so the potential profit on just this one shipment is colossal! That means the boys will be beating the bushes very hard looking for their yummy treats.'

'*You'd better keep your head very low, Harry. I really need you to be invisible.*'

'Gee, Greg. I didn't know you cared.'

'*I don't, you big goose, but you've got one of my best tech specialists out there with you and I don't want her coming to harm.*'

'Yes, Dad. I'll be good. But what's her speciality?'

'*Surveillance — in particular, drones. She's been working with them for a while and has just returned from an advanced course in America and brought back some of the very latest toys the Yanks have let us play with. She's the State's resident expert so don't break her! Please!*'

'Okay boss. I'll look after her. I guess that we'll have to keep our fingers crossed that the boys don't find that idiot Gary Williams. They'll soon find out where he left the goods if they get their grubby little paws on him.'

'Yeah. Copy that. I've got a 'Be On The Lookout' alert out to all car and foot patrols, but he'll probably turn up in the river. At that point, we'll have to assume that he's told where he left the gear and you're going to be in their sights.'

'Yeah. I thought of that and I guess that it won't do any good to just dump the stuff.'

'No, it won't. So you may have to move, but we'll worry about that later. Was that all you had? I've got fifteen people lined up to talk to me.'

'Yeah, just one. I've taken a small sample of the merchandise for analysis. Can somebody come to collect it? I'd rather not go back ashore for a while.'

'Oh, yeah. Good. I forgot to ask you to do that. How about I get the Water boys to swing past on their next run?'

'That'll be fine, thanks Greg, we'll be here. Cheers.'

'Low profile, Harry. Very low...'

I wandered back to the saloon and brought Amanda up to date.

'So we watch and wait for now?'

'Yep. That's about it, kick back and enjoy a paid holiday. There are recorded movies on portable drives you can watch, or e-books if you have a reader, TV if you're really that desperate, or maybe you can do some study for that Detective course you were talking about.'

She grinned at me, 'Yeah. Good idea and I was serious about that, but I'm still a bit too spaced out to concentrate on that, so I might just sit outside in the sun for a while.'

'No problem. I might put this sample into a padded envelope for when the collection service comes around.'

Amanda wandered out and stretched out on the huge daybed, little Krazy kitten leaping up to cuddle in beside her. I found a padded posting bag and tucked the sample safely in its sealed bag inside, along with a note for the local Forensics Lab technicians about its origins and observed effects of a sub-5mg dose on a human.

I'd just finished addressing it to Greg's attention, when there was a hail of, 'Ahoy, *Firebird*.' Closing on the stern was a 25' Rigid Inflatable Boat in Police markings, complete with light bar, spotlights, siren and a pair of gleaming black 300hp Suzuki outboards strapped to the stern. Spotting me, the Senior Constable acting as bowman, Pete Larson signalled the driver to edge forward.

'Gidday, Harry,' he called, 'what have you been up to now that makes us play mailman?'

By then Amanda had sat up, eyeing the guys off with what appeared to be predatory interest that was confirmed by the two small but prominent bumps on the front of her T-shirt, and that caught the crew's attention.

'Well look who's on holidays!' The driver, Sergeant Les Thomas greeted her cheerfully, while Pete just stared, apparently unused to seeing an aroused Senior Constable on duty, 'Gidday Amanda. What the hell are you doing hooked up with this boat bum?'

'Oh, hi Les. Good to see you, but I'm not exactly on holidays.'

I could see that her somewhat ill considered statement had raised both eyebrows and unspoken questions, so I waved them closer and suggested they kill the engines, tie up astern and come aboard for a coffee. Always happy to socialise, they were aboard and sitting around the cockpit table so fast, they almost left skid marks on the deck.

Jasper wisely retreated out of sight, although his fuzzy little sidekick hung around looking for food and attention.

Amanda happily manned the galley to brew tea and coffee, Pete's eyes following her as she moved around, while I tried to explain the situation without giving too much away.

Thirty minutes later, coffees drained, I was wrapping up my

highly modified story about some evidence, vital to a pending case, which was left aboard by a visitor yesterday that needed to be kept away from Southport Station. I was quite proud of my efforts to muddy the waters, and that I hadn't actually told a lie — just left a heap of stuff out!

'So Amanda's the hired muscle, is that the story?'

'Yeah, although more accurately, an extra pair of eyes. It might have looked a bit obvious if there were two or three hairy-chested male coppers hanging around trying to look casual. An attractive lady looks more natural on a boat.'

Amanda blushed slightly as the Sergeant said, 'Yeah, we can't argue with that. But how about we make a point of swinging past on our regular patrols anyway? We can make it look natural, seeing as you're parked 200 metres away from our base!'

'That'd be great if you would, thanks guys. We'd really appreciate it. And just pass the envelope to Greg James. He's waiting for it.'

'Yeah, we know. He's been on the phone three times in the last hour wanting to know where we were.'

They got to their feet, thanked Amanda for the coffee and bickies and wandered aft.

'Okay Harry,' Les said, 'This thing's still a bit suss from my point of view and I can't help think that this has a lot to do with that guy who was found shot over in the Cove this morning, but I'll go along with it. There's obviously things you can't and won't tell me, but if it's something that affects my area of operations, will you let me know immediately? Please?'

I nodded, not happy about having to keep good, straight men like Les and Pete in the dark.

Les added, 'We caught the BOLO alert earlier, so we'll keep an eye out for anything odd at night.'

'Thanks, guys. Cheers for now.'

With no more fuss, they boarded, started and cast off, waving cheerfully as they burbled away.

'I said the wrong thing, didn't I?' Amanda asked contritely.

'Yeah, you did a bit,' I admitted, 'but we've squirmed out from under. They're wondering why a female Senior Constable is officially parked on a boat, but Greg will make sure they don't ask too many questions out loud.' I chuckled, 'At least you being here guarantees their attention at all hours.'

She poked her tongue out and made a rude noise, before resuming her highly decorative position on the daybed.

CHAPTER 10

A very solid, stocky and scruffy man with long hair and a long, unkempt beard was wandering aimlessly up and down a couple of streets, trying unsuccessfully to look as though he belonged in this yuppie's paradise of grossly over-priced real estate. As his attention seemed to be mainly focused on one of the last old rentals in the area, several calls from concerned residents had been made to the Police regarding 'a dirty-looking, homeless man looking like he's planning to break into an old house'.

With the action still happening at Mariners Cove, there was a lengthy delay in generating a response to those calls as there was a shortage of patrol cars available to placate the concerns of the wealthy residents of the long-ago sleepy collection of cheaply built weekenders that had become prime Gold Coast real estate.

Therefore, the battered grey Holden Commodore with two big men inside and looking almost as out-of-place as the scruffy man it pulled up beside, was unchallenged by any form of officialdom as it parked up the street from the old timber two-story house, giving the three large, male occupants a good view of the front and side doors.

'Where the fuck have you guys been?' the scruffy man whinged as he climbed into the back seat, 'I've been wandering around getting dirty looks from everybody. It's a wonder they didn't call the cops!'

'Yeah, yeah. Don't get your panties in a twist,' the driver commented, 'Baz and I were visiting his mother in the Nursing home so we couldn't leave until the hour was up. She gets terribly upset if we leave early.'

'Bloody good thing I wasn't hanging from the guttering by my fingertips that there then, wasn't it?'

'Don't be a smart arse, Billy. She's a dear old thing and the boss knows we visit this time each week. Anyway, we're here now so drop it. Any sign of the boy?'

Billy grumped a bit more then replied, 'Nah. Two chicks wearing some sort of uniform went inside, but they might have just been knocking off work. Other than that, it's been quiet.'

Just then, a very loud hammering on the rear window shattered the glass and scared the crap out of the three men. Standing beside the car was an old lady with a wheelie-walker, wielding a heavy wood walking stick with the skill of a martial arts expert and with which she continued to hammer any part of the car within reach. Unfortunately, Billy didn't think and wound down his window, promptly receiving a backhanded blow to his face that opened a long gash on his cheek and probably cracked his cheekbone.

'I know what you're up to, you rotten mongrels!' she screeched, 'we've been watching you perving on the young girls in that old house. You're all up to no good you lousy bastards and we've called the Police! Take that for starters!'

As Billy fell back in shock from the first blow, blood streaming down his face from the long gash in his cheek, the old dear poked the end of her stick into his face with deadly aim, shifting his entire nose sideways across his face and sending a fresh flood of blood pouring down his face and chest.

Howling in pain and fright, Billy tried to scramble across the seat to escape the attack, the blood from both nose and cheek spraying across the two guys in front.

'Jesus Christ, Billy. Stop jumping around you stupid prick! You're spraying blood everywhere.'

'Well get that rotten old bitch off me,' he screamed, holding his shirt up to his face in a futile attempt to staunch the flood.

The front seat passenger tried to get out to chase their elderly assailant away, only to find himself pinned between his seat and the car door by the wheelie-walker jammed painfully up against his legs, while a series of blows from the heavy handle of the stick opened a gash from his hair-line to his jaw, his blood flow adding to the slaughter-house appearance inside the car.

'Ahhgggh! Get away, you rotten old bitch! We haven't done anything!'

'You *were* about to do something, though, weren't you,' she cackled, prancing around with delight at causing so much damage, 'and don't call me a rotten old bitch, you cock-sucker! I'm not the one bleeding everywhere.'

By now, two more old dears had turned up to help their friend, who plainly didn't need anybody's help.

'Good on you, Gladys! Whack him again,' called one newcomer, 'that one in the back has been hanging around all morning up to no good. Arsehole!'

Salvation of a sort arrived in a most unusual manner as a very large, gleaming black Chevy Suburban eased quietly to a stop in the street beside the besieged Commodore, the front passenger door opening to allow a well-dressed young man in a grey Armani suit to step down. Making a quick assessment of the scene, he looked across at Gladys the Attacker and said in a cultured voice, 'Good morning madam. May I be of assistance?'

Impressed by the large, immaculate vehicle and the calm manner and good looks of the young man addressing her, Gladys settled and replied, 'Well yes, you can if you're the Police. These thugs have been perving on the young girls in the old house over there and that man in the back seat was walking around for ages this morning just casing the place.'

The young man smiled gently and said with a slight accent, 'Detective Edwards at your service. My colleagues and I happened to be passing when we were notified of your call. We will take care of these gentlemen for now if you'd care to return to your home, you have my very grateful thanks for a job well done.'

He carefully and politely shook hands with Gladys and her two friends, before managing to turn them gently toward their homes. Once the old dears were well clear, he approached the old Commodore, while the three men from the Suburban opened doors and climbed out.

'Hi, guys,' he said quietly, letting his suit coat fall open to show the holstered gun at his waist, 'I'm sure that you don't want any more aggro this morning, so I suggest that you sit here quietly with two of my boys to keep you company, while my buddy and I go visit across the street.'

'You won't get away with this, Edwards,' Arthur Davies mumbled, blood still cascading down his front, 'The Undertaker will rip your balls off!'

'Oh, dear me,' Brad said, 'I'm not responsible for your condition, in fact, none of us had laid a hand on any of you. It would appear that you've brought an amazing amount of grief upon yourselves by being stupid. From memory, your esteemed boss doesn't take very kindly to his troops being stupid. I think you might be in for more of the same when you venture back to the Bat Cave.'

The three hapless Undertakers refrained from replying, confining themselves to glaring back as a cheerful Brad and his 2IC Tony Bradford, strode briskly across the road, leaving two large and armed Zombie Eaters standing guard.

Brad and Tony ambled up to the front door, paint peeling in long strips from salt air exposure and zero maintenance for the last fifteen or so years. Knuckles substituted for a doorbell.

A response came in the form of a young and attractive girl, apparently just out of a shower and loosely wrapped in a large towel.

'Oh, hi. Can I help you?' She tried to make the towel more

secure, but it wasn't really working. 'I was expecting someone else.'

Brad gave his thousand-watt smile reserved for attractive females, especially when they are just out of a shower. 'Sorry to disturb you Miss. But we'd like to talk to Gary Williams — I believe he's here?'

She smiled, charmed by his smile and politeness. 'Gary? Oh, yeah. He's out on the back veranda. Do you mind going through. I'd better make myself more decent.'

Brad smiled again, 'You look just fine to me, but do carry on. We'll find our way.'

She even giggled when he gently patted her on the bum as she walked away, peeling off into the first bedroom off the hallway that apparently led through to the back.

'Hey Chloe. Was that Lester?' A male voice from up ahead called out.

A few more paces, then Brad and Tony passed through a doorway to a semi-enclosed veranda where a double bed was jammed into one end and a scattering of worn out old lounge chairs and sofas looked out over a tangled mess of backyard, thickly overgrown with weeds. A narrow path had been beaten to a vintage Hills Hoist rotary clothesline, partly draped with a variety of female clothing and underwear.

A lanky blonde-headed, ageing surfie-type guy was sprawled back in an overstuffed chair, sucking on a scrawny-looking joint, eyes half drooped and un-focused. It took him several seconds to realise that the two guys looking at him were strangers.

'What the fuck...! You're not Lester. Who are you dudes? How did you get in here? Where's Chloe?'

Brad looked carefully around, noting the large backpack propped up against the unmade bed. Looking down at Gary, he said quietly, 'Are you Gary Williams?'

'Who's asking?' Came the rude reply, as Gary belatedly extracted a small amount of bravado from the smoke.

'We're friends who'd like to ask you a few questions, but this may not be the best place to talk, so if you wouldn't mind coming with us, we can drop you back later if all goes well.'

'Bullshit! I don't know you and I'm certainly not going anywhere with you or anybody else.'

'Oh, dear. I was afraid you'd take that attitude. You see, we aren't associated with the people you were supposed to see with your delivery, more like, we're the opposition. But some of those other people are just outside in a car waiting for you and if they were to get their grubby little paws on you, they won't be anywhere near as civilised as we are. So really you have no choice; you have to come with us, quietly and calmly or things will go very badly for you.'

As he stared up at the two tough men, Gary started to shake as the full extent of the mess he was in struck home. 'Oh, shit! This thing has gone wrong from the start! I was going to make the hand-over, but we were late...'

He spluttered to a stop as Brad held up a hand. 'That's enough for now. I want to hear the full story, but for now, please come with us.'

Gary seemed to levitate out of the depths of the chair in a cloud of happy smoke as Tony lifted him bodily and stood him on unstable feet. Brad held one arm while Tony retrieved the backpack from beside the bed.

'Is this all your gear,' he asked, lifting an eyebrow.

'Ah...um...yeah. That's it,' was the mumbled reply.

'Good. Let's go.'

Brad led the way out, tossing a cheery goodbye on the way out to Chloe who was looking very fetching in a pair of brief panties. Tony followed, with Gary in a firm grip with his backpack slung over one shoulder. With no delay, they marched Gary to the Suburban and fed him in the back. As they waited for the two minders to scramble back in, Gary caught a glimpse of the three Undertakers in the old Commodore.

'Holy shit! Are they the guys waiting for me? What'd you do to them?'

Brad laughed, 'Yes they were, and not a thing. Didn't lay a finger on them.'

'Bullshit! There's blood everywhere.'

'Nope. Wasn't us. We don't like strong-arm stuff like that.' He flashed Gary an evil grin, 'Not unless we have to, that is.'

For the third or fourth time today, Gary felt his bowels loosening.

One of the minders beside Gary dug in his pockets and produced three mobiles and a bunch of keys that he passed over to Brad up front. 'There you go, boss. Just so these other turkeys don't try to get clever.'

'Good thinking dude. Wouldn't do to have them getting bright ideas.'

'I also took the liberty of using one of those phones to call the cops when I saw you coming out. I told them that three of the Undertakers involved in last night's mess at Mariners Cove were either in an old Commodore in a Main Beach street, or wandering the area, bloody and beaten!'

Brad hooted with delight. 'Outstanding, Ray! You're becoming superbly devious.'

Ray grinned, 'Thanks boss. I try.'

Three minutes later, while the Suburban was threading its way through the afternoon traffic, with one very unhappy and reluctant passenger, two marked patrol cars blocked the Main Beach street from either end, while a third screeched to a stop beside the grey Commodore, disgorging three large uniformed coppers.

Two Undertakers were retrieved from the grass beside the car, both bleeding heavily from facial wounds and badly disoriented. Their mumbles about a little old lady attack dog were put down to disorientation caused by their injuries. One uninjured Undertaker was found in an alcove behind some large rubbish bins — his hiding place pointed out by a very excited little old lady leaning on a large walking stick.

Her rants about detectives in Armani suits, perverts and young girls were largely ignored.

Based on complaints from several local residents about fighting in the street and threatening violence, the three Undertakers were arrested and held for questioning about their involvement in the Mariners Cove killing.

ZOMBIE EATERS PROPERTY, WEST OF SOUTHPORT

Back at the Zombie Eaters property west of Southport, Gary was parked in a deep armchair with the same two guards from the car watching him. His backpack was dismembered in front of him, but it contained only personal effects and some poor quality weed.

Brad took a seat opposite Gary and regarded him carefully for a while until Gary became so nervous, he blurted, 'You can't hold me here. I've not done anything that involves you. Why don't you let me go? I won't say anything.'

Brad smiled slightly, 'It would seem, Mr Courier, that you're saying a great deal before I've even asked you any questions.'

Gary fell silent, but flinched when Brad hitched his chair closer.

'OK, Mr Williams, I have one simple question. Where is the merchandise you brought to the Coast?'

'I've already handed it over,' Gary blustered, 'so there's nothing I can help you with.'

Brad nodded to Tony, who after dismembering the backpack, had moved around behind Gary's chair. Tony leant over and smacked Gary hard across the side of his face. He screamed as much as from fright as in pain, but it was a solid smack and rocked his head violently.

Brad shook his head. 'No, no, Mr Williams, you've already told me you were going to make the hand-over but were delayed, so please, no more bullshit or Mr Bradford will hurt you some more. Now, please continue from where you were going to say why you were late and missed the exchange.'

Gary seemed to consider some more lies, but then chose wisely. Holding up one hand, he said dispiritedly, 'Okay. That's enough. I'll tell you, but you may not believe me.'

Brad smiled, although his eyes remained bleak and hard, 'Try me,' he whispered, 'I've got a very vivid imagination and love a good yarn!'

Gary swallowed, took a deep breath and told his story about the bus trip; the girl, how the breakdown made them late and they missed the exchange. How all the bikies roaming the area and roaring past made him panic, which was why he hid at the end of the marina. And how two bikies nearly caught him, but a bloke on a boat chased them off and let him aboard.

After very roughly describing the boat to the best of his very limited ability, he also told of trying to sneak inside it but was then attacked by a huge animal of some sort and showed Brad the bite marks to prove it.

'So what did you do with the merchandise?'

'It was made up to look like a rolled up sleeping bag,' he said miserably, 'so I took it off my pack and shoved in down the bottom of a locker at the left end of the rear seats in the cockpit of the boat.'

Brad looked at him, stunned by that revelation. 'Why the fuck did you do that? You just left it there and went walkabout?'

'Yeah. But think about it. I didn't want to walk around town with it any longer than I had to. There were bikies all over the place looking for me, but I wanted to get off that bloody boat and away from that savage fucking beast that attacked me, whatever it was, and hook up with my mate Lester in the house in Main Beach.'

'Why didn't you just hand it over to the first bikie you came across? They're the ones who paid for the stuff in the first place.'

Gary blinked, his brain still slow from the earlier dose of yippee weed. 'I didn't know who the customer was. My people don't tell me that. I just had to deliver it to a bloke in the bar and collect a bag to take back to them ASAP. I was late — he wasn't there — who do I give it to?'

Brad nodded, 'OK. From your moronic viewpoint, that almost makes sense. So to summarise; as far as you're concerned, that container that looks like a rolled-up sleeping bag is still stuffed into the bottom of that locker on that bloke's boat?'

'Yep, that's right.'

'And he doesn't know that it's there? What about the girl? Didn't you say she was sleeping in the cockpit as well?'

'The guy doesn't know, 'cause he was down below asleep and the girl didn't see me put it there 'cause she was asleep too.'

'Okay. So barring accidents, it'll still be there. Where's this boat now?'

'How the fuck would I know? I've been in that flat since last night. When I left, it was tied up to the end of the wharf. Maybe it's there, maybe it's gone somewhere else. You want it — go look for it. Don't ask me anymore dopey questions, 'cause I don't know anything else.'

'He's become a cheeky little shit all of a sudden, ain't he boss? Maybe he needs an attitude adjustment,' Tony suggested, hand poised for another ear slap.

Brad thought a moment, 'Nah! Hold off on that for the moment. I'd really like to throw him in the river with an anchor for a neck chain, but until we check out some of this crap, we'd better keep him here. We might find something better to do with him. Toss him in one of the cells.'

Tony nodded, 'Good idea. C'mon, fuckwit. Your palatial suite awaits.'

'Once he's settled in, come back up. We've got some quick planning to do if we're going to take advantage of this situation.'

A hidden door opening off the entry hallway led down three flights of stairs to the detention centre, where Gary was pushed unceremoniously into a 3m x 2m cell with bed, basin, water and toilet.

'There you go, sport. Two meals a day, all the water you can drink and feel free to yell all you want. You're five metres underground, out of town and on private property. I don't think you'll attract too much attention, unless some of the boys get a bit horny.' Tony laughed at Gary's expression as he carefully locked the door.

THE UNDERTAKERS CLUBHOUSE, MOLENDINAR, SOUTHPORT, THURSDAY – PM

'Undertaker.'

'Boss, it's Mr Davies'

'Why are you whispering, Mr Davies? Please speak up.'

'I can't Boss. They might hear me.'

'Who might hear you, Mr Davies? You're being very cryptic and you know how much I dislike that.'

'It's the coppers, boss. I don't want them to hear what I've got to tell you.'

'You're becoming very tedious, Mr Davies. Either tell me what's going on, or I'm hanging up.'

'Please don't do that, boss. They'll only let me have one phone call and this is it. I'm at the Southport lock-up. We got worked over in Main Beach, someone called the cops and they grabbed us before we could get clear. They keep asking questions about last night. Can you get us out, please boss? Ray and Jimmy are in hospital under guard. They're in pretty bad shape.'

'Okay, Mr Davies. Hold those thoughts until our lawyer

springs you. He'll be there shortly. But tell me this — who worked you over?'

'Ahhh...it was...it was the Zombies boss. A carload of them jumped us, then they grabbed that courier fella as well.'

'That's bad news, Mr Davies, although my contacts tell me that neither the Police nor the Zombies have recovered the money or the merchandise. We'll talk when you are released. The other two might as well stay in hospital and be treated properly.'

'Thanks boss. I'm sorry we failed to get the courier.'

'Very well, Mr Davies.'

After making another call, stirring his lawyer into action to get the unfortunate Mr Davies released, he called his Lieutenant, Jay Fernando and explained the latest situation. The missing shipment and the money were the main topic.

'Was there anything at all last night, that might point to where that fool Gary Williams went after he got off the bus at the main Terminal? Or where he might have stashed the delivery?'

'I was just talking about that to Mr Abrams and Mr Truss who made a walk around of the area at the time and the only odd thing that came up was their encounter with a boat owner down at the far end of the wharf. The dude even pulled a big handgun to keep them off his boat; whereas most boaties would have been scared enough to at least let the boys aboard. Other than that, there was nothing.'

The Undertaker looked thoughtful. 'I'd like you to go have a look around the wharf yourself and see if that boat is still there. Dress up, if you would please. Some of these people don't seem to react to threats, so we'll try the other approach.'

'No problem boss, I'll change and get going.'

'Thank you, Jay. Please call me the moment you have some information.'

Twenty minutes later, a nicely dressed young man strolled casually down the wharf, smiling at a couple of pretty girl deck hands on the charter boats that were finishing up their day. He said hello to some of the live-aboard boaties who were getting stuck into their late afternoon drinks, before pausing at the end of the wharf overlooking the fuelling pontoon.

Which was empty of boats of any description, let alone a large catamaran.

After looking around for a few minutes, he wandered over to the fuel shed where he could see a man working at a desk.

'Gidday, mate,' he said, drawing a non-committal grunt from the white-haired occupant, although a peculiar little dog with a plastic milk bottle tied to it's collar wheezed asthmatically at him and gummed his ankle a few times before he could shake it off.

'Are you the refueller?' he tried again.

The old bloke lifted his head, peering at him through red-rimmed eyes. 'Well I ain't the bloody piano tuner, that's for sure. Wadda ya want?'

'Ahh...A mate of mine is coming in tomorrow and will need a refuel. Do you do private boats?'

'So long as they pay, sonny, I'll refuel a dugout canoe! What's he driving?'

'Ahh...It's a 70-foot something. I'm not sure. Can you fit a boat that size in here?'

The old bloke snorted scornfully, 'That's not so big. I've had 'em up to 120 feet parked there, but the big ones hang their arses out in the channel a way.'

'How about big catamarans? Do they fit as well?'

'Yeah, sure. Look. What's your mate got? A bloody power boat or a big cat?'

'Oh, Ahh...I think it's a big cat. A 70-foot cat he said.'

'Yeah, no problem. I just had a 60-footer in here, but he's moved back out to his mooring. He fitted all right so your mate will be okay. What time's he getting in?'

'I'm not sure, but he wanted me to check that you could fit him in.'

'Yeah, mate. He'll fit. Tell him to call me on Channel 12, call sign Southport Refueller, when he's within range. Now I've gotta get on with these fuel dockets. See ya.'

Dismissed, the young man left, after looking carefully around at what he could see of the Yacht Club basin where boats were tied to moorings out away from shore. The only large-looking cat he could see was not that far away, although there wasn't any sign of movement aboard. Encouraged, he retreated back up the wharf some distance, before pulling out his mobile and calling the Boss.

'Undertaker.'

'It's Jay, boss. I think I've found the boat that the boys got chased off last night.'

'*Excellent work, Jay. Where is it?*'

'It's tied to a mooring out away from shore, but it's not too far from the wharf. I'm looking at it now and from what I've been able to find out, it should be the one. I can't see anybody moving around on board at the moment, but that doesn't mean much.'

'*OK. We need to keep this as low-key as possible, so is it feasible to mount a small raiding party for later tonight? Maybe just two men?*'

'Oh, sure boss. There don't seem to be any occupied boats close by, although we'll need a small boat to get out there.'

'*I'll arrange that, if you choose the two to go. Come back here now and we'll plan from there.*'

'On my way, boss.'

CHAPTER 11

I showed Amanda where all the food and other galley gear was kept, then left her to work out something for tea. I fed the pussies early, mainly to shut the little kitten up as she was permanently hungry and complained loudly if not given her share of attention, but as usual, Jasper didn't object to an early feed. The conniving big cat had probably put little Krazy up to pestering me anyway.

Amanda fitted in pretty well for a land girl and proved to be very pleasant and undemanding company, although I wished that Sandy would hurry up and hand over her temporary position and get back here.

After a simple, but tasty meal of chops and vegies, I treated the cook to one of my famous NQ Teas, which is hot black tea with a double shot of black rum. She approved and we had to have another one to make sure that it would be as good as the first.

It was, but I drew the line at any more, as these things had proved to have a serious bite. So we just chatted and swapped stories while we played with the Krazy kitten that thought having two captive humans to amuse her was the height of luxury. Still, her antics were very entertaining and Jasper stayed close in case a spare scratching was on offer.

One way or another, it'd been a big day, so it wasn't long before we were both yawning. Due to the nature of our cargo, I took a few precautions against intruders, briefing Amanda about them and cautioning her about sleepwalking.

It was just after 2am when the digital radar proximity alarm started a soft beeping through the cabin speaker that caused me to roll out of bed, fully dressed. Jasper's equally soft growl of warning told me that it was trouble approaching, not just some late night fishermen. I went to Amanda's cabin and shook her awake, which took some doing, although I was pleased to see that apparently she didn't believe in wearing pyjamas. I guess she hadn't learned to sleep lightly when trouble was likely, but she'd quickly learn to change if she stayed seconded to duty on the *Firebird*.

I waited outside her cabin door while she hurriedly pulled on some clothes then told her to bring her service pistol that I presumed to be the standard Police issue Glock 22 in .40 S&W calibre.

To her credit, once awake, she got focused quickly. 'Company?' she asked.

'Yeah. I don't know who or what, but Jasper's not happy and that's usually a good indicator of bad guys. We'll wait in the saloon to see if they try to come aboard. They'll be in for a surprise if they do.'

Last evening, apart from telling her not to wander beyond the cockpit during the night, I hadn't gone into detail about my home defence systems, so I half-expected the questioning look I received. The Gold Coast is never totally dark as the night sky is lit by several gazillion lumens of light from the two main centres of Surfers Paradise and Southport, plus all the high-rise unit blocks that have grown like glowing exotic, multi-coloured fungi.

This wash of light allowed us to see a black inflatable dinghy about two hundred metres or so away, being paddled clumsily but quietly toward our stern from upriver with what appeared to be two men aboard. I'd silenced the radar alarm, but hadn't turned it off, so I was surprised when it beeped softly again and Jasper gave another quiet growl. I patted him on the head and told him, 'Good boy Jasper, but we've seen them.'

That reassurance didn't settle him, so as he wanted to see better, I let him jump up onto the dining table, although it's normally out-of-bounds, but he shook his head under my touch and turned to look the other way. Quickly checking the radar display, I was surprised to see another small red blip approaching from the vicinity of Mariners Cove, although it was further away than the one coming from the other direction.

'Bloody hell,' I muttered to Amanda, 'this is getting a bit busy. I hope that second boat isn't coming here as well.' She looked a bit nervous, although it wasn't surprising to have early morning visitors given that we were sitting on at least $4 million in cash and drugs.

'I guess that Mr Williams has shot his mouth off after all,' she observed, only partly comforted by the presence of the Remington TAC-14 short barrel, pump action shotgun I'd taken from a hidden locker behind the nav station.

'Looks like it,' I said. 'That second dinghy is still a fair way off, so if the home defence system looks after the first crew, we may not have to deal with the second.'

'How so?' she asked.

'I've electrified the safety rails with a modified electric fence controller, so the first uninvited guest who tries to open either stern gate is in for a nasty shock. Pun intended.'

'Oh,' Amanda said thoughtfully, 'and just how 'modified' is it?'

'Let's just say that the effect is very different to an electric fence. This one is far more debilitating and painful.'

'Isn't that rather dangerous?'

'Yes extremely, but only if they try to come aboard without being invited. Invited guests don't have a problem,' I added flippantly.

'Shit, Harry! What if it kills someone!'

'Keep this strictly to yourself, but on the last operation it did. Sandy was there and some bad guys came gunning for us. One got what he deserved, since I take a dim view of bad guys thinking they can attack me and mine when they feel like it!'

I felt her look again. 'That's a pretty hard attitude. What if these are relatively harmless thieves or kids even.'

In answer, I flipped on the masthead-mounted infrared camera I'd fired up earlier, and tracked it around to the closest dinghy. Zooming in showed a sharp, bright green picture of two burly men with the unmistakable profile of two shotguns propped up against the sides.

'Yeah, I see what you mean. They're hardly local fishermen, but that's some camera system,' Amanda said, 'you've got all sorts of surprises on this boat.'

'Yeah, I have. But what you see and what happens aboard stays aboard. That's the rule.'

'Seems like we might have a few things to discuss after tonight,' she said quietly, 'I'm not used to this undercover stuff.' Her eyes were fixed on the camera screen as I trained it around 180° and zoomed in on the second boat, still some distance off our bows.

'Well, if you want to hang around here much longer, you're going to have to learn fast,' I said, not unkindly, 'This is the way things happen when you don't have a uniform and a backup squad to hide behind you.'

'OK. Fair call, so I suppose we'd better deal with these turkeys behind us first.'

'Yep. But look at these other dudes. They don't look much like fishermen either; or kids for that matter.'

'I'll concede that point, Harry. And I must admit that those look more like shotguns than fishing rods.'

I grinned, 'Now you getting with it. But it makes me wonder if the two groups are connected? As in — are they working together, or are we seeing both bikie gangs working separately in ignorance of each other?'

It was a fairly rhetorical question, so she made no reply as the first dinghy was almost up to our stern. Soon we felt a slight bump; then a metallic sound followed by a soft curse, then a shadowy figure appeared above the cockpit surrounds.

'Close your eyes,' I whispered to Amanda, 'this may get a bit bright.'

Moments later, there was a bright blue flash like a camera flash gun going off, followed by an unearthly shriek and the thunderous roar of a shotgun discharge. The shadow at the railing suddenly collapsed straight down to become an untidy pile of blackness on the upper step, while a large splash announced the involuntary retreat of the other intruder.

'Oh shit, oh dear!' Amanda exclaimed in shock, 'What the fuck happened there?'

'That's what happens when someone grabs an electrified rail. He must have had the shotgun in one hand with his finger on the trigger. So much for peaceful intentions! That could have taken our heads off.'

She started to move out into the cockpit, but I held her back. 'Wait a moment,' I said, 'let's see what happened to the other bloke and we need to check what the other team does.'

The second question was easily answered as the camera showed that the flash and the roar of the gun discharge caused the second team to promptly turned their dinghy around and head back to the marina. The fate of the second intruder was equally obvious as a frenzied splashing astern and choking gasps suggested that he wasn't much of a swimmer. Hurriedly, I switched the electrified railings off then fetched the long boathook from its mounts on top of the coachouse. After making my way carefully over the body of his colleague, I managed to snag the collar of his leather vest and dragged him to the stern.

He was way too big to haul aboard, so we left him, still choking and spluttering, hanging onto the stern swim steps with a death grip, while we inspected his mate.

There was a distinctly unpleasant smell rising off the slack bundle of clothes that told of voided bowels mixed in with the aroma of burnt flesh, as I poked at him with the boathook.

'Is he dead?' Amanda asked, not wanting to approach too closely.

In answer, I held my breath, leant over and felt the side of his jaw and was unsure whether to be relieved or not to feel a thready, racing pulse.

'No,' I answered her question, 'the piece of shit's still alive, but only just. He'll need medical treatment very quickly if he's going to survive.'

However, for all her concern, Amanda didn't seem to be in a hurry to call for the needed medical attention, so while I was down there, I searched his pockets, coming up with a handgun, and flick knife and a wallet. I passed them to Amanda seeing as she was the official law on board, even though I had a lot of authority, both as Captain of the vessel and as an ACP operative.

Together, we awkwardly dragged his unwieldy bulk clear of the steps into the cockpit then directed our attention to the other bikie, still clinging to the swim ladder.

Nodding towards him, I said to Amanda, 'Care to arrest him, Senior Constable? I'd like to make a complaint about trespass and attempted assault with a deadly weapon. I'm sure we can come up with more later.'

She smiled and with her Glock levelled at his head, went through the arrest procedure.

The half-drowned bikie just stared back at her with blood-shot eyes, still gasping for breath, until Amanda ordered him to climb out of the water. Slowly he did until he was laying in a heap on the boarding platform.

'Face down, hands behind your back. You know the routine,' she ordered and when he'd painfully complied, still without speaking, she quickly nipped down and slapped a pair of hand-cuffs on his wrists then dragged him upright and forced him to stumble up the steps.

We got him seated before I grabbed a mooring line and tied his ankles tightly, tethering the other end to the cockpit table supports. He still seemed vague and unco-ordinated, so I wondered if he'd somehow received a minor shock as well. Certainly, he was quite unresponsive to questioning which was a problem, since I really needed to know what had happened to Gary the Courier.

I had Amanda put the kettle on, while I unloaded my shotgun and stowed it back in it's hidden locker. Reluctantly, I then dialled Greg's mobile, knowing that he'd probably only got to bed a couple of hours ago. Sure enough, after a protracted ringing, he croaked a reply.

'*This better be good, Harry, or I'm gunna come down there and piss on your head.*'

'Well, good morning to you too, Mr Grumpy. I just thought that you'd like to know that we've just had one set of visitors who made it aboard and another set who turned back when they saw the fireworks.'

'*What? What the fuck are you on about? You always do this to me, Harry. I can't understand what you're trying to tell me at times. Now, in words of two syllables or less, please tell me what's happened?*'

'Two blokes in a dinghy came visiting. They carried shotguns and one of them fell foul of my defence system, while the other simply fell overboard and apparently couldn't swim very well, but he's recovering. The first bloke aboard isn't in very good shape and without urgent medical treatment, may not survive. Is that clear enough?'

'*Don't be a smart arse, Harry. I understood that very well, thank you. Now may I suppose that one intruder is in custody, while the other needs medical attention?*'

'Yes, Greg. That's what I've been trying to tell you. I wanted to call you first, since this is your case.'

'*Yeah, thanks Harry for reminding me of that at 03:00. Now what's this about a second team?*'

'Radar and the camera system picked up a second dinghy with three guys in it, complete with shotguns, coming toward us from the Mariners Cove direction, but they turned around when the defence system made a light show and a shotgun went off.'

'*Oh, shit! You didn't say anything about a shotgun going off! I'll have the fucking Main Beach Chamber of Commerce on my back now, raving on about a bikie war! Was anybody hurt?*'

'Not by the shotgun. Can't say the same for our first visitor. Or the second, for that matter — he looks a bit ordinary.'

'*Okay Harry. Let me make a few calls and I'll probably see you soon.*'

'Good on you mate. Drive carefully. There are some idiots on the roads tonight.'

Amanda was amused by the conversation, although she'd stayed focused on watching our prisoner, docile as he was. At least he was more alert now and watching us closely.

'Are you with the Zombies or the Undertakers?' I asked pleasantly.

'Get fucked!' was the response and about what I'd expected.

I looked at Amanda. 'I don't think that backup will be arriving for a while. What if this gentleman were to fall in the water again before they arrive?'

She grinned, catching on quickly, 'Yeah. That could happen if we were a bit careless and he tried to escape. It's a pity that the rope that's tied to his ankles is so long. He can probably get overboard with it like that.'

I untied the mooring line and re-tied the very end of it to the table support. 'You're right. How silly of me to leave it so long.'

Between the two of us, we hauled him feet first out of his chair then started dragging the hapless bikie down the stern steps, his head bouncing off each step with a loud thunk, finally provoking a yell of outrage.

'You can't throw me overboard again,' he bellowed, 'I can't swim!'

'Gee. What a shame,' I remarked as we pushed him overboard, his final yell abruptly cutting short.

He drifted astern, sinking quickly until I hauled in the rope, dragging him up to the stern again. Unfortunately, as the rope was tied to his ankles, that action left his head still underwater. However, a bit of fishing around with the boathook snagged his collar again before he went terminal although it needed the two of us to drag his now unresponsive bulk back onto the boarding platform.

We left him there, although as a precaution against an escape attempt, I pulled the ankle rope up tight and tied it off on a cleat up in the cockpit. Which was probably unnecessary, as the latest near drowning seemed to have knocked the stuffing out of him.

After all that excitement, I felt like a cup of tea, but my last one was cold so I made two mugs and added a healthy splash of rum as Amanda was experiencing some post-action shakes.

'Been in action before?' I asked conversationally, handing over her mug.

She shook her head. 'Not like this. In fact, I've never had to draw my gun in anger. I've always been assigned either to traffic duties or admin. Serves me right for being good at paperwork!'

'I can understand that. It's never like they tell you in training. Especially when a bad guy is trying to kill you.'

'Yeah. That's for sure. Have you seen much action? I mean, I don't even know your background.'

So I gave her a brief rundown on my former career with the SAS and some Afghanistan experiences, but left a lot out.

'So in contrast to myself, you've seen a lot of action with bad guys shooting at you.'

I smiled, 'Yeah. I'm afraid so. I guess that's why I'm never complacent about these amateurs when they start waving guns around. You don't know what they're going to do and half the time they don't either.'

'That makes sense. So you were a Major then, but what rank do you hold in the ACP?'

I never like discussing my ACP service, but she was a colleague and a State Police member, so I replied, 'I'm really just an ACP Agent, but the actual rank they made me is Commander, which is equivalent to Superintendent, although I never use it unless I have to.'

'Oh. So that's what Greg meant when he said that you actually out-rank us all.'

I grinned, 'Yeah. He does like a joke occasionally.'

We'd just finished our tea when I spotted flashing blue and red lights coming downriver at speed and shortly, a 32-foot patrol boat with a pair of rumbling diesels driving water jets, idled up beside us, manned by our earlier crew, Sergeant Les Thomas and Constable Peter Larson.

'What the hell have you been up to this time, Harry? Just five minutes ago the radio started going crazy with the Dispatcher telling us to get here immediately!'

I laughed, as much to ease the post-action tension as anything else. 'We've got some more mail for you, Les,' I joked, 'Special delivery, two over-size pieces for Inspector Greg.'

'Very funny, Harry. We can't leave you alone for a minute, although I suppose you did warn us there might be some trouble tonight.'

'Yeah, I did, but I was hoping for a quiet night. I don't suppose the Ambos are on the way as well, are they. I told Greg that one of these characters was looking rather crook.'

Pete tied off to one of our cleats, as Les shut down the engines and hopped aboard. 'Yeah, he did mention that they should be heading out, but we were upriver helping three ground crews chase some bad guys around the canals. Hang on, I'll radio in and ask.'

A few moments later, he was back. 'They should be on their way in a couple of minutes. They're about to grab a lift from our Base in a RIB.'

'Good oh. He's sort-of still breathing, but his pulse is very erratic. Being challenged by what they thought was a pair of boat bums must have been too much of a shock for his system. That's what bad diet and stress does to you.'

Amanda broke down with a fit of the giggles at my comment, earning her a strange look from Les who was making a quick examination of the bikie with heart problems.

'Shit! This bloke's not too good at all. And he's crapped himself. I hope those Ambos hurry. Where's the other one?'

I jerked my thumb over my shoulder. 'Down on the boarding platform. He's a bit out of sorts at the moment as well. He fell overboard and couldn't swim very well and was too big for us to lug up to the cockpit, so Amanda arrested him and 'cuffed him where he is. I tied a rope to his ankles so he didn't fall in again.'

Les gave me a strange look this time. 'That was very thoughtful of you to think of his welfare like that. I don't suppose he offered any information?'

I grinned, 'As a matter of fact, he did tell us one thing. He admitted he's with the Undertakers OMC, but he wouldn't say why they came out here tonight. I don't really think its 'cause they wanted to take a midnight cruise.'

I copped another of Les' looks, before he and Pete poked and prodded the semi-conscious bikie into getting up and making his way to the cockpit. 'Here's your rope back, Harry.' Les added dryly, 'I don't think he'll need it now.'

'Thanks boys,' I said, casually coiling the rope as the bikie gave me a murderous glare, 'Look after him yourself and make sure that after processing, he's held in solitary for Greg to interview. He's not to talk to anyone except you or Greg. Got that?'

Les nodded seriously, 'No problem. We got a similar word as well, so it'll be cool. We can process him and hold him in a cell at base. He'll be safe, but we'll just secure him down below for now, and then wait for the Ambo's. I think I heard the radio say they're on the way.'

Sure enough, another set of flashing lights headed our way from the Water Police base located adjacent Mariners Cove. It was the RIB Les and Pete had used earlier with two Paramedics and a Police driver aboard.

The Paras competently attended to the bikie, but there was a limit to what they could do on the spot, so after stabilising him, they loaded him onto the RIB and headed for the base where the Ambulance was waiting. After checking that we were okay, Les and Pete took the other prisoner and followed the Ambos.

'I'm glad they're gone,' I said to Amanda, who wholeheartedly endorsed that remark.

'I might just clean up the decks while we wait for Greg to turn up.'

She gave me a hand, as we scrubbed and mopped the places where some blood and shit had collected, until not a trace of the two bikies was left. Jasper and Krazy kitten turned out to help now the excitement was over, but retired again when Greg was delivered in the same Police RIB.

Wearily, he stepped aboard, leaving the driver to shut down the massive outboards and loop a line over a mid-ships cleat. He gave me a knowing smile then turned to Amanda.

'An eventful start to your new posting, Senior,' he commented drily.

'Yes sir, it certainly has been, although most instructive at the same time.'

Greg chuckled, 'That's one way to look at it. But don't catch too many bad habits from Harry. He's been known to take the odd shortcut with regulations at times.'

'Yes, sir. But this one seems to have gone really well.'

'Hmmm. Yeah, all right. We'll see what shakes down later, but for now, you'd both better tell me exactly what happened, then you can both write up another report.'

So we told him what happened, including the electrified railings.

'You'd better leave that bit out of the report, I think. Just say that they were both very surprised to be challenged and slipped on the wet steps. The heart attack was apparently due to a pre-existing medical condition.'

I nodded, 'No problem with that. And we'll avoid speculation about the reason they tried to board us?'

'Hell, yes! Let people wonder all they want.'

Not long after that, Greg took the collection of identity documents, knives, shotguns and handguns confiscated from our intruders and returned to the Water Police base to collect his prisoner, finally leaving us in peace.

'It's 04:30,' I said to Amanda, 'I'm going to get my head down for a few hours. You can do the same, or whatever you fancy.'

'Yeah. I might do the same for a while, although I still feel a bit wound up. Will you be resetting the defence systems?'

'Nah! Jasper will do the job for now. I'll leave you to it.'

'Cheers, Harry. And thanks for taking care of things so well. I wasn't much help I'm afraid.'

I smiled, 'On the contrary, dear lady. You did just great. You didn't panic or lose your focus and that's what counts.'

'Thanks. I appreciate that. But I will try to do better next time, if there is one.'

'The way this affair is shaping up, I think there will be plenty of next times.'

With those disturbing thoughts, I left her to the demands of Jasper and little Krazy kitten and went back to bed.

CHAPTER 12

'Undertaker.'

'Jay here boss. I've got some bad news.'

'That's not very encouraging, Jay. I just don't like to hear that. So tell me.'

'It's regarding Mr Truss and Mr Abrams who we sent out to take a look at the boat that I reported to you earlier.'

'Yes, yes. I remember. They were to search the boat and recover the merchandise if it was there.'

'It would appear that the owner was aboard with a female friend and managed to defend himself very effectively by unknown means. Mr Truss is in the intensive Care Unit at the Public Hospital under Police guard, but it is doubtful that he will survive the next 24 hours. Mr Abrams is suffering the effects of near drowning and is also in Police custody. They have been charged with a range of offences that given their past records, would see then locked up for twenty years. That's if Mr Truss survives.'

'...'

'I'm stunned, Jay. How could such a simple operation go so wrong? I trust that Mr Abrams has kept his mouth shut?'

'So far, boss. But he doesn't know much either, except that the boat owner seemed to be expecting them and somehow had a copper on hand pretty smartly to arrest them. It's all very odd, boss.'

'That's an interesting piece of information, Jay. For them to be so prepared suggests to me that they might be hiding something and don't want anybody else snooping around. Has there been any activity from our dear brothers?'

Jay chuckled, 'Yeah. You'll like this one boss. There were three of them that had set out in a small boat for the target when our guys *beat them to it. They just turned around and headed back to shore as soon as they saw the fuss.'*

'Hmmm. Pity our people didn't plan a bit more carefully before they rushed into this. When I ask for a job to be done, I expect our people to use their heads! I can't do all the thinking for our people.'

'Yes, boss. We'll try harder next time.'

'Is there going to be a next time, Jay? Surely the boat owner will be even more on guard now that this reconnaissance probe has failed. Do we know how he managed to defend against our two Enforcers so effectively? That would be very useful information, don't you think? So do you have any viable suggestions?'

'Not at the moment, boss, except that we should try again when the owner leaves the boat.'

'And would you see that as being a better opportunity, Jay? Regardless of the lack of information about the defences on-board?'

'The owner has to go ashore at some time, doesn't he? I mean; he has to get supplies or do business. He can't stay there 24/7! So if we're ready, we can slip out there as soon as he leaves and search the boat. That won't take long.'

'Hmmm. That might work, Jay. Very well. I'm putting you in charge of organising it. You can draw on personnel as needed, but try very hard not to fail again.'

'Yes, boss. I'll do that.'

ZOMBIE EATERS PROPERTY, WEST OF SOUTHPORT, FRIDAY

'Hey, Tony. Where are you man?'

'In the garage Brad, working on my bike.'

'Well drop that an' get your skinny arse in here. I've got some news.'

After a couple of minutes, Tony wandered in to the comfortable lounge room wiping his hands on a dirty rag.

'Wot's happening, mate?'

'Our spy just called in to say that all that fuss on the water last night when our boys tried to raid the dude's boat, was the Shit-kickers getting the shit kicked out of them by the dude himself! And he's got some chicky-babe on board with him.

One of the clowns is in hospital under Police guard and isn't expected to survive, while the other is locked up in solitary. What a hoot!'

'Shit! How'd that happen? The boys said someone fired a shotgun as well. Was that part of it?'

'Yep. The Undertaker that's about to cark it did that. But I'm wondering if there is something to defend after all.'

Tony looked thoughtful. 'Yeah. Good point. But he must have some very effective defences on that boat to take out two heav-ies. I wonder if the chick had anything to do with it? Still, we'd better be very careful if you're thinking about making a second run at that boat.'

Brad smiled admiringly, 'You can read my mind. But I'll bet that the Shit-kickers are thinking the same thing. That long, skinny streak of pelican shit isn't stupid.'

'No, he's not. So what's our best move?'

'The dude's alerted now so he's waiting for another visit, but our best bet is to be ready if he goes ashore for any reason. It won't take long to search a boat.'

'But if they've had the coppers there, why would they still keep the stuff aboard? Surely it'd be taken to the Police evidence lockup?'

'I've told you before Tony, don't call me Shirley.'

Tony looked blank for a moment as that one went through to the keeper, until Brad added, 'Ha, ha. That's a joke mate. But seriously, from what I can get from my copper mate, the Inspec-tor heading the investigation into the topped bagman doesn't trust the security of the evidence lock up. Particularly with this new stuff that's apparently so potent it can be cut up to 90% and still be super-effective.

So that's why they might be leaving it on the boat if there's such a good security system, although I'd love to know what the hell it is.'

Tony nodded slowly, 'Yeah, weird but okay. I guess that makes as much sense as anything else in this fucked-up situation. So what do you want the boys to do about getting on the boat? They called earlier to see if they should keep hanging around.'

'Yeah, definitely. If they can borrow that inflatable boat they used last night again, have them stand-by where they can keep an eye on it. If they see the owner leave, they should move in and search the thing.'

'Ok, Brad. I'll pass that on.'

FIREBIRD, YACHT CLUB MOORING – FRIDAY PM

Midday was about the time I decided to haul myself out of bed, a bit surprised that Jasper or Krazy kitten hadn't hunted me out much earlier. I did my usual thing of wandering through to my bathroom without bothering to dress, receiving a cheery 'Good Morning,' from Amanda, sitting reading up at the dining table; both cats parked either side of her, asleep.

My lack of dress didn't bother me and thankfully didn't bother her either, since I had no intention of changing my long-established habits. Suitably refreshed, I dressed and checked out the day that had turned windy and cloudy, with some dark clouds in the southeast, but it didn't look like the bad weather was coming in too quickly.

Amanda fetched me a mug of tea, then asked, 'What's the plan now, boss?'

I relished the first sip then said, 'I'd like to go shopping to re-stock the pantry and get a few other things just in case we have to move quickly — something that's looking more likely. With yourself assigned for the duration and hopefully Sandy joining us very soon, we need to stock up.'

So as I sipped my tea and wrote out the growing list, Amanda did most of the checking of our stocks of consumables aboard and deciding what would be needed. I asked her to choose foods that she liked and added those that I knew Sandy and I did. Her eyebrows went up when I asked her to add a carton of Bundaberg Master Blender's edition rum.

'Got to have our NQ teas,' I defended my choice with a grin, 'but please add anything you'd like to drink.'

'I don't mind a good Chardonnay at times,' She said with a grin, 'but I'm not much on remembering the names.'

I added a couple of cartons of a well-known Australian brand that Sandy liked, so they could share. With the food and consumables list complete, I asked, 'How much .40 S&W ammo have you got for your Glock 22?'

She suddenly looked stricken. 'Oh, shit! I forgot to get extra from the guys yesterday like the Inspector told me. Fuck it! Sorry Harry, there's not much. Just my normal load-out of three magazines full, so that's 45 rounds.'

'Don't worry, it's no big deal. I'll just get Greg to organise a few cartons more, 'cause Sandy uses it too. Apart from .44 Magnum rounds, the rest of my stuff is 9mm Parabellum, so I wouldn't mind some but he probably hasn't got any of that still laying around. Still, might get lucky and it'd save a trip out the Ashmore Gun Shop.'

Amanda looked at me in surprise. 'What 9mm have you got and what on earth is in .44 Magnum?'

So, I dug out my collection of weapons, consisting of a LAR Grizzly semi-auto pistol in .44 Magnum, the mini-Uzi automatic machine pistol in 9mm Parabellum, the PMR 30 in .22 Magnum and the Remington 870 express and TAC-14 shotguns with various loads.

To say she was impressed was an understatement and the flood of questions showed that I had a dedicated gun nut aboard. A quick phone call to Greg revealed that he would be happy to send out a few hundred rounds of .40 S&W and he even had several cases of 9mm that had been gathering dust in the armoury and he would be happy to get rid of.

'Well, that's the ammunition shopping list taken care of. I'll phone through a grocery order to the Supermarket over at Australia Fair so they can have it ready to deliver to the dinghy. It's a service they offer to boaties who don't mind paying a small surcharge for the service. There are several boaties around here who take advantage of it.'

Naturally, Amanda picked up on the flaw in my plan. 'But will it be safe to leave the boat unattended?'

'No it won't, unfortunately. As long as they think that the drugs and money are aboard, they'll keep coming at us. There's too much at stake. We'll have a yarn to Greg later, but I'm thinking that we'll have to move from here — probably sooner rather than later. But for now, it means that one of us will have to stay here to defend the castle with Jasper's help.'

She nodded thoughtfully. 'OK. So are you thinking we should set a trap?'

'Yeah. The thought did cross my mind,' I admitted with a grin, 'but I don't like the idea of leaving you here alone, even with Jasper. We've got to assume that they're watching us now and may not come out if they see you leave without me.'

Amanda looked thoughtful for a few moments. 'I'm sensible enough to realise that at this stage, I'm nowhere near able to deal with two or three of these turkeys in a strange environment, so how about this for a plan. I'll dress up like you, jump in the dinghy and head off ashore, but somewhere well away from wherever they're watching from so they don't see me up close. Then if they think you've left, they may break cover and you'll have a much better chance to deal with them than I would.'

I thought a moment, looking for flaws in the plan, but it seemed sound. 'I must admit, I didn't think of that. Great idea, but how are you going to make yourself look like me?'

'I'm less than two inches shorter than you, but at a distance that won't show too much. If I can flatten out my boobs enough with an elastic bandage, put on some of your more baggy clothes and wear a cap to hide my hair, I reckon I can pass for you at a distance.

Remember, people tend to see what they expect to see.'

The more I thought about it, the more it seemed like a simple plan that would probably work, so we set about transforming Amanda to Harry, but before we started, I phoned the grocery order through to the Supermarket and was assured that it would all be ready in about twenty minutes, with delivery to the usual beach about fifteen minutes after that.

First part of the transformation was the task of losing most of her chest measurement and that turned out to be a fun job for me, but less so for Amanda. She wasn't modest about dropping her clothes and seemed to enjoy my appreciative comments, although I tried to be good, reminding myself that Sandy was due back sometime soon — maybe.

Under her guidance I carefully wound a wide, crepe bandage around her lovely bare boobs, squishing her down to what must have been a very uncomfortable and much smaller chest dimension, but it took a couple of attempts to get it right.

She dropped her shorts and we wound a towel around her waist, taping it in place to make that part of her delightful body look less feminine, before she pulled on my shorts. A belt was still needed to stop them falling off, but the final result, with one of my work shirts hanging loose outside the shorts was quite convincing.

The whole procedure had been carried out in a mood of great hilarity before we finally ventured up to the saloon where she grabbed my favourite bright red ball cap and managed to tuck some of her hair up under it, but the rest that stuck out didn't look too different from my unruly locks. I did a time check and saw that we were going nicely.

'Now remember to walk like a man — as in, stride rather than step and swing your arms and not your hips. That'd be a dead giveaway!'

We both had a chuckle over that comment, and she was just about to leave the saloon, when an icy hand grabbed my gut.

'Oh, shit! I forgot to launch the dinghy. You can't do that. They'll spot the difference in seconds. You'll have to give me back my shorts, shirt and cap for a couple of minutes.'

Amanda shrugged, then promptly dropped her shorts and peeled off my shirt and cap, looking both erotic and slightly ridiculous in very brief panties, towel-wrapped centre section and heavily-bandaged chest.

I copped a punch to the arm for laughing at her and as I was still just in my jocks, it only took a few moments to dress again, before going out and making a show of lowering the RIB to the water and tying it up at the right-hand boarding platform. I loaded a bunch of padded carry bags into the bow then returned inside to strip down to my jocks again.

She giggled at the bulge in my jocks that grew more under her scrutiny, an event that I promptly blamed on the view presented by her much briefer lace panties, but before we got too much into discussion about brief underwear and what it did and didn't cover properly, I swatted her neat little bum and chased her out towards the dinghy after issuing a few parting instructions. Fortunately, she was a true professional and made an effortless transition from fun and games to professional.

A few moments later, Amanda strolled out to the stern and gave a fair imitation of me getting in the dinghy and speeding off toward the Southport beachfront, remaining well clear of other boats.

CHAPTER 13

Once I was sure she was heading for the landing area I'd pointed out and wasn't being chased by any bad guys, I went below and dressed, before returning to the saloon where I re-stowed my weapon collection that Amanda had drooled over in their concealed compartments. I kept out my prized LAR Grizzly .44 Magnum pistol, two extra magazines and a box of ammunition, and as I was in the habit of only loading a few rounds in each magazine to avoid over-compressing the spring and risking a misfeed and the subsequent jam, it was the work of moments to fully load all the magazines in readiness.

Staying generally below the level of the windows, even though they were heavily tinted, I scanned every thirty seconds to check on boat or dinghy movements, but there was only the normal daytime to-ing and fro-ing associated with a busy anchorage and marina. I took the precaution of isolating little Krazy kitten in the forward cabin in case trouble did wander my way.

I didn't have to tell Jasper anything; he'd already picked up on the change of dress with Amanda and the general air of tension, so was very alert, sitting up on the dining table seats and scanning 360°. My superb cat was the best early warning system ever!

About then the phone rang. It was Sandy.

'Hi, pretty lady. How's it all going in the wild, wild west?'

'Really good, Harry. I'm enjoying myself being in charge of a station. It's very different to anything I've done before. How're things with you?'

'Funny you should ask. I seem to be up to my armpits in bad guys again.'

She laughed. 'Gee, why am I not surprised? Although Greg did tell me that you got involved with this bikie shooting and the drug thing. And you've gone and stuck your fool neck out again and hung onto all that cash and the new drugs! Isn't that really asking for trouble?'

'Yeah,' I conceded ruefully, 'you're right; it is. But it seemed the best thing to do at the time since Greg was sure the drugs at least would go walkabout if they went to the Evidence Locker.'

'Yeah. He's right, I'm afraid. He told me about last night's raiding party and that he's posted Amanda Burke aboard to help with the guard duties. How's she working out?'

'Great! She's seems to have adapted to boat life really quickly and Jasper and Krazy like her. Of course, this morning's ruckus was a bit of a shock to someone more used to processing traffic accidents, but she'll get over it.'

Sandy chuckled, *'I'm sure she will, hanging around with you. Things always seem to happen to you Harry. You're a trouble magnet. But tell me; have you slept with her yet?'*

'Aww, come on Sandy. She's only been aboard two nights. What do you think I am?'

She laughed again, *'I know exactly what you are, you lecherous, lovable old fart. From what I remember of her when she came to Southport, she's very attractive and very smart. She's the drone expert, isn't she?'*

Groping frantically for slightly safer ground, I replied ambiguously, 'Yeah she is. But I'm a lot older than she is and I've just been appointed her superior officer.'

Sandy laughed, *'Get a grip, Harry. Who do you think you're kidding? You've never used that 'Superior Officer' bullshit before and I'm sure you're not starting now. And as for older! Bullshit! I didn't mind sharing you with Janice, did I? In fact, I enjoyed being with her as well, if you can remember back that far, Grandpa!*

Anyway, I really called to say that I'm going to be out here another week at least at this stage.'

'Bugger! But I get the message, and I'm still looking forward to you getting back here.'

'I should hope so, you horny old goat! Me too.'

'Anyway my darling girl, I'd better go and get ready for the next round with the bad guys. Ciao.'

We'd never been ones for prolonged goodbyes or mushy stuff and the sex thing was very good, but Sandy had always surprised me with her broad outlook on who did what to whom. From the way she was talking, I could only hope Amanda shared that attitude or she'd be in for a shock.

Still, if we were going to continue to cop the attention of two bikie gangs, I'd be a lot happier having Sandy aboard helping defend our cargo, as she was a trained martial arts expert, hand-to-hand combat expert and Instructor-rated firearms expert.

My musings were rudely interrupted by Jasper's warning growl, so I scanned around and spotted a dinghy approaching from the vicinity of the Yacht Club with two large men aboard. Being daylight, no weapons were visible, although I didn't doubt that they were coming my way and would be armed with something more than abusive words.

I patted Jasper and left him to watch the approaching dinghy while I stayed low and moved to the saloon doors that I opened slightly. I decided to turn on the electrified railing system again as a first line of defence, in order to avoid if possible, a shooting exchange in the Yacht Club's hallowed waters in daylight.

Staying below window height as much as possible, I watched as the dinghy closed on my stern where it was hidden from my view for a short time. In a close repeat of the previous evening, I felt a gentle thump followed soon after by an ugly head capped with an unruly mass of dark greasy hair, cautiously appearing above the cockpit coaming. His eyes swivelled around looking for signs of life, but the dark tinted windows shielded Jasper and me from view. As he slowly climbed the steps, I saw that he was armed with a pistol held low by his side, his finger on the trigger and a long suppressor screwed to the barrel. His mate appeared two steps lower behind him and it seemed safe to assume that he was armed as well.

'Bad men, Jasper,' I whispered, resting my hand gently on his head in warning, although I was sure he'd worked that out for himself when he gave a soft growl in response. The first guy reached the top step and reached out for the safety railing that Amanda had closed across the entrance.

Apparently last night's surviving colleague hadn't worked out what had zapped his mate, since this one grabbed the rail with his free hand, causing an initial bright flash of blue light accompanied by a loud crackling sound as he danced and shook on the spot for a few moments, thankfully soundless for a change. Finally, he slumped to the deck, tearing his hand off the railing, his gun clattering to onto the step below him without going off. There was a frightened yell from his mate, who then climbed up to check out his fallen leader.

Which seemed a good time to make my move and although he had a gun in his hand, it was down by his side and no real match for my .44 Magnum levelled at his chest, whose barrel looked like a railway tunnel when viewed from the wrong end less than 2 meters away.

'You might like to drop that gun,' I said quietly, 'then unlatch the railing and step this way. Very, very carefully.'

He must have been the resilient kind who recovered quickly as he came back with a quick, 'Fuck you, Jack! You ain't gunna shoot.'

'Oh, dear. You haven't even got my name right,' I said with an evil grin, 'and here I was trying to be nice. Now I'll ask you once more; drop the gun and step through the gate. Last chance!'

'Or what, arsehole!' He sneered, arm muscles twitching as he prepared to swing his gun hand up.

'Or I'll take other measures to ensure your compliance with my request. And I'm afraid you will find those measures very unpleasant.'

'Big words, little man. Such as what?'

'Such as my assistant, who dislikes people who come aboard without invitation! Your mate hasn't fared very well so far.'

'Yeah. I dunno what you did to him, but it doesn't matter now. He's out of it, and I'm here. It looks like a Mexican standoff to me.'

I smiled gently, 'I'm afraid you're a little bit mistaken if you think you are in a bargaining position. My assistant is ready to fix that misconception.'

He seemed to tighten his grip on his gun, 'You're fulla shit! What's this assistant crap? There's nobody else here. The other guy left. We saw him go, although there was supposed to be some moll here with you.'

'Ahh...but you didn't see this one.' I turned my head slightly and said in a firm voice, 'Jasper. Bad man. Don't kill. Get him!'

There was a blur of black that launched past me like a missile and hit the guy square in the chest with a massive set of razor-sharp claws that dug in and held, so that the long, white fangs could get a hold on his throat. He gave a single howl of fright and pain as he fell over backwards, the gun falling from his hand as he struggled to free himself from the incredible crushing pressure that stopped his breathing. The loud thump as his head smashed onto the boarding platform didn't help his disposition at all, particularly as Jasper kept a choke hold on his throat.

'Jasper,' I called, 'don't kill. Just hold him.'

Despite my plea, there was a copious supply of blood staining the pristine white gel coat of my stern, but with a bit of luck, it wouldn't be too life threatening.

I took a good look around to see if the antics so far had attracted any attention, but all seemed quiet, so I cautiously made my way past the crumpled mass of the fallen leader, smelling yet again the stench of voided bowels, the thought occurring to me that it must be something about the volts or amps settings of the electric fence controller that always caused this problem. I mean three out of three now was conclusive proof that the fence controller was the problem.

I picked up both guns on the way down the steps, flicking the safeties on automatically. My caution proved unnecessary as the dude was way out of it. Jasper still had him by the throat, but as he'd held back from ripping it out, there were only a few puncture wounds that still bled rather well. The back of his head under his greasy, matted hair felt a bit spongy, so I diagnosed severe concussion and left him there, calling Jasper off and telling him what a good boy he was.

He obeyed me, but I scored what passed for a dirty look from him and a distinct 'Huffff' of displeasure that he hadn't been allowed to finish the job properly. He always did take pride in his work and hated to be interrupted. I fastened a rope around the ankles of the dude at the top of the steps and using one of the electric sheet winches, dragged him into the cockpit and parked him on a plastic sheet out of casual sight, repeating the manoeuvre with the concussed and bleeding one at the foot of the steps.

I admit to being tempted to just push him overboard, but that might have lead to a bigger mess, so I reluctantly parked him beside his mate, letting Jasper sniff him while I washed the blood and shit from the steps.

I took the time after that to clean Jasper and inspect the guns while I brewed a welcome mug of sweet tea as a way to dissipate a little bit of the adrenaline still pumping hard through my system. It really doesn't matter how often one goes into combat or any other high stress situation; the aftermath is always the same where it takes time to wind down and burn off adrenaline. I'd really like to be able to go for a run to accelerate the process, but no sort of physical activity was possible at the moment, so I did the next best thing and made a phone call.

'Gidday Harry. How's it going?'

'Good now, Greg. But I'll need a pickup crew again, if you don't mind.'

'What! You're doing it again, Harry. What are you talking about?'

'I've got another two bikies here who fancied their chances

trying to knock me off. One's in bad shape while the other appears to have severe concussion and some lacerations to the throat and chest. He's bleeding quite a bit, but still breathing.'

'*Well fuck me! Not again! I almost don't believe it and if it was anybody but you I wouldn't. You've really got to stop bashing these bikies up, Harry. They'll be getting pissed off with you if you keep going like this!*'

'Yeah. I was thinking that too. Maybe it's time to think about getting the flock out of Dodge.'

'*Yeah maybe, but how's Senior Burke? Did she handle herself alright?*'

'Oh she's fine. We dressed her up to look like me and I sent her off to pick up the groceries over at Australia Fair. The bad guys must have thought it was me and came out to do a spot of break and enter. But that sort of backfired on them. Ha, ha.'

'*Okay Harry. I'll send the Ambos and I'd better come out myself. Is Senior Burke still at Australia Fair? I can catch a ride if she is.*'

'Hang on a moment Greg. I'll call her on the other phone and find out.'

I dialled her number on the boat phone and found out that she was still on the beach in front of Aussie fair, just loading up, so I asked her to wait for Greg. She giggled and said, 'He's welcome, but he'll be sitting on top of the booze. The dinghy's pretty full.'

'Yeah, she's still there Greg. There's not a lot of room, but you'll squeeze in.'

'*Okay. I'll be there in five minutes and the Ambos are on the way. They'll come out from the Water Police base.*'

'Goodo, thanks mate. I'll see you shortly.'

I realised that I'd forgotten to tell Amanda about the attack, but figured she'd find out from Greg. While I waited, I checked the two pistols more carefully and was very surprised to find that they were both very expensive weapons, one being a Coonan .357 Magnum and the other was a compact L6 Desert Eagle, also a .357 Magnum. They were a bit scuffed and scratched, but otherwise in good condition. Both magazines had full loads, but as much as I would have liked to keep them, I was obliged to turn them over to Greg as evidence that my intruders intended harm.

Of course, I could always ask him to let me mind them afterwards!

CHAPTER 14

Amanda and Greg just beat the Ambos to *Firebird* and I was very pleased to be on the receiving end of a very hard, close and personal hug from Amanda, who suddenly realised that she was being less than decorous with one senior Officer while another looked on, and backed off blushing and stammering an apology. I patted her bum in a very unprofessional manner as she broke away.

I was partway through the story to Greg and Amanda, when the Police RIB eased alongside with the same two Paramedics aboard.

'Good afternoon, Harry. We believe you've got some more trade for us?'

'Gidday fellas. Yep. Same as last night, I'm afraid. One with suspected cardiac problems and the other with lacerations and severe concussion from hitting his head when he fell down the stern steps.'

One grinned at me, 'You didn't push him, by any chance, did you Harry?'

I gave the Boy Scout salute, 'I can swear that I wasn't within reaching distance when he fell. I think something gave him a fright. The same with the other bloke, I was nowhere near either of them.'

They worked on the cardiac patient for a while and managed to get his heart settled down enough to move him onto the RIB, before turning their attention to the concussed dude.

'Where'd he get these scratches, I wonder?' one asked the other.

I gave my suitably blank look that drew a glare from Greg, but at least he kept his mouth shut for now. 'Don't know fellas. I think he had them when he turned up, so maybe he was in a fight just before he got here.'

'Yeah, I suppose that could happen. The fall might have opened them up again, although these marks on his throat look a bit odd. It looks like a large dog has bitten him. You don't have a dog, do you Harry?'

I shook my head with Amanda's head turning back and forth like at a tennis match.

'Sorry fellas. No dog here. That might have been pre-inflicted as well.'

Greg rolled his eyes; Amanda stifled a giggle and I was grateful that the Ambos didn't know me that well or they'd be aware of Jasper who had wisely retired out of sight. I belatedly asked Amanda to go and release Krazy kitten from her confinement in my dressing cabin.

Her appearance raised a few laughs and some references to 'killer kitten' while they cleaned up the concussed bikie who was still unconscious. Finally, both bikies were loaded onto the RIB and it returned to Base.

We pressed Greg into service helping to transfer all the groceries from the dinghy to the galley, where Amanda started to stow things away.

'Jeeze, you've bought a lot of stuff, Harry,' Greg commented.

'Well, there's a good reason for that and I wanted to chat with you about it, 'cause I'm inclined to think that we should bail out of here as soon as we can. Two attacks in 24 hours are getting a bit much and as you said on the phone, they must be getting pissed off with losing crews. Plus, we can't keep getting lucky fending off these characters. They'll get smart soon and hit us really hard. And I'm willing to bet that the other mob, the Zombie Whatnots have been watching us as well since the prize is rather large.'

Greg nodded, 'I hate to agree with you, but I do. This area has become much too hot for you. But where will you go?'

'Well, for your ears only, probably up to Moreton Bay at first. There are a lot of places to hide, but if necessary we can just move on further north when they pick up our scent again.'

Amanda had stopped unpacking food and watched us carefully, while Greg looked thoughtful. 'Yeah, I guess that's all you can do. After the ruckus last night and today, I'd transfer the money and the drugs ashore, but the situation with the Evidence Locker is getting worse. And the Undertakers will probably still keep chasing you on account of what you've done to them, whether you've got the stuff aboard or not.'

'Yep. That about sums it up. Therefore, I'd like to get out of here tonight in the dark. We're fuelled, provisioned and when the extra ammo turns up, fully armed and in good shape.'

'I'm not too happy about just the two of you being so far away from immediate back-up,' Greg stated, 'can I put another Officer aboard?'

I thought a moment, 'Sure, if you want. I don't have any problem with the idea, but Sandy won't be free for at least another week and if possible, I'd like her skills with us when she does turn up. Do you have anybody else in mind who could go right now?'

Greg looked at Amanda, 'What're your thoughts Senior? You know the situation better than I do. Is there someone you'd recommend to pad out the team?'

She cleared her throat, 'Actually, Sir, there is. It's Melissa Briggs. She's just been made Senior Constable and has done the Intermediate Drone course and Advanced Firearm training. She's also passed most of her study Modules for Detective the same as me. She's on General Duties at the moment, and I think she'd fit in really well to this slightly unusual environment. She's the best I can suggest, Sir.'

I shrugged at Greg as he thought a moment. 'Okay Senior.

In lieu of any other suggestions, we'll go with Senior Constable Briggs. I don't suppose that you have a contact number for her?'

Amanda fished her phone out of her/my shirt pocket and looked up a number. 'I think she's on duty at the moment, sir. Would you like me to make contact?'

Greg flapped his hand for her to go ahead, so she pressed buttons to make it happen.

'Hi Mel, it's Amanda.'

'Hi Mandy, where the hell have you been. Nobody knows what happened to you after the big turnout yesterday morning at Mariners Cove. Jackie said you didn't come home last night, but some of your gear seems to be missing. Is everything OK?'

'Yes, I'm fine thanks. But I'm in a hurry and so are you. Are you at work now?'

'Yeah. Ploughing my way through a foot-high stack of traffic accident reports. I thought when we made Senior we were past this shit! I wish the boss would get some more Constables or civvies to do the data entry.'

Amanda rolled her eyes theatrically, 'Mel, you're babbling and you really need to shut up and listen to me. This is serious shit!'

'Ahhh...What's going on Mandy? I've never heard you talk like this before. It's creepy.'

'It'll be a bloody sight creepier if you don't shut up. I'm trying to tell you what's going on!'

'Oh, OK. Sorry.'

'That's better. I've got Inspector James here and he wants to talk to you about a deployment. Here he is.'

'Oh, shit! Sorry.'

Greg took the phone with a wry grin on his face, 'Senior Constable Briggs?'

'Yes sir, Inspector. Go ahead.'

'Senior Briggs; you've been recommended for an unusual, important and very urgent assignment by Senior Burke, but based on what I've just heard, I've now got serious doubts concerning your suitability for this task. You don't seem to listen very well.'

'I'm sorry, sir. That was just my concern for Senior Burke's safety that made me talk so much. I'm not usually like this, sir and it won't happen again. So how can I help you, sir?'

I could see Greg struggling to hold a straight face as he wound her up a bit more, 'If, against my better instincts I do assign you to this Multi-Jurisdictional Task Force, do you think that you can keep your tongue in check, your ears open and actually do the job assigned to you?'

'Ahhh...Yes sir! Absolutely! I certainly can do just that and won't let you down. I'd really appreciate the opportunity to be involved in whatever you assign me to.'

'Very well, Senior. Despite the fact that you seem to be babbling again, I'm assigning you to an undercover detail as of this moment with the Multi-Jurisdictional Task Force mentioned previously. Everything you hear from this point on is to be regarded as Top Secret and may not be discussed with any other person at the Station, unless you have my personal authorisation. You will be under the direct supervision of Superintendent Stevens of the ACP and will do as instructed by him. He and I are the lead Officers on this case. Are there any questions you need to ask me directly?'

Ahhh...No sir. Not for now, but there are several hundred I'll need to ask later.'

'That's the most sensible thing I've heard you say, Senior. Now, I have some instructions for you, but do not discuss any part of what I say with anybody. If questioned by a Superior Officer, refer them to me. Understood?'

'Copy, sir.'

'Good. I want you to stop what you're doing immediately and go to the Armoury. There are a number of heavy boxes that the Armourer will sign over to you. He will arrange for them to be loaded into your personal vehicle and you will then leave the Station as quickly as possible. Go to your home and pack minimal civil, casual clothing appropriate for a three-week holiday. I suggest taking something warm as well, but no uniforms or cocktail dresses are required, although you are to take your full kit of Police issue hardware including your firearm. Copy so far?'

'Copy, sir.'

'Excellent. You may tell anybody who asks that you have been placed on Administrative Leave for a few weeks. Despite the sound of that, it will not reflect badly in your record; in fact, very much the opposite, so don't be concerned. Once packed, soft bags only please, you are to proceed to the Water Police Base on SeaWorld Drive, Main Beach where they are expecting you and your cargo and will direct you from there. Please call Senior Burke on this number to advise that you are leaving your accommodations. I need you to expedite your movements, Senior Briggs, so chop, chop. Get going.'

'Yes, sir. Thank you sir. I'm gone!'

Greg handed the phone back to Amanda, frowning slightly, 'I do hope that you've made a good choice here, Senior Burke. She still sounds a bit flaky to me.'

'With respect, sir, she would have been a bit intimidated by all that but I have every confidence that she'll be an asset to the team.'

He nodded, 'I hope so. If not, Harry will ream her out quick smart. Please remind her that she can and will be replaced at a moments notice if she screws up.'

'Yes, sir. Will do.'

Greg turned to me, 'Anything else you need for now?'

'Nah. I don't think so, thanks mate. Our job at the moment is to stay one or two steps ahead of the bad boys, so the extra pair of hands will be very useful since we'll keep on the move as much as possible. Just keep us updated on any developments locally with the bikies.'

'Yeah, will do, Harry. Take care, mate.'

Amanda ran him back to the Southport beach in the dinghy where he'd left his car and was back aboard ten minutes later.

UNDERTAKER'S OMC CLUBHOUSE – FRIDAY – LATE AFTERNOON

An immaculate black Harley-Davidson Fat Boy motorcycle burbled around the building that constituted the Undertaker's OMC Clubhouse and parked in the rear yard. It's rider swung off the machine with a degree of urgency and hustled inside. In a comfortable corner office that was fitted out as a lounge and small meeting room, the President, who liked to call himself the Undertaker and to be called by his boys 'Boss' was leaning back in his tilting chair, his gleaming black boots propped up on a desk draw, sipping a red wine from a fine, elegant glass.

'Come in, Jay. I'm guessing you've got things to tell me.'

Jay Fernando, his 1st Lieutenant, edged nervously into the room. 'I'm afraid so, boss. I've got more bad news.'

'It's very unfortunate that I'm getting used to that, Jay, so you'd better go ahead and ruin my evening.'

'Ahhh...Yeah. Sorry boss, but we've lost two more of the boys.'.....

'Don't tell me; let me guess. The two clowns you sent to search that triple-damn and blasted boat?'

'Gee. How'd you know that boss? I just found out when the Ambos turned up to cart them away.'

'I suppose that I'm just psychic Jay, although there is a limit to the extent of my second sight, so please tell me what happened. And try to keep it simple.'

'Oh. Yes, boss. Well, we were watching the boat from the Yacht Club outdoor lounge area like we talked about and as soon as the owner left, I sent the boys out to the boat. It was difficult to see properly all the time with other boats in the way, but I definitely saw them go aboard and they must have got inside the boat all right, 'coz I lost sight of them pretty well straight away. But then nothing seemed to happen for about ten minutes until the owner came back again, but this time he had another bloke with him.

I saw them go aboard and although there were some boats in the way at times, I still didn't see anything happen and it was just a few minutes later that the Ambos arrived in the Police boat again. They must have already been on their way out boss, 'coz the owner and this other bloke had only been aboard a couple of minutes.

Anyway, the Ambos weren't there very long before they took them ashore on stretchers. I've just heard that Andy's being treated for a heart attack and Joey has a severe concussion and what look like bite marks around his throat and deep claw marks down his chest. He lost a lot of blood.'

'Are you trying to tell me that this owner and another bloke just drove up in their dinghy without our guys hearing them, then surprised and took out two armed men just like that? In just two minutes and without you seeing or hearing anything?'

'That's how it happened boss. There was nothing to see! It's really weird there being no fight or anything. This is seriously spooky stuff, boss. The rest of the boys are getting edgy and aren't real keen to try again. They reckon there's some bad magic going on with that boat, especially with the teeth and claw marks nearly bleeding Joey out. I mean, there's no dog on the boat, so what made those marks.'

'That's a load of crap, Jay. I don't want to hear any more talk like that about voodoo or other stuff. There's an excellent chance our money and merchandise are on that boat and I want it back. Now we can either fold our tent and move on, or we can fight.

But I reckon this place is way too lucrative a market, particularly with this new version of 'Molly', so I say we fight back, reclaim our stuff and dig in.

Call all the boys in for a War Council, even though that other mob don't seem to be involved.'

'But we don't take on Civilian targets, boss. You've always said that's bad for business 'coz it'll just get the coppers stirred up and they'll create one of those Task Force things.'

'Yeah, yeah, Jay. I know what I said, but this is one guy, and even if the coppers seem to be supporting him, he seems to be declaring war on us. We can't just lie back and take that, now can we?'

'I dunno, boss. Taking on one guy is OK, but if the coppers are involved in this mysterious stuff, that's not a rumble I reckon we should start!'

'Wise council from you, Jay, but what about this idea. What if we were to talk to the Zombies with the aim of joining forces to firstly reclaim the money and Molly, then to handle this new stuff properly?

If we work together instead of fighting, we can be much more effective.'

Jay shook his head, 'I dunno, boss. I mean the boys really hate those Zombie arseholes. It'll be a hard sell to tell them were going to be working together.'

'Well, that's just it Jay. We'll be working together, not fighting with them. We're not marrying the bastards either. It's just a business deal to market the Molly more effectively.'

Finally Jay nodded. 'Yeah, righto boss. I might be able to sell that one to the boys. I can see that it would be good for business, so long as we can get a steady supply of the stuff.'

'Yes. That's always the problem, but I've managed to make some connections in Korea where the stuff is made. If it works out, we might be able to bypass the Sydney mob and get part shipments direct when it comes in by freighter. There's a drop expected in about a week into Moreton Bay where they pick it up using some of the trawlers that operate in the Bay. We've been promised one container that is 50 kilos. I don't have to remind you that's a huge quantity, especially when we can cut it by up to 90%.'

Jay's eyes were spinning trying to keep up with the flood of information. 'But what about paying for it, boss. I mean, that 10-kilo package cost two mil, so is 50 kilos going to be ten mil? That'll pretty well clean out the stash.'

'Ah. Good point, but the price won't be quite that high since we're cutting out the middleman in this case. The quoted price is $8M and that's where our new partners get to kick in their share up front. If they're going to share the distribution, they'll have to pay for it. And we take an extra cut, since we organised it in the first place.'

Jay nodded, 'OK boss. That might work, but we'd better talk to them very soon. And are we still going to try to get our cash and Molly back?'

'Hell yes! We can't afford to write that off, even if we do get this co-operative venture going. I want a plan to hit that boat as soon as we can with a decent crew, not just two guys.'

'Okay. I'll get a few boys together and we'll kick ideas around. I'll try to have something by the morning.'

'Good, Jay. But that stuff about the shipment is for you only for now, so keep quiet. And with the boat raid, don't try to get too clever. We just want to hit that bastard hard and take him out permanently if possible. If it happens to be an accident, that'll be best.

Now go do your stuff but don't go too far away. I might need you after I've made some phone calls.'

CHAPTER 15

'This is Brad.'

'Good afternoon Mr Edwards. This is Mr Jones.'

'Oh, gidday Henry. How're they hangin'?'

'I'm very well, thank you for asking. To 'cut to the chase' as you Americans like to put it, a situation has developed that could be very beneficial to both of us, but we need to put our differences aside for a time and have a meeting immediately. Perhaps just you and your 2IC and me and mine.'

'Wow! That's outstanding Henry! I can't remember us ever sitting down together, unless we were trying to shoot each other. This could be historic! I'm excited!'

'I'm very pleased you find the concept so exciting, Mr Edwards. May I presume that you are in favour of a truce for the duration and will meet at a neutral location?'

'Shit yeah! Why not? Let's hear what you've got to say, big fella. This is huge!'

'Kerb your enthusiasm, Mr Edwards. I require you to be very objective about this. I have not made this offer of a meeting lightly, but there is much at stake. The time is now 17:30. May I suggest the lounge in the Benbow Tavern at 18:30? Only my lieutenant Jay Fernando will accompany me. No other Club members will be in the vicinity. May I count on you to do the same under a general truce?'

'Hell yeah! We'll go along with that, Henry. You've got me real curious now. I'll even shout the first round of drinks. We'll be there.'

'Thank you, Mr Edwards. I hope that these talks will be fruitful.'

'Good on ya mate. See you soon.'

BENBOW TAVERN – 18:30 FRIDAY

It was only the Tavern Manager and the senior barman who recognised the mismatched pair of characters who entered the busy lounge from opposite sides of the building that Friday evening. The very tall, lean man with huge hands, wearing an immaculate black Armani suit and the shorter, stocky man in yellow baggy shorts, joggers with no socks and a voluminous garishly coloured Hawaiian shirt had never been seen in public together, and certainly not in what seemed a convivial social setting.

The manager sent a waitress out to scan the carpark for groups of bikies, but she reported back that all was quiet and that there were only the two silent big men accompanying the legendary leaders of the two most feared bikie groups in the State.

Based on that information, the Manager decided to hold the call to the Police for the moment and instructed the staff to treat the four men as normal customers. True to his word, Brad sent Tony to the bar to get a round of drinks, although the two deputies stayed with a schooner of squash each.

At their table outside the lounge to escape most of the noise, the two leaders eyed each other off dispassionately. For all his brash, apparently carefree ways, Brad Edwards was a very tough and astute man.

'Okay Henry. Here we are and we've got the Manager over there absolutely shitting himself seeing us sitting here together, having a drink. It was your call and your idea so you lead off. You've got my undivided attention.'

The Undertaker cracked a small, wintery smile as he sipped a quite acceptable Merlot, 'I must admit, Mr Edwards, that I also find the situation quite amusing however, to business. You are aware of the difficulties we have been experiencing lately?'

'Yeah. Bad luck running foul of a bloke like that. I can't understand how he and some sheila took out four of your best men. I mean that's crazy. You must be really pissed! And to lose the cash and the Molly as well! Dear oh dear.'

'I must confess that I am quite upset by the turn of events, but we are still proceeding with plans to recover the items and exact some form of retribution for the damage done.'

'That's the spirit, Henry. Nothing like a good dose of retribution to get the guys fired up. But do go on and forgive me for the interruption.'

'Thank you, Mr Edwards. As I was saying, despite the setback which is temporary, it has highlighted a situation where I believe that both our groups could benefit financially if we were to collaborate in a purely business arrangement.'

'Okay Henry. So far I've got no problem if this is just a business deal. Keep going.'

'Thank you. To continue; I have managed to make direct contact with the producers of this enhanced product and they have agreed to let me have a part of the next shipment which is expected in seven or eight days. The only drawback is that we must take one complete container that holds 50 kilos of pure product and they want $8M up front to secure it. That, as I'm sure you know, is a substantial discount on what we paid for the lost shipment.'

Brad looked admiringly, 'Henry. As much as I think you're a stuck-up arsehole, you really do have a great head for a deal!'

The tall man inclined his head gravely in acknowledgment of the great compliment he'd been paid. 'Thank you, Mr Edwards. I appreciate your thoughts. Now. If you are in favour, I propose that we agree to pool our finances to purchase this part shipment and decide on how the territory should be split up so each group can protect it's distribution rights from each other and from outsiders. There is too much money to be made for us to squabble between ourselves over petty issues, but there must not be any poaching of clients and only you and I will fix the price and not offer any discounts.

That should make things fair and stop either group gaining an advantage. Your thoughts?'

'Sounds good to me Henry. But I presume that you will want us to tip in a bit extra so that you are compensated for hooking up directly with the manufacturer in the first place?'

Henry inclined his head, 'That is so, Mr Edwards. I thought that a 60:40 split in the payment would be reasonable.'

After a couple of seconds, Brad's calculator brain fired back, 'That works out at just 3.2 from you and 4.8 from us and looks a bit too lop-sided, I'm afraid. How about 55:45. That's 4.4 from us and 3.6 from you, which is effectively a payment of $800K for a few phone calls. Not a bad payday, Henry.'

Henry smiled, acknowledging Brad's expertise, 'Very well, Mr Edwards. At the risk of appearing to give in easily, I must say that the pie is too large to quibble over peanuts. It shall be as you say. When would you be able to have your share ready for transfer? The client requires the full sum immediately.'

'Would tomorrow morning be OK, Henry? We can lodge the funds with a neutral party with a trust account. Either ours or your Solicitors will be acceptable to me.'

'That's very trusting and generous, Mr Edwards. In that case, we will use your people. We will make the transfer also in the morning and I will email the payment details for you to instruct your people as to the transfer to the client.'

'How about the division of sales territory, Henry?'

'We have some time before we receive the shipment and be in position to make sales, so how about we agree to continue normal operations under truce conditions until the new product becomes available. By that time we can have another meeting to work out the territory split.'

'Done, old mate. I agree to all we've said and we have a recording, as I'm sure you do as well. How about we get together again in five days? Same time; but a different place to be advised just before the meeting. Then we can carve up the territories.'

Henry stood and held out his hand to Brad. 'We will never agree on outlook or philosophy, Mr Edwards, but if we can maintain this business alliance and protect each other from outsiders, then between us, I believe we can take over much of the East Coast market and make a substantial amount of money.'

Brad took Henry's hand and gave it a firm shake. 'Hear, hear on that Henry. But let's make sure we stick very firmly to the letter of our agreement in these early stages so there's no misunderstandings.'

Henry looked Brad in the eye and replied, 'I agree and you have my word that we will do as we have agreed.'

The Tavern manager's jaw dropped open to see the two feared leaders shaking hands amicably on some sort of deal and he couldn't wait to dig out his phone and call a friend in blue.

FIREBIRD – YACHT CLUB MOORING
– FRIDAY LATE AFTERNOON

Amanda was keen to finish stowing the groceries, as we'd be departing in a couple of hours, but desperately needed to change out of her disguise that was killing her boobs.

I was still pretty wired after the brief action with the two bikies, but agreed wholeheartedly when she commented, 'Bloody hell! I'm glad that's over and we've got something positive to do. I was worried about you. That shit with the two goons could've gone badly.'

I gave a rueful smile, 'Don't I know it! The number of times in Afghanistan I've seen simple plans come totally unglued when something doesn't work out as hoped. That's another reason I want us out of here. As long as the bikies even think we've got their shit aboard, we're a floating target with a giant carbon-fibre flagpole saying, 'here we are."

Following that cheerful observation, she disappeared below to change while I made ready to move by hauling the dinghy up into its stowage place under the huge rear day bed. I guessed that our new crewmember would be at least an hour or so getting organised, but I didn't want to leave until it was dark which was in another hour and fifteen minutes, so there wasn't any hurry.

I noted that there was very little breeze, so we'd have to travel under power until we found a secluded anchorage for the night. My ponderings on this and that were interrupted by a plaintive bleat from the aft cabin.

'Harry, help please.'

I made my way below to find Amanda standing minus shorts and shirt. She'd managed to unwrap the towel around her waist, but couldn't reach the tape that I'd used to fasten the bandage around her boobs. She looked very erotic, standing there with just the wrapping around her top and those very brief, lacy panties that were nearly transparent.

'I can't undo the tape,' she said, 'you did a good job, but the bandage is killing my boobs.'

I chuckled as I eyed her appreciatively, 'Apart from the strapping, you look very sexy.'

She grinned, 'I didn't think you'd notice.'

'Oh, I noticed all right,' I said with feeling. 'But you need to turn around a bit to let me get at the tape end.' I found the end and with some difficulty, pulled it free starting the process of unwrapping her chest. We'd used a lot of bandage to flatten her in the first place and I tried to unwind it gently. As the final length came free, she gave a groan of pleasure as her lovely boobs were freed and stood up more or less as they were supposed to. She gently cupped them and massaged them with a sigh of pleasure.

'You should know that that looks extremely erotic, young lady,' I said with a grin.

Naturally, she was now wearing very little and when she

giggled, I saw that she was looking at the front of my shorts that were considerably distended.

With disarming candour she observed, 'Goodness me, Harry. That can't be a gun in your shorts, but it's certainly big enough. Is that really all you?'

I always became uncomfortable when females discuss my erections, which happen way too frequently for comfort, but it had been a long time since Sandy left, so I replied, 'I afraid so. All me.'

'Excellent! Of course, it would be totally inappropriate for you to let me see it, wouldn't it?'

I grinned, 'Yes. That would be completely out of line, but clothing accidents do happen at times.'

'Is now one of those times?' She asked, busily undoing the buttons and zip of my shorts, letting them drop to the deck.

'I guess it must be,' I said, letting go a big 'Ahhh!' of relief as the pressure was released.

'Oh wow!' Amanda said. 'Just look at that! He's a very big boy! I might have another clothing accident myself, if that's okay with you?'

I didn't get a chance to reply as she slipped her panties off in seconds, before hoisting herself up onto the side of the bed. I didn't need any further invitation to move in between her parted thighs and join with her, my normal urgent need heightened by the adrenaline still circulating in my system.

For a first time between virtual strangers, it was very good for both of us, although mutual urgency made for a reasonably short session. She didn't seem to mind that at all and was very happy that I stayed with her afterwards. She was even happier when after just ten minutes I pushed her over on her back again.

'You're kidding,' she said, 'Already?'

'Yup!' I grinned lecherously, 'I'm afraid so. It's a bit of an affliction I can't control.'

She grabbed me enthusiastically, things automatically going where they should. 'Oh, goodness me, yes. Look Ma, no hands!

But what a lovely affliction you have and don't you dare try to control it!'

So I didn't and things went even better the second time around, lasting much longer to Amanda's frequently repeated delight. When we finally separated, she was wrecked, covered in sweat, but with a broad grin on her pretty face.

'Oh you lovely man! I think just I set some personal records, although I might have lost count a few times! I might add, if you don't mind, that you seem to be...Ahh very productive! I'm a mess.'

I chuckled, 'Sorry about that. Another part of the affliction I'm afraid. Always have been like that, but never noticed it myself. It's not something that guys get around to comparing.'

That made her laugh, 'Don't apologise. It's amazingly lovely and I hope you don't think I'm too greedy, but I hope Sandy takes her time getting back!'

I laughed at her enthusiasm and patted her smooth, firm bum, it being the nearest part of her anatomy to my free hand. 'I'm glad you're pleased. I am too. And even when she does get back, I have to warn you that with her broad view of relationships, she may surprise you. In a very nice way,' I added hastily.

Amanda raised her eyebrows at that remark, but didn't have a chance to follow it up, as her phone chose that moment to ring.

'Oh, hi Mandy. It's Mel. Am I supposed to report to you that I'm about to leave my place? I thought Inspector James was still there.'

Amanda giggled, 'Just as well he's not!'

'Pardon? Did you say that he's not there, or glad that he's not? You sound a bit funny.'

Amanda composed herself, although with some difficulty under the circumstances as she was still damply draped half over me, before replying, 'Yeah. Sorry about that. Yes, you were supposed to report to me that you were leaving your place for the Water Police station. Do you know where it is?'

'*Yeah. We saw it yesterday going to Mariners Cove. It's virtually next-door. But who do I see there?*'

'Just drive in the second entrance along and there'll be a white sliding gate ahead of you. Blow your horn when you get up to it so it'll open, then drive around to the left into the main courtyard. You'll be met by a couple of Water Police guys who'll unload you.

At that point, I want you to just text me that you're there. Then wait and don't answer any questions. I hope you don't need to pee, 'cause you should've done before you leave home. The guys will wait with you and shouldn't try to question you either.'

'*Mandy. This is getting seriously creepy! If it wasn't you and Inspector James involved, I'd say 'stuff it' and go back to paperwork. And who's this Superintendent Stevens? Is he OK?*'

Amanda laughed, 'Don't worry, Mel. All will be revealed shortly, as somebody once said, and Superintendent Stevens is just fine.' She stroked me in a sensitive place to make that point. 'We'll be seeing you shortly. Just follow instructions exactly and don't try to second-guess things.'

There was a big sigh from the phone, '*All right, Mandy. I'll be a good little Copper, but this had better not be a wind up! I had a nice guy to go out to dinner with tonight and I was hoping it'd turn into an all-nighter back at my place. But since Inspector James called, I've been rushing so much, I still haven't eaten.*'

Amanda laughed again, 'OK. We've both got to go, but to make up for all the run-around, I can promise you a lovely dinner tonight with a very nice man in a wonderful setting at the best table with the best water views in town. Will that do it?'

'*Yes, of course it will. But how the fuck are you going to do all that?*'

'All will be revealed, little one. Have faith. Bye now and hustle.'

CHAPTER 16

As it had taken us a little while to clean up, any further fooling around was postponed for now, although there was little doubt that we both wanted a repeat session or six. Amanda had shamelessly announced that she was very keen to try to improve on her PB score, now that she knew what was possible.

To save time and forsaking clothing, I'd nipped up top and fired up the engines, letting them warm up while I went below for a rudimentary clean-up. Amanda had more time to do so more thoroughly. She giggled at the sight of me returning through the saloon.

'Is a lowly Senior Constable allowed to tell her Commander that he looks particularly sexy like that?'

I grinned back, 'It's probably prohibited in some HR manual, but who gives a stuff.'

Minutes later, I was fairly clean, dressed and ready.

'What can I do,' Amanda asked, as I switched on the nav lights, but turned all other lights off.

'Nothing for the moment, but when I take us into the Base jetty, you can hang a fender over the right bow since we won't tie up. I'll just hold that bow against the fender with the engines so you can get Melissa and her gear on board ASAP. Ignore her questions until we're under way, then we can give her a full briefing.'

She nodded, 'No problem. But what's that little box you've got?'

'It's a controller that's a full function remote for letting me drive the boat if I want to be away from the main steering station.

I can change gear, throttle setting, steering and raise or lower the anchor with it from any place on the boat. It operates on Bluetooth® and is really good for single-handed docking or manoeuvring in tight positions. I've got a hard-mounted version here at the chart table for when I don't want to go outside into the rain and cold but tonight, I can drive the boat from up the bow where I can see exactly where we are.'

'Neat!'

Just then, Amanda's phone buzzed with an incoming text message. 'It's Mel. She's at the Base and two of the guys are with her. What should I reply?'

'Text, 'Stand-by'. That should do it.'

We went forward and dropped the mooring buoy. Once free, I moved us slowly through the cluster of moored boats in to the Police base jetty, where I wedged our starboard bow in against a piling. There wasn't much room as a Patrol boat was taking up most of the space, but we only needed a small space to poke the bow into.

The coppers had seen us coming and had moved three heavy boxes down to the jetty, a small female figure that must have been Melissa tagging along behind, two soft bags in hand and looking quite bewildered until she spotted Amanda standing tall on the bow.

'Evening Harry,' called Sergeant Les, part of the clean-up crew from last night, 'we heard you've been busy again. I wish you'd leave a few for us.'

'Yeah, gidday Les. You're welcome to all the rotten bastards. You know me — I just want the quiet life. All this aggro is very upsetting for my constitution.'

He laughed as he and Constable Pete heaved the small but heavy boxes up onto the bow where Amanda humped them back a few metres out of the way. 'Yeah, bullshit, Harry. You love it. But seriously, the bad boys aren't very happy with you at the moment. That's four you've taken out so far.'

'Yeah, I know. But what can you do? They just keep coming at us.' They laughed again as they finished with the boxes, then threw Melissa's bags up to Amanda, then helped Melissa scramble awkwardly up and over the bow railing.

'Is that it, Harry? A crew change or an addition?'

'Just an addition for the moment, fellas but thanks for your help. We'll be away for a little while, so see you when we get back.'

'Take care Harry. We'll be happy to back you up anytime. Just call.' echoed across the water as I backed us up quietly, turned and headed at low speed toward the channel leading north. As soon as we were going straight for a few minutes, I turned to our new crewmember and held out my hand, 'Hi Melissa, I'm Harry. Welcome aboard *Firebird*.'

She was small for a Policewoman, and looked way too young to even leave home, let alone be a Senior Constable with unarmed combat training, expert firearms rating and drone technician qualifications. Nevertheless, even in the dim light on deck she moved with lithe grace, despite her ungraceful scramble aboard and seemed to have a slim, neat little body with all the right bits that I could see. She and Amanda had shared a very enthusiastic greeting that seemed to suggest a close friendship that would be good for our working and social relationship.

She had a firm grip that belied her size and spoke with a sexy, husky voice. 'Thank you, Sir. Or is it OK to call you Harry?'

'Bloody hell, woman!' I protested with a grin, 'we're undercover, so it's always first names, and would be even if we weren't on the job. This boat is my permanent home, so things are done my way and that's casual. No official bullshit here! But seriously, because we're undercover you need to start role-playing immediately.

Basically, I'm a retired, wealthy playboy who likes boats, booze parties and girls. When we're around civilians, you two get to lie around in bikinis all day, suck up booze and act like bimbos. You even get paid to do all that!'

She chuckled at that then said, 'It all sounds a bit too good to be true.'

'Well, it's not. This is the job. I'll explain more shortly, but basically, because we're carrying a very valuable cargo and the bad guys are a bit cranky with us because it's their cargo, we're going into hiding, as much as we can with a 60 ft cat. And apart from the dumb bimbo bit, normal day-to-day life isn't much different as we're just going to be moving from place to place fairly often. Your role-playing really kicks in when we are around other boaties or civilians. That's when you can't afford a slip-up and we must appear harmless; hence the bimbo act and the lack of uniforms aboard. I want you to tuck away all your Service ID and hardware where it can't be easily seen, but make sure it's quickly accessible. I'll fill you in on background to the assignment in the briefing.'

I scanned the channel ahead for obstacles like sleepy or stupid fishermen who thought that the middle of a main channel was a great place to anchor, before continuing. 'For now though, while I navigate us clear of some of these drunken idiots trying to drive boats, I'm going to get Amanda to show you the workings of the boat which means how not to sink us by mistake, clog up the toilets or waste all the water. She'll then settle you into your cabin which will be the palatial and spacious forward port queen, right down there in fact.' I pointed at the big hatch almost at our feet. 'But first, we'd better go through the routine of you meeting my cat, Jasper. He's had his eye on you since you came over the bow and is busting to see whom else we've dragged aboard. He's also our best early-warning system for bad-guys and the main guard for our cargo, although we have a kitten now as well, but she's got a lot to learn.'

Melissa looked like she thought we were crazy, but nodded and let herself be led aft.

I followed the girls, appreciating their stern view, and after cautioning them about not turning on any white lights for now, switched the remote across to the main steering station when

I reached the cockpit and set myself up to follow the channel north. I'd roughly planned to get as far as the Jumpinpin area for the night and anchor well away from the high traffic channel.

At our comfortable cruising speed of 14 knots, it should only take about an hour, and after putting our rather devious, meandering course into the chart plotter, it politely informed me that we would arrive at our selected anchorage at 20:17 precisely, or in 61 minutes. I decided that we could have the promised 'water-view restaurant' meal as soon as we anchored. That way there'd be no engine noise to disturb the peace and no mozzies if I anchored at least a few hundred metres away from shore.

That all done, I turned George the Autopilot on and let him steer the course as dictated by the bossy Chart Plotter. That let me talk to Melissa while I kept a careful lookout for boats in our path, although the digital, close range radar would also warn of any conflicts

Melissa displayed the usual reaction to meeting my beautiful big sort-of Chausie cat for the first time and was amused by his introduction routine, but was immediately and totally won over by Jasper's gentle nature. Krazy kitten also helped the feline welcome routine by curling up in her lap and kneading her crutch. After seeing her do the same to Amanda, I resolved to come back in my next life as a cute, fuzzy little cat!

I let Amanda continue with the tour guide bit and sat quietly, watching out for other boats whose skippers may not be so vigilant at night. Finally, the girls joined me in the cockpit, at which point I suggested the meal plan to them. They were very happy with that, especially when I suggested the fresh rib-eye fillet steaks bought just that afternoon, so Amanda ducked into the galley to make some nibblies to tide us over, then to make early preparations with veggies, but she popped out briefly to hand Melissa a Chardonnay and me a beer.

'So this is going to be my promised 'lovely dinner, lovely man, best-table and water-views in town' eatery', Melissa said cheekily.

'Afraid so,' I replied, 'Amanda does have a way with words, but you'll have to suffer her cooking since I'm a bit too basic in the culinary department for decent company.'

'From what I hear, I don't think that there's much you couldn't turn your hand to, Harry. But I admit to being a bit blown away by this whole thing, the boat, which I love already, Jasper and his attack ability, the bikies and all the rest of the drama. Mandy's told me what she knows of the tactical situation, but she didn't say why you guys are being chased by the bikies.'

I was relieved that she'd lost the 'frivolous attitude' that Greg was worried about and seemed all business, so I gave a short history of what had led to our current situation.

'Crap! You mean we're sitting on two million in cash and about ten times that in drugs? That's insane!'

'Think it through for a moment, ' I said quietly, ignoring her outburst, 'if the Evidence Locker is compromised, what else is Greg James going to do with it?'

She thought a moment, a small, intense person with straight shoulder-length blonde hair and a neat little figure, 34 maybe on a really good day, I thought irreverently, although they were very nicely shaped. 'Yeah, okay. I see your point and I didn't mean any disrespect. I'm a bit new to this stuff. General Duties doesn't really equip you for any real Policing like catching bad guys, let alone fighting them, so you've got to teach me all you can.'

I was surprised by her intensity, but replied, 'Sure thing, I'll do what I can. I'll talk; you listen and ask questions. OK?'

She grinned, transforming into a different and much more relaxed person, 'Deal! You know, you really aren't like any other Commander or Superintendent I've met before.'

I smiled, 'Ah, that's what undercover work does for you. No uniforms, no formality. It's very refreshing and you might get used to it'

'I like it already.'

As we cruised quietly along at a deceptively fast speed, we

exchanged information so that by the time we were nearing our anchorage, she was up to speed on most of our recent happenings. I'd made no mention of our afternoon romp while waiting for her call, figuring that if Amanda wanted to do the girl-talk routine, she would, but it'd be very obvious at bed-time, since I was pretty sure Amanda was as keen as I was for a repeat performance as she had been a happy and very satisfying partner. In hindsight, the choice of steak for tea was a good one.

I had no idea how Melissa was going reconcile Amanda being very intimate with the boss, but that was up to them to figure out. Still, I was happily looking forward to seeing Melissa in a bikini.

I'd offered to do the steaks on the Weber BBQ, hung out in the cockpit to keep gas vapours out of the interior, but Amanda insisted on doing the lot, so she was busily trotting to and fro, timing things so that she could serve shortly after we dropped anchor. Melissa showed a very healthy interest in the running of the boat, something I was very happy to encourage. And like Amanda, she was also very interested in the weapons I had aboard and curious about the contents of the small but heavy boxes, currently parked in the cockpit out of the way. I'd ignored them for now and decided that tomorrow was soon enough to see what Greg had given us.

I found a decent anchorage about a 100-metres off a sandy beach, to the west of the main north-south channel, where there were no other anchored boats and apparently little or no traffic. The slight breeze had dropped and the water glassed off, so that with the dim cockpit lighting, it was a genuine million-dollar setting and Melissa was utterly delighted. The meal was excellent and Amanda deserved the praise we heaped on her. With dishes cleared away, I volunteered to make my now trademark NQ teas, a strong, dark tea with a double shot of dark rum liquor added. It took the breath away for an instant then became plain bloody good.

Two were enough to loosen tongues; three would make a saint raid a nunnery. I kept the girls to two, figuring that Amanda was already looking rather predatory and sitting a lot closer beside me than was really necessary. I was sure that subtle signals were being passed between the two girls and for sure Melissa had guessed that things were cosier than would be normal.

Melissa's tongue was certainly loosened, although she was disciplined enough to stay slightly in control, as she rattled on about her almost non-existent sex life, even detailing her preferences for bedtime activity. Therefore, the conversation turned very raunchy, very quickly, although both girls were happy and giggly which made it a fun evening. As the first serious yawns appeared, dirty dishes were piled in the dishwasher and good nights were wished. The girls went their separate ways to get ready for bed, while I made sure the cat's toilet mat was clean, the anchor secure, then closed the cockpit doors, but didn't lock them. With Jasper on duty, I had no fear of an intruder.

I showered, then climbed into bed, hearing murmuring voices and some muffled giggles coming from Melissa's cabin, separated by several deck lockers from mine, although sounds passed disconcertingly freely when the deck hatches were open as they were tonight.

I was indulging in one of my favourite pastimes, reading, when there was a timid knock on the open cabin door and a tousled blonde head poked around. 'Care for a visitor?' Amanda asked shyly.

I just smiled and folded the bedclothes back in invitation. She was in there with a flash of bare tanned limbs — her only garment a long T-shirt that she left draped over the end of the bed.

'I was hoping you'd want me to join you tonight,' she said softly, 'I've been buzzing all afternoon and couldn't wait to do it again. It's never felt like that before and was all so intense that I almost scared myself, so I wanted to see if it could happen again.'

I was more than happy to assist with the experiment and

shared her pleasure as she set a new PB after a very prolonged session. As she showed no sign of wanting to leave, we curled up and went to sleep. That luckily lasted until just before dawn when there was a fairly serious repeat bout that threatened to challenge her previous PB, but fell a bit short. Neither of us was concerned about that and Amanda fairly bounced out of bed, fizzing and bubbly and went to shower, leaving me to lie in for a while.

She came back, naked and with wet hair to retrieve her T-shirt.

'Stay there and I'll bring you a mug of tea,' she offered.

'I should get up,' I said, 'but I'd certainly appreciate a cuppa.'

'Okay, I'll make it, you work out where you want it.'

I did get up, had my ablutions and sallied forth to greet the day, taking my steaming mug of tea forward to my favourite early morning spot in one of the bow seats. On this occasion, Amanda joined me with Jasper tagging along as soon as he'd finished his breakfast, with little Krazy kitten scampering along behind, swiping at his long tail that he obligingly allowed to drag along the deck, suffering the needle stabs of her claws for her pleasure.

'Thank you, Harry, for everything so far. It's been wonderful and I'm not exaggerating when I say that I think the last 24-hours has changed my outlook enormously. But enough of that stuff — this is a peaceful spot. Where are we?'

'The south side of Crusoe Island. This area, as well as the passage through to the ocean is called Jumpinpin. The bar itself is just around the corner, but it's very dangerous to cross unless the sea is calm. We get to pass in front of it when we head further up the passages to get to Moreton Bay which will be our hangout area for a while.'

It *was* a pretty spot, even though the scenery was a bit drab, but the only traffic was a couple of tinnies that ran past, rods poking up in all directions, the occupants either cheery if they'd been successful or glum if not. I made a mental note to try the girls on fishing to supplement our supplies.

The water in our channel was a slightly murky colour that

didn't invite swimming, although a sandy beach was close by, so I resolved to launch the RIB to take Jasper for a good romp on the beach and that maybe we'd stay here until tomorrow.

It was about then that Melissa poked her head up through the hatch over her bed, 'Good morning you two.'

'Good morning back at you,' Amanda replied, 'I suppose you want a coffee in bed.'

'Yum oh,' she said, disappearing back down but leaving the hatch flipped fully open. As we hadn't kicked up any salt spray last night, the decks and gear were clean and didn't need washing down, so I could relax and enjoy the serenity. Amanda reappeared with three mugs in hand and handed Melissa's coffee carefully down the hatch, giggling at something as she did, before handing me a tea.

'What's going on with you two,' I asked casually, watching a nearby pelican diving for his breakfast, his huge, expressive black eyes fixed on us in between dives in case there was a free feed on offer.

'I was laughing at Melissa,' Amanda said. 'She doesn't wear anything to bed and was asking if she would shock you if she came on deck like that. I suggested that it might be a bit early and a bit cool.'

I looked at her; 'It's never too early for a lovely naked lady. Remember, you guys have a reputation to live down to. Melissa seems to have grasped the idea very quickly.'

'Oh. So it really is okay to run around naked if we want?'

'Of course. When we get amongst other boats, you'll see a lot of naked bodies, male and female. In fact, up at the Whitsunday's, it's getting hard to spot clothing! And that's only a slight exaggeration,' I added. 'When I'm by myself, I rarely wear clothes. It saves on washing. Nobody minds unless we're in a crowded harbour. So you can pass that onto Melissa if you want.'

She looked carefully at me, nodded then said, 'Okay, I will.' And went back to the open hatch, knelt down and they had a quiet conversation. When she came back, I asked, 'Have you done any fishing in your past life?'

'Oh, yes. My dad was very keen and taught all us kids. I really enjoyed it.'

'Excellent, 'cause we've got a bunch of fishing gear aboard and it's a very good way to extend our supplies as well as being a very tasty change from meat.'

'No problem, I can do that and I'll get Mel up to speed as well. That is if I can stop her flashing herself in front of you all the time. She quite fancies you already.'

It was my turn to be surprised. 'Really? We've only just met and I'm sharing a bed with you.'

She made a puffing sound that I took to indicate contempt for male reasoning. 'Oh really, Harry. She's always been a randy little thing, but tries to behave herself for the sake of the job. But suddenly, here we are, away from our workmates on a lovely boat with a lovely man and being paid to act like bimbos. What's a girl supposed to do? Plus she heard everything last night and was terribly jealous. So you've got two randy females on hand, who won't have any problem acting out our roles.'

The last was said with a lecherous grin and I feared the standard of shipboard discipline might be slipping.

Breakfast was hot toast with honey, served on the foredeck when Melissa made an appearance, fully clothed for now, and the girls had fun bouncing on the trampoline nets when they'd finished eating.

'They're a great place to sleep on a hot night, or to sunbake on, especially when we're sailing,' I suggested.

'Oh, that'll be great,' Melissa said, 'will we be able to do any sailing?'

'Sure, but in the confines of these narrow passages with the shifting sandbanks, it's not practical. As soon as we enter the Bay proper north of Russell Island I'll gladly stop the engines. I normally try to sail everywhere if possible, but we'll stay here today and head up to Peel Island tomorrow, depending on the weather.'

After breakfast, I decided to have a look in the boxes Greg had sent. They were triple-layer cardboard and heavily taped up. The first contained many boxes of standard issue .40 S&W rounds in boxes of 20. An inventory showed that there were 2000 rounds in 100 boxes and that should keep the girls banging away for hours with their Glock 22 Service pistols and I made a note-to-self to make the girls practice whenever possible to keep their skills sharp.

The second box contained Greg's old hoard of 9mm Parabellum and that size suited several of my own weapons, including a highly prized mini-UZI machine pistol that spat 9mm bullets at a rate of 950 per minute. My other prized weapon was a .44 Magnum and Greg couldn't help with that size round, but luckily I had plenty in stock.

The third and smallest box held a lovely selection of shotgun cartridges in normal and Magnum loads and included 00, SG and two varieties of rifled slugs. He'd generously given me a thousand rounds altogether, so together with what I already had, there would be plenty for practice. The final treat made up the lower two layers in the box and consisted of twenty boxes of Winchester .22 Magnum rounds for my pair of Kel-Tec PMR-30 pistols.

CHAPTER 17

Despite it being Saturday, two large financial transfers were made from accounts in the Cayman Islands to a Solicitor's Trust account in Southport, and after receipt of an email, all the funds were then re-transferred back to a different account at a different bank in the Cayman Islands.

ZOMBIE EATERS OMC PROPERTY

Brad Edwards wandered through the sprawling house, sipping from a glass of fresh orange juice. 'Tony. Hullo! Where are you mate?'

There was a yell from the garage, 'Out here Brad.'

'Come inside a minute, would you, dude? I want to run an idea past you.'

UNDERTAKER'S OMC CLUBHOUSE

'Undertaker.'

Gidday, Henry. It's your new partner, Brad.

'Of course it is Mr Edwards, no one else calls me by my given name. Plus your quaint mixture of Australian slang spoken with an American accent renders your voice unmistakable. What can I do for you?'

'That's a fascinating observation, Henry. Thank you. But I'm

calling to let you know that the funds transfers have been executed as required.'

'Excellent, Mr Edwards, in fact, I have just received confirmation of payment from the manufacturer of our...goods and I'm about to email you the expected place and drop-off times of our shipment. I've been warned that they are not precise as a ship is involved and minor changes to the schedule are possible. The initial collection procedure is handled by a contractor and is detailed in the email, but we have to make appropriate arrangements to collect our shipment from them immediately after the initial collection. I'm informed that a strict time element is enforced — one hour in total, I'm told. I've made some calls already in an effort to secure a suitable boat, but nothing so far.'

'Thanks Henry. I'll see what contacts we have and get back to you. But the main reason for my call was that I thought in the spirit of co-operation that's been giving me such a warm, fuzzy feeling, I'd throw you a bone in the form of Mr Gary Williams, ex-courier and alive and fairly well. He has confirmed that he did leave your merchandise on that boat, but claims to know nothing further than that. But I'm sure you'll double-check all that when you receive him.'

'That's a very generous offer, Mr Edwards. Where has the gentleman been these last few days?'

Brad laughed. 'Locked up in my cellar, I'm afraid Henry. But I'm tired of having to feed the prick and he never stops whinging, so be warned. I nearly dumped him in the river days ago, but it occurred to me this morning that you might like to have him.'

'Thank you, Mr Edwards. That gesture is greatly appreciated. Although for now, in light of the impending large shipment, I've suspended further operations against that boat and I rely on you to do the same.'

Brad chuckled, 'No problem there, Henry. I don't want to lose four men in mysterious circumstances either, so ops are suspended for now.'

'Excellent, Mr Edwards. So when can we expect Mr Williams?'

'How about I send him to you now. We'll drop him off at your place, or anywhere else if you'd prefer. I hope your lads will behave themselves?'

'Have no fear of that, Mr Edwards. All members will be on their best behaviour from this point on, unless pre-agreed lines are deliberately crossed. At our place will be fine, thank you.'

'No problem, Henry. We'll talk again soon.'

Less than thirty minutes later, a dark blue current model BMW M5, eased to a stop in front of a freshly painted factory building in an Industrial estate in Southport's west, the 4.4L twin-turbo V-8 burbling quietly at idle, giving little hint of the vast amount of power held in check. Four large, brawny men stood waiting impassively at the kerb, ready to receive the very reluctant passenger.

'I don't want to go with those blokes,' ex-courier Williams, bleated, 'I don't think they like me very much!'

'I'll give you a tip, sunshine,' growled Tony Bradford from the front seat, 'we don't like you at all. In fact, we fuckin' well hate you, so shut the fuck up and get out of the car before I throw you out.'

'But they're going to hurt me!' Williams bleated again.

'They'd better or I'll come back and show them how, you useless bloody wombat!' spat Tony, jumping out and yanking the back door of the gleaming sedan open. 'Get out you pathetic, whining goose. Now!' he reached in and hauled so hard on Williams's arm that he shot out the door and sprawled on the grass verge, almost at the feet of the four impassive Undertakers.

'There you are, fellas. Here's a special delivery to your Man from ours. Good luck with him.'

'Thanks, Ahh...mate,' one of them said, still having trouble adjusting to the terms of the unprecedented truce agreed to by their leaders, but secretly pleased to be able to talk normally to a fellow bikie with similar aims and interests, instead of having to try to kill him.

'I don't think the Boss is very happy with him.'

Tony laughed, 'No. I expect not, but anyway, he's all yours, although I think he's told all he knows.'

FIREBIRD – SATURDAY – JUMPINPIN

The rest of the day was spent doing very little. Jasper got his long awaited romp on the beach and we all went on that, the boat quite safe as it was in sight at all times. There were too many people around to have any gun practice, although I was keen to try out the Isis 22 suppressor that a mate in Customs had passed on for testing on the PMR-30, so that was postponed for now. Nobody felt like swimming, so we lazed around, ate lovely food prepared by Amanda and played with the cats.

As the day warmed up nicely, the girls decided to do some sunbaking on the for'rard trampolines. They had the choice of the vast daybed hung over the stern between the hulls, but seemed to prefer up front. Naturally, it wasn't long before they both removed their tops, Melissa proving to have small, but very nicely shaped boobs with small, pink nipples. Amanda was about halfway between Sandy and Melissa in size, but also shaped very nicely.

To play the perfect host and get to examine Melissa more closely, I made up some cold drinks and took them forward, sitting chatting with them for a while. Two fast boats travelling together whizzed past, their crews cheering at the sight of the topless ladies.

'There you go ladies,' I said with a grin. 'That's what people expect to see. Pretty girls without much in the way of clothes on.'

Melissa looked at Amanda and they both started giggling as she said, 'As a Police Officer, I should be highly offended by being looked at as just a blonde bimbo, but fuck it! I don't care, 'cause that was fun and I'm enjoying myself. That was the first time I've ever been topless in public and cheered by strangers!'

That comment started the conversation down the track of

public performances with neither girl showing a lot of interest in personally indulging in sex in public. Public nudity seemed to be a different thing however, as Melissa glanced at me and said, 'I do hope you're not going to be offended Harry, but I'm taking my pants off. I've always wanted an all-over tan and this might be the best time to get it.'

I grinned and Amanda giggled, 'I'm never offended by a lovely lady taking her pants off for any reason.'

Melissa grinned back and without sitting up, lifted her hips and wriggled the tiny bikini bottoms off, quite happy to do so under my scrutiny.

'Ahh. What the hell!' Amanda said with a grin and slid hers off as well providing a pervert like me a delightful opportunity to compare the attributes of two lovely naked girls.

Unfortunately, the ringing of the satellite phone rudely interrupted my highly stimulating inspection of my crew.

'Hello?'

'Hi Harry, it's Corrine. How the hell are you?'

Corrine used to be a SAS sniper and 'wet-work' specialist in the Middle East and circumstances had conspired that after she was badly wounded during a firefight with a bunch of Taliban bad guys, I was able to rescue her, something neither of us forgot since I also got shot as a consequence. I hadn't seen her for several years until she popped up on the wrong side in an investigation I'd become accidently involved in not that long ago.

Because they joined the side of righteousness and light, some high-level intervention meant that Corrine and her partner Dave had managed to avoid a stretch in jail and also managed to retain possession of a very fast and luxurious 68 ft Italian powerboat that they used for high-cost Executive Charter.

'Hi Mouse. It's great to hear from you. I'm fine, but how are you guys?'

'Dave and I are really good. Business took off after you left us and we've been flat out making lots of lovely legal money, but now that

the rotten Melbourne winter weather has kicked in, things have gone quiet. What the weather like where you are?'

'I'm just North of the Gold Coast and it's beautiful. In fact, the crew are up for'rard sunbaking.'

'Ahh. And I'll bet that the crew are female and don't have many clothes on?'

'You always were a perceptive little trooper. Good guess!'

She laughed. 'Hey. If you've got crew aboard, does that mean you're on the job? Or are you just being your usual randy self and shagging a couple of young lovelies?'

'It's a bit complicated, but for your ears only, I can say 'yes' to the first question and 'no, it's work' to the second.'

'Outstanding, Harry. But to business, I might have something of interest for you. First thing this morning, we had a call from some dude who wanted to charter a very fast, sea-going boat for an unspecified job in Southern Queensland waters. The job was to happen in about one week's time and might last a couple of weeks.

When I tried to get him to be more specific, he became very evasive, so when I said that we don't do illegal stuff, he hung up. Stupidly, he hadn't blocked his number, so I can give that to you if you want to look further into it.'

'That's very interesting, Corrine. Was there anything else you could get from him?'

'Nah! Clammed right up when I knocked back the big charter fee he offered that included the long ferry up there. Although, now I think of it, there was one odd thing. I asked why he didn't just charter one of the hundreds of fast boats already up there and his reply was that he'd heard that we were the fastest boat in Australia in this size range that could safely go to sea, had long range and that we didn't mind doing jobs that weren't exactly kosher.

He got a bit huffy when I said that the boat was under new ownership and it wasn't available for that stuff anymore. He hinted that he thought we were still bent and were just holding out for a bigger charter fee. When I still knocked him back, he hung up sounding a bit upset.

I don't suppose it'd be worthwhile coming up anyway? It's too fucking cold down here to be just sitting around.'

I thought a moment. 'I'm sure there's heaps of work for a boat like *Seeker,* although that's not my area of expertise. At this stage of the job, there's nothing I can throw at you for the moment. If you don't mind burning a whole lot of diesel getting up here, I'd certainly like to have the pair of you close by, but I can't pay you. You'll have to earn your keep with normal charter.'

'We're not worried about work or getting paid, but I'll explain that when we see you. So does this phone enquiry sound interesting. And how long is your job? I don't suppose that my info has anything to do with it?'

'I truly can't say, 'cause I don't know until we chase up that number, but I have a bad feeling that it might be linked.'

'Yes! I knew there was something going on. All right, Harry. Dave's heard all this so we'll have a chat, but since the coffers are sort of overflowing at the moment, we might just zip on up and hope you're onto something. We miss the excitement!

It's a good thousand nautical miles, from here to you, so even with the calm seas we've got at the moment, it'll still take nearly two days to get there. Will that fit in with your plans?'

'For reasons that I'll explain face-to-face, we're doing much the same as I was last time, so we won't be far away. Call when you're in the area.'

'Nicely cryptic, Harry. OK. Dave's nodding so I guess we're on our way, probably within the hour, so we'll call you in a couple of days. Cheers, Harry.'

'Cheers, Corrine. Drive carefully.'

I went for'rard and brought the girls up the date on the phone call. They were both intrigued by the implications of the phone call, and curious about Corrine, Dave and the boat.

'Were they part of the last operation?' Amanda asked shrewdly.

'Yes. But I'll tell you about it at a later date. It's a long story'

'Sounds like we'll have plenty of time to hear that story,' she said with a smile, although the rather careless positioning of her legs made it hard to concentrate. I made a mental note-to-self not to try to have important discussions with this pair while they were naked.

'Later for stories,' I said, 'but for now, I can call in to check this number, but it might be better if you guys do it.'

Melissa immediately jumped up. 'I'll do that,' she said, 'if I can use your phone?'

So I led the way aft, grateful that she spared me some distraction by pulling her skimpy panties back on, and sat her at the nav station where the sat-phone resided. She was familiar with it's use and was quickly onto the Station where she requested a reverse listing check on the number Corrine had supplied. Lack of clothing didn't affect her professionalism, although it kept my blood pressure up and maintained a healthy bulge in my pants.

While she sat and I stood waiting for a response, she looked sideways to where I was standing beside her and giggled. 'That looks like a dangerous weapon, Harry. Amanda has certainly been impressed. But doesn't it ever go down?'

I immediately felt uncomfortable, but managed a flippant reply, 'Not while two lovely naked ladies are draped around my boat.'

She smiled prettily at that compliment then focussed sharply on the handset as it squawked at her. Grabbing a pencil, she scribbled on a message pad.

'Yep. Yep. Did anything red flag? OK, copy that, thanks Andrew. We'll get back if we need more. Cheers.'

She terminated correctly, then jumped up, giving me a hug that made me feel even more uncomfortable in my shorts. And she felt it too, the little tease, giving a little wiggle with her hips before letting go!

'Bingo! It belongs to the listing we have a watch on for the Undertakers OMC! How about that for co-incidence and how dumb of them not to block their number.'

She raced out to tell Amanda the news, while I followed more slowly, trying to fit that piece of the puzzle into place. By the time

I was up for'rard again, Melissa had her pants off again and was stretched out beside Amanda telling her. They were slightly less distracting this time, so I asked their opinion of the information.

They looked at each other before Melissa said, 'I might be jumping to confusions, but I really think it means that there's another shipment of drugs coming in by ship and they want a decent boat to be able to pick it up.'

'How do you make that leap of logic?' I asked.

'You said that Corrine's boat was big and very fast. Why else would they want a boat like that?'

I gave her a serious look, 'Maybe to search for us if they think we've done a runner. Don't forget we've still got that pile of cash and something like ten million in Super MDMA on board.'

Her face fell. 'Oh, bugger! I didn't think of that!'

I shrugged. 'That doesn't matter. We could both be right, so I'd better call Greg and see if he's got anything.'

So I got on the phone again, interrupting him in a meeting.

'*You must be psycho, Harry. We're just talking about you in connection with some information we've had phoned in by a snitch.*'

'Yeah? Well I've got some info too, but you go first.'

'*OK. The word is that the Undertakers and the Zombie Eaters have agreed to an alliance to buy, process and distribute some of the new MDMA derivative. Maybe you don't realise how big a deal this is. These guys normally never even speak to each other, but here they are meeting in public and shaking hands on the deal. They also have managed to bypass the Sydney mob that imported it in the first place and are buying direct off the Korean manufacturer.*'

'Bloody hell, Greg. That is huge! It means that we can't rely on the usual inter-gang warfare to create some distracting mayhem and confusion.'

'*Exactly! But wait, there's more. There's a whisper that a very big shipment is due in to Brisbane in about a week's time. The time frame is still a bit loose, but for the Gold Coast alliance, their portion will be the first of the direct shipments, although we don't have any more info at this stage as to how, when, or where they plan to make the pickup, although it's a fair bet that it'll be by boat.'*

'That's fascinating and it ties in with a phone call I just received from a contact in Melbourne who operates a very fast, sea-going powerboat. She had a call from an unidentified person looking to charter the fastest sea-going boat in Australia for a job in Southern Queensland waters for about three weeks, starting in about one week's time. Senior Briggs checked the number and it originated from the Undertakers.'

'That is way too much of a coincidence. Did your friend agree to take the job?'

'No. And the dude got quite miffed when she said they don't do illegal stuff anymore. But they're going to come up anyway, if only to get away from the Victorian winter weather.'

'I take it that you've worked with these friends before? 'Cause I'm not sure how all this is going to fit together.'

'Likewise. And yes, I have worked with her, both here and in Afghanistan — she is ex-Special Forces like me. But she and her partner are really just coming up to get better weather and see what's going on, as apparently, they aren't strapped for funds at the moment.

However, Senior Briggs came up with the thought that the bikies might need a fast sea-going boat so they can make a water pickup of their portion of the stuff and be able to make a run for it if chased.'

'Hard to outrun a Police helicopter, Harry.'

'True. But helicopters normally only have a three hour endurance, whereas a decent fast boat is good for 24 hours or better.'

'Good point. So we'd better be prepared, but in the meantime, we need more intelligence.'

'Exactly! Call when you get some more, mate. Cheers.'

I dutifully reported to the crew, but they couldn't come up with anything fresh, so we let our minds work on the problem in the background while the girls enjoyed the sun and I enjoyed looking at the girls.

MORETON BAY AREA, SUNDAY

Saturday evening had passed without any major mental revelations, perhaps helped by a liberal serving of NQ Teas that rendered the girls pissy and made all three of us sleepy at a decent hour. Amanda seemed to have moved in with me until Sandy returned, which was no real hardship, although our activities that evening were somewhat more subdued than previously.

Melissa had retired without too much comment, although she had a gleam in her eye I didn't really trust. I was very grateful that the four-legged pussies had moved in with her at night, as Jasper was way too big and heavy to share a bed with two people. That was also the night that I heard a strange buzzing sound as I was drifting off to sleep.

'What the hell's that?' I demanded struggling to sit up with Amanda draped half over me.

She giggled, 'Oh come on, Harry. Don't you recognise a vibrator when you hear one?'

'Vibrator? Why on earth would I recognise a vibrator? I wouldn't know one if it bit my big toe! Is that Melissa?'

She settled me down, my mind still foggy from sleep and NQ teas. 'Of course that's Melissa. There's nobody else aboard. I told you she's a horny little thing. She needs some relief as well.'

'Oh,' was the limit of my reply at that stage, so I drifted back to sleep.

Sunday morning dawned bright, clear and warm, so breakfast on the foredeck was even more of a pleasure than usual. More boats had droned past in the night and several went past as I sat with Jasper and Krazy kitten, their crews waving cheerfully. I noticed that there seemed to be a lot of kids aboard nearly all the boats and made a note-to-self to check with the girls when they woke up if it was school holidays. The sight of all the kids had given me an idea to help us hide, inspired by my last operation down south.

It also prompted me to call my Controller on the encrypted sat-phone, an anonymous, but pleasant-sounding lady no doubt buried in a drab office in Canberra. She was always contactable, day or night, and unfailingly pleasant, despite what my reports had to say. On this occasion, I brought her up-to-date with happenings and listed my plans. She offered some suggestions generated by her razor-sharp mind and as always, I considered them carefully, before signing off. Her suggestions made me modify my plans a bit, but I needed to talk to the girls when they were fully awake.

It was a while later before the crew showed any signs of life and I was on my second mug of tea and a second plate of toast and honey, half of which Jasper pinched, before Amanda showed up with a sleepy Melissa in tow.

'Good morning sleepy heads,' I greeted them cheerfully.

'What the hell did you slip into those teas last night?' Melissa asked, 'I don't think I woke up once. Great sleep.'

'Nah! It's not the NQ tea it's *Firebird*. She has that effect on all visitors. But before I forget, I must ask, is this the start of school holidays?'

Amanda thought a moment then said, 'Yep. Two weeks I think, or is it three? Anyway, the little darlings are running around loose. Is that a problem?'

'No, it's a help. I was thinking about where we go from here. I want to get further up to the Bay proper since it's a bit too quiet here and we'll be too obvious if we stay here too long. I mean the water's a bit dirty, the scenery is dull and there's traffic to and from the bar, so sooner or later, word will get back to the bad guys.'

'So what's the plan?' Melissa asked, looking more awake.

'Simple. We go and anchor where the biggest cluster of boats are. That way, we're just another boat amongst many others. For the next two or three weeks, we can move from group to group, hiding in plain sight.'

The girls looked at each other, before Melissa said, 'Sounds logical to me.'

I let them go get tea, coffee and toast, before holding a meeting on the foredeck.

'My people are happy with what we've been doing and are planning to do. They're particularly pleased that you two are aboard and are able to role-play the blonde bimbo thing so well to reinforce my role as wealthy, dissolute playboy. They see our presence here as a really great opportunity to find out the guts of the importation process of this new MDMA.

They suggested that the best way to achieve that is for us to play up the part to the best of our ability and be seen slightly drunk and disorderly all over the Bay so it won't look strange if we're loitering somewhere near when that ship comes in.

I addressed Amanda, 'You're the resident drone expert. What equipment have you got that would help us maintain surveillance if the stuff is being dropped off a ship coming into Brisbane?'

She thought carefully. 'I've got some really great gear at Southport, although it depends what range and endurance you want. Do we need live video, or will recording be good enough?'

'Live video would be really good. As for range and endurance, that'll depend on how close we can get to the ship when the dump happens. If we're in the right place, we could need as little as 30 minutes and a 5-kilometre radius. But to be safe, let's work on a 10 kilometre radius, but a 2 hour endurance.'

'Hmmm. That narrows it down a bit. Do we need to launch and retrieve off the *Firebird?*'

'Yes. We can't afford to go looking for somewhere long and level to launch and retrieve.'

Melissa spoke up. 'Maybe I'm missing something, but why don't we request a light aircraft or helicopter to track the ship?'

'Mainly because to keep a close eye on things, we'd need them to be well under 5,000 feet and we don't know where they'll drop. If the guys pushing this stuff overboard see any aircraft tracking the ship, they'll abort and do nothing. We've got to catch them in the process, but with the shipping lanes being right beside Brisbane airport, it would be very odd to see a light aircraft or helicopter just floating around in circles and the airline drivers get a bit edgy about other aircraft floating around too close to their airspace. I suppose from that point of view, the drop spot has been chosen rather well. If it was further north on the approach channel, helicopter surveillance would be simple.'

'OK, I'll go with that, but why wouldn't they just push the stuff over when they're well offshore and put a radio beacon on it?'

'That was the old method, but a lot of shipments were lost. Beacon failure, or the containers leaked and sank before they could be picked up. There could be other reasons, but virtually all drops these days are close inshore, in fairly shallow water and with the retrieve crew not far away.'

She nodded and grinned, 'Just playing Devil's Advocate.'

I smiled, 'That's just what we need. A wise person taught me that random brain-storming could solve almost any problem.'

Amanda carried on, 'So with those requirements, there isn't much that I've got back at base, even though I brought some great stuff back from the USA. But to be honest, the only thing that fits this need is a prototype UAV that a very dear old friend out in country NSW sent me. He was a pilot for forty-odd years and flew just about everything but when he retired, he started designing UAVs. He's quite brilliant, but nobody was prepared to take him seriously because he doesn't have an Aeronautical Engineering degree.

A cheap foam remote control toy inspired the concept for his UAV. Apparently, most people in the industry forget that drones and UAVs are just very expensive model aircraft, so the work this guy has been doing is based on ideas that actually work and based on designs that have been tested by thousands of R/C modellers worldwide!

Anyway, to get off the commercial, this prototype is a fixed-wing UAV with vertical take-off and landing ability; fully-autonomous flight performance, plus forward flight at any speed from hover to walking pace to 80 knots. Endurance is four to five hours at a cruise speed of 55 to 60 knots, or seven hours at 25 knots. It can carry a variety of instrument packages, but this one is fitted with stabilised Electro-Optical HD colour and Infrared cameras.

It offers full live streaming of the 1080P video image so long as the antennas can see each other. It can also be re-programmed in flight for a different task, or to return to a different home base. It's fairly quiet, silent beyond 300 metres and virtually impossible to see, so long as it stays more than 1,000 feet from the target. He's called it the *Dragonfly*.'

I blinked at the torrent of information she'd just fed us. 'Wow! That sounds exactly what we need. This guy must be something else if he's designed a UAV that is better than anything else on the market.'

'Yes, he really is good, although without the massive funding the big Aerospace companies throw at their UAV programs, his *Dragonfly* looks a bit rough, but it's proved itself to be rugged and strong where it counts.

But remember, there are UAVs that use some of the features on the *Dragonfly*, but nobody has combined all these things in one package before. The Germans are the closest in capabilities, but they've gone all electric, which limits their range and endurance. I have a smaller, all electric version that's good for about 20 minutes and a number of 6-motor drones in different sizes, but they aren't suitable for this particular job.'

'Hmmm OK, what would it take to get this *Dragonfly* and a selection of smaller drones to us? Say in the next day or two at the latest?'

She grinned, suddenly fired up with enthusiasm for her speciality, 'No problem. They're all packed and ready to go with all the control and support equipment in separate carry boxes. We just need to arrange the pick-up and delivery.'

'I'll look after that, if you can tell Greg what you need.'

'No problem. Call him now.'

I laughed, 'Yeah. Good idea. Get him working.'

So I placed the call and found Greg very receptive to the idea, particularly when I mentioned that my people were really asking us to do it.

'*No problem, Harry. If Amanda can tell me exactly what she needs and where it is, I'll get it picked up. But how can we get it to you?*'

'We don't want to go to Brisbane to get it, so how about you get it to the Water Police base at the Port of Brisbane and ask them nicely if they could deliver it to us at Horseshoe Bay on Peel Island?'

'*Yeah. I guess that'd work. But won't that make you stand out a bit? I mean if you're trying to go low profile, having a Police boat pull up alongside isn't a good look.*'

I laughed. 'Good thinking. But if the boys were doing some safety checks amongst the holiday crowd, that would be normal, wouldn't it? And maybe do it tomorrow so that some of the weekend crowd has gone home.'

'*OK, Harry. That sounds like a plan. Stick Amanda on before we finish and I'll get the info.*'

'Yeah, righto Greg and thanks mate. Just let us know ASAP if you get more info on the lolly shipment.'

'*No trouble, Harry. Great work so far. Now stick Amanda on, please.*'

I handed over and she explained where the stuff was stored and what to send.

'Well done crew,' I announced. 'That's sorted out a few problems, so all we have to do is get ourselves to Peel Island.'

'How far is that?' Melissa asked.

'Only about 20 nautical miles so we should be there just after lunch, or even sooner if this wind keeps picking up.' A brisk south-easterly was blowing and looked like it would hold, although it would be a pain to try to sail in the close confines of the twisting passages, at least until the waters opened up past Russell Island. We motored on at a steady pace, the girls taking turns at the wheel, although I stood close, pointing out the beacons that were keeping us off the sandbanks lining the narrow channels.

They both enjoyed steering and Amanda got to make morning tea.

When the water widened sufficiently abeam Macleay Island, I left Melissa on the wheel and made preparation for sailing by attaching the various sheets to the correct bits of the sails, retracting the cover over the mainsail that was hiding in the boom and closing hatches. I turned into the wind before pulling the engines out of gear then hauled the small staysail up first to get some way back on the boat. The big mainsail was next and the electric halyard winch dragged its fluttering bulk up the mast, the girls staring in apprehension at the huge area of stiff, white fabric unrolling out of the boom just over their heads. Turning back on course, the breeze was back on our stern quarter, so the main wasn't setting very well until we picked up some speed. Then it drew well and I was able to winch in the main sheet. The enormous screecher or reaching spinnaker followed, it's purple mass divided horizontally by a broad yellow chevron. *Firebird* really kicked up her heels once that was sheeted in and we were soon hissing along at better than 20 knots.

The girls were a bit afraid at first to see such a huge area of sailcloth straining overhead, but soon the exhilaration of sailing so fast, barely heeling over and almost in silence took over and they both had broad grins stitched on their faces. I let them take turns on the wheel as there was plenty of water either side of us and they quickly became addicted to steering a big cat at speed.

'This is fantastic, Harry,' Melissa said, having to fight the wheel a bit as gusts off the low hills upwind hit us.

'Yee ha!' was Amanda's response.

I grinned at them, 'I guess this means that you like big cat sailing?'

Their grins said it all as we powered on north, the low shape of Peel Island showing off to our left front, the tiny blob of Goat Island in front of it to the right. I reminded myself that there was an extensive area of mixed coral and rock to the west and south of Goat Island that it would be wise to steer clear of.

About a mile from Goat Island we jibed so we were heading almost West, a manoeuvre that kept the boat speed up for a bit longer, then after a while with Peel Island well off to our right, we jibed again to make a fast run north. As the south easterly was still blowing quite hard, I decided to stay away from Horseshoe Bay which was wide-open to the wind and would be choppy and unpleasant, and head for the more protected little anchorage on the western side of Peel Island.

However, as I had feared, all the other boats that had been in the Horseshoe felt the same way and had either gone around to the north side to a small, sheltered bay called the Lazarette, or were clustered in a tight mass in the anchorage known as 'The Corner'.

Luckily for us, most were of a size that needed more water than we did and had anchored out a comfortable distance from the rocky shore, whereas despite our size, we could lift our dagger-boards and slip inshore of them, only needing 2 feet of water to float in.

Finally anchored safely, the girls made lunch while I checked around the decks and made sure the anchor had a good bite. The wind was reduced in the lee of the Island and with the sun shining brightly the air was delightfully warm. With lunch over, the girls decided to sunbake topless on the trampolines, after noting that my predictions about how well bare skin and boats mixed, as there were many others with topless female crew.

Melissa was standing up on one of the bow seats, inadvertently striking a modern-day figurehead pose, bare breasts and all, while peering at the Island. 'Harry. I think I can see a building over there. Do people live here?'

'No. But back in sailing ship days, this was the Quarantine Station for Brisbane — then later on it was a Leper Colony. At the time, all types of Leprosy were thought to be contagious, but apparently that strain isn't. Anyway, the old buildings are still there, although the whole thing is Heritage listed. You can go for a wander around if you want, but it might be easier getting ashore when we go around to Horseshoe Bay.'

A varied collection of power cruisers, smaller cats and a few monohull sailing yachts surrounded us; the crews had all waved and called out cheerfully as we'd slid amongst them. More than a few called out invitations to come over for drinks later that afternoon.

'What do we do about the social scene?' Amanda asked. 'They seem such a happy lot, it'd be rude to ignore them.'

'You're quite right and it would be out of character if we did. Remember that we're rich, laid-back yachties and here to have fun.'

Melissa laughed, 'They really do look happy and most seem to be family people. Not too many drugs amongst this lot.'

I agreed. 'You're right. Most of them are hard-working people who just love their time away on the boat with the whole family. Their biggest concern is finding bunks for everyone aboard and keeping up the booze supply. Therefore we need to fit in with them, rather than stand out.'

The phone rang soon after with Greg on the other end.

'Hi Greg. What've you got for us?'

'Gidday Harry. With regards your delivery, it's all assembled and will be taken by a crew-cab Ute to the Pinkenba Water Police base shortly. Amanda didn't say how large one of the boxes was. It wouldn't fit in a car so I hope you can find room.'

'Yeah. No problem. We'll fit it aboard somewhere. What's the arrangement with the Boat Boys?'

'*Oh, yeah. Sorry. Can you be in Horseshoe Bay on Peel Island, tomorrow at 08:30?*'

I laughed, 'I think we can manage that. We're about 600 meters away at the moment. The southerly made things a bit choppy for comfort in there, so we're just around the corner.'

'*Oh, OK. The boys took your suggestion and will be conducting a series of random safety checks, so they'll pass the gear over then.*'

'Sounds good, mate. Thanks for doing that. Is there any more info on the delivery?'

'*Nah. All quiet, but we should hear something soon. The drop is supposed to be next Thursday or Friday. I'll call you immediately we hear.*'

'Goodo. That'll do thanks Greg. Cheers.'

'*Yeah. Cheers, Harry.*'

UNDERTAKER'S OMC CLUBHOUSE – SUNDAY

'Undertaker.'

'*Hi ya, Henry. It's Brad again.*'

'Of course it is, Mr Edwards. What is it now?'

'*I got to thinking about us having to pick up our merchandise from that trawler in Moreton Bay. You said you hadn't been able to hire a boat, 'cause nobody wants to get involved, is that right?*'

'That is correct, Mr Edwards. What are your thoughts?'

'*Well. Why don't we go and buy one and drive it ourselves? It can't be that hard. Looking at the profit to be made on this deal alone makes it worthwhile. We could share the cost and if we don't think we'll need it again, we'll sell the bastard. Put it down to operating expenses.*'

The tall man was silent for a few moments. 'There is some merit in what you say, Mr Edwards. Do you or any of your people know anything about boats?'

'*Not really, old mate. But Tony here has been fishing a few times with a couple of mates, so he'll know enough.*'

'I admire your confidence in nautical matters, Mr Edwards. How much are you proposing to pay for this boat?'

'*I dunno Henry. I guess that we need something bigger than a tinnie or runabout. And it should be fairly fast. How about I look at what's available here on the Coast and get back to you?*'

'Very well, Mr Edwards. That is an acceptable plan, but please do so quickly. Friday is the deadline and we cannot afford to miss this opportunity.'

FIREBIRD

It was getting on for rum time, so after I got the girls a wine each and made myself a rum and coke, we set up in the cockpit with a plate of cheese and bickies Amanda had prepared. Our nearest neighbour was a pretty 35 ft motor cruiser with an extended family aboard who had also set up the traditional 17:00 salute to all nautical gods.

'Come on over and join us,' one of the men called.

'Thanks,' I called back, 'but maybe you'd like to all come over here. There's a bit more room.'

He laughed, 'I can't argue with that, brother. Don't mind if we do, thank you. Won't be long.'

Amanda gave me a concerned look. 'What about Jasper? It may not be wise to introduce him to a whole bunch of people!'

'No problem. He's used to the occasional influx of strangers, so he'll tuck himself away right up for'rard in my dressing room. Although I don't socialise like this very often, he doesn't mind other people coming aboard so long as they don't go wandering. And I'd rather do this today when we don't have the drones aboard. We'll get invited to their boat tomorrow.'

She smiled, 'Good thinking, but maybe Mel and I should put something on top.'

I agreed and they went below to cover up a bit.

Our new friends arrived shortly; two families with three kids each, ranging from ten through to about seventeen for one girl and one boy. They brought their own drinks in two large eskies, plus more nibbles, but raided my icemaker and stored more booze in the cockpit fridge.

They were all real boatie people, just like I'd told the girls earlier — very happy unpretentious boat-lovers. I gave a brief tour of *Firebird* to lots of appreciation, but I didn't show the special features. There was no shortage of conversation and I was pleased that the girls joined in, giving plausible explanations for our presence along the lines of — I was the rich playboy, and they were the attractive friends. Having a real sailing boat and not acting stuck-up also went a long way toward acceptance and I was well satisfied with our acceptance as harmless, pleasant boaties.

Another family joined us, the party spreading to the spacious fore deck, so the evening ended a lot later than we'd planned. We brought out extra food and the three wives went to get more from their boats, so it all ended up a grand party where all the adults got quite pissed, but in a happy way. To the amusement of their wives, the two men had a lovely time making fools of themselves flirting with the girls. Even the kids, being raised in the boatie tradition, didn't haul out an iPad or iPhone and amused themselves playing around between the vast foredeck and the cockpit, an area they'd never seen on a boat before, as well as playing with Krazy kitten who loved the attention, while Jasper remained hidden.

Later, when our visitors had all left and we just got into bed, a very spaced-out Melissa wandered in naked, and crawled in between us, promptly falling into a coma-like sleep and couldn't be budged.

I shrugged and grinned; 'I guess that's it for tonight. Will she be OK?'

Amanda looked more embarrassed than upset, 'Yeah. She should be, although she doesn't often get like this. She'll be a bit doughy in the morning.'

Even comatose, Melissa was very pleasant to lie beside, but I was a good boy and behaved myself, even if my erection showed that I was ready, willing and able to misbehave, much to Amanda's amusement.

CHAPTER 19

The day dawned bright, clear and windless and Melissa woke up feeling and looking surprisingly bright and chirpy. She was, however, initially appalled to find herself in bed with us with no recollection of how she got there, but Amanda soon filled her in on that, including the lack of anybody doing anything last night, and chased her out to get dressed. She was reluctant to go once she got over the first shock, but Amanda was insistent and I decided to follow since we'd slept in somewhat and time was getting on.

Therefore, while the girls did the necessaries, then made lovely toasted bacon and egg sandwiches for breakfast, I fired up the engines and raised the anchor, conning *Firebird* remotely from the bow as we threaded our way through the tightly packed cluster of boats. It was one of those times when I was really glad we had two engines driving props so far apart, so we were very manoeuvrable. Our three skippers from last night were just out of bed, sitting up in the bow of each boat and peering blearily around with coffees in hand as we slid quietly past.

'Where you heading, Harry?' Gerry called.

I held us in position just a metre off his bow with the single joystick controller, much to his interest and amusement. 'Not far, mate. Just around the corner to the Horseshoe to get a good spot before you lot pinch all the best places. I promised the girls a nice sandy beach for swimming and I want to scrub the slime off the waterline. Where do you guys normally go?'

He coughed and replied, 'Ahhh...We usually head for the east end, or wherever there's a bit of privacy away from the other boats. There's quite a few of us here belong to a Naturist Club, so we take the opportunity to strip down when the weather co-operates, like it seems to be doing at the moment. There may be a few more boats coming over for the day if it stays nice and you're all very welcome to join us if you don't mind some bare skin. We don't make a big deal about it and none of the other boaties seem to mind.'

I smiled, 'No problem for me, Gerry. I'll mention it to the girls and see if they want to join in. I'm guessing that they probably will, so we might head up that end of the bay anyway, in case the sou'easter kicks back in this arvo.'

He waved understanding. 'Either way you'll be very welcome, Harry. We all had a great night last night, so when we can kick the crews into action, we'll see you there later. Everyone's a bit slow this morning for some reason.'

We shared a laugh before I eased around a few more boats, their owners calling a series of cheery 'Good mornings'. It was the sort of boating conviviality that I really enjoyed and made me glad to be part of the scene.

We hadn't even turned the corner into The Horseshoe when the sat-phone rang. There were only a select few with the number, so I was intrigued when I throttled back and put Amanda on the wheel while I grabbed the off-key warbling device.

'Yo!'

'Gidday Harry. It's Corrine. How're things?'

'Corrine,' I exclaimed delightedly, 'how the bloody hell are you? Or more to the point, where are you?'

'Dave and I are in Port Macquarie. We hit some bad weather and decided to sit it out since there's no real urgency. The seas are still fairly rough, so if there's still no urgency, we can be there by Wednesday if that suits. So where'll you be?'

'We're at Peel Island in Moreton Bay at the moment with a bunch of other boats belonging to members of a Nudist's Club, but I'm planning to be in a more isolated spot on Wednesday morning.'

Corrine laughed, 'Jeeze Harry, you don't change and I guess that's a good thing. Is Sandy there? That'd suit her right down to the ground!'

'No, she's still relieving, but I do have two other young ladies with me to officially keep me company. Now on Wednesday, we'll probably be at an anchorage called Myora. Call me when you leave Southport after re-fuelling and I'll give you co-ordinates. It might be wise to fully fuel and re-stock at Southport, just in case. Things might be starting to move here, but Wednesday will be a good time to get here.'

'OK, mate. I'll hold the questions for now. Is there anything else we need to bring or be ready for?'

'No. If you've still got the good hardware you had when we last parted, that should be enough. We've got plenty of standard size supplies to suit.'

'Ahh. Say no more. We'll be prepared and see you for sure on Wednesday morning. I'll call again when we're leaving Southport.'

'Thanks Corrine. I'm looking forward to seeing both of you again. Bye for now.'

SOUTHPORT POLICE STATION – MONDAY MORNING

At the same time as we were rumbling quietly across the limpid, aquamarine waters of Horseshoe Bay, an incoming email gonged for attention on the computer of Southport Police Station Manager, Superintendent Bob Casey. Thirty seconds later, he was yelling out his open door for Inspector Greg James to 'get his arse up here ASAP'.

Puffing slightly, Greg trotted in a few minutes later, 'Yes, boss?'

Bob Casey waved a sheet of paper, hot off his printer. 'Look at this! We've just been told that an ACP Assistant Commissioner and a Commander are on their way from Canberra as we speak to have a meeting with you and me about the situation with local bikie gangs and the new drugs coming in.'

'That's not a lot of notice, Bob,' Greg ventured cautiously.

'Too bloody right it's not, mate! Seems like someone cocked up and forgot to send it on Friday! Silly pricks! Still, at least after that last clean out, there are some half-decent fellas in there now.

'When do they get here, Bob?'

Bob looked at the email again, 'They land at 10:00, which is nearly now, so we'd better schedule for 11:00. You'll be available, I trust?'

Greg gave a rueful grin, 'Yeah. I guess I don't have a choice, do I? Seeing as this last clusterfuck has landed in my lap, thanks to Harry. Do we need to arrange transport?'

'I already did that while you were trying to climb the stairs. One of our newest Highway Patrol Falcon's will do the duty. I've told the crew to be on their best behaviour.'

'Goodo, boss. I'll go finish up what I was doing and get my files ready for 11:00.'

'OK. Thanks Greg. You never know, maybe for once we'll get some help from these blokes instead of a hard time.'

Promptly at 11:00, Superintendent Bob Casey, Inspector Greg James, ACP Assistant Commissioner Michael Davies and ACP Commander Roger Norris, were sitting around a finely crafted Tasmanian Oak table in the spacious conference room on the upper floor of the Southport Police station. A side table held tea and coffee and a selection of sweet treats filled a large serving plate in front of them.

Even though pleasantries were exchanged, almost palpable waves of animosity washed across the table from the local Officers, causing the two ACP officers to go to some lengths to placate them as to the reason for their presence and perceived level of interference.

'We're here to help, Bob,' Michael Davies stated, 'we formed this Task Force with Roger at the head because this thing with the bikie gangs has gone Interstate and is getting way too organised. This latest information about your two gangs getting into bed together is a new and very worrying development.'

Slightly mollified, Bob Casey replied, 'Yeah, fair enough, Michael. So far, we've relied on natural hatred for each other to keep them too busy fighting to get too serious about flogging too many drugs. But that has suddenly changed. Both leaders are very astute businessmen and have apparently seen the potential in forming an alliance to market this new version of MDMA properly over an expanded territory.'

The ACP Assistant Commissioner nodded, 'That's why we're here. We want to help co-ordinate what assets we have and get more information flowing to help you guys doing the work up front. We've come straight from a weekend meeting with your Sydney Central counterparts. Also, there's this vague report of a big shipment coming in to Brisbane by ship later this week.'

Bob nodded his head. 'That one's a real worry. We don't have a lot to go on at the moment. We're relying on an insider we have in the Zombies to feed information and so far, that's been working well, but we need to know a lot more about this shipment. We've also seconded two officers undercover to your man, Harry Stevens. We hope that by placing them in the right position, we can nail these clowns properly.'

'Ah, yes. I'm glad you're using Harry. He's been a remarkable asset for us so far. An incredible SAS history, but he seems happy to be an undercover agent on that boat of his. We gave him the rank of Commander, same as Roger here, even though it's really meant to be an administrative position, but he's not particularly fussed about it. What's his current situation?'

'They're hanging around Moreton Bay, posing as a trio of wealthy layabout fools with too much money and time and so far, they seem to be playing the role very well. One of my Senior Constables is our leading drone and UAV expert and we've just delivered several units to cover any surveillance tasks that might come up.'

'That sounds excellent planning, Bob. We know Harry's able

to look after himself, but I hope your men are just as good. With what's at stake, these bikies aren't playing softball. Things can get very serious very quickly when their income is threatened.'

Bob coughed and flicked a glance at Greg. 'Well actually Michael, my two Officers are female.'

Both ACP Officers raised their eyebrows. 'That's a bit risky, isn't it Bob?' Michael queried, 'I really mean it when I say that these people will stop at nothing to defend their income source. Especially with something as potentially lucrative as this stuff!'

Bob smiled, 'We've no reservations about either of them. As well as being very competent in all aspects of self-defence, they fit into the legend of a wealthy playboy far better than two hairy-chested males would. And remember that one has already helped repel two attacks from the bikies, who thought that the first drug shipment was still aboard the boat. Those encounters put three bikies in hospital, with one still on life support and another locked up.'

'Oh, yes. We read those reports. There were some strange aspects to both incidents, but if you're happy, we are too. I must say that the end results were excellent for us, and that's really all that matters! So what are your plans at this stage?'

'We're still waiting on confirmation of the delivery point and timing, although Friday seems to be the day, with the drop occurring from a cargo ship somewhere in Moreton Bay. We've directed Harry to be as prepared as possible and to use the long-range UAV to follow the freighter once we've identified it and have an arrival time.'

'OK, we're good with that part. But what are your plans once the drops have happened. There'll have to be a boat or boats to pick up each container.'

Bob shrugged, 'We don't have that info yet, but however it is picked up, I know that Brisbane would like to follow the stuff to see where it's delivered, then try to wrap the local distribution network up in one move.'

Roger spoke, 'But isn't that also a bit risky, Bob? As in, you don't know how many containers are to be dropped, only that the Gold Coast one is to be picked up separate from the rest. What if there's three or four containers, and there are that many separate pickups? They'll be very hard to follow and you might lose track of several containers. That's not a good outcome.'

Bob nodded grimly, 'That's the big flaw in the plan. The planning geniuses in Brisbane are dead keen to try to track the individual containers, but I'd much prefer to grab the stuff as soon as the primary pickup boat has it aboard.'

Michael leaned forward, looking excited, 'That's more like it, Bob. Canberra really wants to stop this new shit hitting the streets. We hear that there are some weird side effects, as well as a very high addiction rate. We need to grab this stuff — not let it go floating about South East Queensland where there's a very good chance we'll lose it. We're heading to Brisbane next to push this point and try to change their minds about being too adventurous.'

Bob nodded. 'Yeah. I got a report from Harry, in fact, about the side effects of this stuff. One of my Senior Constables tried a micro dose, in the name of official testing, and said that the immediate loss of inhibitions it caused was frightening. We could have people doing all sorts of strange or dangerous things that'd be very detrimental to law and order. But although I agree wholeheartedly that grabbing all the shipments straight away is the best idea, I wish you the best of luck selling that to Brisbane!'

Roger spoke again, appealing to both senior men. 'If Harry, his boat and crew are our joint asset and he's got by far the best surveillance system in the area, even though this drop is in Brisbane's territory, surely we can dictate how it's to be done?'

Michael grabbed that one, 'It's a bit of a hot potato unfortunately. We have to respect Brisbane's jurisdiction and if they want to let the individual shipments get picked up, all we can do is offer assistance. We hope to dissuade them later today, but I'm not hopeful.'

Bob looked thoughtful. 'We're waiting for further details from our inside man, so what if somehow we were able to just move in and grab them ourselves? You know — the old 'easier to ask forgiveness afterwards than get permission first!'

For the first time, Michael and Roger laughed. 'That would be an excellent outcome,' Michael said, 'Canberra would be very pleased. But how can that be arranged? Harry can't charge in with his boat. It's not exactly the quickest or the most inconspicuous getaway vehicle!'

Bob shrugged, 'Let me put it to him. I was going to call him later anyway.'

'Well, we've told Harry that he's at your beck and call and naturally has our full logistic support if there is anything needed. Just call Roger directly at any time. Naturally, we'll immediately pass on any information we hear that might help. We really need to nail this one down as quickly as possible.'

That effectively concluded the meeting and the Highway Patrol car was summoned to transport the two ACP Senior Officers to their meeting in Brisbane Central.

GREG JAMES

After seeing the two ACP Officers safely away, Greg hadn't long been back at his desk, filling out reports, when a seldom-used phone buzzed in his pocket. The number read-out on the screen was 'Private' and wouldn't have meant anything anyway. As per agreement, he didn't speak, although the voice in his ear had plenty to say. The call finished abruptly, and the phone went dead, as Greg hastily made some notes, before hustling up the stairs to Bob's office again.

'Well, bugger me! Two visits in one day. People will start talking if you keep this up, mate. What's the problem?'

After carefully closing the door, Greg caught his breath before answering. 'I've just heard from my bikie contact, with the times and details of the drug drop on Friday. It seems that they dump the stuff overboard at the designated spot and one of the Bay trawlers scoops up the consignments in its net. There are several individual consignments and our boys have been allocated one this time. Each consignment will only be released on the reciting of a password and must be collected off the trawler within an hour or it gets dumped back overboard. Our local boys are having trouble hiring a fast boat to make the pickup, since they don't own one and no one who does wants to get involved in what is obviously a dodgy and dangerous deal.'

Bob thought a moment, 'OK. Better fire that off to Harry and crew immediately so he can plan the surveillance. We want that ship tracked from well before it enters Moreton Bay just in case they dump early.'

'OK Bob, I can do that. But what's your plan to grab these guys? That is, of course if you want to grab them and not just track them to their distribution point where we can round up a lot more of these weasels.'

'You were at the meeting, Greg. We have to find a way to grab that stuff before it walks. All we can do is hand-ball it to Harry to see if he has an idea, since he usually does.'

UNDERTAKER'S OMC CLUBHOUSE

'Undertaker.'

'Gidday Henry, it's your old mate Brad.'

'I have reservations about that, Mr Edwards but please, do continue.'

'Yeah, well. I just wanted to let you know that we're the proud owners of a boat! Tony and I went looking yesterday and went back this morning and bought one. It was only 60-grand, so I just went ahead and got it. I know that you're a bit strapped for cash at the

moment, but you can kick in your share later. I don't mind. I mean, anything to help a mate. So wadda you reckon about that!'

'I utterly delighted, Mr Edwards, can't you tell? But being practical, is this boat going to be suitable?'

'Of course, Henry. We checked that out first. It's 25 feet long, has a big V-8 engine, a couple of beds, and a dinky little kitchen with a 'fridge and it even has a shitter! You'll love it!'

'That's very doubtful, Mr Edwards, but if it will do the job, then you have my reluctant approval.'

'No problem, Henry. It even comes with a trailer so we don't have to worry about keeping it in the water somewhere. I'll keep it here. Tony had a go with it and reckons it's a piece of piss to drive so there shouldn't be any problems making the pickup. We can even tow it up to Brisbane on Friday to save a long trip by water.'

'Thank you, Mr Edwards. I do hope your optimism is well-founded, however, you won't mind if I supply two of my men to assist with the operation on Friday?'

'Hell no, Henry. I don't mind at all. In fact, why don't you send three or four of yours and I'll just send two. That way you're assured we're doing the right thing.'

'That's very generous of you Mr Edwards, I might just do that. Do you have a suitable towing vehicle?'

'Yeah, sure thing. I've got a Ford F-350 crew-cab with a bloody great diesel engine. It'll pull the trailer an' carry five guys no problem.'

'Very well, Mr Edwards. Shall we meet in the Broadwater car park at 06:00 on Friday morning? If you'll attend to setting up the boat, I'll have my three men there. I must warn you that they will be armed; not to cause trouble with your men, but in case we encounter problems with the pickup.'

'That's a wise move, Henry and thanks for letting me know up front. Mine will be too, as you say, just in case. See you at 06:00 on Friday.'

PEEL ISLAND – MONDAY

Even without rushing, we were dropping anchor five minutes later right up in a little pocket of beach at the far eastern end of the 2.5 kilometres of white sand beach that was of an unusually very coarse texture. By anchoring close in, it promised to provide reasonable shelter from even a south easterly if necessary.

The coarse beach sand didn't detract in the slightest as the shallow water was a stunningly beautiful shade of aqua over a sandy bottom. Casuarina trees and the occasional majestic Moreton Bay Fig lent a semi-tropical atmosphere to the glorious view, in complete contrast to the rather drab view at the western anchorage last night. To say the girls were impressed was an understatement.

'Harry, this is absolutely fabulous,' was Melissa's opinion.

'Couldn't agree more,' came from Amanda, 'I'm going swimming.'

'Don't forget our, or rather your delivery is due. It could be soon.'

'Oh, fuck the delivery. I'm going swimming!' was her response and Melissa seemed to be of like mind as they stripped down to panties only and jumped in. I copped a teasing from both for being an old fart, but when I saw a large powerboat curve around the western end of the island, a white froth of wash streaming off the bow, I guessed that our delivery was inbound.

As payback for the 'Old Fart' comments from my nubile crew, I refrained from mentioning the approaching Police boat as they throttled back a hundred metres out and gently approached our stern.

The first my semi-naked crew knew was when I was hailed by the bowman, a Constable with a line in his hands and a huge grin on his face when he spotted the girls in the water.

'Commander Stevens, I presume?' He asked, cracking up laughing over the hoary old joke.

'Very funny, I'm sure,' was my response.

'Ahh...Yes sir. We have your items as delivered from Southport station. They're marked for attention of Senior Burke. Is he available to sign for them?'

Exacting my revenge, I leant over the side and pointed to Amanda's golden locks bobbing beside Melissa's above the clear, transparent water. 'I think you'll find Senior Burke right there, although she may have some difficulty signing the release at the moment, unless she cares to get out of the water.'

It was worth the crap I was going to cop later to see the look of horror on her face, but I took pity on her and went on.

'However, as her Senior Officer, I'll sign for the delivery and spare her the trouble of showing herself while she's out of uniform.'

Naturally, the Constable in the bow had been joined by the Sergeant who was the Coxswain and was highly amused by the to and fro discussion and the red faces on the pretty, bare-topped Senior Constables in the water.

They introduced themselves as Sergeant Brian Thomas and Constable Derek Lance.

The Sergeant cleared his throat, 'As I believe you suggested, we've been carrying out some safety checks on random boats, so we'd better tie up here for a convincing amount of time while we transfer the gear. Good thing you're alone up this end of the bay. Makes it easier.'

I laughed. 'If you *were* able to hang around, you'd be inundated with boatloads of naked people shortly. There's a Naturist Club parked at the western end of the island and they're all heading up this way shortly.'

I almost laughed aloud at the look on their faces.

'Oh, really?' The Sergeant asked politely, exchanging a look with his Constable bowman.

'Yep. I'm afraid so, Sergeant.' I said sternly, 'As you've possibly been told, we've been going to some lengths to establish a cover as a rather degenerate trio just bumming around. The two Senior

Constables were getting into their roles early. It's very important that we are able to maintain a credible cover at all times.'

'Yes, sir. I can appreciate that sir. We'll do all we can to back up your cover.'

I grinned, 'That's good, Sergeant. But all we need at the moment is the cases you've got for us and for you to treat us like any other possibly pissed boatie in the bay this morning.'

'Understood, sir. We'll just unload the freight and pretend to do a safety check, if that's the go?'

'That's fine, Sergeant. I appreciate your efforts.'

'Actually Sir, your security must be good, since we weren't told that there was a major undercover operation in progress. But can we help in any other way?'

'Not for the moment thanks, Sergeant. Unfortunately, I'm not able to give you any more information for now, but in the next few days, if you or another boat weren't too far away, that could be useful.'

'Very good, Sir. I'll act upon that and pass it quietly on to my other crews.'

'Thanks Sergeant. Now we should pass the freight across and I'll brew up some coffee while we let the Senior Constables regain some dignity by getting out of the water.'

While they busied themselves transferring the various boxes from their cabin to their bow ready for transfer, my crew quickly hauled themselves out of the water, grabbed the towels I'd left on the boarding platform and headed below to dress.

'Your arse is toast, *Commander*!' Amanda whispered as they scurried below under the lecherous gaze of the two Water coppers, hands clutching towels over boobs as best they could, although the nearly transparent panties went unshielded.

'Likewise!' was Melissa's comment. 'Totally toast! No nooky for at least six hours! Cop that, young Harry!'

I laughed at them and managed to swat Melissa on the bum as she went past.

To maintain a semblance of cover, the coppers only tied up beside us for a short time, just long enough to enjoy a hot coffee and exchange some cheeky banter with the girls. They then headed off to conduct some more 'safety checks', allowing the small flotilla of boats from last night's anchorage to slowly filter in.

While most chose to anchor in the middle of the bay, five or six came up to where we were, our new friends Gerry and his mates with all their families. Once again, being of very shallow draft, we were able to tuck in very close to the beach, having made allowance for a falling tide later that afternoon.

We were about to move the drone boxes when the cell phone rang as we were in range of the Dunwich tower.

'Hi Harry, It's Greg. How're things?'

'Gidday, Greg. So far, all's well. We just took delivery of Amanda's toys, but haven't looked at them yet. We've got some friendly visitors around so we're just putting them out of sight for now. What's new with you?'

'Two things. Bob and I just had a meeting with a couple of heavies from the ACP wanting to make sure the incoming shipment of stuff isn't allowed to go walkabout. The Brisbane Central coppers want to let each package be collected, then follow them to their destination so they can haul in more of the local distributors.

The problem as Canberra sees it is keeping a close track on three or four packages without alerting the collection crew so to be safe, Canberra wants all the stuff grabbed as soon as it gets picked up from the water, while Brisbane wants to let it be dispersed so they can follow each container to the distribution point.

We think that's asking for trouble and support the Canberra viewpoint.'

'Yeah, copy that, mate. Brisbane is being silly if they think they can track each container. There will be several; well, three at least, so I'd agree with you and Canberra. We should grab them as soon as we can. So what's the second thing you wanted to tell me?'

'We were hoping you'd feel that way about the drop. The second thing is that our inside man has come up with details on the drop. Ready to copy?'

'Yeah, mate. Go ahead.'

'Friday morning. The container ship 'Atlas Dawn' registered Liberia, will enter Moreton Bay via the Spitfire Channel maintaining a speed of fifteen knots and will turn abeam Salamander Bank at 10:20. Nearly two nautical miles along the Main Channel from the Salamander 4s Flashing Red Beacon, there's another Flashing Red, a 2.5s this time with a 2.5s Flashing Green opposite. The drop is scheduled to occur right at the second Red beacon.

There will be a Bay trawler with a net out, loitering on the northeast side of the Main Channel. That boat is the collection vessel and will move into the Channel immediately after the 'Atlas Dawn' passes, following in her wake and scooping four plastic barrels up with its net that will be set to trawl shallow. After the pickup, it will haul the net and head for Pumicestone Passage. The transfers to the various collection boats will be made on the run and within one hour, or the containers get dumped. A password is necessary for the pickup and that is, 'Atlas Dawn today'. Not very original, we thought, but go figure.

We are also informed that if the ship or the trawler drop crew see any suspicious surveillance boats or aircraft of any description, the whole lot is dumped.'

'Copied that, thanks mate. I suppose you and Bob want us to go and grab the whole shipment? Is that what you were going to ask next?'

'Shit, Harry. How'd you guess that! You must be psycho or something!'

'Yeah, or something! Just makes sense. But as difficult as it seems, I might just have an idea forming on how to do it. The only requirement for you is to make sure that there is no surveillance other than us out there on Friday. No Police boats, no aircraft or helicopters, no nothing! Just us. Is that clear?'

'Okay Harry. I'll talk to Bob and do what we can, but Brisbane will be having fits if they've got nothing out there.'

'Just make it happen, Greg. I don't want to be tripping over coppers disguised as fishermen with rifles as rods or mermaids with sub-machine guns stuffed down their fake fins, or any other bloody thing!'

'Yeah, I hear you mate. We'll fix it, but be very careful and keep us informed all the time.'

'Yeah of course. Talk soon. We've got some planning to do. Cheers, Greg.'

After we had stowed the drone and UAV boxes well out of sight right forward in the two dressing rooms, I announced to the girls, 'I'm going overboard to scrub around the waterline. If you feel like another swim, you can grab a scouring pad and help.'

They'd forgiven me the mild embarrassment of their exposure to the Police boat crew, even though they'd be the butt of jokes for months to come, and willingly stripped off again and jumped in, still just wearing panties. With three on the job, it didn't take long to do all four sides. The girls were fascinated by the schools of tiny, brightly coloured fish that hung around feeding on the green clouds of weed and slime as they were scrubbed off the hulls.

By the time we'd finished, several more boats had moved in around us, as we seemed to have become to focal point at this end of the bay and soon our new friends from last night, plus a lot more, were in the water paddling around us, all without clothes.

It was the girls and my first time with a Naturist group and apart from the slightly unusual sight of everybody from little kids, teens and adults being naked, you couldn't have met with a happier or more relaxed bunch of people. They all knew each other well from past trips to the Island and made us feel welcome, so in deference to their unwritten code of behaviour, we removed the rest of our gear.

Luckily I'd been having a lot of practise lately keeping my body under control, so major embarrassment was avoided when it was time to join our new friends for lunch aboard their boats. There was a constant stream of naked bodies coming and going with food and drink, with many small groups choosing to sit in the warm, shallow water to eat. This seemed to me to be a terribly practical of way consuming food.

All in all, it was a delightful way to spend the day in such a picturesque setting and there were no awkward questions about the Police boat visits; just happy people enjoying themselves, and although there were some laughs about 'safety inspections' the Water Police were held in high regard since they spent so much time helping boaties in trouble.

The girls adapted really well and came in for more than their fair share of appreciative looks and a lot of full on, but good-natured flirting from the males. It was good that we weren't going anywhere that day since we all drank too much again and staggered back aboard for an afternoon siesta.

The girls were very giggly as we washed the salt off under the stern shower, and they deliberately stirred me up with a lot of close body contact and very provocative comments that only increased my problem. Given the excess of naked bodies we'd been exposed to all morning, plus the heavy flirting from the males that got the girls excited, I guess it was inevitable that we all ended up in my bed together, where Melissa proved that she wasn't so shy after all and Amanda was pissy enough to enjoy herself just as much. After keeping the two of them happy, I needed some rest, so it was dark before we sleepily emerged to a warm, soft dusk.

The girls stayed very close and clingy after all that and I suspected that it was their first three-way experience and they'd surprised themselves. I also suspected that it might not be the last, and after experiencing the delightful Melissa for the first time, I didn't mind the prospect.

CHAPTER 20

We'd spent all of Tuesday in Horseshoe Bay, enjoying the company and sights of our new friends enormously and even getting some mild sunburn on those places normally kept covered. Bedtime was again lots of fun, but all good things come to an end and while we were anxious to test the UAV and drones that had been delivered at great expense, I was very conscious of the Friday deadline.

I also needed to discuss the situation and my tentative plans with the girls — something I'd not been able to do since *Firebird* had become the centre of activity for our new naked friends.

Therefore, early on Wednesday morning, we headed out, telling our new friends that we wanted to roam the bay a bit more.

They only wanted to stay at their quiet, semi-private beach, which eliminated the worry of tag-alongs.

'Where are we headed, Harry?' Amanda asked, handing me a mug of tea and a plate of hot toast and honey, as we slid quietly out past the wreck of the old *Platypus* steamer on the southeast point of Peel Island, staying under power as the distance was too short to bother with sails in the light airs that prevailed in the early morning.

I showed her on the Chart plotter an odd-looking little bay that lay north from the small town of Dunwich, in an area called Myora, where a long spit comprising several skinny, shallow sandbanks in a long line closed off a series of sheltered anchorages.

'So much for hiding in a crowd,' I commented ruefully, 'but hopefully, there won't be too many boats there and we can get the testing done quickly, then maybe re-join them. There's an anchorage close to Dunwich called One Mile that most boaties seem to like holing up in, although I've never really liked it, particularly when it gets crowded like it will be these holidays. But Myora has a good anchorage at the southern end that we should be able to use quite comfortably.'

While we motored quietly around the end of Peel Island and across to the start of the Rainbow Channel running down past Myora to Amity and the notoriously fickle and dangerous bar crossing, I brought the crew up to date on the delivery details and briefly discussed my plan for grabbing the shipment.

'That sounds a bit risky,' Amanda observed, 'won't these people be ready for some sort of nonsense?'

'Possibly, but if we use the old 'overwhelming force' routine, things might be biased a bit more our way.'

That earned me a pair of very old-fashioned looks and a thoughtful silence that lasted until we entered Myora.

My prediction about One Mile had been correct and we saw as we motored past that it was jammed full of all the boaties who like to nest together in one spot and stay there for the duration. It wasn't far past One Mile to the turn-in to Myora and although there were a couple of small tinnies pulled up on the inner shore, the anchorage was otherwise deserted.

We dropped anchor at the northern end over a fairly shallow bottom of mixed weed and sand, the water crystal-clear and inviting. The girls wanted to swim, but I insisted on work first, so they put some clothes back on and went to get the big prototype UAV from my dressing room. I was intrigued to see this product of the ingenuity of a retired pilot and life-long aero-modeller from the country and I wasn't disappointed when it was unpacked.

With a commendable sacrifice of function before beauty, it had a simple, boxy fuselage that bulged considerably just behind the front wing, and was a little over a metre long, with two rectangular planform wings of 1.5-metre span each, one mounted right at the tail and the other set back a way from the bulbous nose that seemed to be made from a single piece of crystal-clear plastic. A large, swept-back fin adorned the rear end, while each of the four wing panels sprouted a slim, streamlined nacelle at the tip with a large two-blade propeller smoothly integrated into the front of each. Two low-set, streamlined skids protruded from the underside supporting the airframe on the ground, with two thin wire support struts attached to outer section of the rear wing.

Overall, it did look remarkably like a dragonfly, except that it was painted a mottled light blue-grey colour on the underside and a darker mottled shade on top.

'What's the power system?' I asked Amanda.

'Cunningly, it's a hybrid design with a lightweight twin-cylinder, two-stroke petrol engine fitted with a high-output AC generator mounted directly on the motor shaft along with a cooling fan, buried in the centre of the fuselage. That supplies power to drive four low-KV electric motors connected directly to the large-diameter propellers. The nacelles can rotate through 100° so the UAV can take-off and land vertically or even move very slowly, but will then transition to wing lift once it's airborne. The cruise phase of flight is much more efficient with the propellers providing horizontal thrust and the wings providing the lift. Vertical take-off and landing use a great deal of power and is very inefficient for horizontal flight.

That's why multi-rotor drones have relatively short range and endurance. This design is the best of both worlds — long range and endurance, with the obvious benefits of vertical take-off and landing in a small space.'

I was impressed and said so. She smiled, 'The guy is brilliant. He just borrowed the concept from a Radio-Controlled toy and made a platform that can be operated from a confined area, but with great range and/or endurance. Other designers have done something similar, but they've made theirs all electric which has reduced the payload, range and endurance by having to lug a heap of batteries around.

And that's where this design is unique and so much better, in that it doesn't have to carry the weight of batteries, even lightweight Lithium types. It has a fully autonomous autopilot that can follow a pre-loaded flight plan or be re-programmed in flight if necessary. As I mentioned the other day, it's fitted with a full-colour, 1080P HD, Electro-optical and Infrared, gyro-stabilised camera system with 30X zoom.

Full time telemetry has enough bandwidth to allow real-time HD video of a target and it can loiter at low speed for up to 8 hours, or fly out 150 kilometres, loiter for 5 hours and return home. Within telemetry range, it has a target-tracking function that will keep the camera focussed on a designated target, regardless of what manoeuvres the UAV has to do, but beyond a maximum of 75 kilometres, the live signal drops out and Solid State recording devices keep a dual record of the video images for download on return.

If necessary for long-range live viewing, a satellite relay can be activated, but the bandwidth is much reduced and only HD snapshots can effectively sent back. Still, even they have proved very effective and in some cases, are better than video. The auto-pilot has a Return-To-Base function, but if the base station has to move during the mission, a beacon tracking function will still bring it home, provided the base beacon on the landing pad has been activated. The Auto Land function is accurate to within 150mm or 6 inches.'

'Fantastic! But does it actually do all that stuff, or is that just what it's supposed to do?'

'She smiled gently, 'Oh yes. It really does! When I get it setup, I'll flight plan it to fly back to Peel Island and orbit our friends at 1500 feet a few times, then return to base and land. You be the judge from there as to how good it is.'

'OK. That'll be a good first test. Can I help with anything?'

'Not with this for now. Melissa needs to learn about it, but you can watch all you like.'

So I watched and learned as she competently filled the fuel

tank with a petrol/oil mix, topped off the small backup batteries that were also used briefly for remote engine starting, then carried out a full function check of all systems, including tilting the nacelles through their full range of motion. The two-bladed propellers had to be moved to the horizontal for that test, as they would hit the deck with the nacelles horizontal.

A waterproof Pelican case held a big-screen laptop nested in foam that was the main Ground Control Station with its own power supply and connected to transmitters and receivers for the telemetry link. It could be powered from its own batteries or plugged into external power when available, which is what we did in this case.

There were no flight controls as such as most deployments were fully-autonomous, but there was provision for non-autonomous flight by inputting changes of direction, height and speed required then letting the autopilot work things out from there.

'Where is it going to take-off from?' I asked.

'On top of the cockpit roof will be fine, Harry. But you'll need to swing the boom aside and lash it out of the way, and I'll tell the Autopilot to take off sideways to avoid the backstay. I'll put a radio beacon on the deck to make sure it finds us again.'

Shortly after, with the boom safely pulled aside, Amanda laid a blanket over some of the solar panels to avoid scratching them if the UAV slid, placed a matchbox size beacon in the middle then had us pass the UAV up to her. It was surprisingly heavy and I had doubts that even four electric motors would be able to lift the thing at all.

It wasn't long before Amanda had finished setting up the Ground Control Station in the cockpit and had programed the flight plan. With power on both the UAV and the Ground Control Station, she started the engine remotely, an immediate but subdued and throaty purr announcing all was well. A full set of digital instruments on the GCS screen gave engine health readouts as well as the navigation plot.

'I'll let the engine warm up for a minute,' she said, 'but then it's just a matter of switching control across to the autopilot and activating the Flight Plan.'

One minute on, she threw a mechanical switch, pressed a button on the touch screen and moments later, the engine obediently revved up to a governed maximum power RPM and a soft whirring came from the four propellers as they spun up to speed. I couldn't help but step back to the stern where I could see and it was almost surreal the way the machine lifted smoothly into a low hover, pivoted to the right away from the lashed-out boom and flew slowly away from the boat. The engine exhaust noise deepened as the UAV's nacelles rotated slowly forward, picking up speed smoothly as the wings took over the lifting duties before accelerating away in a fast climbing turn out over the Rainbow Channel and back toward Peel Island.

Within seconds, the muted purr of the engine exhaust and the multiple whirring of the props had faded completely, and the UAV was just a shrinking dot in the blue sky, the colour scheme helping it disappear.

On the GCS screen, a detailed map of the area was overlaid by the flight plan course, with a yellow dot representing the *Dragonfly* moving along the blue line of the plotted course directly toward Peel Island. Readouts on the panel showed the direction was 230°, speed was 60 knots and height 1500 feet, time to station was just 3 minutes, and distance to run 3 nautical miles. At this point, to me, it was just like a video game, except that the yellow dot represented several hundred thousand dollars' worth of complex aircraft and camera systems.

Amanda tapped another touch button and the navigation display realigned itself up the right-hand side of the screen and a steady picture of the water took its place, steadily streaming from top to bottom.

She zoomed out by sliding her finger along a slider bar and the picture instantly pulled back to show Peel Island approaching at the top of the screen, every detail in razor-sharp, shake-free high definition. As the autopilot brought the UAV over the top of the group of boats in the east pocket where we'd been earlier, Amanda used a multi-mode trackball to create a set of cross-hairs that she laid on Gerry's boat near the beach and clicked once. The camera then faithfully stayed focused on the boat as the UAV went into its pre-programmed series of orbits over the top. She was able to zoom in so well that we could see Gerry and his wife Beth in fine detail, sitting in the cockpit, sipping on mugs of what looked like coffee, the picture totally sharp and shake-free.

'Fantastic!' I enthused, 'is that the zoom limit?'

In reply, she tweaked a knob and we seemed to dive right into Gerry's mug of coffee, even seeing little wisps of steam rising off the surface.

'OK. You've convinced me. That's terrific. But now I want to see it come home without hitting something.'

'The Flight Plan calls for it to do three orbits there before returning, so just one more lap and it'll come back by itself.'

Sure enough, after the next orbit, it broke off the turn, the camera staying locked onto Gerry's boat until Amanda cancelled the tracking function, and headed away from Peel back toward us. About three minutes later, I picked up the tiny dot coming our way, growing rapidly larger in silence until it passed overhead, curving around in a tight turn, losing height. The engine noise was just a soft purr as the UAV smoothly curved around behind us, slowing down as the propeller nacelles smoothly rotating to the vertical, until it came to a steady hover just five metres out from our right side.

It then turned 90° left and drifted gently in over the deck, rotated again to face forward and lowered down to a gentle touch-down on the blanket set up as a landing pad.

I couldn't help but applaud the performance. 'Absolutely flaw-less,' I exclaimed, 'I've heard how good they can be, but reality is so much more impressive in this case. What a terrific machine. Congratulations!'

Amanda beamed with the praise as she went through the shut down checklist and all went quiet over our heads. 'It really is, thanks to my dear old friend. It can loiter around an area for up to eight hours if needed or go a couple of hundred kilometres away and back at dash speed just take a quick look at something.'

'Well, I'm highly impressed and it's going to be a terrific addition to our surveillance arsenal when we have to keep a discrete watch on happenings. I noticed that when it was coming in overhead, it was very hard to spot and quite silent until it got quite low and close. I'm guessing that if it were holding station on a ship or boat, with no relative motion, it would be impossible to see.'

'You're right. That's what we were taught. To try and avoid relative motion as much as possible and stay as high as possible and use the image stabilisation and the zoom function. Then the UAV is nearly invisible.'

The phone rang at that point, so I let her and Melissa get on with post flight checks and cleaning, while I answered.

'*Hi Harry, it's Corrine. How're things?*'

'All good here Corrine. I take it you're leaving Southport?'

'*Yeah. Your friend Ray with that dysfunctional fucking dog says 'Hi'. We're fuelled, stocked, locked and loaded! Anything for us to do yet?*'

'As a matter of fact, there just might be, but I'll wait until you're here for the briefing. Is *Seeker* in good shape?'

'*She gave an excited laugh, 'Better than ever, Harry. You won't believe what we've done to our baby, but that can wait for now. Where are you?*'

'It's an anchorage called Myora and the co-ordinates are S27.27.36, E153.25.14. It's about 35 nautical miles, though most of the way is via shallow, winding, narrow passages so I guess you'll be a good couple of hours even at your normal cruise speed. There's a fair amount of holiday boating traffic so be careful.'

'*OK Dad. We'll be careful. See you soon. Bye.*'

The girls had overheard the conversation. 'She's a cheeky thing, Harry. I gather you know her well?' asked Amanda

'Yes. She's ex-SAS and was in Afghanistan where our paths crossed on a couple of occasions. She was also involved in the last operation down south.'

That caught Amanda's attention, but as Melissa looked blank, she hadn't heard the story, although I was sure Amanda would fill her in before long. By now the girls had broken the *Dragonfly* down to its component parts again and were stowing them in the travel case. Minutes later, the cockpit was clear of boxes, cases and UAV stuff.

'Why don't you have that swim now,' I suggested. 'Corrine and Dave will be a couple of hours, although it may be a bit less. *Seeker* is pretty fast.'

'It won't matter how fast it is,' scoffed Melissa, 'those narrow channels can't be taken at speed.'

I thought a moment, 'I dunno. They used to run the Russell Island Ski Boat Race years ago from the Gold Coast to Russell and back and that was pretty quick. Anyway, they'll be a reasonable while. So enjoy your swim then we'll have a quiet lunch before they get here.'

The time at Peel Island had got the girls much too used to being naked all the time so they automatically dropped everything and jumped in. I didn't really mind watching, convincing myself that I was watching out for any nasty, bitey things, whereas reality said that I just liked perving on pretty, naked girls. They splashed around for a while before getting out and hosing off.

After they had climbed out and rinsed off, Melissa wanted me to dry her off. However, I was learning that nothing is simple with Melissa and it wasn't long before her standing in front of me, braced with both hands on my shoulders to steady herself, I was gently rubbing a towel over part of her front that seemed particularly sensitive and which she said needed a lot of extra drying, and who was I to disagree with such a request. Amanda was most amused by the carry-on as she sprawled erotically on the daybed letting the sun do the work. I had reached a stage in the process where the towel seemed to have slipped to the deck and I was carrying on the job with just my hand, when Melissa's imminent explosion was rudely interrupted by Amanda saying, 'I think that boat's coming in here.'

I stood up, my intense contemplation and manipulation of her nether regions shattered, to see a large and familiar red-hulled speed boat coming off the plane as it turned in from the Rainbow Channel.

'OK. I guess I was wrong. That's them,' I announced lamely to the girls who glared at me before heading for their clothes. 'They must have decided to set a new speed record for Gold Coast to Myora. That was only about 40 minutes.'

'Yeah. And maybe they told you porky pies about when they left,' Melissa said, regretfully pulling up her shorts.

CHAPTER 21

FIREBIRD AND SEEKER,
MYORA ANCHORAGE, WEDNESDAY

'Holy crap! Look at the size of that thing,' Amanda exclaimed, stunned by the appearance of the long, sleek red hull that eased alongside us, her deck well above ours and the engine sound a deep bass growl that seemed to shiver the air, even at idle. The boat was immaculate, even after the voyage from Melbourne, the white upper works and deck gleaming in the bright sun, contrasting with the blood-red hull, the heavily tinted windows concealing any glimpse inside the rear-set cabin.

With barely a bump, the monster came to rest, just touching the fenders I'd placed along our side, before the engines cut.

In the ensuing silence, a small female figure with long, flowing red hair darted out of the cockpit, flung herself over the rail and jumped up into my arms.

'Hello, my darling Harry!' she cried, hugging and kissing me deeply, her finely muscled legs clamped firmly around my waist. I was finally able to pull back enough to draw breath and respond.

'Hello back at you, dear Mouse. Wonderful to see you again, my lovely girl.'

'Hi Dave,' I called out over her shoulder to the tall, lean young man with the beaming smile, busy lashing *Seeker* to *Firebird*.

'Hi ya, Harry. Good to see you again mate. You're looking well.'

'You too. The boating life still agrees with you.'

'Shit, yeah!' was his response.

I finally managed to prise Corrine off me and return her to the deck, but she kept a hold of one arm as if I was about to evaporate. My crew were giving Corrine and me some very strange looks, with Amanda saying in a dry tone, 'It would seem you two know each other?'

I laughed, but Corrine answered for me as she stuck her hand out to the girls, 'Sorry about that. I'm Corrine and I always remain extremely fond of someone who's saved my life at least twice!'

That statement pushed their eyebrows up, so to forestall that line of discussion, I jumped in quickly and made introductions. 'Corrine, this is Senior Constable Amanda Burke and Senior Constable Melissa Briggs of the Queensland Police. Ladies, this is Corrine Johns and the tall, genial gentleman is Dave Robson of the *Seeker*.'

Dave chose that moment to jump down into the cockpit so I was able to shake hands and exchange heartfelt hugs. He and Corrine greeted the girls formally then hugged them both. That did a little to ease the puzzlement showing on their faces.

'Come and sit down, I'll make you coffee; we have a lot to say to each other, not the least of which was how the bloody hell did you get here so fast without fibbing about when you left Southport?'

Corrine punched the air laughing. 'See Dave, I told you he'd ask that first up. That's $10 you owe me.'

Dave grinned ruefully, 'Yeah Babe. I should know better than to bet with you when Harry stuff is concerned.'

'Come on, sit and I'll get tea and coffee,' I urged, 'There's a lot to cover and we've a deadline to meet.' I also had to call Jasper out to re-acquaint him with Dave and Corrine, but he remembered them without trouble. They both loved little Krazy kitten that adored having extra laps to jump onto.

Amanda forestalled me by shoving me down into a seat at the table and saying, 'Sit, Harry. You need to talk to Corrine and Dave and I can listen through the open window while I do lunch and the drinks. Mel and I have had the briefing anyway.'

So I did as instructed and tried to bring Dave and Corrine up to date with the complete background to the operation, before finally outlining my plan for the drug pickup operation. While I spoke, the girls served a lunch of toasted sandwiches with tea and coffee that went down very well. When I finished, Corrine thought for a while.

'Not a bad plan, Harry, although we don't know how many guys will be on the trawler and how hard they'll resist having the load hi-jacked.'

'I was counting on the fact that they'll just be contracted for a fee to make the pickup. If it's not their shit, they shouldn't be too concerned who takes it. But I figured that to dissuade them from argument, we'd all be on *Seeker* armed to the teeth as a massive show of force.'

'Pretty good reasoning, but what about the pickup boats? There are four containers; presumably there'll be a separate pickup crew for each. They definitely won't meekly sit back and let us grab the lot!'

'True. But if we get in first and move quickly, we can beat them to it. And I'll bet that they won't have anything that can touch *Seeker* for speed. Which reminds me — my plan is still very flexible, so before we go any further with it, you'd better show me how you made that run this morning.'

Dave and Corrine grew huge grins and Dave said, 'Oh, you'll love this, Harry. But we have to tell you one thing and we'd like it kept a secret.'

My girls looked at each other, before Amanda said, 'I presume that this secret happened Interstate and some time ago, so it doesn't concern us officially. Please go ahead.'

Dave and Corrine smiled gratefully before Dave continued. 'After you left and we registered the boat in our names, we were going through cleaning very thoroughly in preparation for Corporate Charter stuff, when I found a hidden locker under the bed in the Master stateroom. All the time I've been looking after the boat and sleeping in that cabin, I had no idea it was there, but I suppose I had no reason to go looking for things like that.'

Corrine elbowed him sharply in the ribs, 'You're waffling, Dave. Get on with it.'

He sucked a few painful breaths then said. 'We found where Xavier had been keeping his nest egg. We'd heard that his bank accounts didn't amount to much at all and there were no safe deposit boxes that anyone could find, so the Victorian Police didn't look any further since the boat was off the books anyway. We just re-registered it in our names and the job was done.'

I gave him my 'getting pissed Major' look. 'What was in the locker, Dave?'

'$3.65 million Aussie dollars all in hundreds, along with a small collection of cut diamonds, plus a few emeralds. They are all around one to four carats in size and vary in colour from pure white to blue and even a couple of red ones. We thought that the blue ones were medium-coloured sapphires and the red ones were rubies, but Corrine took them to a jeweller friend and he nearly fainted. The red ones are rarest and most valuable and together they weighed just over seven carats. There were some intense blue ones like really good sapphires, that he said could be really valuable and there were six of those weighing just over thirty-five carats. Strangely, he wouldn't give us an estimate of the value, but from what we can gather from the Internet, there was possibly another five or maybe six million in coloured diamonds and emeralds. We've locked them up for safekeeping, but we've kept three of the pretty blue ones out; one each for you, Sandy and Janice as our way of saying 'Thanks for everything'.'

They both got a bit emotional and had to stop for a moment to recover, before Dave said, 'Enough of that. You know what we owe you, but come and see what we had such a lovely time spending some of that money on.'

As he led the way onto *Seeker* I commented, 'So I guess that you guys aren't going to be applying for Unemployment Benefits anytime soon?'

Dave laughed and shook his head, 'That's for sure, Harry. In fact, we haven't decided what to do with the stones at this stage, since the cash alone has let us be very picky with what charters we take on.'

He chuckled, 'It's really odd in that now that we don't have to work, we keep getting charter offers thrown at us! But then, the pickier we become, the more in demand we are. We've doubled our rates and still have more business than we want to handle, but so far, we're still enjoying the life and having fun.'

'That's all you have to worry about,' I commented. 'If you stop having fun, get out.'

So while Corrine took the girls on a general tour, Dave took me to the engine room. It was as immaculate as when I'd first seen it, many months ago in the Gippsland Lakes. The two massive white-painted MAN V-12 diesels squatted like two barely restrained monsters anxious to be woken up again to bellow their glorious song to the uncaring sea.

But a new piece of hardware sat innocently on the deck between the rear of the two diesels looking like a large generator unit, so I said so.

'But you've got two generators already, Dave. What do you need another one for?'

'Look more carefully, Harry. In fact look behind it.'

So I did and spotted a few things that generators don't usually have, namely; a very large diameter pipe coming out of the middle and going up through the deck head, a rear section made of champagne-coloured shiny metal that looked like it became quite warm in operation, and with a drive shaft protruding from the back end and running out through the rear bulkhead between the other two drive shafts.

I turned to Dave and met his grin with my own. 'You sneaky buggers! You've installed a gas turbine!'

'Yep. Up to 5,600 horsepower extra which is 50% more than the diesels combined, but at just 21% of the weight of the diesels. It drives another Water Jet installed on the centreline. It uses diesel, the same as the main engines and because it's a water jet drive, there's no drag if we don't use it. But when we do fire it up, there's a quite dramatic boost to performance!'

'I'll bet there is. So tell me; just how fast are you now?'

'Well, we used to be able to hit 63 knots with the diesels, but the best we've safely seen so far is 84 knots! And there's still more to come 'cause that's only using 70% rated turbine power, since we're still getting the feel of the boat at that speed. It's both terrifying and exhilarating at the same time to be going that fast in a boat this size, but she really just sits nicely and doesn't jump around or feel unstable! The designers did a great job!

Of course, we installed full-harness seat restraints for the high-speed runs in calm water only. Otherwise we just use the diesels as usual since they're a lot better on fuel consumption.'

I shook his hand. 'Fantastic job, Dave. I might have to factor this extra capability into my plan for Friday, provided you guys are willing to take part?'

'Hell, yeah! We wouldn't miss it for anything.'

I clapped him on the shoulder as we left the engine room to re-join the ladies.

'What'd you think, Harry?' Corrine asked eagerly, 'Is that some toy or what!'

I grinned at her enthusiasm that matched Dave's in intensity.

'Bloody brilliant Mouse. I've got to use this in my plan. Let's sit and talk it through again.'

Before we adjourned to *Firebird* for the briefing, Corrine ducked below, returning moments later with a small black velvet bag that she held out to me. 'They don't feel like much, but it might be best to put them somewhere safe just in case they are worth something.'

As we were out in the cockpit, I prudently didn't open the

little bag that felt like it had three small marbles in it, instead just shoved it into my pocket while thanking them both profusely for their extreme generosity.

By late afternoon, we had what seemed like a very complicated, but maybe workable plan hashed out and I went into the saloon to place a call to Greg.

'Gidday Harry. How's it going?'

'Good thanks Mate. I've got a bit of a plan worked out and need something done to help it work.'

'OK. What's the plan?'

'Can't give you the whole thing at this stage as it's still in the making, but I do need you to arrange with the Brisbane Water Police to have one of their bigger boats hanging around at the mouth of the Pumicestone Passage on Friday from no later than 11:00 on. I strongly suggest they task Sergeant Brian Thomas and Constable Derek Lance with the job since I've already met them and they seem competent. The task will be to pickup our two Senior Constables and myself from a red-hulled cruiser and return to the *Firebird* wherever we've parked it ASAP. Copy that?'

'Yeah, copied that, but jeez Harry. You're really pushing things this time. If there's a cockup that loses the drugs, everybody's going to be pissed off with you and my nuts will be in the same wringer as yours! Can you at least tell me what your ultimate outcome is for all this? The way you're heading, Firebird is going to be the floating drug centre of Australia!'

'Yeah, sorry about that Mate, but this is the only way I can think of to keep all the good guys happy. I will emphasise that we aim to grab the whole shipment and hang onto it until you're ready, willing and able to take it off us!

But call me back as soon as you have confirmation from the Water Police that they'll play ball. I'd prefer you to ask them nicely and not to have to pull rank and lean on them myself.'

'Well thanks for the reassurance and we are working to try to find *and seal the Evidence Locker problem, but aren't you taking this a bit personal? You're going to tread on a lot of toes doing this. And not only the bad guys!'*

'OK. That's a fair comment, but what if we do let the coppers loose with their flash boats, aeroplanes and helicopters? Then see how much dope they get and how many of the bad guys they catch. It, and all the bikies, would disappear in a flash!

Would that be a result that everyone is happy with? No toes would be trodden on, but the poor dude on the inside of the Coast bikie gang is going to be toast as soon as they figure out that all their private info was leaked. The net result will just be to drive everybody underground and burn a precious asset!'

Greg was silent for a few moments. 'Yeah, you're right again, Harry. I can't fault that logic. I'll do as you ask, but can you let me know what's happening as soon as you can? Please?'

'Yeah, okay mate. I promise that I'll let you know as soon as we get the plan set. How's that?'

'All good, thanks, mate. I'll call the Water Police and get back shortly.'

'Thanks Greg. Cheers.'

Everybody was looking at me strangely as I hung up, so I grinned. 'What? Sometimes people need to be leant on a bit to get things happening.'

Corrine looked at me, 'Yeah, fair enough, but I'm sure you realise that you're setting yourselves up as a target for all the bikies groups who've got a stake in this shipment.'

I beamed at her. 'Yep! That's the idea. This way it looks like we're independent pirates and there's no connection with the Police, State or Commonwealth and we have a better chance of causing some serious attrition amongst the ranks of the bad boys. It won't take long for them to start suspecting each other of forming this pirate group. Besides, we're still carrying the merchandise and cash from the first shipment that came onto the Coast so the Coast boys are still on the warpath.'

Corrine stared. 'Did you forget to mention that, or were you going to tell us later?'

'Settle petal! That's why they've been chasing us and why we've burned up four of their best men so far.'

'So what've you got of theirs?'

I grinned, 'Just two million in cash and 10 kilos of pure, modified MDMA.'

Corrine just shook her head in disgust, but Dave broke the air of doom and gloom by laughing. 'Good one Harry. I'm with you. This'll be a hoot!'

I grinned back, 'Thanks Dave. Have you guys still got some weapons aboard?'

Corrine jumped in, 'Yep. We've still got the original shotgun with SG loads and some Brenneke solid shot, plus two PMR-30's in .22 Magnum. Plus we found a couple of Coonan .357 Magnum pistols in with Xavier's stash. They're virtually new and there's a heap of ammo for them. They beat the hell out of the old 1911 .45 ACP!'

I had a chuckle to myself since I'd last seen a Coonan in the hands of a bikie sneaking aboard *Firebird* not long ago, but I'd had to turn it in to Greg along with the bikie.

'That'll be good,' I said to Corrine, 'but the frame would be pretty big for your hands. Have you tried it?'

'Yes, I have and you're right. It is big to the point of being too awkward to be effective, so I'd prefer not to use it.'

That seemed to wrap up the official business for the day, so as it was drinks time, I broke out some of everyone's choice and the party began as we discussed more pleasant subjects. The girls pumped Dave and Corrine for stories about the last operation down south and after a nod from me, they told what they knew.

Those stories, plus the usual ones about the Afghanistan experience generated a lot of laughter and some incredulous looks from my crew and I knew I was in for a quizzing later when they had me alone.

After a while, Corrine was pissed enough to take her shirt off and show where she'd been shot through the side. Her bland announcement that she was a 'wet-work' specialist as well as her team's sniper also generated some looks of awe and guaranteed I was in for a *lot* of questions later.

Dave and Amanda teamed up to make a simple dinner of steak and veggies and I followed that with a round or three of my now-famous NQ teas. By the time the third round had finished, we were all shot ducks and everyone staggered off to bed. I made sure Corrine and Dave made it safely over the rails between the two boats, before stumbling below where I found the bed occupied by two pissed females who were already snoring softly.

So I did the gentlemanly thing and crawled in between them and went to sleep.

The accumulation of alcohol in our systems ensured that we actually did sleep most of the night, although first Melissa then Amanda woke, went to pee then returned to bed wanting to play. Therefore, the sun was well above the horizon before we crawled out of bed and ventured up on deck to find Dave and Corrine sitting in their cockpit having breakfast.

'About time you lot got up,' Corrine observed dryly, 'Dave's got brekkie ready for you if you can drag yourselves across the rails.'

It smelled too good to refuse, so we went and that set the mood for the day, where we ate too much, lay around either in the sun or in the cockpit, chatting, where my crew dragged more war stories out of Corrine that sometimes horrified them. Some involved me and were a little embarrassing to hear repeated.

There was a serious session in the late afternoon where we all dug out our weapons and checked them over carefully as well as to tally what we had. It totalled up to be: 3 x 12-gauge shotguns, 4 x PMR-30 .22 Magnum, 1x Grizzly .44 Magnum, 1 x Mini-Uzi 9mm machine pistol, 2 x Glock 22 in .40 S&W and 2 x Coonan .357 Magnum.

With weaponry checked and ammunition sorted, we went

over my very simplistic plan again and decided on who'd carry what. I elected to have the Uzi since I intended to be in front and the wicked-looking little black gun had a decided calming effect on anybody it was pointed at. The .44 Magnum Grizzly was my backup.

Corrine chose my short barrel TAC-14 shotgun with SG loads and a PMR-30.

Dave, who'd been trained by Corrine, took their shotgun with SG loads and a Coonan .357 Magnum.

Amanda and Melissa stayed with their service Glock 22's in .40S&W, so I talked them into taking a PMR-30 each as backup.

Amanda and Melissa also checked over the *Dragonfly* UAV very carefully, since it would be playing a major part in the operation and were watched with great interest by Dave and Corrine.

Everyone was a lot more subdued that evening and went to bed at a reasonable hour, since we needed to be on station at the kick-off point by 08:00 in the morning.

CHAPTER 22

At 08:00, *Firebird* was laying at anchor with several other boats at The Wrecks anchorage on Moreton Island, in shallow crystal-clear water, just north of the former whaling station, Tangalooma Resort. Jasper with Krazy kitten in close attendance was looking forlorn since he'd been left in charge of the boat, the drugs, the cash and the diamonds. I'd tucked the small packet containing the three oval-cut, deep blue diamonds that Corrine and David had given us into the hidden locker in my dressing cabin with some other stuff.

I chuckled to think that *Firebird* was currently the most valuable 60-foot boat in existence.

Before leaving Myora early that morning, we'd loaded the *Dragonfly*, along with its GCS and support equipment onto *Seeker*, along with Melissa, Amanda and the weapons and hardware we'd selected. I'd motored *Firebird* across to The Wrecks alone and secured it before transferring to *Seeker*, then had Dave move us further north along the west side of Moreton Island to the Curtin Artificial reef just off the tiny trickle of fresh water called Cravens Creek.

Even though it was a good fishing spot, there were no other boats here yet, so Dave dropped an anchor with just enough chain to hold us in the southeast breeze that was stirring into life yet again. The forecast suggested that it would become quite strong later in the day, but one way or the other, we'd hopefully have our business over and done by then.

Dave, Corrine and I sat back and watched Melissa and Amanda prepare *Dragonfly* for flight with a maximum fuel load, and set up the GCS in the cockpit. It would launch off the vast, un-obstructed foredeck of the *Seeker* that could easily handle a full-size helicopter. Amanda programmed in a flight plan along the lines we had discussed that would allow us to identify the ship, then loiter along behind it at sufficient altitude and distance to avoid detection.

One refinement I was keen to try was to take the UAV's downlinked video signal and re-transmit it via my VSAT hi-power satellite link to Greg James and Bob Casey at Southport. Amanda and I had spent some time fiddling with patch cables to make the link and were hopeful it'd work.

Another backup tool we planned to have available was one of Amanda's short-range drones with camera and she had set this up in case we needed it for close surveillance.

It was a small six-rotor drone that was fully autonomous and able to be flown by even a total newbie such as myself. I'd had a couple of runs with it at Myora and was happy that I could launch and direct it where required, although the range and endurance was very limited.

I asked Amanda to launch *Dragonfly* as soon as she was ready and while our immediate area was clear of other boats.

Within five minutes, the engine fired up, and after warming up, the UAV floated smoothly off the deck, tilted its nacelles and accelerated forward as the wing neatly took over the lifting task from the propellers.

I placed a call to Greg who was with Superintendent Bob Casey's in his office.

'I'm switching on the satellite upload feed now Greg,' I announced.

Thirty seconds later he responded, '*Got it! That's bloody brilliant, Harry. We've got a solid picture, shake-free in hi-definition. That thing is worth any price! What a superb surveillance tool!*'

I laughed, 'Talk to Amanda about getting more if you're that keen. She knows the designer pretty well. He's some sort of an eccentric living on the pension in outback New South Wales. Go figure!'

I left them to their delight at being able to view an operation live in HD, full-colour video in the comfort and safety of their office and went back to watching our own monitor.

The initial waypoint for the *Dragonfly* was the top end of the ship channel off Caloundra Heads and the UAV headed there at an economical 60 knots, the 22 nautical mile trip taking just 20 minutes with the help of the southeast breeze. Amanda had the camera feed running from the start and once in position, the aircraft entered a wide oval search pattern at 2000 feet, immediately relaying the clear images of three ships heading southeast along the channel. One we discounted straightaway as it was a bulk carrier, but the other two were container ships.

Amanda directed the UAV to sweep across the sterns of both at suitable height and distance off, and by zooming the camera in, we were gratified to see the last ship in the little convoy was indeed the *Atlas Dawn*, a typically ungainly-looking container ship with the aft accommodation and control decks peering over the stacked arrays of multi-coloured containers. She then activated the tracking function, and after placing the cross hairs on the rear-most containers as most likely to hold our items of interest, the autopilot smoothly adjusted power to hold our 'eye-in-the-sky' firmly in position. She left the wide-view mode active so we could see where the ship was until it entered the expected drop zone.

There wasn't much of interest to see for a while, apart from the occasional crewmember that wandered around the deck having a smoke, or a cook's assistant tossing garbage overboard, although Amanda did spot one guy with binoculars who seemed to be scanning the sea and sky a little too often to be just a crewman interested in Bribie island.

'Are you sure that he can't see us?' I asked.

'Yep. Not a chance. He's not looked straight at us at all so far, or stopped his scan, but this is the third time he's had a good look around, so I reckon this is our boy and we're effectively invisible.'

I took the opportunity to look around our area and was surprised to see that several boats had pulled up to the beach, or anchored just off it like us, as the presence of more wrecks and artificial reefs close by made the fishing prospects very good.

Most crews I discounted as just fishermen working the quite strong tide flow, but one that stood out was a boxy-looking 25-foot fast cabin cruiser and it caught my attention since it had five large men aboard, none of whom appeared to be doing anything much, especially fishing!

It also appeared to be dragging its anchor in the strong current flow along the edge of the channel and was being set down onto a serious fishing boat with several guys aboard who did know what they were doing and had set multiple rods from every vantage point. The cruiser crew didn't notice their predicament until yelled at by the fishermen.

The ensuing heated vocal exchange and panic on the cruiser did little to resolve the conflict until the dragging cruiser hit the fishing boat square on, sending rods, lines and angry fishermen in all directions. To compound the problem, some genius on the cruiser fired up the engine and tried to power out of the mess, without even first clearing the fishing lines or hauling up the ineffectual anchor.

On impulse, I switched on the little drone we had waiting and launched it, camera active, over toward the two locked-together boats. I had it in mind to get some video of the guys in the cabin cruiser, in case, as I suspected, they were from a bikie gang. Directing it where to go was easy and I managed to get a very good look at the five big men aboard, including video of guns beings waved around. I left it in place, happily videoing the escalating mess below, until some clown on the cruiser squeezed a trigger. That's when I brought it back before it got noticed and shot at, and managed to tell it to land on the foredeck, which it successfully did.

The screech of tortured stern-drive bearings momentarily overcame the yelling of angry fishermen and a cloud of smoke from the engine announced that several lines had wrapped around the prop and seized the whole drive train. I could see at least one fish-killing billy club raised in anger, to be countered by several pistols brandished by the inept but raging cruiser crew. Inevitably, another trigger was pulled, followed by several more as the farcical situation degenerated into a free-for-all brawl, the fishermen being put down quickly by the gun-wielding cruiser crew who nevertheless paid a steep price with blood flowing freely from several heads.

Needless to say, as both boats were effectively lashed together with fishing lines, neither was going anywhere in a hurry and I could imagine that several Police help calls had hurriedly been placed by other boaties.

'I think that one boatload of pickup crew has just eliminated themselves,' I announced to the crew.

'Good,' Corrine said, 'but there must be at least two or three more out there.'

I went back to looking around with binoculars and although there weren't any more prospects in our immediate vicinity, there appeared to be several boats of various types generally hanging around the area, although they were in positions that could just as easily be good fishing spots. While I could, I noted the boat's registration and placed a quick call to Greg.

'*Yeah, Harry. We've still got a good picture.*'

'That's good, but we've just had a boatload of big guys who look like they'd be more comfortable on motorcycles, run foul of a bunch of fishermen. Can you run the rego for me please?'

'*No problem. Do you want to wait?*'

'Nah. It looks like we're close to kick off so I'll get back later.'

As the *Atlas Dawn* came closer to the drop point, tension ramped up in the whole crew with Amanda zooming in to a tighter picture of just the stern of the ship. Only the guy with the binoculars was visible and Amanda quickly zoomed in to record his face before pulling back a bit. He made another scan around sea and sky, then waved his hand and two more crew darted out from the accommodation tower and quickly unlatched the doors on a container that was at deck level, one stack in from the outer edge.

As they swung open the doors, we saw four yellow containers like 60-litre oil drums, lined up across the width of the container. Each drum had a short length of chain and a small red buoy attached to its top. In short order, the two crewmen heaved them out one by one and threw them over the side.

Within a minute, the yellow containers were gone and the shipping container was locked tight and what looked like seals had been re-applied to the latch bar clips.

I looked at my crew. 'By the way they heaved them over, I'd say that the estimate of 50 kilos per load is fairly close.'

With the drop over, Amanda moved the tracking cross hairs from the ship's stern to the cluster of small red buoys, bobbing in the disturbed wash of the big ship's wake, causing the UAV's autopilot to set up a circling orbit around the drop point. She zoomed out to get the bigger picture and as predicted, we spotted a small Bay trawler moving straight in from the west side of the channel. As we watched, it slowly turned so that it was lined up with the remnants of the ship's frothing wake.

I turned to ask Dave to get ready, but he'd already started both big diesels and had the anchor chain clattering in over the bow roller. The breeze blew the big boat aimlessly for a few moments until Dave held station with the jet units and the bow thruster, keeping us pointing at the trawler closing in on the small cluster of red buoys and the trawler that seemed to take forever to close up on them, bobbing in a neat line about ten metres apart.

The skipper neatly positioned his boat so the buoys passed very close down the side where two large crewmembers were waiting with short boathooks to snag the floats.

I was puzzled that he hadn't used his net like we'd been told, but this pickup method did seem a lot easier, as the four buoys and their lengths of chain were collected in a bundle at the stern. The trawler slowed even more as the drag load came on and they turned away toward the northwest and presumably Pumicestone Passage as we'd been advised.

'Looks like they're going to leave the containers in the water and just tow them,' Corrine commented, 'Why don't they pull them aboard?'

I chuckled, 'Pretty smart, really. Maybe because they have one extra, but I think it's so they can drop them instantly if they see Police or Customs moving in, without being obvious about throwing stuff overboard. They're just adapting to circumstances.'

I called over to Dave at the wheel, 'I think we should move now, please mate. Not too fast, but make a bit of a show.'

He flashed a grin at me and engaged the jet drives and shoved the throttles forward partway. Luckily I'd warned the girls and they were hanging on, as the massive boat just seemed to jump half out of the water under the instant surge of thrust from the two Rolls-Royce water jets. Even at reduced throttle, there was something like two thousand horsepower instantly converted to jet thrust and the acceleration was brutal as we went from rest to 35 knots in a few seconds.

With a pair of huge rooster-tails of shredded white water arching up behind us and pushing half the boat out of the water, we must have presented a dramatic sight to the trawler crew as we bore down upon them. I hoped that we didn't scare them into releasing the containers, but it was obvious that we weren't Police or Customs boat so they let us close up without panicking too much.

Dave brought us expertly alongside, where as part of our plan, I stood on the deck beside the steering position holding the wicked little Mini-Uzi while Corrine, a bandoleer of shotgun rounds across her chest and snugged down tight between her breasts, stood further forward with the brutal-looking TAC-14 shotgun in hand, where she had a direct shot at the Skipper on the wheel. The others were in a group in the cockpit, weapons in hand, but pointing down at the moment.

The Skipper glared at us, only looking slightly worried as Dave planted the big boat close alongside. 'Yeah? What the fuck do you want?'

'Atlas Dawn today,' I replied easily, a smile on my face, 'we're here to make a pickup.'

He nodded, 'Jeeze, you're on the ball. I didn't even see where you came from. That's one hell of a boat you've got there! But there's no need for guns — get someone to toss a rope over and we'll hook up a container.'

I nodded to Amanda who tucked her Glock into her pants for a moment and threw a mooring line over where one of the trawler crew caught it and tied it around one buoy chain. She tied her end off to a sturdy cleat.

I called across to the Skipper again. 'I know that at least one pickup crew won't be coming, so we'll just take all four, if you don't mind.'

He took a moment to process that statement then said, 'Oh you stupid, dumb fuckwit! Have you got any idea who you're going to be pissing off? Your arse will be toast in about five minutes, I reckon. Just as soon as these other three boats get here.'

I smiled and shook my head. 'The only thing that should concern you, my smelly, bearded friend, is what will happen to you and your boat if your crewmember doesn't tie that line onto all four marker buoys instead of just one. Now!'

He hesitated, then stupidly reached for a pistol lying beside the instrument console, so I nodded to Corrine who had a wolfish grin on her face as she racked a round into the stubby 12-gauge shotgun and pulled the trigger. The cluster of SG steel shot took out half the wheelhouse windows, sending shards of glass and splinters of timber framing in all directions. Since a fair share of them had ripped into the Skipper's upper body, hands and face, he was screaming in a mix of pain and rage as she racked another round and took out the rest of the glass, destroying most of the instrument panel as well.

'Stop! Stop!' he screamed again. 'Take the fucking things. You can argue the toss with four groups of very bad-arse bikies as soon as they catch you.' He staggered out to the open stern and waved to the crew. 'Tie that line to all four quickly before that maniac bitch shoots anymore of the boat from under us!'

As payback for that remark, and even though the deckie hurriedly re-tied the rope around all four of the marker buoy chains and released them from the trawler so they then trailed astern of *Seeker*, Corrine casually put another five rounds into the wheelhouse, driving the screaming skipper right back to the stern.

Reloading again with solid shot Magnum rounds from the bandoleer adorning her chest, she pumped a series of shots into the hull just at the waterline, tearing huge, jagged holes in the wood that let streams of water pour in since they just kept going right through the hull sides and out the bottom.

Another scream of outrage from the Skipper brought the two Glocks in our cockpit up to cover and control the group huddling at the stern.

As Dave and Corrine came aft to haul in the containers, I called out to the Skipper, waving the Uzi as emphasis to my words, 'Now might be a really good time to see how quickly you can launch that dinghy strapped to your foredeck, Skipper, 'cause your boat's on its way down as we speak.'

He'd already felt the change in motion as tonnes of water flooded the bilges, making his boat wallow instead of bobbing, so interrupting a stream of cursing, he called back, 'You've got to let two of us forward to launch the dinghy.'

'Did I hear a please? Or am I suddenly hard of hearing?'

'Please can we go forward and launch the dinghy? Our feet are getting wet!'

'Oops! I guess my crew are a bit enthusiastic when it comes to dealing with scum!'

The Skipper looked up from where they were frantically undoing the lashings holding the dinghy down, 'And what do you call yourself arsehole? You're just a bloody pirate, but you're robbing the wrong people. Talk about dead men walking! Fuckwits!'

Corrine didn't bother asking permission — just fired two more solid rounds into the transom of the dinghy making two very large holes that effectively removed it from the dinghy and would let it float only if they clustered in the bow to keep it above the water. Flying splinters shredded the arm of one guy, so I reminded them, 'I wouldn't let too much blood get in the water if I were you Skipper! As fishermen you know what Bull sharks are like if they smell any and I believe there are heaps around here. That unfortunate girl at Amity Point was taken by one or two, wasn't she? Anyway, Whitsunday's here we come.'

They just glared back as they finally got the dinghy free and hastily threw it over the side, before rather more carefully climbing down to keep the transom above water. *Seeker* had already drifted clear, so we finished pulling the containers aboard before I asked Dave to get under way, but slowly until we emptied the containers and dumped them.

Wax was used to seal the large screw tops, but with that removed, they screwed off easily to reveal thick, heat-sealed plastic bags containing a fine, white powder. Each bag weighed about five kilos and there were ten bags per container.

As soon as each container was emptied, it was shoved overboard where the weight of the chain took it to the bottom. The bags were dry, but we wiped them carefully before stacking them in the stern storage garage beside the dinghy under the cockpit floor.

'How's the traffic situation,' I asked Dave who had his digital radar on as well as scanning all around us.

'Two boats seem to be headed this way from the south,' he

reported, 'and although they were moving quite fast, they've slowed down a lot in the last few minutes. Maybe since they lost sight of the trawler. The same for the one coming from the Redcliffe area and although still moving quickly, he's a long way off.'

I looked aft and saw that the trawler had disappeared, leaving an oily slick forming with a stream of bubbles and the small, pathetic sight of a crippled dinghy bobbing sickeningly in the small swell to mark it's passing. The sight of three heads ducking up and down as they desperately tried to bail water out made me grin.

'They'll be right,' I said, 'One of those possible pickup boats will do the rescue bit, but it'll give us more time to get clear and do the transfer. Time to put the hammer down, Dave.'

He grinned, called out a warning to the girls to hang on and smoothly shoved the twin throttles forward. The engine exhaust note rose through a roar to a frantic bellow, then further up the scale to a shattering howl as 38-tonnes of boat shot forward, absolutely smashing the small swell and wind chop into a seething mass of white foam and spray.

Amanda and Melissa were startled for a few moments, then manic grins spread across their faces as they joined Corrine in howls of delight.

At 60 knots, the ride was remarkably smooth and the run across the Bay to the entrance to Pumicestone Passage, the mostly narrow waterway that makes Bribie a true Island, took just 13 minutes and left any potential pursuers far behind. Nothing short of a full-on race boat was anywhere near as fast as *Seeker*!

I was delighted to spot the unmistakable colour scheme of a large Police launch anchored on the west side of the channel as requested, near a green beacon not far short of the Bribie Bridge. Dave eased our crazy speed as we came into the estuary, until we drifted up sedately up beside the coppers and greeted our previous acquaintances, Sergeant Brian Thomas and Constable Derek Lance, both of the Brisbane Water Police.

They looked at *Seeker* rather suspiciously, until they recognised Amanda, Melissa and myself, Sergeant Brian even throwing a salute and calling me Commander, although I'd asked him not to.

'Are we allowed to ask what this is all about, Sir,' Brian enquired, looking even more confused as the *Dragonfly* seemed to appear out of nowhere and tracked to its homing beacon to smoothly land back on *Seeker's* foredeck.

'Yes, you are, but it will have to wait until we transfer some cargo and you take three of us back to *Firebird* anchored off Cowan.'

The pair of them looked a bit frustrated, but leant a hand transferring the forty bags of powder from Seeker to their cockpit, as Amanda and Melissa got the UAV under cover and dismembered it to stow in it's travel case. 'Does this, ahh...stuff need to be stowed securely, Sir? I'm presuming that I'm not looking at forty bags of icing sugar?' Sergeant Brian asked.

'Nah. She'll be right, don't bother. We'll be tossing it on *Firebird* as soon as you drop us off.'

'With all due respect, Sir, but is that wise? I mean this looks like drugs — heroin or pure cocaine. I've never seen so much in one place before — it's amazing! It needs to be to be locked up securely.'

I stopped shifting the load for a moment to stand in front and look him straight in the eye, 'Sergeant Thomas. You're a good man and I respect that. But on the way back to Cowan, we're going to have a serious talk where I will explain to you what's going on, including the part you've still got to play. At that point you'll have a choice of following my instructions, which could result in promotions for both yourself and Constable Lance, or finding that both of you will be removed from your lovely boat and placed in protective isolation for the duration of this operation. That will have to do you for the moment. Understood?'

I'd never really had the chance to practice being a 'pissed-off Commander', so I'd reverted to my 'severely pissed-off Major' version and let him see a hint of the depth of blackness that lurked like a caged beast behind the normally benign front I put on for most people. He swallowed and said contritely, 'Sorry Sir. It'll be as you say. We're here to help.'

I patted him on his tensed-up back and said reassuringly, 'As you most certainly are, Brian and will continue to be. Now let's finish up and move on. Bad guys are incoming as we speak.'

He looked startled, 'What bad guys, Commander? You didn't say anything about bad guys!'

I gave him an exasperated look, 'Was there a radio call for a boat to respond to an incident over at Cowan a little earlier?'

'Ahh...yes. We couldn't respond as we'd been told to wait here.'

'OK. I was the one who asked that you be tasked to wait here and the incident was that five suspected bikies were involved in a fight with a bunch of fishermen where guns were discharged. They were part of several groups of heavily armed bad guys currently heading this way to try to regain this merchandise, so if you can hold your doubts and questions until I have a chance to talk to you, we really need to finish shifting this shit and get the flock out of here! Now! Then *Seeker* has to get through the passage and head further north.'

'Sorry, Commander. I didn't understand.'

'No, Sergeant, but you soon will, as long as you get your finger out of your bum and move it!'

So in a far better spirit of co-operation, we quickly finished the task of transferring the forty bags of Super MDMA, along with my TAC-14 shotgun and the drone and UAV cases, and bid farewell to Dave and Corrine. I waited until Brian and Lance re-boarded their boat to speak. 'I've just had another idea concerning hiding in plain sight and since I'm still working on it, I'd like you guys to stay well out of sight for now. Even though Tin Can Bay is still our next layover port, I'd like you to stay completely away from it or any other human contact if at all possible. Can you find a small inlet or creek down the southern end of the Strait that will float this great lump of over-powered aluminium and still let you stay out of casual sight?'

They looked puzzled, but Dave answered, 'Sure, Harry. We should be able to find somewhere. I think the western side of the Strait has a lot of small creeks or estuaries and we've got plenty of fuel and food.'

'Good. Keep your freshwater tanks full, if you would. We might need extra if this plan works. I'll call you on your sat-phone when we get close, probably tomorrow afternoon or Sunday.'

'Okay, but you're sounding very mysterious as usual. So I guess we'll find out more when we see you.'

'Yup. That's about it. Remember, low profile — no drag races with the locals. Cheers, guys. Keep having fun and take care.'

I watched fondly as the sleek red boat burbled quietly away north, although I didn't fancy Dave having to thread the ridiculously narrow channels on the inner passage to Caloundra in a 65-foot boat, even if it was water-jet drive with very shallow draft. Instead, I turned to Sergeant Brian and said, 'When you're ready Skipper, we can head for Cowan. Economy cruising speed will be enough. We'll keep an eye out for suspicious boats and characters, but they aren't going to bother this boat, especially as our very obvious red herring is heading the other direction.'

Sergeant Brian looked like he was struggling to come up with either an answer or a question, but wisely decided to keep quiet.

CHAPTER 23

On the run back to Cowan and *Firebird*, I brought Sergeant Brian up to date on the reasons for all the mysterious happenings in his territory and gave him the new bits of my plan. I also called Greg at Southport and issued some strange, but very specific instructions. He and Superintendent Bob Casey were still over the moon about the perfect video they'd recorded, including close-up of bikie faces and the Atlas Dawn crewmen, so only became moderately flustered about my requests and instructions. At least they promised immediate action.

I resumed talking to Sergeant Brian. 'So please understand that this is an on-going operation and any word out of place could sink the whole thing, as well as possibly wipe out an undercover operative or six, including the two Seniors and myself.'

'Yeah. I get that, but why are you going to sit on 200 kilos of this Super MDMA? It really needs to be in the Evidence Locker.'

I looked at him. 'C'mon Brian. Let me tell you something for your ears only — the Southport Locker is already compromised with serious pilfering and has an investigation underway as we speak, so how long do you think 210 kilos of Super MDMA plus two million in cash is going to last there? And with that level of temptation, how long would it last in anybody else's Locker for that matter once the word got around? And believe me, the word would get around so fast the bad guys would know where it was before it even lobbed there!'

He thought for a moment then reluctantly agreed. 'Yeah, fair enough. But how can you maintain security on a boat, for Christ's sake? I mean all that shit's worth millions!'

I grinned, 'Actually, we roughly estimated that because of its unusual and very powerful effects, it could be cut 90% which could mean that one kilo of raw is worth around five million on the street!'

He gaped as the numbers spun around his head, finally coming up with, 'But...but that means that that pile out there in the cockpit could be worth around $1 billion!'

'Yep. That's about right. And toss in the 10 kilos already on my boat and there's a neat $1.05 billion waiting to be cut and distributed on the streets.' While he mulled over those figures, I nodded over at Amanda and Melissa, sitting up in the wheelhouse chatting to Constable Lance. I was too far away to hear what they were saying, but he was blushing almost continuously, which reinforced my belief that my two Senior Constables had been most thoroughly corrupted by my boating lifestyle.

'They're my security guards, plus my cat. Between the four of us, we're in good shape.'

'But you went and left the first shipment of cash and drugs on your boat this morning with nobody guarding it at all! Even that's worth $50 million! With all due respect, Sir, that's surely a bit irresponsible?'

I laughed, 'I'd like to challenge you to try to get aboard and break in to my boat right now, Sergeant, but I don't want you dead! That's what would happen to any intruder who tried to come aboard — especially if I'm not there. There are two bikies in hospital at the moment, one critical, who did try. I was there watching and didn't touch either of them.'

He looked strangely at me. 'I'll have to take your word for that, sir. It all sounds very strange, but I have too much respect for what you've achieved already to be challenging you. So how can we help further?'

'I've told you why we're being chased, but remember that the bikies don't know for sure that we have the money and drugs aboard. And at the moment, they think that a bunch of pirates on a red boat snatched the lot. They just can't find them at the moment, and the strength of our defences on *Firebird* has made them curious. Therefore, they'll keep coming at us, except now we've just upped the ante considerably and we have at least three Brisbane gangs joining the hunt, if only for revenge.'

'I hope you've got a plan to cope with that, Sir. Otherwise I don't think I'd like to be in your position. Those guys play very dirty.'

I nodded, 'Yes, they certainly do. So the plan is to apply as much misdirection as possible and sow confusion to the enemy at every opportunity. It's worked for me before and I'm certain it'll do so again. Now, listen very carefully, I vill zay zis only once, since zis ees your very important part.'

That classic saying from a classic TV series went straight through to the Keeper as far as Sergeant Thomas was concerned although he got that worried look back on his face as my plan and his specific instructions unfolded.

'But Sir, that seems like a very complicated way to achieve your objective!'

I beamed at him, 'Thank you. Yes, it really is and that's exactly the point. Hopefully, the bad guys will think that as well and become increasingly confused looking for ulterior motives under every bush, to mix the odd metaphor or two!'

Brian shook his head, 'You've lost me, but OK, sir. We'll do our part, but forgive me for not really understanding your plan. It seems that you're sticking your neck along with the two Seniors out a long way.'

'I'm afraid so,' I admitted ruefully, 'but under the circumstances I can't come up with anything better. Can you?' I asked hopefully.

He shook his head, 'Not for the moment, except that maybe if certain things were to be leaked to the press, that might add confusion. My sister-in-law is a reporter with the Courier-Mail if that'd help? She's always on my back for tips and insider info.'

I thought a few moments as the powerful big boat droned smoothly on toward the Tangalooma Wrecks, riding in a pronounced bow-up attitude. 'Yes, you're right, that's good, Brian. Give me your mobile number and I'll call you at the right time with a series of anonymous statements to issue. Can you get her to attribute them to 'a highly placed Police Service Official'?'

He was still puzzled, but happy his suggestion was going to be useful. 'No problem sir. Coming from you, it'll be the truth! She loves getting any insider Police information I can feed her.'

Soon after, Constable Lance smoothly swung the 45-foot Police boat around and parked it neatly beside *Firebird*, fenders taking care of the rubbing as our wake caught up with us, bouncing both boats around for a few moments. The sheltered anchorage only had a few boats still at anchor or pulled up on the beach as most seemed to have found other much safer locations to fish for the day.

The excellent relations the Water police have established with the majority of boaties was evident by the number of cheerful waves and calls they received and it was considered quite normal to have them tied up alongside my big cat. We tried to conceal the to and fro of persons with freight as much as possible, leaving all the freight piled up in the saloon while we socialised out in the cockpit for the benefit of onlookers.

We suffered through the exuberant welcome given by Jasper and little Krazy kitten, although this time I didn't have to personally introduce Jasper to the Officers, as he seemed to recognise officialdom in its various forms and behaved himself.

Brian and Derek were more than impressed with Jasper and after seeing his fangs and claws on display, were more than willing to believe that he could readily defend the boat against intruders, although I refrained from discussing my other defence secrets.

Nevertheless, after a very eventful morning, we were very happy to be able to sit and relax while we drank tea and coffee and nibbled on an array of tasty snacks that Amanda whipped up. Brian and Derek seemed to be more comfortable with things, although they both, with some misgivings, kept eyeing off the great mound of plastic bags of white powder stacked up in the saloon as if it wasn't everyday that they saw one billion dollars handled so carelessly.

Finally, with morning tea disposed of, they took their leave, instructions firmly imbedded and expected to both see and hear from us before long.

For our part, I decided to sail quietly back to Myora as part of the post-action unwinding process. There were other parts of that process, but they would have to wait 'till later. As we were anchored at the more open north end of the anchorage and well clear of the main wreck of an old dredger, I left the engines off and raised the main first, letting it flap loose before unfurling the staysail. Sheeting it in hard, it forced the bows around until we were facing west and picking up speed steadily. The acceleration increased as I sheeted the main in then picked up still further as I let the huge screecher unroll off the bow roller furler. With it sheeted in, *Firebird* took off like its sacred mythological name-sake, the Phoenix, with a burnt tail.

While nowhere near as dramatic as opening the throttles on the *Seeker*, doing 20+ knots with only the hiss of passing water becomes its own sort of dramatic and the girls were once again delighted with the sensation, particularly as we only leaned over a few degrees. As there was no immediate urgency to return to Myora, I decided to take the long way home, tracking initially southwest toward Wellington Point, taking advantage of the strong southeast breeze before tacking to head straight for Myora, passing just north of Peel Island and since it was high tide, across the shallows of the Amity Banks to Myora. The only drawback with that route was that I had to pull the deep daggerboards up to avoid ripping them off in the shallow water.

It was worth the extra leeway caused by the lack of daggerboard area in the water, to see and hear the delight of the girls as we flushed many stingrays, a couple of turtles and even spotted a family of three dugong feeding on the sea-grass that now grows in abundance across the shallow banks, allowing this beautiful, but threatened species to slowly start to rebuild its numbers. It was early afternoon by the time we had dropped anchor in the peaceful beauty of the Myora anchorage and the phone rang.

'Hi Greg. How're things going?'

'*Getting there, Harry. We found a carpenter who agreed to do a rush job and they'll be finished by 17:00. The plan is to send it all up there with two Constables in plain clothes in one's personal Ford F-150 to cut down on attention. We have a booking for the 07:00 ferry that gets into Dunwich at 07:50. But there seems to be a problem with access to the water close to where you say you're camped. How about back at the Public Boat ramp at the Little Ship Club? Is that too far to come in a dinghy?*'

'No, not far at all. That sounds great, thanks Greg. I'll be at the boat ramp from 08:00 on. How'd you go at organising ballast?'

He laughed, '*We raided the two local catering stores for bulk bags of cooking salt. Apparently, restaurants use tons of the stuff, so 200 kilos wasn't too big a deal.*

I sent the two Constables home to change first and they thought it was all a hoot getting away from the office for a while. After I swore them to secrecy, I told them we needed to weigh down two makeshift coffins with what looked like drugs, so there are forty bags at five kilos each. They shouldn't be too hard to handle, but I hope your dinghy is up to it.'

'Great. Yeah, the dinghy should handle the load. Are you sure your men can keep their mouths shut for a few days?'

'*I'm sure. But feel free to read the Riot Act yourself. A bit more of that 'I'm an arse-hole Commander' bullshit should do the trick.*'

I laughed. 'You cheeky bugger. But I do owe you and Bob for swinging this so quickly. But how about the Brisbane Water

Police station crew and the whole Central mob. Will everybody play ball?'

'*They're understandably a bit nervous about maybe provoking a head-to-head, but otherwise they're happy to go along with the plan so far. They reckon that at worst, it'll make a good exercise. They'll have your mate Sergeant Thomas and his sidekick with you at 10:00. Is that all correct?*'

'Yep. That's exactly right, thanks mate. But there are just a few more things I'll need and according to the Internet, one is available in Brisbane, so you'll need to get it sent down ASAP so your boys can bring it in the morning. The other items are available at Bunning's locally, so that's easy.'

Greg gave a groan, 'Yeah, righto Harry, what are they?'

He grunted some more when I told him.

'*I don't even want to know what you're going to be doing with this shit, Harry! You get the weirdest ideas sometimes.*'

'I do, but they usually work out. Anyway, if you can get that stuff as well, we'll be good to go and I'll be in touch as things unwind.'

'*Will do. Cheers, Harry.*'

UNDERTAKERS OMC CLUBHOUSE – MOLENDINAR, SOUTH-PORT – FRIDAY AFTERNOON 17:00

'Undertaker.'

'*Gidday, Henry, this is Brad.*'

'Good evening, Mr Edwards. You don't sound your usual chipper self. May I presume that you've received the same news that I have?'

'*Yeah. I just got off the phone to my Lieutenant, Tony. He's in Brisbane Central Police lockup with another of my men and three of yours. I've got my legal guys on it and presume you've done the same, but there are some heavy charges on account of some goose started*' *popping off with a handgun at those bloody fishermen. It turned into a total clusterfuck!'*

'I hesitate to remind you that you claimed that the boat operation was totally under control. It seems that your nautical experts didn't anchor properly, but that's past now. I'm only interested in getting our people out and recovering the merchandise. Once again, we seem to have paid for something we don't have. I feel more drastic steps will have to be taken to recover our goods and safeguard our investments in the future.'

'Yeah, I agree, Henry. And I do apologise for my boy's poor performance, but as you said, that's past. I also heard that some pirates in a red boat grabbed the entire shipment, so the Brisbane crews are howling for blood. This was their first shipment of this new shit as well.'

'Yes, I heard that. I believe that the trawler crew have disappeared as well, so it wasn't only their boat that has sunk!'

'Did you just make a joke, Henry? I'm impressed. But getting back to our situation, do you have anyone on the inside in Brisbane Central?'

'Yes, I do, Mr Edwards. I expect a report sometime this evening or tomorrow. Shall I call you when I have that information?'

'I'd be grateful, thanks Henry. It's no good both of us sending troops all over the place until we know whose heads to start busting.'

'True, Mr Edwards. I believe that there was some concern that the trawler crew might have tried to do a side deal with these pirates who, I might add, haven't been seen or heard of since the grab when they were last seen heading for the Pumicestone Passage, but I have been reliably informed that their very large boat couldn't possibly fit through the narrow passages, so we believe that either they are hiding somewhere in the lower Pumicestone Passage area or have come south into the Bay again.

'Good info, Henry, but if they've come back south, they could be anywhere.'

'That's why I have my men and most of the Brisbane groups searching the entire Moreton Bay area, right up to Caloundra and Mooloolaba, seeing as that's a big boating place, as well as back down here on the Gold Coast.'

'*Good oh, Henry. That should cover things for now. Please call if you need more troops, but I'd like to hear from your Brisbane Central guy before we charge off half-cocked.*'

'Very well, Mr Edwards. I'll call when I have news.'

FIREBIRD - MYORA ANCHORAGE - MORETON BAY - SATURDAY MORNING

Last night, the girls had been still quite wired from the day's events and needed to unwind. Some wine before dinner and a couple of NQ teas afterwards took care of most tensions, but a very athletic romp on my queen bed had resolved the rest. The girls were absolutely delightful to be with as well as in, but were quite different in their own ways. Things had gone so well, that there had been a couple of replays through the night with both girls obviously still feeling like more of the same, and I was delighted to oblige where I could. At one stage, they tried some cautious experimentation with each other and that seemed to work extremely well, judging by their reactions to what was apparently a new experience for both.

The morning started early, for me at least, but I wanted to check that the next piece of the Grand Plan was working before I made the 10-minute trip to Dunwich in the dinghy.

I turned on the TV to the local news and was rewarded with a dramatic report that the Police had seized a massive shipment of a new Super drug that had been dumped overboard from a ship entering Moreton Bay. Overnight raids had arrested three crew-members on the ship for their part in dropping the drugs and charges were being laid against the Captain and the ship owners.

A related story stated that a gun battle between rival gangs had occurred near the drop point in Moreton Bay, with a trawler, suspected of being the drug collection boat, being sunk and it's crew murdered. Two bodies identified as crewmen were found some distance to the west of the scene of the gun battle and appeared to have been attacked by sharks, several of which were sighted in the area.

The other boat in the gun battle had been forced to depart the scene by the timely arrival of a Water Police patrol boat that managed to note the position of the dropped containers of drugs. As the water was shallow on the Salamander Bank where the gunfight had taken place, Police divers were planning to search for and recover the drug containers at first light.

The picture then cut to a live helicopter shot of a cluster of Police boats with black-clad divers in the water, dramatically back-lit by the sun rising over Moreton Island. A graphic artist had added red arrows and sketches of a trawler and another boat to show where the Fatal Gunfight had taken place. I could imagine the cursing of the whole group directed at the idiot who suggested that they stage this whole dramatic search in the dawn chill, although at least they had a sunken trawler to poke and prod at. Naturally, I was that idiot, but it was at least a productive suggestion and potentially far more useful than anybody else had come up with.

And sure enough, a few minutes later, a couple of inflatable, orange salvage buoys popped up over the wreck, live and in full colour in time for the early breakfast viewers to get their dose of daily vicarious thrills. A breathless, pretty but stupid, talking head tried to whip up even more interest by suggesting that there might be more bodies and drugs to be found in the wreckage of the sunken trawler. Somehow, the blonde bimbo managed to restrain herself sufficiently to avoid dragging drug-smuggling submarines or the Colombian Connection into the report.

The Producer then cut back to another roving reporter at Police Headquarters where the Commissioner was giving a press conference, where he announced, amid the usual pile of waffle, that the massive drug shipment that had just been recovered would be transferred from the Water Police Base at Lytton to the Central Police Headquarters at 11:00 that morning under heavy escort.

I mentally rubbed my hands in glee, as this was an important piece of the plan and showed that so far, everyone was co-operating. The girls had dragged their lovely little bare bums out of bed when they heard the TV and were snuggled up against me to get warm.

'So is that what you hoped to achieve?' Amanda asked.

I smiled, beautiful memories of the previous night revived by their presence, 'Absolutely, or even better than I'd hoped. Now all we need is for the delivery and Sergeant Brian with the lustful Constable Derek to be on time, but I'd better go get the props.'

I grinned at them again, 'As much as I love seeing you both like that, perhaps you'd better dress for our visitors or we'll never get rid of them.' They giggled and waggled their bums at me before disappearing below to clean up and dress.

Shortly before 08:00, I was standing beside the dinghy pulled up on the rough and rocky boat ramp beside the charming and hospitable Little Ship Club in the quaintly named Yabby Street in Dunwich. Ten minutes later, a rumbling, red F-150, with wide, gleaming alloy wheels turned in through the car park and stopped at the top of the ramp. Two tall, lean young men hopped out and greeted me.

'Commander Stevens? I'm Constable Story and this is Constable Jakes and we're very pleased to meet you.'

I shook hands, already impressed with their professional attitude, even though both were in basic civilian casual clothing. 'Thanks for bringing all that stuff, fellas' I said, 'was there any trouble fitting it all in and getting here?'

'Oh, no sir. Plenty of room in the Ford, but it's going to be a bit of a squeeze for you in the dinghy going back if you take it all at once.'

We'd walked up to the truck and immediately saw what they meant, since two large pine crates sat side-by-side, looking very much like slightly short, but wide coffins. A pile of heavy plastic bags sat in the load bed beside them, all neatly heat-sealed. The crates looked well made and thankfully had decent rope handles at each end. A 20-litre plastic drum, a large, colourful cardboard box and a smaller plain box completed the load.

'Good work. There is a lot of stuff. Did you two do the bagging? They look just like the originals!'

Constable Story gave me a curious look as he replied, 'Yes, sir. We borrowed the sealing machine and it all worked a treat after we had some practice.'

'Well, you both done an excellent job. I won't forget this. Now. You're right about fitting it all in the dinghy. Two trips are definitely in order' I said to them, 'How long before the ferry takes you back?'

'Oh, plenty of time, sir. We don't leave until 11:00.'

That confirmed the two-load decision. 'OK. We'll split the load as best we can per trip if you'll help load this end.'

'No problem, Commander. One of us could come with you to help unload at the other end if that would help?'

'No, thanks. I've got crew there and we need to keep the dinghy loads as light as we can.'

'Okey doke,' Constable Story agreed cheerfully, his easy manner making me wish I could use them in the operation somehow, but I couldn't think of anything they could help with for now, but I'd remember these two. We quickly had the dinghy loaded, the first wood box taking up most space. We put the bags and some other stuff inside it for ease of storage, but they would make the box too hard to get onto *Firebird,* so would have to come out first.

I advised them to move their truck to clear the ramp and that I'd be about 30 minutes.

'No problem, sir. We might just go grab something to eat at the store back down the street, it that's OK. We'll be back in time.'

I smiled, 'That's fine thanks, fellas. Enjoy your breakfast.'

They sketched a salute, jumped into the F-150 and burbled away as I launched my rather overloaded dinghy under the curious eyes of a couple of early fishermen and headed to Myora. It was an uneventful trip, and although we had to be very careful unloading, we soon got the crate emptied of half of my extensive shopping list into the cockpit and the bags of 'drugs' stacked close by.

The Constables were waiting when I got back and had me loaded in a couple of minutes. I shook their hands and thanked them for a very good job.

'A pleasure, Sir. We've heard that interesting things seem to happen around you, so if you need any more assistance, please ask for us. If I may add, we've been through the SERT course and qualified Expert on all hand and long guns in the Service. So far, there hasn't been any chance to put that training to good use, so we'd be delighted to get involved in whatever it is that's going on.'

I seized on that opening. 'I appreciate that, Constable Story, but I must also caution you that this is an active undercover operation with a number of Service personnel at serious risk if information is leaked inadvertently. Even discussing the work you've done and the items you've brought here today is forbidden and while I don't want to come the heavy, you can't discuss anything to anybody other than Superintendent Casey and Inspector James.'

They didn't take offence, but smiled their easy, confident smiles. 'Understand completely and there's no problem with that, sir. Inspector James already threatened us with permanent assignment to Archive Filing Duties in Outer Woop Woop if we even ask too many questions let alone talk, so we have a story made up that's far enough away from the truth to be safe. We just wish we could do more.'

'Thanks, fellas. I appreciate that and if there is a chance to use your talents, I'll call.'

'That'll do, thank you Sir. Good luck and take care.'

CHAPTER 24

'Undertaker.'

'*Jeeze, Henry. Don't you ever sleep? Anyway, this is Brad.*'

'Yes, of course, Mr Edwards. I dare say that you're calling about the revelations on the idiot box regarding the loss of our merchandise?'

'*Yeah, that's right. You're good, Henry. I'll give you that.*'

'Damned with faint praise indeed. Thank you, Mr Edwards. Allow me to pre-empt your questions with a statement. Yes, I have already dispatched most of my troops to assist our brothers in Brisbane who are putting together a plan to regain the entire shipment.'

'*Good one, Henry. You're being very pro-active today. But I'm not happy with the way the coppers suddenly ended up with the merchandise, when it was the pirates that grabbed it and shot up the pick up trawler. Does that smell a bit to you?*'

'No, it doesn't, Mr Edwards and I find it interesting that it does to you. As that Police press release explained, a Police boat that was already in the area sorting out an 'altercation between two boat-loads of fishermen where firearms were discharged', came up on the pirate boat as it was starting to get the containers aboard and they had to dump them and run. Apparently it was too fast for the coppers to catch it, so they stayed with the sinking trawler and marked where the containers had sunk. They didn't know about the bodies until later.

It's a pity they didn't survive to say exactly what had happened, but it seems to me that if our boat crew hadn't made such a mess of anchoring, and then getting into a fight with those fishermen, there wouldn't have *been* a Police boat hanging around in the first place.

Although there still would have been those bloody pirates or whatever they are. And how did they know the pick-up details?'

'I'd say Henry, that there were too many persons in the loop on this one. How many of the other Clubs were to share in this shipment? To me, it was inevitable that the details had to leak, or maybe one of the other Clubs decided to get greedy and become pirates. Anyway, I'll take that at face value for now so long as we are making a serious attempt to get the stuff back. Do you know what their plan is yet?'

'Yes, or I should say, most of it. It was very kind of the Police Commissioner to shoot off his mouth about the transfer of the merchandise. I suppose that there will be some sort of ambush involved and knowing the inventive ways of the planning committee, I expect not only success, but a very embarrassed Police Commissioner showing up on TV later today.'

'That sounds impressive Henry, but surely they will be expecting something like this?'

'Of course they will! But I have faith in our Brisbane brothers to come up with something unexpected...Just a minute please, Mr Edwards. I have a call coming in, please hold a moment...'

'I apologise for the delay, Mr Edwards. I wanted to get the latest information to pass on since you are a major stakeholder in this enterprise. The plan is this: the Police will make a big show of transporting the merchandise in a commercial armoured vehicle from the Water Police base to State headquarters. The armoured vehicle will be escorted by an impressive number of Police cars and bikes and a helicopter will track the convoy overhead. However, the armoured vehicle will be empty, as the merchandise will actually be taken by water in a single, un-escorted fast RIB to the North Quay Public Ferry terminal that will be temporarily closed for the transfer. The merchandise is contained in two wooden crates that, very appropriately, look like small coffins and will be loaded into a marked Hyundai iLoad van, then driven the short distance to Police headquarters in Roma Street. The Brothers will take control of the van in advance and wait for the arrival of the cargo. As the Police wish this part of the operation to be as unobtrusive as possible, there will only be a small reception squad, and they will be overcome with a display of overwhelming force with the intention of preventing any firearm discharge in such a public place, even though the area is beneath the expressways and is not heavily trafficked except at peak times.'

'*Bloody hell, Henry. That's some plan, but I guess that it could work if the coppers don't have too many men at the ferry terminal.*'

'That is the expectation Mr Edwards. As I just said, the Police don't wish to attract extra attention, so if forces are as light as we are informed, the take-down should be relatively uneventful.'

'*If they're playing around with helicopters, why wouldn't they just fly the stuff in?*'

'Simply because there's no helipad close by and the roof of their HQ isn't stressed for the load. The reasoning is that, if they have to take it via the streets anyway, they might as well leave the helicopter out of the equation since those things always attract a lot of attention.'

'*OK. Have you got your boys back from Brisbane yet? My two just arrived, but haven't anything new to report.*'

'Yes, they have and likewise, there is no further news since they were effectively sidelined because of that stupid altercation with the fishermen.'

'*Well, thank you Henry for all that information. If there is something else you require from me, please call.*'

'I'll do that, Mr Edwards. Watch the news unfold and a good day for now.'

FIREBIRD – MYORA ANCHORAGE – MORETON BAY – SATURDAY MORNING

It was just after 09:00 that the now-familiar shape of Sergeant Thomas's Police boat turned into the small anchorage, dropping off the plane as the water shoaled. Thankfully, we were still alone without any close-by curious eyes.

'Morning, sir and to you, Senior's,' Sergeant Brian greeted as he expertly placed the 45-footer alongside *Firebird* with scarcely a bump.

'Morning Brian. Hi Derek,' I responded. 'Coffee's ready, but we need to get you loaded and back to base by 10:00.'

'Oh, that's all doable, sir. We can make thirty knots and with the high tide, can cut the banks north of Peel for a quick run straight to base. It'll only take 30-minutes to get back and won't look out of the ordinary, so as soon as we're loaded, a coffee would be great.'

They were surprised by the cargo we had ready, but my warnings yesterday were enough to keep the questions at bay, although I threw them a bit of a bone as we wrestled the crates over to their spacious cockpit.

'What you're looking at is a deception and misdirection package all-in-one,' I said cryptically, 'But you will understand more later if the plan unfolds as I hope. It's still important that this part stays secret between us, so what we'll do is load these bags of powder into the crates with twenty bags per crate then screw the lids down.

No one should ask what's in them but if they do, you know nothing! You must be very clear about that. OK?'

They both nodded seriously. 'Yes, sir. Our Superintendent is busting to know the full story, but we've already told him that we can't say anything.'

'Good. Everything will be explained or become obvious in due course. One last thing — these two crates are not to be opened for any reason and there will be steel banding straps put around them at your base. You'll notice that the crates have been lined with plywood to stop inquisitive fingers trying to find out what's inside.'

Sergeant Brian nodded, 'Understand, sir. But just between

us, may I hazard a guess and say that those bags that look very much like the ones we carted yesterday, aren't the same ones?'

I smiled grimly, 'True, Brian. But if you voice that opinion out loud, your career will come to an immediate screeching halt. I don't approve of threats, but this is deadly serious, as you'll hear later today if my judgement is correct. Just stay with your boat for the rest of the day and get away from base on patrol again, if possible.'

I saw in his eyes that he didn't like the threat, but I had to make the point and the Sergeant's making idle speculation would be very unhealthy for all concerned. When the remainder of my words sank in, he relaxed a little. 'I guess that's a good tip, if ever I heard one!'

'Count on it!' As I tightened the last screw in place, I said in a more friendly tone. 'C'mon. The ladies have coffee brewed and I can see that Derek is keen to go chat up Melissa again.'

Derek blushed, but didn't mind hopping back to *Firebird*, although I made sure their coffee break wasn't too prolonged and managed to get them moving by 09:20.

As the drug bust, the firefight, the sinking of the trawler and the deaths of the crew had been major news items all morning, the transfer of the drugs was a terrific piece of extra drama that was mercilessly flogged to death by all the TV news channels. At 11:00 sharp, a live picture came in from a TV helicopter with the usual breathless talking head wearing a headset this time, spruiking about the impressive escort being assembled into a convoy around the armoured car.

Although it was briefly and accidently in camera shot, no notice was paid to a 25-foot Police RIB that pulled away alone and unescorted from the jetty and accelerated away upstream at high speed, just two Constables aboard for the 12.5 nautical mile journey. Two 250-horsepower Suzuki outboards easily pushed the RIB along at a steady 35 knots, allowing them to complete their twisting journey in just over twenty minutes.

NORTH QUAY FERRY TERMINAL

At about that time, a white Hyundai iLoad van with Police badges on the doors pulled up in the Loading Zone near the North Quay Terminal entrance. The driver sighed, undid his seatbelt and tried to get comfortable with the sundry bits of required hardware strapped around his waist and upper torso digging into his anatomy. His companion, a rather more corpulent young man dug in his bag for a sandwich and pulled out a ham and cheese with creamed raw garlic dressing.

'Oh, no. No more of that bloody garlic, please!' He gasped as waves of the pungent mash washed across his sensitive nose.

'Yummo! It's really good for you. I mean look at me. No coughs or colds for four years so it must be working.'

'Yeah, maybe it is, but your social life has gone down the tubes. Nobody's brave enough to go out with you.'

His partner considered a moment, 'I must admit that there's a bit of a girl drought on at the moment, but that'll turn around, just you wait and see.'

'I'll be a hundred and ten before you get a girl into bed,' The driver scoffed, then sparked up and said, 'But speak of the dear little devil's, look! There are two nice girls walking past, why don't you get out and look at them and spare my nose for a few minutes.'

'Oh, all right. Maybe I will just stretch my legs a moment.'

He stood by the front of the van, munching his smelly sandwich, idly watching the girls who also had the attention of the driver. Therefore, both failed to notice the six very large men who quietly moved up both sides of the van from the rear. While one slid smoothly into the passenger seat via the open door, three more surrounded the garlic-muncher, while another pulled open the driver's door and pulled the Constable out by clamping hold of both wrists to forestall any attempt to reach for his gun.

'Come along, sonny and don't try to be a hero,' the driver's captor growled, guiding the startled Officer toward the rear of the van. The passenger suffered the same treatment and with the six large men glaring at them, they were relieved of their utility belts, vests and radios. A few strips of gaffer tape secured their wrists, ankles and mouths then they were pushed unceremoniously into the back of the van.

'Just stay quiet thanks boys, and no harm will be done to anybody,' the squad leader growled softly. The Senior Constable driver had time to see the six men pulling on dark blue official-looking dustcoats, before the rear doors closed.

Two men climbed into the front seats of the van, the other four fading back into the shadows cast by the expressway overpass above. They didn't have long to get settled, however, before a two-tone whistle sounded as the Police RIB pulled up to the Terminal jetty. An older, distinguished-looking man in a smart dark grey suit joined four of the big men before they all walked smartly down the deserted ferry ramps to meet the boat.

'Good morning Constables,' the suit-clad man called, flashing his ID card in a flip case.

'Superintendent Peters. I'm to receive the shipment. You've had no trouble, I hope?'

The boat driver looked reassured by the civilised tone of the senior man and grateful for the presence of the four large officers in blue dustcoats so that he and his mate wouldn't have to lug the crates by themselves.

'No sir, no trouble at all. A very pleasant run this lovely morning, in fact.'

The Superintendent beamed at them, 'Excellent! You've made really good time. These officers will carry the crates up to the van if you'll just help lift them up onto the wharf. You're then released to return to Base.'

'Yes, sir. That'll be fine. There seems to be a lot happening this morning. The radio's going crazy.'

The Superintendent chuckled as the Constables heaved the second crate up onto the wharf for two of the dust-coated men to pick up, clearly relieved to be able to stay with the boat and not do any more lifting work.

'Yes, there is a lot happening, so we'd better keep moving. Thanks for your good work, Constables.'

'Thank you sir for helping with the lifting. We'll be off then. Cheers.'

With that, the Senior Constable driver fired up the big Suzuki's again and with the bow rope released, swung back out into the river and headed downstream at a more subdued pace.

Back at the van, the two trussed Constables were pulled out of the van, had their ankles freed, then with many rude comments about the passenger's breath, were led over to an old Falcon sedan parked down the road a short distance. Both were pushed into the front seats, their caps, utility belts and vests carefully stowed in front of their seats.

'There we are, boys,' the only one of the big men to speak said to them. 'That was painless, although I imagine it's all rather embarrassing. Still, it's better than having someone hurt. This car isn't ours by the way and if someone doesn't release you soon, we'll be calling in to let your mates know where you are, so you won't have to suffer being tied up for long. I do apologise for the inconvenience and thank you for your co-operation.'

A savage glare and muffled grunting was the only response, as he laughed, clapped the driver on the shoulder. 'Ta-ta fellas. Do try to hold your bladders while you wait. That really would be the final embarrassment, now wouldn't it?'

The men left, two in the van while the other four discarded their blue dustcoats and walked up the street, climbing into a nondescript brown Commodore once they were out of sight of the two stranded Constables.

It was just as well that there was plenty of traffic noise from the expressway that no one saw or heard a small, mottled grey, sort-of aircraft-shape that moved around, at times quite close-in, while trying to get the best angle for its cameras to record the action.

FIREBIRD – MYORA ANCHORAGE – MORETON BAY – FRIDAY MORNING

I kissed Amanda and hugged Melissa.

'Well done both of you. Perfectly executed operation. No one hurt — goods in the correct hands and lots of mystery with more to come. Bring *Dragonfly* home, please Captain.'

I dialled a well-used number.

'How's that, Greg?'

'Fantastic, Harry. Bob and I are over the moon with the video we collected and we have some officers on the way to release the two at the Terminal as we speak, although their boss won't be too happy with their performance!'

'Tell their boss from me that they did exactly what they should have. We didn't want a firefight down there on the edge of the City, there was too much chance of collateral damage.'

'Yeah, righto, I'll do that. For your information, the main convoy is just approaching the south side of the river on the Expressway, so they should finish the decoy operation shortly.'

'Great work, Greg. That's all worked very well. Now we just have to wait to see what the gangs make of their find and what they do about it.'

'Yeah, righto Harry. What's your next move?'

'We're going to bug out now before the bad guys start trying to find what's going on and who's jerking who around. I'd rather be out of sight while that's happening 'cause I reckon there'll be some shit flying around. I'm hoping that these characters will start to blame each other and that you good guys can collect a heap of them when they try to take each other out.'

'Yeah, that's a plan all right. I suppose that you're going to hang out with those highly visible mates of yours from down south?'

'Yes but keep that quiet. I have a plan to reduce that risk, but we'll see how that works out. I'll be in touch, otherwise call if needed. Cheers, mate.'

ZOMBIE-EATERS OMC – WEST OF SOUTHPORT – FRIDAY MIDDAY

'Gidday Henry. How's it all going?'

'And a very good day to you, too, Mr Edwards, although I have very unsettling news.'

'Uh, oh. I just knew something was wrong! What's happened?'

'Our brothers anticipated a false transfer of the merchandise and executed a perfect intercept of the delivery. The trouble is that the merchandise is not what we paid for. It consisted of 200 kilos of cooking salt, bagged the same as the Manufacturer would.'

'Oh, shit, Henry! So who's having a bit of a lend of us? The manufacturer, the pick up crew on the trawler, the pirates, the 'Brothers' or the coppers?'

'An excellent question, Mr Edwards, and one that is being debated in numerous Clubs across SE Queensland right now. At the moment, everybody is under suspicion and all contact or communication with each other is suspended, except at executive level, like you and me.'

'I agree, Henry. A number of nasty possibilities pop into my mind and I don't like any of them. I still say it was a bit too convenient that the trawler crew were killed. And those so-called pirates sound very suss. They would have to have very secret information to pull that one off the way they did.'

'You make some sense Mr Edwards and I tend to agree with you. It is always possible that a leak has occurred from one of the other groups involved in this shipment. I believe that six or seven Clubs as well as ours put up money for this purchase.'

'OK. So that means there are way too many possible leaks, given that at least two of each Club Executive are privy to the finer details of the delivery. I suggest that we do some investigating by ourselves. Are we together on this one, Henry?'

There was a sigh over the phone. 'Yes, Mr Edwards. We shall stick together on this, but we must both tell our members that they are to only trust members of our two Clubs. It's a terrible thing that we have such division in the Clubs at a time like this. Being on the verge of such a lucrative deal is very bad timing.'

'Yeah, sure Henry. But isn't it a bit coincidental that just as we, the newcomers to direct dealing, ante-up for our first shipment, the whole thing goes sour? I regret to say that I have deep suspicions of our 'Brothers' to our north.'

'Understand. I agree that we pool our investigative assets, Mr Edwards and report frequently, if that suits you?'

'No problem, Henry. I'm with you on this.'

CHAPTER 25

So we sailed from Myora and headed north and I told the girls that we'd stop at Noosa Heads for the night.

'It's a bit too far to make it to the Tin Can Bay area by dark and I don't want to run the bar at night, so we'll do it the easy way and rest comfortably overnight.'

'Ooh! That'll be fun,' Melissa said with a cheeky grin, 'will it be as comfortable as last night?'

I grinned back, 'I don't see why not. What do you think Senior Burke?'

Amanda smiled, 'It was rather nice. I've not done stuff like that before and wouldn't mind trying it again. I take it that you didn't mind, Harry?'

'Of course not! Its all just good fun and I have my share of it as well, don't forget.'

'Oh there's no way I'll forget about you having your fun!' She laughed and gave me a very fond look, 'but tonight we must have a couple of towels with us. You do make a lovely mess.'

We scooted on through the afternoon with the brisk south-east breeze broad on our starboard quarter. Having the breeze behind us meant that there was very little spray being tossed around and with the warm sun, the girls were tempted to strip down and sunbake on the trampolines. With only a low swell, I relaxed my rule about wearing lifejackets on deck, provided they hung on carefully when moving around.

Our course took us right past the scene of the hi-jacking and the trawler sinking, of which there was no sign now apart from a lone orange buoy on the Salamander Bank. We had to dodge a few freighters and cruise ships entering and leaving port, the crews and passengers giving hearty cheers at my naked crew who were so relaxed they didn't bother to cover up, just cheerfully waved back to each passing ship.

It didn't take long to clear the shipping lanes and at a steady 15 knots, we fled the scene of the latest marine drama, all the spoils of war safely tucked below, although because of the sheer mass of drugs, I'd had to stow the bags of powder in all sorts of odd places to maintain the correct boat trim.

We stayed a couple of miles offshore the Sunshine Coast, even though we shouldn't be on anybody's radar this far up, but I was being careful for once and glad I'd told Dave to do the same. It was going on 17:00 when we rounded Noosa Headland into Laguna Bay and lined up for the entrance to the Noosa River. The bar crossing was quite easy. Although there was a fair swell running, the high tide meant that there were no serious breakers to contend with. For safety, I still came in under power, having stowed all sail some distance out. The river was quite shallow in some spots, but with dagger boards raised we had no problems following the twisting channel.

After consulting the local port guide and a satellite map, I decided to bear around to the left once into the estuary and anchor in Woods Bay. There were a lot of other boats already there, but we found a clear spot to settle for the night.

'This looks a pretty spot, Harry,' Melissa commented, 'I've never seen Noosa from the water before.'

'I checked the local map and from here, it's only a short run in the dinghy to Hastings Street with lots of lovely wine bars and restaurants, so I thought we might have a run ashore tonight.'

That drew a very enthusiastic response from the crew, so after securing the boat, we cleaned up, changed, told Jasper and Krazy to mind the store, then headed ashore. I found a spot to tie up the dinghy beside the Ferry Wharf and we wandered up past the Sofitel resort to the famous Hastings Street.

It was just as well that there was no Water Police breathalyser that night, as we sampled several bars before the girls demanded food. We didn't have to search far for places to eat, but when I suggested that we try my world-famous Wandering Eating Adventure, the girls enthusiastically agreed.

They were quite pissed from all the cocktails they'd been sampling, and I had trouble stopping them giggling, but then as part of the eating plan, we stopped at the first place in the fabulous and long, non-stop cafe/bar/restaurant area that is Hastings Street, where we had an entree of whatever took our fancy. After finishing that and the accompanying drinks, we moved on to the next place where we repeated the process — then again and again until we were full of both food and lovely booze, as we'd become quite attached to rum cocktails earlier on.

As it was still only 21:00, the girls didn't want to go back to the boat yet, so we just wandered, taking in the sights that consisted mainly of other totally pissed tourists doing exactly the same and having a great time doing it. The girls attracted a good deal of attention with several brave young men suggesting that they could do better for themselves if they dumped 'Grandpa' and went with them for 'a really good time'.

In most cases their fits of giggles drove the wannabe studs away, but one very persistent young buck with a skin-full of piss kept pestering Melissa who looked a lot younger than Amanda tonight for some reason, probably to do with the super-tight slashed shorts and the tight, brief top she was almost wearing.

Finally, after politely telling him that her needs were very well served by 'Grandpa' she turned into his latest advance and grabbed him by the front of his too-tight shirt with one hand and grabbed his nuts firmly with the other. With the drunken goose effectively immobilised, she hissed, 'Back off, cockhead or I'll rip your nuts off an' stuff 'em down your throat! Go ahead and make my night!'

We didn't see him again that night.

Finally, after several nightcaps and some funny exchanges with other pissed patrons, we wobbled back to the dinghy and managed to fall aboard it instead of into the wet stuff. It only took me three tries to get the outboard functioning, and the brief excursion upriver instead of down I passed off as just a sightseeing detour. We finally found *Firebird* after almost boarding several other similar looking big cats in the dark, to be greeted very enthusiastically by Jasper and Krazy kitten demanding food, even though they'd been fed before we left.

I managed to retract the dinghy into its parking space under the daybed before I went below to wash up and join the ladies who I'd thought were winding down. But I found that they were still very excited from the evening's good times and were ready to see if last night's fun and games could be repeated.

Apparently, we discovered, good times can be re-created!

FIREBIRD – WOOD'S BAY – NOOSA HEADS – SATURDAY

Accordingly, we were very slow getting up next morning, and any thoughts of actually going anywhere that day were quickly forgotten. With a startling burst of good sense, I proclaimed, 'I think we'll stay here for the day.'

That brought a subdued round of cheers from the crew who were in the process of raising the blood pressure of all the males in easy sight of us in what was a crowded anchorage, by wandering around the decks quite unconcernedly naked, before sprawling on the trampolines to soak up some more Vitamin D.

That set the tone for the day, although some couples from neighbouring boats dropped by to say 'Hi' and for the men to perve on the girls who pulled just their panties on to socialise with the visitors. That behaviour reinforced our cover very nicely.

After the first bunch left, I roused myself sufficiently to call Dave and Corrine to see where they were.

'*Hi Harry. How are you all and where are you?*'

'We're at Noosa at the moment, recovering from a heavy night on Hastings Street, so won't be with you until tomorrow. It's only about 45 nautical miles, so if the wind holds, we should be there late morning. Did you find somewhere good to hide?'

'*We're well up Kauri Creek, which is the inlet almost opposite Wide Bay Bar, just below Tinnanbar. We've been able to get quite some way up the creek and are about 500 metres further up from the junction with the very aptly named Mosquito Creek! You'll see it on your chart. There's very little civilisation in the area — just a house near the mouth and a few tinnies fishing, but nobody seems to come this far up or at least we haven't seen anyone yet. It's interesting country with some mangroves and other scrub, but the bottom and banks are all sand, not mud!*'

'That sounds a great spot. We'll come straight there tomorrow, then we've got some work to do before we can visit the delights of Tin Can Bay Township.'

'*I hope the work won't take too long. The mozzies are fierce at dawn and dusk, but there's hardly any through the day, thank goodness.*'

I chuckled, 'That'll be fine. Our work will be through the day so we can be buttoned up behind the fly screens well before dusk. And my crew doesn't like to rise at dawn if they can help it.'

'*Goodo Harry. We'll see you tomorrow. Take care. Cheers*'

The rest of the day wandered along at the same pace as it had started, with a few more happy boaties stopping in on their rounds of the anchorage to be alcoholically sociable. To be fair, they all invited us back to their boats as well, but we pleaded a heavy previous night and stayed put. Happy hour saw more roaming packs of boozing boaties on the prowl and having the biggest cockpit, we ended up with fifteen or so in the cockpit at one stage and as they'd brought their own booze, they weren't in a hurry to leave until it was all consumed. Amanda and Melissa whipped up some finger foods and served them while still just in their flimsy lace panties, much to the delight of the men in the group, although I did notice a couple of the wives casting carefully calculating looks at them.

The crowd of visitors slowly decreased until we were left with just three, two guys and a woman, the three of them well tanned and attractive. With all the chatter and press of bodies through the evening, I'd forgotten their names, but they were very pleasant company so I whipped up a batch of NQ teas, that combined with all the alcohol we'd already consumed made everyone very pissy.

Sitting around the cockpit table, we discovered that our new friends were two surgeons, Roger and Peter and their favourite theatre nurse, Erin. The inhibition-dissolving effect of the NQ teas caused Erin to disclose that the three of them took two weeks holiday several times a year to hang out together on Peter's boat, a 45-foot catamaran. Erin started telling me how wonderful it was for her to have the attention of two such virile men all the time and how busy they kept her.

Following another round of fortified tea, Roger suggested they all were overdressed compared to my crew and promptly stripped down to brief jocks. The other two followed, Erin revealing a luscious, well-rounded body that was reasonably distracting, particularly the way she enjoyed displaying it. The men were well-toned and appeared quite excited by either their companion or by my crew's lack of clothing.

It was Peter who suggested that a supper of scones, jam and cream would top the evening off very nicely, so when Amanda and Melissa went inside to the galley to start proceedings, he followed along to 'supervise'.

I tried to keep an ear open as by now the cockpit lights were dimmed, as was the galley lighting. Erin had launched into a slightly slurred, but highly graphic tale of their more memorable romps on board their boat, but the predominant sound from the galley was the buzz of the hand-held whishing machine and lots of feminine giggles.

After a while, Amanda appeared with a plate of toast with jam on top and a dish of whipped cream. She was very giggly, half-pissed and sported smears of whipped cream and jam all over her, boobs and belly. There was even some in her hair, and one large dollop of cream that clung tenaciously to its perch, obscured one nipple. The other nipple looked remarkably clean, given the state of the rest of her upper body.

I laughed at her appearance and asked, 'What happened to the scones?'

'Oh, we sort of got involved with the cream and jam first and Peter thought that he should test it out, but that it would taste better if he licked it off us. I dunno about the taste, but it surely felt nice being removed!'

I didn't doubt that the removal process would feel nice, especially where some of the smears were headed, so I followed her back inside, leaving Erin to continue her blow-by-blow discussion with Roger. In the galley, Melissa was still giggling, but had lost her panties and was even more covered in cream than Amanda.

Or rather she had plenty of smears where the cream had been, which told the tale that Peter's aim had been well south of her boobs and nipples. That respected gentleman had also lost his jockey briefs and was in the process of applying cream to the throbbing tip of his very prominent erection. He made it very clear that his intention was to use his applicator to apply the cream to Melissa in her most delightfully sensitive spot, but she was having none of that and with a giggle, dodged away from his first drunken lunge that made him spear painfully into the vertical gap between the fridge and freezer.

The pain of that encounter was quite sufficient to cause an instant deflation and an end to Melissa's concerns about impalement, accidental or otherwise. It wasn't long after Erin had administered first aid along with a stern lecture about keeping his pants on in future that they thanked us and departed.

After that bit of excitement it ended up being a relatively quiet night, especially after we had worked off our arousal, and we slept very peacefully.

FIREBIRD - WOOD'S BAY - NOOSA HEADS - SUNDAY

Next morning dawned clear and warm with the south wind forecast to blow again, so we didn't rush getting underway, preferring to wait for the breeze. I decided over breakfast that we could usefully fill in some time by re-fuelling. Although the Yanmar 80 horsepower diesels were very economical, we'd had a lot of motoring in calm conditions and I get nervous heading into unknown territory without full tanks.

Once we up-anchored, we threaded our way through the mooring calling out to our many new friends who were staying for the duration of the holidays. A check of the river chart showed that the refuelling facility, Cormorant Marine Fuels, was just few kilometres upstream. A quick call told me that the dock was empty at the moment and they'd be very happy to fill us up.

The facilities at Cormorant were clean and modern with friendly, obliging staff. While the tanks slowly filled, the girls wandered up to the shop to get some fishing bait to supplement the lures they'd been using and came back with a selection of souvenir T-shirts for each of us, along with some fresh bread, milk & magnum ice-creams. By the time the tanks were full and paid for, the breeze had picked up nicely, so after reviewing the river chart again and noting the breeze was still blowing off the shore, I decided to sail out.

It was pure showing off, I guess, but I reasoned with myself that it kept my sailing skills sharp to have to negotiate a winding series of shallow channels to reach the bar under sail alone.

So with the Cormorant crew watching with some trepidation, I unfurled the staysail, had the girls cast off the bow and stern mooring lines then sheeted the staysail in, letting the southeast breeze take us smoothly and quietly away from the pontoon. As soon as we picked up steerageway, I jibed back downriver and let the boom-furler mainsail haul the huge mass of fabric up the 73-foot high carbon fibre mast. With that sheeted home, we accelerated smartly and were soon threading the channels leading to the bar. There were only a few guys fishing in tinnies, or heading for the bar as I tried to keep us in the deepest part of the channel. The girls helped by staying ready to lift or lower the dagger boards if it became too shallow.

The bar crossing went smoothly and the breeze picked up as we cleared the land. We stayed fairly close inshore for the short run north and had a late morning tea cum lunch on the way. 12:30 saw us crossing the Wide Bay bar on an easy swell under full sail and I was able to lay a course direct for the wide mouth of Kauri Creek that only had a narrow navigable channel.

Well before getting too close to Kauri Creek, I stowed all sail and fired up the engines to poke carefully into the estuary that narrowed very quickly. There were mangroves lining the shore and a lot of mud banks mixed in with sandbanks. But intriguingly, they soon gave way to crystal-clear water over fine white sand the further up Kauri Creek we poked. We passed two tinnies with a couple of guys in each and they waved cheerfully, calling out that whiting and flathead were biting well.

Fortunately, while the channels were narrow, there was just enough water depth to let us motor quietly through, although the props stirred the sandy bottom quite often. It wasn't the sort of place where I'd like to try to pass another cat our size. Jasper and his little Krazy kitten were having a wonderful time up in the bows looking at the shallow bottom sliding past, with the occasional flurry of a stingray or big flathead taking off out of concealment in the sand.

Finally, we carefully eased around the outside of a left hand bend to see a small creek coming in on the right, while ahead of us, about 500 metres up from the small creek mouth, lay the long, sleek red hull of *Seeker*, Dave and Corrine waving from the bow.

They had anchored at the mouth of another tiny creek entering from the west, but there was still plenty of room for us, although the water looked to be only waist deep.

I eased up alongside them, tied up and cut engines, before we enjoyed an affectionate reunion, even though it'd only been a few days.

Over an early afternoon tea, we brought them up to date on all the latest happenings and plans. Finally, Corrine rounded on me and demanded, 'What's this work we've got to do that involved us hiding out up this overgrown storm drain in Mosquito Central?'

I waved her objections down and said, 'As I said earlier, there seem to be too many stories being passed around about a red pirate boat, so I thought that we might have a colour change.'

She and Dave just stared at me for a few moments, 'What? You want to repaint *Seeker?*' Dave exclaimed, 'No way, and even if we wanted to, we'd need a large boatyard slip and a ton of equipment.'

I smiled, 'Hang on a moment and let me explain. But read this first.' I ducked into the saloon and retrieved a brochure off the chart table, flicking it into his lap.

'Easy Skin?' He read, a frown furrowing his forehead, 'what the bloody hell's Easy Skin?'

'Read on, brother,' I urged, 'it's the prefect solution for pirate boats! And it's DIY!'

He read on then passed the coloured brochure to Corrine.

'Well, I must admit that sounds like it could just work. But what are we doing here? We still need a boatyard!'

I grinned, 'Uncle Harry thinks of everything. We can do it right here, 'cause I've got all the gear, courtesy of Greg James. The stuff's quick drying, and once dry is even water-blaster proof. You have to lift one edge and peel it off. It's good for years if you want to leave it that long. The only drawback is that it's only in matt colours and I've already chosen a tasteful shade of dark blue for you.'

Dave and Corrine exchanged looks, shrugged and said, 'Sounds good, Harry. We actually were a bit concerned about our very high visual profile, but short of a boatyard job, we didn't know what to do about it, so this seems ideal.'

CHAPTER 26

The weather was settled and we had all the equipment, but the crew were slow to get motivated so I lit a fire under their collective backsides and got things moving. We launched both RIBs and with a couple of buckets of hot water and metho in each dinghy, we split the crews and gave the vast expanse of *Seeker's* red hull a quick wash down to remove salt and other residues.

It didn't take long and with the warm wind blowing, I could see the surface drying quite quickly as we moved along.

Then it was out with the rolls of masking tape with the attached plastic sheeting. As the red area had all straight lines, except around the registration numbers and letters, that part didn't take long. Dave dug out a 240-volt extension cord and plugged in the main sprayer unit. The 20-litre bucket of Skin Fast was very heavy and needed stirring thoroughly, although it was able to stay on deck and was moved as needed along with the sprayer body. I practised on a test sheet to get the pattern and density right then it was on with the mask and start spraying.

The plastic brew was quite thick and covered the red paint very easily. The low pressure, high volume spray gun was also very effective and there was very little overspray. The spray part of the job took only about an hour and we were able to strip the masking off almost immediately.

Apart from being a matt finish, Dave and Corrine were delighted with the transformation of their boat from Rosso Red to a beautiful shade of Royal Blue. Wading ashore to view it from a distance, the change to the appearance of *Seeker* was radical!

I was so impressed with the result that I decided to use what was left of the plastic skin to add a broad line to each of *Firebird's* hulls. After a quick cleaning wipe and thanks to Corrine's excellent eye for a straight line, the masking didn't take long. I guessed that there was enough material to cover a 500mm wide band from bow to stern, being deliberately conservative to avoid running out partway through the job.

There was enough, although dusk was falling by the time we'd finished spraying, pulling the masking off and cleaning up the gear. Once again, the results looked excellent, but the final appraisal would have to wait until the morning light.

Even in the failing light, we could see that the dark line made *Firebird's* hulls look lower and leaner, that in turn changed the look of the whole boat.

It was a tired, but very happy crew that celebrated with drinks and such a steady supply of tasty finger foods from both galleys that we didn't bother about the evening meal.

MONDAY

I kicked the day off making myself very unpopular by rousting both crews out of bed two hours before first light.

'I want us out of this creek and across the Strait to a little sandy beach at Elbow Point, almost opposite the mouth of this creek before it gets light. If we leave at a normal time, there'll be too many people around who will take note of two distinctive boats our size making an appearance out of a tiny creek. It'll look like we've just completed a big drug deal!'

I hoped for a laugh at the last line, but it fell as flat as last week's pancakes.

As it was, my plan almost backfired, since despite having forward-looking sonar, we had to idle our way down the narrow, twisting waterways with all our spotlights blazing but we only encountered two tinny-loads of fishermen. By the way they pretended we weren't there, they also must have thought we were big-time drug dealers. Finally clear of the shallow creek and the building swarms of mosquitos, it was a brief run across the Great Sandy Strait to a pretty little sandy beach where we dropped anchor and with everyone's mood improving now that the coffee addicts had their first fix or three, the ladies prepared a lovely hot breakfast.

While the brekkie things were being cleared away, Dave and I fired up our respective mounts and motored sedately across the Wide Bay bar to the Tin Can Bay inlet where we joined a regular procession of small boats going to and fro in the wide, winding channel upstream. I was also surprised at the number of boats anchored in the bays just before and on the east side of Tin Can Bay township itself, although we took the narrow channel that lead to the town itself and the more established boating facilities.

A phone call to the town marina had reserved two berths for a week and the promise of unlimited hot showers, bar and restaurant sealed the deal for the crew. The cheerful, welcoming marina crew even put us side-by-side, with *Firebird* in an outside berth. Once standing on the floating pontoon beside the two boats we were all impressed with our new paint schemes — even viewed close-up, they looked quite professional and the matt finish could be passed off as extreme weathering or just a bad choice of paint.

Jasper and Krazy kitten were keen to explore the new environment, but with so many people around, I decided to confine their walks to nights only or run them across Snapper Creek inlet to a small beach opposite the marina.

We spent the rest of the day wandering around the small town having a feed and drinks at the Marina restaurant. Almost by accident during the afternoon, we found a pub that looked like a house, tucked down a side street not far away. We'd walked across a sports oval from the marina and as we were about to cross the road, a pair of black Harleys rumbled by with their distinctive exhaust beat, the riders unusually being two attractive girls who handled the big bikes with great familiarity and competence.

They seemed to eye us off very carefully and I was happy to reciprocate given the pleasant shape they appeared to be in. Inside the pub, we were greeted like old friends and in keeping with tradition, tried the local beer and wines both of which were very good. The publican, a retired fisho called Jack and his staff made us very welcome and the afternoon boozily and happily drifted along.

At some stage, I registered the sounds of big bikes pulling up and noticed that what seemed to be the two girls from the drive-by earlier, came into the bar, camping at a table over the other side of the room, sucking on schooners of beer. I wasn't so far gone that I didn't feel a tingle of warning when they seemed to pay rather more attention to our group than to others.

The girls were dressed in classic bikies gear, right down to the tight jeans and what appeared to be colours on the back of their leather jackets they took off as soon as they entered the bar, stopping me from seeing what the badge was. I watched to see how they were treated by the bar staff and was interested to see that they received a fair amount of deference from all the staff. They only stayed for two drinks, then left, their bike's exhaust roar fading into the distance.

Our drinking session seemed likely to continue into the evening, so we got them to feed us as well. Accordingly, it was a rather wobbly crew that meandered back to the marina and after a few fumbles, managed to find the right gate to the pontoon arm leading to our boats.

AUSSIE AMAZONS OMC
– OUTSKIRTS OF MARYBOROUGH – MONDAY PM

'AA. This is Etta.'
  'Hi Etta, it's Chloe.'

'Yeah, Hi Chloe. How's it going?'

'You gave Dianna and me the Southern area to search and we're down at Tin Can Bay at the moment. We didn't get away until Dianna got a baby-sitter for little Jason. Then we wasted time looking at Rainbow Beach first, but of course there's no harbour there, so we came back through Cooloola Cove, but there's fuck-all water activity there too.

Anyway, we're in Tin Can Bay and we checked out the town marina and found there are a big catamaran and a big powerboat parked together that came in this morning. Dianna undid most of the buttons on her shirt and pulled her jeans up even tighter and one of the yard apes nearly tripped over his dick trying to tell her anything she wanted to know. Bloody men!

The only problem is that the powerboat has dark blue sides, not red like you said. The big catamaran that came in with it has a dark blue stripe along each side, but you didn't say in your briefing if it had a stripe or not.'

'Good spotting, Sister. I'll check the boat colour with Henry and let you know but I'm sure he said the powerboat was red. But have you seen the crew yet? The cat should have a guy with two bimbo-looking tarts with him, but we don't know what the powerboat has for crew. Can you guys hang around there and see if you can get some eyes on the crew?'

'Actually, we've already done that and may even have a line on the crew. After spotting what might have been the boats, we were cruising around the town looking for likely groups when we spotted five persons going into the pub. They seemed to have arrived there on foot, so it's possible they're off a boat, but there are quite a few tourists in town at the moment. This group was two guys and three girls and we sat near them in the bar and had a couple of beers, but didn't overhear anything of importance, although there was some talk about boats. There was something about fast skin, but I'm buggered if we could work that out.

Anyway, what would you like us to do? Just remember that if we stay much longer you'll have to organise something with Dianna's babysitter. It's nearly a hour's ride back home.'

'No problem. But you might as well come back now. I'll call Henry and see what he wants done. We might have some planning to do.'

'*Will do, Sis. See you soon.*'

AUSSIE AMAZONS OMC
- OUTSKIRTS OF MARYBOROUGH - MONDAY PM

'*Undertaker.*'

'Hi Henry, 'tis your sister with some news.'

'*Good evening dear sister. Good, I hope.*'

'I think so. Firstly, yesterday morning, my Lieutenant in Noosa spotted what seems to be the catamaran you've been looking for. Secondly, two of my girls down in Tin Can Bay spotted what seemed like the catamaran and the powerboat. They found out that they came in together and have booked space for one week, but the only trouble is that the powerboat is dark blue, not red, so either someone made a mistake, or there's another pair of boats almost matching the descriptions running around.'

'*That's brilliant work, Sis. I don't know about the red boat thing. I heard from one of my guys who were involved in a fight with fishermen not long before the merchandise pickup was due. He said that there was a red boat not far away, but I suppose that he might have not seen it clearly, especially if they were in the middle of a fight at the time. Regardless, this is the best lead we have so far and the presence of the catamaran suggests that this is the correct powerboat and the colour was a mistake. Did your girls get a look at the crew?*'

'Yes, they did. There's five altogether, two men and three girls. My Lieutenant told me that the catamaran has a man who's the owner and a couple of bimbo's along for the ride, so the other two must be from the powerboat. Do you need us to take any action?'

'*I'd like to move on this myself, but I can't get away for a while and I don't want to see them disappear again, so I must ask if you*' wouldn't mind perhaps doing a snatch for me. That should hold them in one spot long enough for me to get the boys together and get up there. My delay involves some other business that requires my personal attention here tomorrow, but perhaps if one of the bimbos were to be taken for a ride tomorrow afternoon or evening and held quiet for a couple of days that would do the trick. No damage to the goods would be best and we can be there Wednesday morning to sort out this fellow on the catamaran.'

'Yeah, we can do it, but won't a snatch bring down a lot of attention? You don't want the coppers running all over the place looking for missing girls. And may I presume that the rest of the boat crew won't actively retaliate?'

'Firstly, we don't think they'll be running to the coppers or they would've complained already about our boys lobbing on their doorstep in the middle of the night. And secondly, the information we have is that it's just some rich, dopey boatie with a couple of bimbos tagging along for the booze and sex, so we don't expect any trouble from them. We don't know about the other crew, but if it's just another rich guy and his little chicky-babe, that shouldn't be a problem for you and your girls, should it?'

'Maybe not,' Etta replied thoughtfully.

'Although,' Henry went on, 'I must admit that something strange happened to my two crews when they went calling on the boat at Southport and I've still not been able to talk to any of them yet to find out what happened, since the coppers have them wrapped up tight. Maybe there is a dog on-board, but that won't be a problem if you make the grab on-shore. We're the ones who'll have to worry about a dog if we hit the boat directly.

Anyway, just make sure your crew does it right, doesn't attract public attention and make her disappear for a day or two then you can let her go unharmed. You should still have those homemade stun guns I sent you. A quick shot with one of those will keep her quiet at least until you get her to a car.'

Etta laughed, 'Oh yeah brother. They really do work. I tried it out on one of the girls and it sat her on her arse! Didn't you say they were half a million volts?'

'*Yeah. That's about right. My lieutenant, Jay, put them together. Oh, one more thing, when you can you might like to ask her about the merchandise that's supposed to be aboard the boat. If she can confirm that it's there, it'll make my job much easier when we get up there on Wednesday.*

And if you're still worried about the snatch, remember that the coppers won't react that quickly to a missing person report, especially an adult.'

'Yeah, I suppose you're right. OK. I'll put a crew down there tomorrow and hopefully the targets will go to the pub again in the afternoon so we'll try to cut one out once it's starting to get dark. We'd better bring her up here to the Clubhouse and bung her in a cell until you say we can release her. We'll blindfold her as well.'

'*Thanks Etta, that sounds like a good plan — I'll owe you one. I'll be in touch tomorrow, or perhaps you call me when it goes down.*'

'OK Henry. That's how it'll happen. But I think this'll be worth a piece of that new merchandise action when everything is resolved.'

'*You drive a hard bargain, little sister, but I guess you're worth it.*'

'You'd better believe it, brother. I'm more than worth it! Bye for now.'

Hanging up, Etta grabbed a legal pad and began scribbling notes, before reaching for the phone again.

CHAPTER 27

The crew slept in Tuesday morning, making up for our very early start the previous day and with nothing really planned, we had a late brunch, letting the girls slack around while Dave and I caught up on a few maintenance items like an oil change on the other engine. There was a Yanmar agent at the marina and I stocked up on some fuel and oil filters while the girls roused themselves enough to go for a walk, telling us they'd be back in time to head for the pub for 'afternoonsies', which meant another piss-up was planned.

With stuff fixed, Dave and I sat around in the cockpit of *Seeker*, chatting to a few locals who wandered past, but the party grew until we ended up with 5 or 6 guys sitting around telling fishing or boating yarns, so we cracked a few beers with them, getting a head start on the girls.

On a couple of occasions, I heard the sound of large, two-cylinder motorbikes rumbling around town, but didn't sight them.

The impromptu meeting of the Marina Men's Shed was broken up by the arrival of our ladies, sounding off because we'd had a couple of cold beers and they'd been having healthy, fresh fruit juices. Our new friends chuckled, eyed off the girls appreciatively, before wandering back to their own boats

'Rotten pigs!' Amanda laughed as she punched me on the arm, 'imagine starting without us!'

'I'm sure it won't take you long to catch up,' I bounced back as they headed below to pee and freshen up. Consequently, it was late afternoon when we wandered off to find the pub. Crossing

260

the sports oval, I noticed there were several bikes parked outside, that on closer inspection proved to be Harleys of various models and vintages, the newest of which was the latest Fat Boy with the much-improved engine and chassis. I'd not been much of a Harley fan in the past, but the new Softail models seemed to have thrown a lot of the old conventions away to create truly modern bikes that were much more appealing and tempting to my taste.

'You're not thinking of getting one, are you Harry?' Dave chuckled, 'although I can just picture you roaring around the Gold Coast scaring LOL's!'

'Actually, I wouldn't mind,' I replied seriously. 'I took a couple of test rides a few years ago and that convinced me that the only good thing about Harley-Davidson was the skill of their marketing crew in being able to make excessive weight, excessive noise, bad handling and an inefficient, agricultural engine from the 19th Century into a cult icon that every self-respecting biker type person wanted to have.

Now, with the new Softail series in particular, they designed an engine and a bike that compares quite well with what's available from Japan and the UK. I particularly like the look of the Fat Bob. It's a neat package.'

Dave laughed at my description as we wandered inside to catch up with the ladies who'd already ordered drinks and were halfway through the first one. Publican Jack greeted us happily like old friends as we went to our table.

I noticed a group of leather-clad girls at a table just outside in the veranda area that I presumed belonged to the bikes parked out front. My weird mind found that a group of girl bikies was odd enough, but when I thought about the numbers and came up with three bikes and five females, it was even stranger. Most bikies don't like carrying a pillion. I also couldn't help but notice that even seated, one severely attractive girl towered over her companions and had a very distinctive mane of white hair she kept brushed back from her forehead.

The other standout in the group was a stony-faced woman who seemed to be glaring non-stop at our group. There was nothing pleasant about her features at all, to the point where her look was particularly malevolent. She wore just a sleeveless denim vest that was unbuttoned to the waist, showing the inner half of each heavily tattooed breast.

It was when she turned to make a comment to the white-haired woman that I saw the same distinctive tattoo of a female warrior down the outside of her left bicep that I'd seen on a naked and pissed nurse last Saturday night on board *Firebird* when she was trying to talk me into a threesome or foursome or something that I'd had very little trouble resisting.

That was when the penny dropped that the presence of these bikie women was no accident. It took a hard kick in the shins to make me realise that the others had been trying to attract my attention for a couple of minutes.

'Hello Harry. Anybody in there?' Amanda inquired with a chuckle.

I pasted a big, dopey grin on my face and spoke quietly, 'I'd really like you all not to react, but those bikie females are paying us way too much attention and it's giving me one of those really bad feelings.'

Corrine was sitting just past Amanda picked up on my tone and the comment and knew exactly what I meant, so she casually sat back and shifted position so she could see the group in the corner of the mirror over the bar.

She gave a slight giggle that sounded pretty false to me. 'Gotcha, Harry. You're right again. Maybe a good time for us to bail out?'

I nodded, 'Yeah, good idea. This is definitely a case of discretion being the better part of getting in a bunfight, or some metaphor like that. Let's finish our drinks and go, but do so casually and quietly.'

'I've gotta go pee first,' Melissa announced as she finished her wine well ahead of my schooner of beer, 'I won't be a minute.'

'OK. We'll all wait here,' I said, noting that as she did, two of the bikie chicks had left their table and gone outside, leaving the other three to pretend that they weren't watching us. I was almost glad that one of the ones who'd left the table was the unpleasant woman who seemed to have been glaring the most.

It was a couple of minutes later that the remaining three bikie females casually got up and left, the one with the white hair showing how tall and well built she was when she stood. Moments later, as their bikes fired up in perfect unison and rumbled off down the street, there was a minor commotion of raised voices behind the bar. Jack the publican hurried over to our table, an urgent tone to his voice as he said, 'Harry. My cook just spotted two of those bikies loading what looked like one of your girls into a car parked out the back! Did one of you go to the toilet?'

I felt like a rush of ice water hit me. 'Oh, shit! Yeah, Jack. Melissa did. Those bikies had been eyeing us off since we arrived and we were about to go. The rotten bitches must have been waiting for one of us to go pee and Melissa was the first. Who are they and where would they be going?'

He didn't seem to hear me at first, since he said, 'I've got someone trying to call the coppers, but our local fella is away giving evidence in court in Brisbane. The Gympie boys are at least 30 minutes away.'

I thought quickly, trying desperately to suppress the rage that was threatening to overwhelm me and managed to push it down into a back corner of my consciousness where I closed a mental door on it for now. I quickly stood and waved Amanda forward as I turned to Jack, speaking quietly to save stirring up the other drinkers. 'No! Hold that call please. For your ears only, we are coppers! We'll deal with this directly. But we need all the information you have on who they were and we also need to borrow a car if you don't mind!'

Jack looked a bit bewildered as Amanda dug in her purse and flashed her Police ID card in his face, but at least he called to one of the bar staff to hold the call.

'I couldn't get through anyway, Jack,' he said plaintively, 'the lines are busy.'

Jack looked quite distressed, as was to be expected, so I got his attention and said, 'We'll take care of this, thanks Jack. I can tell you in strict confidence that this is part of an on-going Inter-State and Inter-Force operation, but our shore-based backup crews are in the wrong place for now, which is why we will need a car and any information you have on them.'

Amanda looked at me sideways at this mild distortion of the truth before Jack eyed me briefly, nodded as though he'd reached a decision then inclined his head toward the office behind the bar so we followed him in.

'Ok. You guys seem like the real deal. You didn't quite measure up like the average boatie we get in here, so I'll help all I can.' He took a deep breath and went on. 'Those girls are known as the Aussie Amazons and they're the only all-female bikie group in Australia. The very tall white-haired one is their leader, Etta Jones, and I've heard that she's the older sister of the leader of another bikie club on the Gold Coast. She's not too bad, but that one with the unbuttoned vest is a very nasty piece of work. There are some bad stories floating around about her — her love of torture and gratuitous violence are just some of them so you'd better move fairly quickly.'

'That's not good,' I said, not liking the thought of Melissa in the hands of a sadist.

'No, it won't be,' Jack added, 'but I can show you on a map where their Clubhouse is. I reckon that's the most likely place they'll take her. And by the way, the cook said their car was a dark blue VF Commodore Calais.'

He dug a detailed map of the Maryborough area out of a drawer and pointed out a semi-rural property on the outskirts of an outlying suburb called Tinana. 'It's quite distinctive since there's a big, red barn-type shed set away from the house, with a driveway that circles around the back of the house to a large, sealed parking area.'

'That's a very detailed description Jack,' I said, giving him searching looks. 'I wonder how you might have come by that?'

He winked and gave a wry grin as he reached into the filing cabinet and produced a manila folder. 'Last year, the ladies had a bit of a snot on with one of the clubs in Hervey Bay and came down here on the warpath. There was a fearsome rumble outside with cars trashed, two of my motel rooms wrecked and all the tables and chairs out on the veranda smashed. Somehow they dodged the coppers and didn't respond to my threats to take them to court for damages, so a mate took me up in his Cessna 180 and I got a heap of photos of the place.'

He opened the folder and a stack of blown-up, high-resolution photos spilled out, showing the property as he'd already described.

'May I borrow one of these?' I asked.

'Sure, Harry. Help yourself. I didn't know what I was going to do with them anyway. They're a very tough bunch — even the other Clubs steer clear of them. As for a car, here are the keys to my wife's Chevy Silverado crew cab truck out the back. Just try not to bend it. She loves it.'

I nodded. 'Thanks Jack. We'll be prepared for trouble.'

'I'm glad to help, Harry, if it's going to help shut those bitches down. They act as though they own this area and cause a lot of trouble. The local copper has his hands full with dopey bloody tourists most of the time and doesn't need bikie gangs bashing each other up in public places.'

I took the keys. 'Thanks for your help Jack. We'll get going. There's some stuff to collect from the boats first, then we'll hit the road. How long is it to Maryborough?'

'A bit under the hour should do it, mate. But take care approaching that property. There's not too much cover.'

I flashed him a grin. 'That sounds like an old soldier talking now. Vietnam?'

He grinned back, 'Yep. Three tours. You'd think I'd learnt my lesson after the first, but I backed up for more. Anyway, get going and rip those bitches a new arsehole each.'

With a wave, I led the remainder of our crew out the back and drove to the marina where we held a quick council of war.

MELISSA

When Harry agreed with Corrine that they should leave, Melissa finished her wine, but needed to pee. The toilets were at the rear of the Hotel at the end of a hallway with the kitchen on one side and which opened to the carpark at the end. As she got to the Female toilet door, one of the bikie chicks was just coming out, while another was entering the hallway from the carpark.

The girl coming out of the toilet swung her hand up with what looked like a mobile phone in it, except that Melissa felt it shoved firmly into her chest, then felt what seemed like a hard punch and a sharp pain. Within three seconds, a series of punches and a rapidly increasing amount of pain occurred until her legs gave way and she just fell straight down, the second bikie grabbing her before she hit the floor.

Semi-conscious, Melissa was hauled out the back door supported between the two bikies, her head lolling as though she were drunk and quickly bundled into the back seat of a car parked close by with the door open and engine running. One bikie jumped behind the wheel while the other slid in beside Melissa.

'Fuck it!' She dimly heard the woman next to her exclaim in disgust. 'The stupid bitch has pissed herself!'

Her accomplice in the driver's seat laughed. 'I did say that you should have grabbed her on the way out *after* she had a piss, but you had to be in a hurry. Anyway, you'd better shove something under her or Etta will be really cranky if her back seat is soaked in piss!'

The back-seat girl cursed again, but ripped Melissa's shirt off and stuffed that under her bum. 'Aww! I think she's crapped herself as well! Fuckin' hell. What a fucked up mess this is turning out to be!'

Her companion laughed again. 'Better wind the windows down, we've got a way to go with that stink in here. And while I think of it, you'd better give her the dose of sleepy stuff that Erin made up for us, before she starts to get over the shocks.'

Avoiding Melissa's messy lower regions, the girl opened a water bottle and carefully tipped a small amount into Melissa's mouth. As instructed, she pinched her nostrils closed briefly and was rewarded with the captive swallowing the brew. Repeating the process several times until Erin's recommended dose had gone down, the bikie capped the bottle for later and watched as after a few minutes, Melissa slipped into what appeared to be a deep sleep, snoring softly. The muscle twitching from early seemed to have ceased.

'Keep a close eye on her, like Erin said,' the driver reminded her companion. 'We don't want her carking it on us.'

'Yeah, yeah. I'm on it, but Jeez she stinks! Are we nearly there yet?'

'Stop whinging. Your shit stinks too, as I remember.'

'Get fucked, Sally.'

The sedan droned steadily on toward Maryborough, an escort of three bikes keeping it close company. On arrival, the driver pulled around the back of the low, ranch-style house and stopped, the girl in back flinging open both back doors and stumbling out as soon as they stopped.

'Thank Christ for that. Finally, I can get away from this stinkin' bitch!'

The three escort bikes pulled up near the back door to the

house, long denim or leather-clad legs swinging over the low-slung seats, helmets pulled off and stowed over rear view mirrors.

Etta, the tall, white-maned leader, approached the car, nose wrinkling at the smell.

'Ok, ladies. Let's get her out, strip her down and clean her up properly.'

She glared at the girl from the back, 'and clean the car seats while you're at it, Jackie. You should have been better prepared for something like this. You're lucky she didn't do some projectile vomiting!'

'Ok, boss,' said Jackie sullenly. 'Can Marie help as well? I can't handle an unconscious body by myself.'

Etta waved her hand casually. 'Yeah sure. Marie. Please help Jackie with the clean up. I want her squeaky clean so I can sit her in a chair shortly and ask some questions. Wash her clothes if you can, otherwise chuck 'em, but leave her naked. She looks rather good. And don't forget to clean the car!'

Fifteen minutes later, a naked, pink, sweet-smelling, but largely un-responsive Melissa was half carried, half dragged into the kitchen and propped up in a chair, but had to be held there or she'd slide off.

Etta grinned at Jackie and Marie. 'I hope you two behaved yourselves in the shower with her?'

Jackie looked a bit smug. 'Mostly! We had a bit of a play, although she's so far out of it, I'm not sure she noticed.'

Marie giggled, 'Oh, she noticed all right! It's like she's half-asleep, not fully knocked out.'

Etta eyed off the semi-comatose Melissa with a mounting sense of frustration. 'Fuckin' hell! This is weird shit! She's supposed to be awake enough to talk. How much of Erin's dope did you give her?' She asked Jackie, 'I need to ask her questions about Henry's dope before this night gets on much more.'

'Just what Erin said — about three swallows.'

'Well, it must have been too much. She's too far out of it for now! We might as well put her on the bunk in the back room 'till she wakes up.'

Jackie gave Etta a cheeky grin, 'Ok boss. We'll make sure she's comfortable!'

Etta shook her head, 'Not you, Jackie. I'd like you to go finish cleaning out the car, please. I'll help Marie shift the girl then she can sit with her and try to get her awake and aware, but don't damage her and no bruises. Henry wants her able to go back in one piece.'

Jackie grumped and after rounding up some cleaning stuff from under the kitchen sink, slammed out through the back door, muttering curses under her breath, while Marie smiled as Etta helped her wrestle the naked and slack Melissa into the small bedroom and dumped her on the bed.

'Look after her now. And don't let that nutso Dianna any-where near her. I meant it about no damage. We all know what she's like, especially with fresh meat!'

'No problem boss. I think Dianna and Chloe are doing watch in the barn, but I'll make sure that nothing will show. And I'll call if she starts to make sense.'

'Yeah, do that and try to make it soon, huh?'

Left alone in the small bedroom with their captive, Marie re-arranged Melissa's naked form to her liking and commenced having fun, all in the name of waking her up. However, despite her best efforts with various devices, she was unable to rouse her, although she was pleased with the series of moans and groans her efforts produced and presumed that she was getting through on one level at least. After nearly half an hour, Marie took a break to have a coffee, reporting the lack of helpful progress.

'Don't we have an antidote or something?' Etta asked.

'Nope. All Erin gave us was the Scopolamine solution. She just said to be careful not to overdose 'cause the reaction would be unpredictable and possibly fatal.'

'Terrific! I just hope we haven't done that, since there's no way

I'm going to take that risk for Henry. A drugged and kidnapped girl is one thing, but a kidnapped dead one from an overdose is a whole world of hurt and I'm not taking us there.'

'Fair enough. I'll go back to baby-sitting shortly. There's not much different I can do to wake her, although some part of her sub-conscious does seem to like what I'm doing.'

Sally, a tall blonde, wearing just brief panties, wandered in to get a mug of coffee and heard the last part of the conversation. 'What about letting her sniff some of the ammonia cleaner we've got for getting bloodstains off stuff? If you're careful and don't let her get too much of a snootful, that should bring her around. It fair makes my eyes water!'

Etta eyed off her lush body appreciatively as she always did. 'That's not a bad idea. Do you know where it is?'

'Yeah. I used it the other day when I cleaned my baseball bat after the dustup with that mob from Bundaberg. It's in the pantry — I'll get it.'

Both Etta and Marie appreciated looking at Sally as she stretched her long, lean length up to reach the bottle of Cloudy Ammonia on the top shelf.

'Just a brief sniff,' she warned Marie sternly. 'Too much can cause serious damage to the nasal passages and lungs, so be very careful.'

Marie took the bottle gingerly as if the fumes might attack her through the glass. 'OK. I'll be careful, I promise.'

FIREBIRD - TOWN MARINA - TUESDAY EVENING

I sat everyone around the saloon dining table for some privacy. 'Ok. I have a bit of a plan, but we have to move quickly.'

'I hope you intend taking all of us, Harry,' Corrine said. 'This is a bit personal and deserves an appropriate response.'

I nodded, 'Yeah, you're right. We all go, but I need to include

Jasper as well. I want to make the biggest possible statement to these jerk-offs. Do not mess with us!'

I looked at Dave, 'Has Mouse been teaching you firearms and unarmed combat?'

He nodded and Corrine added, 'Yep. He's not quite SAS standard yet, but very close.'

'OK. That's what we need, but Dave and Amanda, you must be prepared to shoot first or be shot. These people won't mess around when we're on their property, so don't hesitate or hold back asking them to surrender!'

They nodded soberly.

'Right. My grand plan is that we all dress in tight black or dark blue — no loose clothing, and arm ourselves with everything we've got. Especially the shotguns with SG rounds, no solid shot. Wear bandoleers for extra loads so there are no loose, flapping things to catch or make noise since I want to go in covertly as far as we can. Alright so far?'

Everyone nodded, although Corrine as my 2IC in this sort of situation, suggested, 'How about you and I go point, with Dave and Amanda hanging back a bit to cover our arses?'

'Yep. Good idea. No offence guys, but Corrine and I have done this stuff a lot. We know that there are only a maximum of eighteen of them and some may be away working or whatever, but as usual, we plan for the worst case and hope for the best.'

Twilight had slipped its soft, purplish veil over the town as we made final preparations by feeding the pussies, checking each others gear then locked up *Firebird* with Krazy kitten inside, complaining bitterly at being separated from Jasper who sat quietly with us in the cockpit, watching as we pulled jackets on over our black or dark blue tight-fitting outfits. Corrine and Amanda looked very sexy in their tights, with the bandoleers of extra ammunition across their upper bodies covered by loose jackets, despite the warm temperatures.

We also had Gerber Mk II combat knives in sheaths to strap to our lower legs once we were on the job. I tried to tell Jasper what we were doing and to the vast amusement of the others, I actually think he understood. At least he huffed at me, which normally means that he knew what I was talking about and that my repetitions were totally superfluous. We wore our balaclavas rolled up into crew caps to avoid spooking our neighbours, some of who were still wandering to and from the various bars and eateries around the marina area. I clipped a lead onto Jasper and hoped that nobody looked too closely at my black 'dog'.

Nevertheless, we still looked like a 'Mission Impossible' hit squad as we hustled up the jetty.

Fortunately, we only met two couples on our trek to the carpark and they were too pissed to take too much notice or us. The trip to the outskirts of Maryborough in Jack's HSV Silverado took well under the hour and was conducted mostly in silence, with Jasper perched up on the middle of the rear seat where he could look ahead and make the most of this rare treat of a car trip. The only down side to having Jasper along was that he farted twice, nearly gassing everybody and requiring a hasty lowering of all the windows to clear the noxious pall. The on-board GPS Nav system directed us to a rural area west of the suburb of Tinana, where a series of 5 and 10-acre blocks gave a fair degree of privacy.

As we had aerial photos of the place, I killed the headlights well before the target, driving on park lights only. I then found a convenient dirt road turning in to somebody's vegetable patch about 500 metres from the start of the Amazon's property and parked the truck.

'OK. We'll keep off the road, so we go through the fence and follow it until we cross onto Amazon land. I don't think they'll have any sophisticated alarm or defences set up, but Corrine will wear night-vision goggles that will spot anything strange. Hopefully, they won't be expecting any raid, or at least not this early, so there's a good chance we'll take them by surprise.'

As we'd discussed at length who was to do what, we shed jackets, checked that all weapons, firearms and other special gear were secure, pulled our balaclavas down over our faces before I let Corrine lead off with myself two paces behind.

Dave and Amanda spread out a little on either side with Jasper on a lead that was just looped through his collar, both ends then held by Amanda, so that letting go just one would free the black killing machine.

Despite the palpable tension, he loved the rare walk through the scrub, his wet, black nose working overtime to take in all the fascinating new smells.

Five minutes of careful and quiet walking brought us undetected to a small clump of trees just west of the main house that was a long, low building with a couple of arms tacked on for extra accommodation. Our position allowed a good view of the front of the building, and as shown on the photos, a driveway split in front of the house, one curving around in front, the other went behind to a sealed parking area.

A dark blue Holden Calais sedan with both rear doors wide open stood close to the back door of the house, its interior light casting a dim pool of illumination onto several bikes parked nearby.

A large barn-type building was about 50 metres directly behind the house, with several roller doors along its front face and several personnel doors on the side.

There was a small garden shed about 10-metres off the southwest corner of the house, so with hand signals, I indicated that Dave and Amanda should remain in the trees with Jasper to watch the house front while Corrine and I should re-locate to the cover of the shed. We made the move un-detected so Corrine removed the NVG's and stowed them in her compact, conformal backpack. Suddenly, the back door of the house opened and a woman wearing black jeans and a blue denim shirt marched out, slamming the door behind her in what appeared to be a fit of anger. Producing rags and lotions from a bucket dangling from one hand, she started cleaning the rear seats of the car.

I chuckled softly and murmured to Corrine, 'I'm guessing that Melissa either threw up or pissed herself in there from whatever they used to quieten her down.'

She nodded and murmured back, her lips close to my ear, 'I agree. Do you want me to take her out? It'll be one less.'

I thought a moment then nodded. 'Yeah. Do it now, but don't kill her yet. We need to find out how many are in there.'

She gave an evil grin, shrugged out of her backpack and faded into the shadows like she was one. I had always marvelled at her spooky ability to blend into the landscape in daylight or night. I suppose that's what made her so effective at quiet, close-range killing as well as sniper work.

The woman cleaning the car seats had just moved around to the other side to finish up, when a shadow seemed to merge with her from behind. Moments later, she slumped soundlessly over the car seat, before Corrine effortlessly hoisted her over a shoulder and faded back into the shadows, re-appearing beside me moments later, her breathing hardly elevated.

I relieved her of her slack-limbed burden and we quietly retreated to the clump of small trees.

'What did you use?' I asked Corrine. 'A choke-hold?'

'Yep. She should be coming around any moment.' She competently tied the woman's hands and ankles with nylon zip-ties as groans announced that she was awake, so I clapped a hand over her mouth, the other hand under her jaw.

'Struggle or try to call out and I'll break your neck! Understand?'

She glared at me for a moment then nodded grimly.

'Good. Now. How many are inside?'

She grunted to indicate that she wanted to speak, so I relaxed my mouth-covering hand slightly.

'Fuck you!' She announced loudly, so I clamped my hand back over her mouth and nodded to Corrine who reached over her shoulders from behind and stabbed a protruding knuckle into each of the cavities just behind the jaw.

Immediately, our captive arched her back, her eyes trying to bulge out of her head and she shrieked in agony against my smothering hand. I waited a few moments until she settled down then quietly asked the question again, adding that Corrine was quite happy to continue doing her part all night.

Unfortunately for our captive, it took two more repetitions before she broke down with tears streaming down her cheeks and nodding furiously against my grip, so I slightly loosened it and said, 'OK. Go ahead, but remember...'

Slowly and quietly, she spoke, 'There are 8 of us here tonight. The rest are working or away.'

'How many guns are inside?'

'There are plenty of pistols and shotguns, but they're stored in a cupboard — none very ready for instant use.'

'Ok. Good so far. Now, what's your name and were you on the snatch run?'

'Jackie and yes.'

'Where is our girl being held?'

'She was in the kitchen, but I'm pretty sure she's still too dopey to talk, so she might be in a bedroom off the kitchen at the back of the house.'

'What's her condition?'

'We cleaned her up after she pissed and crapped herself, but she's still half asleep. Otherwise she's unharmed.'

'What did you give her?'

'We used a stun gun to put her down initially, then fed her a brew of Scopolamine.'

'Is everybody inside, and what's in the barn?'

She hesitated a moment, which I took to mean she was about to lie, so before she could speak, Corrine jammed her fingers down behind each collarbone, in against her neck. The pain spasm was so intense that she couldn't even scream and it was nearly a minute before she could speak.

'Now. That was because you were about to lie, so I presume that there is someone in the barn. How many and are they armed?'

I felt her draw in a wavering breath and clamped a hand down, but before I could nod to Corrine, our captive motioned that she wanted to speak.

'Don't let her do that to me again. Who are you people?'

'We're about to be your worst nightmare, because you dared to mess with us at a personal level by snatching our girl! Now, answer my question or she'll do it again.'

'Fuck me, mister. You already *are* my worst nightmare! I can't imagine how it gets any worse, but I want no part of it. There're two girls in the barn, Dianna and Chloe. Dianna is one really tough, mean bitch and both are armed with shotguns. They were supposed to hit any rescue attempt from behind, although we weren't expecting you to get here this quickly. In fact, we didn't really expect you tonight at all.'

'Tough! Where in the barn are they waiting?'

'Just inside the first personnel door.'

'Are all the doors unlocked?'

'Yeah, but they'll hear you coming if you try to go in through another one.'

'Don't worry about us. Worry about yourself if we find out you're telling more lies.'

The wild look in her eyes suggested that she'd play it straight.

Slapping a piece of gaffer tape over her mouth, we dumped her on the grass with a big cable tie around one arm and the thin tree trunk then moved away to have a quiet conference.

'You don't intend going into the barn I hope?' Amanda asked, 'That doesn't seem like a very healthy move.'

'No, that would be silly, so we need to draw them out.' I looked at our captive thoughtfully. 'She's about your size, Amanda. Take your balaclava off, whip her shirt off and pull it over your top. Then I want you to go and lie down on your front, not far from the first barn door. Leave your shotgun with Dave but tuck your Glock into the bandoleer belt under the shirt at your back.

Then I want you to make some painful, hurt-type noises as you crawl towards the door, calling softly and weakly to Dianna and Chloe by name. They'll have to open the door to see what's going on, since there's no window there. Do you think you can act that out?'

By way of answer, she promptly handed Dave the short stock TAC-14 shotgun from *Firebird* and with some difficulty stripped the denim shirt off Jackie, leaving her naked from the waist up, her full, firm breasts quivering in frustration in the dim combination of house light and moonlight. She slipped it over her skin-tight top and the cartridge bandoleer full of fat, red-cased shotgun rounds, but had to adjust the position of the bandoleer between her breasts, before looking at me.

'Shall I go now?'

I grinned. 'Good girl. You, Corrine and I will go to that shed then you wait until Corrine and I take up station on the handle side of the door. Then you come in and do the Aussie Land Crawl from about 5 metres out from the door. Don't be too noisy — there's supposed to be intruders in the house who've taken out everybody except you.

She nodded, surprisingly giving me an excited grin. 'No problem Harry, but make sure you guys take them out quietly and quickly. I'll be a bit exposed out there like a stranded starfish.'

I nodded, holding up a short, fat cylinder with a leather thong that wrapped around my wrist, 'No problem there, not with our handy-dandy flick batons.'

CHAPTER 29

Corrine and I slipped quietly into position, crouching down on the handle side of the inward-opening door, and thirty seconds later, Amanda was belly-down on the concrete path near the door, dragging herself slowly forward, calling out softly, 'Dianna, Chloe — help, it's Jackie.'

She only had to repeat it twice when the handle quietly moved and the door opened a small amount. In the dimness, they would have seen a female form wearing Jackie's shirt, moving painfully toward them. They were cautious, but not used to covert operations, so moments later the door opened fully and both girls stepped out, checking toward the house for a threat, but forgetting about behind them. Corrine was in front by choice and distained my use of a flick baton, preferring to use bare hands, in this case a double-handed, hand strike to the side of the neck on the girl bringing up the rear and therefore closest.

As usual with anything Corrine does that involves violence, her target dropped straight down like a sack of potatoes, with only a heavy thump as she hit the ground. The girl in front, who turned out to be the super-tough bitch Dianna, spun around, startled by the sound, placing herself nicely to be met with a scything side kick to her solar plexus from Corrine who had stepped up onto the fallen body to get some extra height.

As Dianna doubled over with pain and a muted 'woof' of forcibly expelled air, Corrine knuckle-punched her behind the left ear and she dropped straight down like her companion, her head thumping hard on the pavement before she flopped in an untidy, sprawled heap on the pavement. I was halfway disappointed that I was deprived of the chance to whip some arse with my you-beaut flick baton, but perhaps I'd have a chance later.

For now, however, the job was done with a minimum of fuss, almost zero disturbances and a huge heap of hurt on two bad girls. That added up to three down and just five left, although the ones in the house didn't know about the drastic reduction in numbers yet.

Amanda scrambled thankfully to her feet and between us, we dragged the unresponsive bodies back to the tree shelter where we'd left Dave, Jasper and Jackie who was very upset to see the Amazon's prime enforcer so easily reduced to a slack bundle of arms and legs dumped unceremoniously on the ground.

Taped at mouth, wrists and ankles, and secured to separate trees, they posed no threat, even if they did wake up sometime soon.

Retreating from Jackie, the only conscious captive, we held a quick planning session.

'What's the next move, Harry?' Amanda asked.

I thought a moment or two, refining a plan that had occurred to me earlier.

'Given that there are five left and all are inside, we need to split them up further. Here's what I think — anytime soon, someone is going to come looking for dear Jackie or even Dianna and Chloe.'

I looked at Corrine, 'Would you mind doing the honours again, please. I'd like whoever comes out the back door taken down quietly first. The other four we'll hit hard with Amanda, Jasper and me ringing the front doorbell and barging in, taking down whoever is there. As soon as that distraction happens, Dave and Corrine will enter the back door that they seem to leave unlocked, and deal with whoever's left. Does that sound reasonable?'

Corrine was the one I expected to respond and she did. 'Yeah. Good plan, Harry. But what about using guns? Can we shoot if necessary?'

'Absolutely!' I replied, 'just because shit-for-brains Jackie said all their weapons are locked away, doesn't mean she's right, so be prepared to use overwhelming force. No fucking around with this lot!'

Corrine gave her evil grin that I'd seen so often in the Afghanistan, just before going into action and that usually meant bad things were about to happen to the bad guys.

'Excellent, boss. Just what I wanted to hear.'

'But,' I cautioned. 'If you do have to shoot, be careful as I'd like them alive if at all possible. I've got a bit of an cunning plan hatching for these clowns that might make a nice statement.'

Corrine laughed quietly and said to Amanda, 'When Harry hatches what he calls an 'cunning plan', it's usually a ripper!'

I grinned, 'Yeah. I think you'll all like this one if things go well. But for now Corrine, will you get into position at the back door? Maybe kill that light if you can.'

She smiled and slipped away, Dave, Amanda, Jasper and me moving over to the shelter of the garden shed to watch how the next phase went down.

I was gratified to see that it went almost as if scripted, or maybe I could predict bad guys behaviour all too well. Corrine had only been in position a few minutes, the back area now well shadowed apart from the weak light from the car's interior light still burning since the back doors were left open. She was just a deeper pool of shadow on the handle side of the door when it suddenly opened and a tall, half-naked blonde clad in just a brief pair of panties called out through the opening, 'Hoy! Jackie, where the fuck are you? Etta wants a word.'

The lack of response prompted the blonde to step forward, pulling the door closed behind her, whereupon a black shadow merged with her dim form, both flowing down onto the concrete path. I trotted across to join them just as Corrine started to haul the unconscious blonde upright. Between us, we made short work of getting her back to the clump of trees, the slack body slung across my shoulder, her bare breasts bouncing heavily against my back as I walked. More gaffer tape rendered her helpless and she was dumped with the others, much to Jackie's distress.

'Four down, four to go,' Corrine stated. 'Do we proceed with the next bit now?'

I nodded, the moonlight bathing the house and surroundings in a cold, washed out glow. 'Yep. You and Dave wait until you hear a commotion at the front door before you enter the back way.'

'OK.'

So Amanda, Jasper and I moved carefully to the front door where I quietly unscrewed the globe out of the coloured glass holder beside the door, Dave and Corrine moving to the garden shed, then to the back door, taking up station right in front of it.

I'd let Jasper sniff all the accumulated captives, including a terrified Jackie, telling him they were bad persons who had hurt Melissa. He growled softly when I'd told him, and again when Jackie tried to push away from his searching nose, baring his fangs at her for good measure. In the dim moonlight, and from her position on the ground, he must have looked like the devil-cat straight from hell!

When ready, I knocked on the door normally — not too loudly, and 30-seconds later, it opened to reveal an unpleasant-looking female built like a wharf piling. She took several seconds to take in our black outfits and the wicked little Mini-Uzi machine pistol I held, as well as Amanda with a Glock at the ready.

'What the fuck...'

She was fast, and started to close the door, but Jasper was way ahead of her reactions and launched through the doorway like a heat-seeking missile, the long, sharp claws on his forepaws digging deep into her chest while his jaws clamped sideways across the lower part of her face and bit down hard.

She went over backwards, a heavily muffled shriek of pain, fright and terror issuing strangely from several new openings in her nearly destroyed face and hardly covering up the spine-chilling sound of bone crunching. As her shirt flew up from the impact with the floor, I saw the handle of a knife showing above her waistband and as we followed Jasper inside, I grabbed it as I went past, its razor edge neatly slicing through the waistband of her jeans. I left Jasper to gnaw on what was left of the human he'd been allowed to rip into and walked on carefully into the house.

It was just as well that we did, since the intimidatingly tall, white-haired woman with the dramatic, powerful build we'd last seen at the pub, shot out from the hallway to my left, a pistol in her hand, already swinging toward us. Unfortunately, being right-handed added to the time taken to swing the gun onto a target, so as I had my flick baton ready for action, it was just a quick flick of the wrist to bring it smashing up under her fore-arm with an sickening sound as both the ulna and radius bones shattered, causing her to drop the gun, drop to her knees and clutch her floppy arm to her imposing chest with a howl of agony.

I kicked the gun back to Amanda with my foot, before planting my sneaker-clad foot as heavily as I could into her side where I had the satisfaction of hearing several ribs crack and drawing another chocking scream of agony from her. With another hard kick to the inside of one knee to make sure that she wasn't going to be too active for a while, I pushed on further into the kitchen where we saw that Dave and Corrine had the remaining two ladies well under control. In fact, both were unconscious on the floor, one with a trickle of blood seeping from her ears.

Hearing strange noises from the front of the hallway, I returned to the open front door to find that the facially mauled bikie was attempting to crawl outside, but Jasper hadn't finished playing games. The saving grace for her was that she hadn't actually tried to attack me, or else Jasper would have just ripped her throat out straightaway.

As it was, he had a firm grip on one ample bum cheek and by shaking his head violently, was giving a very good imitation of a White Pointer shark trying to break away a lump of flesh. The girl was feebly trying to escape, clawing at the ground while making inarticulate noises but Jasper was having way too much fun to let his new chew toy get away that easily, as gouts of blood and chunks of denim and flesh were splattered and sprayed over the walls and floor.

Amanda came up beside me, eyes wide, looking horrified at the gory scene. 'Aren't you going to stop him?' She whispered.

I appeared to consider that thought for a few moments, while the girl managed to drag herself and Jasper another metre across the pavers out front, extending the broad, bloody trail she'd left before replying, trying to sound reluctant. 'Yeah, I guess I'd better. Jasper's probably had enough fun by now.'

'Had enough!' Amanda almost cried, 'He's fucking well ripped her apart!'

I patted her shoulder and showed her the knife I'd taken from her waistband. It had a blackened, double-edged, 9-inch blade, and was wickedly razor-sharp. 'This was about to be drawn and stuck into either of us. She's not as helpless as she might have liked to appear, the rotten bitch. And don't forget, she's part of this whole stinking group that kidnapped your best mate, Melissa.'

Like most people, Amanda was badly frightened of knives and shuddered at the sight of the black, evil-looking device I held loosely in one hand. 'Yeah, sorry Harry. I forgot things for a moment, but maybe Jasper should stop anyway.'

I smiled to ease some tension. 'Yeah, OK. Jasper, stop please. You can leave the bitch alone now.'

Thankfully, he obeyed instantly, stepping back a few paces to watch as she collapsed unconscious, facedown on the tiles in a spreading pool of blood.

With that one not going anywhere under her own steam for a while either, we returned to check on the fallen leader, still trying to cradle her shattered arm, while she leant against the wall at an odd angle trying to ease the pain of several broken ribs and a knee that would probably need major work if she wanted to walk properly again.

We all met up in the kitchen where I outlined the next stage in my diabolical plan of retribution and as they were well into the same mood as mine that drew a bunch of delighted grins and chuckles from the crew. Corrine had already checked on Melissa and reported that she was still out of it, but appeared otherwise unhurt, so after Amanda checked as well, she left her there, covered with a blanket.

We went and retrieved the four bikies we'd left in the clump of small trees, finding only Jackie was still awake, and brought them inside.

We searched the house and barn for the simple materials my plan called for and managed to find all of them. One of the finds was a normally harmless white powder that Amanda mixed with water in proportions not recommended by the label. The bottle of ammonia retrieved from Melissa's bedroom proved very handy in waking them all up enough that they could at least drink some of Amanda's potion. Seven of them got a healthy dose down without choking, then Corrine went to work with her magic little knock-out kit, left over from her time with her very ex-employer, currently languishing for the next ten years or so in one of the Victorian Government's Hotels California.

In short order, all eight had been injected with a very small dose of the drug and were sleeping fairly peacefully. We took the opportunity to splint and secure Etta's arm from further harm by strapping it roughly across her chest with a roll of plaster found in the medicine cabinet, as well as administer some very basic first aid to Jasper's new playmate, but there wasn't much we could do apart from untidily binding up everything that leaked blood.

There wasn't much of her face to see when we'd finished, but not one of our crew showed the slightest sign of sympathy.

Especially when we recovered a bottle from Melissa's bedroom marked, 'Scopolamine solution — 20ml per dose only.' This we added to our collection of booty. We decided to leave her where she was and to proceed with the plan with the other seven.

All seven bikie girls were then stripped of all clothing, a difficult job made easier by using the razor-sharp knife that the doorperson had tucked in her jeans. They were then left snoring where they were until we searched the house and barn very thoroughly, turning up some interesting finds like a large collection of hand guns, shotguns, full automatic sub-machine guns and a few long rifles. These we left in place without touching them, except for a very nice, near new, H&K MP5 SD6 suppressed sub-machine gun in 9mm, with an integrated suppressor. This, plus several thousand rounds of 9mm ammunition I decided would be 'spoils of war' and would be a welcome addition to *Firebird's* armoury.

There was a very large stash of drugs of various types that were bagged and appeared to be ready for shipment to dealers, so they too were left untouched. The barn yielded an interesting collection of plastic explosive, readily identified by Corrine and me as Semtex, a very effective plastic explosive made in Czechoslovakia. There was something like 150 kilos of the stuff in several wooden crates, so I couldn't help myself and took six, one kilo packets, a tin of pyrotechnic detonators and a coil of safety fuse.

CHAPTER 30

Dave went to retrieve Jack's Silverado from down the road, and once parked at the front door, we loaded Melissa who was waking up, but still very woozy into the back seat. The bikie girls were loaded, still naked, into the rear load tray, along with the rest of my shopping list. My confiscated weaponry was stowed out of casual sight under seats. The savaged girl was left where she was, propped up outside the front door and we hoped the presence of the rudimentary first aid would confuse the ambulance crew and the Police who we were about to summon, as soon as we were clear of the property.

The last task was a thorough cleaning of the house and barn of any fingerprints we might have left. The sealed driveway wouldn't hold tyre tracks so it was safe. It seemed odd to the others that we were taking such careful steps to avoid involvement with the Police when we *were* the Police, but undercover means just that, and it was a lesson it had taken me a long time to learn that retreating back into the arms of the Force every time some shit went down was the quickest way to blow cover and the operation at the same time.

I had to explain it to the crew, hopefully for the last time, before the queries stopped.

Then it was just a case of all squeezing into the big crew-cab, so Jasper was delighted to be sitting up front with Dave, leaving room for our three girls in the back, although Dave wasn't quite so comfortable as Jasper was still damp after being washed down following his 'put down' job on the bikie. Melissa was wrapped in her blanket, propped up and seat-belted in the middle of the back seat as Amanda and Corrine still had some work to do. With the help of the GPS navigator, I drove into the centre of town to a large Supermarket complex. At this time of night it was closed and deserted. Out front of the main entrance was what I was hoping for, a row of flagpoles flanked by various signs mounted on steel poles.

We initially parked away from the entrance and waited for the security guard to do his rounds, which luckily didn't take long before we saw the flash of his torch on the door locks from the inside. Given the size of the complex, there would be plenty of time for what we had to do, even if he was conscientious enough to do his rounds on a regular basis.

Giving him time to get clear, I started the engine again and without lights, rumbled as quietly as a 6.6 litre V8 turbo diesel can, up near the main entrance.

Without banging doors closed, four of us hopped out and unloaded some supplies.

Several rolls of Gaffer tape were the first things to be stacked near the flagpoles, followed by Etta, the Amazon queen in all her naked glory. Her badly broken arm was still strapped in place across her magnificent chest, so we tried hard to avoid bumping it. The arm was already swollen very badly and it was clear she'd need urgent medical treatment. We awkwardly carried her over to the centre flagpole, stood her up against it, then used windings of gaffer tape to bind her to the pole and hold her upright. A final piece of tape sealed her mouth with a small air hole poked in the middle with a pen to help her breathe.

That task was repeated with the other six and didn't take long. The next task was to spray paint each naked body with a water-based acrylic paint in whatever colours we had found in the barn. Red must have been popular at some stage since there was more of it than anything else. While the paint was still wet, a pre-printed sheet of paper was stuck to each bare belly and each sheet read the same in large point print.

'*I am an illegal drug-dealer who sells drugs to school kids as well as adults in this region. I am also an illegal gun dealer selling firearms to anybody willing to pay for them, including young kids. As a member of the Aussie Amazons Outlaw Motorcycle Club, I take delight in terrorising innocent people in this area and love telling the Police to get fucked. If you believe that I am telling the truth about how bad I am, please leave me here, like the vermin that I truly am, for the Police to collect at their convenience. To prove how full of shit I have been, please see my other side. That's not brown paint!*

You cannot touch me as I am an official crime scene and can only be released by the Police!'

Our final job was to move along each girl in turn with the open bottle of Cloudy Ammonia, waving it under each nose. Etta was the first to react, jerking her head wildly in a desperate but futile attempt to get away from the fumes that were attacking her sinuses and causing so much pain. Her broken arm was temporarily forgotten.

After peeling the tape off her mouth for the moment, the four of us stood in front, balaclavas carefully in place, calmly regarding her painful climb back to full consciousness.

'Who the fuck are you and what have you done?'

I stepped forward. 'We're the crew you very unadvisedly decided to mess with by kidnapping one of ours. Retaliation has been swift and very sure, although the fun is only just starting. The massive dose of painkillers we gave you for your broken arm should be wearing off about now, so that should focus your rotten little mind on the error of your ways. But just in case it doesn't, there's something else.'

As I guessed, she couldn't help herself and asked, 'What something else?'

By way of answer, I asked, 'How does your gut feel?'

She glared at me. 'You arsehole! What did you give me? It's churning like a bloody washing machine! Let me down, I need a toilet!'

I looked at Amanda and laughed. 'Well done my lady. What perfect timing! Oh, sorry. It's just a massive dose of Epsom's Salts — like about six times the recommended dose for constipation, so you just might feel a bit cleaned out when it's over.

Oh, one more thing. We dosed the other six as well so you can all appreciate each other's stink.'

She glared murderously at me and tried to turn her head, but it was taped firmly in place as well as the rest of her limbs. 'Where are we? You can't leave us here.'

I laughed, 'Perhaps you should have thought of that before you decided to kidnap one of our crew, an act of declared war that invited massive retaliation. Therefore, should you be stupid enough to try to lash out at us again, we'll come back and totally wipe you out. You and you little group of unhappy campers will be crushed like bed bugs under a size 12 boot.

However, to answer your question, you're all tied to flagpoles outside the Plaza Shopping Village where I reckon you won't be found until about 08:00 in the morning when the doors are due to open to the public. Staff and the security guard changes happen through the rear of the complex, so the public will probably get to find you first and will see a lot more of you than even you would like.'

My chat session was interrupted as Etta gave a groan of pain and voided her bowels in a massive, explosive stream. Without wind to blow the stench away, we had to step back quickly to avoid the worst of it, but not before I darted in to slap the tape back over her mouth. As I backed away, she convulsed again and dumped another load.

Although only two others had more or less recovered a measure of consciousness, as we moved away towards the truck, it was proved that the bowels work as part of an automated system, when one after another noisily and malodourously commenced the bowel-cleansing process.

As I drove away and found the highway out of town, Amanda

took great delight in phoning in an anonymous report to the local Police station of gunshots at the bikie headquarters address. She hung up when they requested her name. She also called the local TV and newspaper to report the shots fired at the Club and promised that there was a 'very newsworthy happening in the local drug and bikie gang war at the entrance to the Plaza Shopping Village', and if they went there ASAP, they would even beat the Police to the scene.

Both enterprises were very interested and promised to send crews immediately, especially the TV news desk as they could have something juicy to show on the early morning news.

We waited until 06:30 before calling the Police again claiming that there were naked girls dancing and running around the Plaza Shopping Village parking lot, but were told that the whole thing had already been aired on the early breakfast news and was being repeated every fifteen minutes in live, graphic detail. By that time, we were safely back in Tin Can Bay, Jack's unscratched Silverado parked back behind the pub, fuel tank filled and had put Melissa to bed on *Firebird*, pleased that she now appeared to be recovering quite quickly with normal vital signs.

I tuned into the local TV news and we saw that both the Amazon Club house attack and the Plaza Shopping Village Amazon display had received massive coverage that had been picked up by all the National networks and was being repeated endlessly by talking heads who speculated wildly as to who had done what and for what reason. The current line was that a rival bikie gang had attacked the Amazon's: a wild dog or dingo had attacked a bikie and that a vigilante group had somehow taken advantage of the opportunity to display seven naked Club members and make a statement.

Several community groups weighed into the argument, mostly in favour of cracking down hard on bikie gangs and drug pushers in general, while several church groups deplored the violence and condemned vigilante action at any time.

Another anonymous phone call to the producer at the TV channel revealed that the early-arriving news crews had gleefully heeded the warning on the signs hung around the girls necks and refrained from freeing them, but had spent their time while they waited for the Police by capturing every possible angle of every girl in Hi-Definition detail. While the images had to be heavily sanitised for breakfast TV, there were no such restraints required for the production of a YouTube video that also incorporated the Amazons Clubhouse battleground and the mauled bikie. By 10:00 that morning, the hasty production had already gone viral worldwide and as it was currently logging one million hits per hour, it promised to make some relatively serious money for the production crew.

CHAPTER 31

It was late morning and we were sitting around in *Seeker's* cockpit having morning tea with crumpets and honey, being way too wired to sleep, when the phone rang.

'Hi Greg. How's it going down there in the land of the working stiff?'

'Just tell me, Harry, that you're nowhere near Maryborough?'

'Well it's great to hear from you too Greg and I hope the family are well. And for the record, we're about 75 kilometres away from that place. That's pretty far for someone who has a boat, not a car. But what's the problem?'

He actually screamed, or at least made a sound that was suspiciously like it.

'Have you been watching the news, any news broadcast this morning? All hell is breaking loose up around there and its kicked off some serious trouble between most of the bikie gangs in SE Queensland. There's talk of all-out war being declared between them if something isn't done to defuse the situation!'

'What situation is that, Greg?'

He made the same strange noise again before composing himself.

'Allow me to summarise what's happened since this operation first started with a report from you Harry; in dot pints obviously!'

A bagman for a Gold Coast OMC is found shot, execution-style, at Mariners Cove.

A bikie succumbs to injuries received while raiding a private yacht in Southport.

Three bikies are seriously injured in raids of the same private yacht — all arrested.

Six bikies arrested after guns are discharged in a remote anchorage in Moreton Bay and a subsequent fight with a bunch of fishermen, three of whom are injured.

Three crew of a trawler engaged in a drug pickup in Moreton Bay are deceased in strange circumstances and when their sunken trawler is re-floated, it's found full of very large bullet holes.

Persons unknown raid the Clubhouse of the Aussie Amazons OMC in Maryborough and the Police are tipped off by an anonymous phone call well after the event. Upon attending, they find one female Club member seriously injured by what is described as a large, very vicious wild dog or dingo, probably rabid, going by the extent of the injuries. There are serious doubts that she'll recover, due to blood loss and shock, according to the hospital.

An inspection of the house yielded a large quantity of guns, cash and drugs, as well as a large, hidden cache of Semtex high explosive, detonator cord and primers.

The other occupants of the house, who were all Amazon Club members, were found bound, gagged and naked, tied to flagpoles outside the Plaza Shopping Village and covered in their own shit. The media were alerted well before the local Police were and Ambulance crews also were called long after the media had plenty of time to have a good long look at them. Paramedics suggest that all the bikies showed signs of being sedated and had been fed some sort of very strong laxative.

Several of the group suffered from a variety of injuries including a double fracture of their leader's right forearm. Oddly, all wounded persons, including the dingo-mauling victim back at the house, had rudimentary first aid administered that went a long way to reduce to long-term effects of their injuries.

Signs stuck to wet paint on the bodies of the Amazons seemed to point to a vigilante group, rather than a rival bikie gang.

Now have I missed anything off the list, Harry?'

'Well you could add in that a large quantity of very potent drugs, cash, firearms and high explosives have been taken off the open market, but that's not really for me to say, now is it? But that's a real clusterfuck all right, Greg. I'd hate to be the copper who's trying to sort that lot out or make much sense of things. Although it would seem from what you've told me, that the bad guys lost and the good guys won this round? Mate!'

'Yeah, I'll give you that one, Harry, but we're still looking down the barrel of a bikie war in SE Queensland, not just on the Gold Coast! They're all accusing each other of knocking off the drugs and cash payments.'

'May I make a suggestion? It's a bit radical, but it might just help smooth things over.'

'Yeah, anything! Bob and I are at our wits end and the big cheese in Brisbane is threatening to make us Probationary Constables if we don't come up with something very soon.'

'OK. Try this. Call the heads of the two gangs, oh, sorry, Clubs on the Gold Coast, Brad Edwards and Henry Jones, and suggest a meeting with you and Bob at a neutral place like the Benbow Tavern. I believe they know where it is. Explain to them that the drugs are gone — the money's gone — the Amazons got hit because they messed with the wrong people when they pulled that kidnapping stunt, but they got off very lightly considering what will happen if they, or anybody else tries for a bit of payback.

You might like to suggest that the wrath of God will be mild compared to what will happen if there's a next time!'

'OK, Harry. That's a radical idea all right, but it might get Bob and me off the hook, although I hesitate to say that it'll be a fun meeting.'

'Earning the big bucks isn't always fun, Greg — it goes with the territory. But don't let Bob try to come heavy-handed or bullshit with these guys. Play it light and be reasonable and obliging. That's my advice.'

'Ok, mate. That's good advice and we'll do that. I'll let you know the outcome. Cheers.'

'Cheers, Greg and be careful. And for Christ's sake, let me know when you've got a leak-free Evidence Locker. This stuff's burning holes in my hull bottoms and I'd like nothing more than to be shot of the lot of it!'

'Greg tore you a new arsehole?' Amanda queried.

I laughed, 'He tried, but I pointed out the upside and suggested he and Bob tell the Commissioner to pull his silly bloody head in if he wants the results he's been getting so far to continue. But there does appear to be some rather heavy fallout from our antics of last night that may bring the wrath of little brother Henry of Undertaker fame down on us.'

'So might this be a good time to change location?'

'Excellent thinking, dear girl. I think we might go into retreat for a short time. How are your supplies, Dave?'

'Heaps, mate. We can feed all of us for four or five weeks at least.'

'OK. That sounds good. Are we about the same?' I asked Amanda.

'Yeah. No problem, although we don't have the freezer space that *Seeker* has. Still, if we do some fishing to supplement the larder we'll be fine for a couple of months.'

I shook my head. 'I had no intention of hiding out for that long. Just enough to drop out of sight for a while and probably no more than a couple of weeks at most, before we head up to the Whitsunday's for a while.'

I looked at Amanda again. 'Two questions — is Melissa OK to travel or should we stay close to a doctor for a while? Second — do we need any more bread-making stuff? I've grown very fond of your latest brew.'

She laughed. 'Melissa is recovering quickly and I don't think that there will be any relapses, so she's right to travel. Secondly, we could use some more bread-making stuff and some more long-life milk. I could take a taxi to the supermarket and be back in thirty minutes.'

I nodded, 'OK. Can you make a quick list and do just that, please. As soon as you're back, we'll leave.'

She jumped up and Corrine offered to go as well and help, so they made a list to cover both boats, called the taxi and went to the head of the marina to wait for it. Meanwhile, Dave and I checked our boats over and made ready to get going, after which I went to the marina office to inform them that we had to leave within the hour to meet friends down at Noosa. As I'd pre-paid for both boats, I refused the refund and that generated more goodwill and thanked them for making our stay so pleasant.

'What's the sailing plan?' Dave asked.

'I think we should head off shore for a while. The closest suitable places are in the Bunker group of Islands with Lady Musgrave Island at the bottom end. Most are coral cays, but there are a few with a small island where we could get inside the reef, anchor in shallow water and be safe from a blow. If we can stand hanging around there for a couple of weeks, we might head for the Whitsunday's. Race Week is coming up soon and that should be a hoot to be around for.'

He grinned, 'Good plan, mate. I don't think that Corrine or I would complain about some peace and quiet at some deserted islands for a while. And Race Week sounds interesting.'

'Good oh. We might make the run in two legs, though. It's about 45 nautical miles to an anchorage called Sandy Point on the northwest tip of Fraser Island. With the sou'easter still blowing, I plan on about a 12 to 14 knot cruise, so that's going to be about three and a half hours for us. If you don't mind burbling along quietly, stick with us, otherwise you guys just blast on ahead and we'll meet up there.'

Dave grinned, 'Nah. Sometimes the slow road works just fine. We'll stay in convoy — I'll just use one engine to save fuel.'

Shortly after that exchange, the girls returned and I was able to report that Melissa was talking rationally and even being a bit cheeky, so she was well on the way to total recovery. She'd loved the story about what we'd done to the Amazons and insisted that it was repeated several times to make sure she hadn't missed any juicy bits. I'd copied the uncensored viral video and let her watch it to her heart's content on a laptop.

Fifteen minutes after the girls returned and I'd passed on my Melissa report, we were rumbling and puttering quietly down river toward the broad entrance channels. As it was still well before noon, I expected to be at Sandy Point by mid-afternoon.

Once clear of the river channels, I hoisted sail to take advantage of the brisk sou'easter blowing and we scooted north at an excellent pace, Dave hanging easily off our port quarter.

Amanda kept me company after she'd stowed all the food stuff she'd bought, ducking down below to check on Melissa every fifteen minutes or so, until the girl in question showed up in the cockpit, wearing trakkie-daks and an oversize jersey, giving me a surprisingly hard hug. 'Thanks for rescuing me, Harry. I'm so sorry to have put you all to so much trouble and danger, but I just wasn't expecting them to want to snatch me!'

I stroked her back gently. 'That's OK, lovely girl. That's what we do for family. The bad guys messed with us; we fucked them over big time.'

She gave a devilish grin, 'I so loved that video! And your story about the raid on their house was brilliant!'

I grinned back. 'Yeah! I thought it went down rather well myself. Everyone did a great job, especially Amanda lying on the ground, pretending to be hurt and crawling up to the barn door. I was afraid she'd gravel rash her boobs, but she says they're OK. I haven't had time to check.'

That made her giggle, another good sign as we scooted north under full sail. I deemed it sensible to drop sail when we got into the confined passages of the Great Sandy Straits, then relied on the engines wound up to 75% power, pushing us along at 14 knots and without the need to mess around with sail settings all the time, it was an easy passage. Once clear of the channels, I hoisted sail again and we continued up to Sandy Point in relative silence.

CHAPTER 32

'Undertaker.'

'Hi Henry, it's Etta, the cops have got us and we're in trouble.'

'Hi, Sis. You don't sound too good and I sort of gathered that there were problems from your less than photogenic appearance on National News this morning and in rather more graphic detail in that YouTube video. I must admit that I haven't seen you naked since we were kids having a bath together. You have grown very nicely.'

'Stop being a smart-arse, Henry. This is my only phone call, so I need to pass on some information so you can get me and the girls out of here.'

'Steady, sister. I already have our tame lawyer on the job, but he tells me that getting you lot out of there is going to be harder than prising a Catholic priest off a choirboy. I mean Semtex, drugs and automatic weapons? And you kept them around the house without security?'

'Stop busting my tits, Henry. We cocked things up a bit, but we didn't expect to be attacked by a squad of SAS troops.'

'What SAS troops? There wasn't any mention of the SAS involved in that shitfight?'

'Well there had to be. You should've seen the way they picked the girls off one or two at a time, and they had some sort of an attack animal with them! It wasn't a dog, was black and sort of looked like a cat, but it was way bigger and much more ferocious than any other cat I've seen outside a zoo. It must have been bred specially for attacking and killing! That thing just about ripped June's face and half her bum off before they called it off! Christ, it was hideous! These arse-holes

have got to be made to pay for this, Henry! I'm counting on you to do some heavy payback on my behalf.'

'What's wrong with you doing it when you get out on bail?'

'Cause, dear little brother, in addition to the double break to my right arm, I've got three broken ribs and may need some kind of knee surgery before I can walk again.'

'Ah, shit! I didn't know that, Sis. So do you know who it was? I mean you were rattling on about the SAS a few minutes ago.'

'Yeah, I do. The leader spoke to me when they tied us to those fucking flagpoles and he was the one who beat up on me. I mean, just because I was trying to shoot him at the time is hardly any reason to get that physical, now is it? He's the bloke that Erin identified off the catamaran at Noosa! He and the two bimbo's are now travelling with a big power boat with a guy and a small girl.'

'It's not red, by any chance, is it?'

'Nope. I told you that last phone call; it's royal blue and white. C'mon Henry, get your shit together!'

'OK. But explain the SAS reference. I really don't get that.'

'Sorry. I've been a bit spaced out with painkiller medication. The coppers have June and me in the Base Hospital under guard. The mob that raided us was dressed like SAS troopers in tight, black overall suits with ammo belts, strap-on knives and pistols, and carrying either sub-machine guns or military-grade shotguns. They moved like military people too!'

'Terrific, Sis. So you want me to send my boys against a bunch of ex-SAS troops. No wonder four of my guys got trashed trying to get on that bloody boat! One died yesterday, by the way. Anyway, even though they've attacked you and your ladies, I'm going to have a hard time convincing my guys to take them on. This isn't a good time for a bunch of guys to be racing all over the countryside looking for these people, with most of the other Brothers at each others throats trying to find that shipment. And we've got a funeral to stage for my guy! The Zombies are going to ride with us!'

'Yeah, sorry to hear that. It'd be a great ride, but after that, can you get your arse into gear and get after these turkeys? C'mon! This is your big sister who's been bashed up and is lying in hospital! And remember that June may not survive either! Even though they wrapped her up with bandages, the Doctors say that there was massive system shock and blood loss. She wasn't pretty to start with, but if she does survive, she's going to look like Frankenstein's Monster having a bad hair day!'

'Settle down, Sis. She knew what she was getting into and you've all been in fights before, so what's the big deal?'

'I know we've been in fights before, but this was different! They were stone cold merciless; seemed like they'd planned every move and seemed to really enjoy tying us to those flagpoles and feeding us that fucking Epsom Salts brew so we'd shit ourselves! And how convenient was it that the TV and newspaper reporters all turned up together before the coppers?'

'Stop whining, Sis. This isn't like you, so build a bridge and get over it! I know I said there wouldn't be any serious reaction to the kidnapping of one of their girls and yes, I know it was me who asked you to do it in the first place, so I guess we'll try to do something to help. I'll ask some of the Brothers further north from there to have a look around first and try to get a lead on them before we make a move.'

'OK, Henry. They've told me I've gotta go. Just do what you can, as soon as you can and get us out on bail at least.'

'Bye Sweetie. Try not to molest the nice policemen. I'll be talking to you soon.'

KOFFEE AT KITTYKATS IN THE CENTRE OF MARYBOROUGH

The creak of protesting cane strands accompanied the movement of a heavyset man in a rumpled suit, as he impatiently shifted position, the street behind him temporarily quiet. Another man, this one tall and slim, dressed impeccably in a dark grey Hugo

Boss suit with an expensively subtle sheen, sat down opposite and delivered a broad smile and a firm handshake.

'Good Morning, Jim. Lovely to see you again, especially under these circumstances.'

The big man growled, but held his response until the slim waitress in a distractingly tight body suit with a yellow apron tied around her waist, delivered two large, steaming mugs of their best flat white coffee. The slim man studied her name badge, pinned just above her small left breast and gave her a beaming smile.

'Thank you, Clarisse. That looks terrific.'

She smiled back, quite taken with the dapper, polite man. 'You're welcome, sir. Call if there's anything else you need.'

He smiled acknowledgement, then turned all his attention to Barry, who cleared his throat and said, 'Thanks for meeting me here, Jim. My clients are all here, so it seemed best.'

'No problem, Barry. I would have been coming up here in a day or two anyway, since this has become the centre of bikie activity at the moment. I mean it's not often that seven naked, female Outlaw Motorcycle Club members get strung up, so to speak, on National TV.'

'Alleged Outlaw Motorcycle Club members, if you don't mind thanks Jim.'

'We can dispute that one, Barry, since their leader, this very tall dramatic, Amazon-looking woman, what her name — Etta Jones — calls them that, but let's move on. As the Police Prosecutor on this case, let me show you mine and then I guess you'd want to show me yours? Am I correct?'

'That's one way of putting it,' Barry growled, his normal way of speaking, but quite off-putting at first exposure, 'so tell me what I have already guessed.'

Jim beamed. 'Delighted to, my dear fellow. Firstly, we have kidnapping, then false imprisonment, offences connected with explosive substances, (suspicious possession will have to do for that one since your clients didn't actually blow anything up

— yet), a whole host of gun laws, most of the controlled drug offences and drugs of dependence, including supply of drugs to children and trafficking, tax evasion and unlawful assembly. There are a few others were still considering, but that's enough to start with, don't you think?'

Barry put on his bored, 'I-don't-give-a-shit' look and by way of reply, took three pieces of paper from his pocket, unfolded them and laid them on the table, face down.

Jim looked at them, putting on a disappointed look. 'Is this trade-off time already? I expected a bunch of outrageous denials and a chance to fine-tune my courtroom argument. This is very disappointing, Barry.'

'The people who did this to my clients are guilty of more offences than my clients, Jim, but they have magically disappeared and seem to have some heavy protection from higher levels. Regardless, I cannot in all honesty dispute the charges you have levelled at my clients and I've advised them accordingly.'

Jim raised his eyebrows, 'That's a new one from you Barry, but I suspect that you have an offer for me to consider?'

Barry nodded. 'Yes, I do.' He turned the first sheet of paper over and pushed it across to Jim.

'Disclosure of all the end users for the weapons that were found at your client's premises. That's useful and may be worth a small reduction of sentence. What's next?'

Barry turned over the next sheet and slid it across.

'That's better. The full list of all the pushers your clients have been supplying. That's worth a decent chunk of sentence reduction. Now, let's see your last card.'

Barry repeated the showy revealing and pushed it across the table.

'Ah! This is interesting. In return for a ridiculously low bail for all of your clients involved in this bunfight, they will reveal details of the super MDMA shipment that has all the bikie gangs in SE Queensland up in arms. But we already know much of this,

Barry. In fact the Brisbane Central boys thought they had their grubby little paws on it for a while, until it was pinched off them in turn by bikies unknown. This might not be worth so much. Is that it? No more?'

For once in his less than illustrious career, Barry was stuck for a witty response.

Jim nodded thoughtfully, 'I can see that you've been dealt a dud hand Barry, but there's not much we can do about it. Your ladies are in some serious trouble and while some of what you've offered will help, they aren't going to walk out on bail that easily. But, I'll leave the door open to further trade if they can come up with something a lot more useful.

That's the best I can offer for now, I'm afraid.'

Barry nodded miserably, hating to be helpless. 'Yeah, I got it Jim. I'll try to get some more, but you know how it is. Sometimes the client only tells you what they want you to hear.'

'Yes. I can appreciate that, so do your best. We really would like more information on the missing shipment of super MDMA.'

On that note, they finished their coffees, left a tip for the pretty waitress and went their separate ways.

UNDERTAKERS OMC CLUBHOUSE, MOLENDINAR, THURSDAY AM

'Undertaker.'

'*Good Morning, Mr Jones. This is Inspector James of the Southport Police. How are you this lovely morning?*'

'Ahh...well. Good Morning Inspector. I'm very well thank you and it's good to hear from you although things are rather in a bit of a muddle at the moment, I think you would agree?'

'*Indeed, Mr Jones, although much of that muddle could be resolved by some old-fashioned confession. As the old saying goes, 'it's good for the soul'.*'

'Yes, I do agree with that basic sentiment Mr James, however, I believe that maintaining my personal freedom is even better for my soul, so unfortunately I'm unable to take advantage of your offer, if that was the purpose of your unexpected phone call.'

'*Actually, Mr Jones it wasn't, although it is related. I'd like to invite you and your opposite number, Mr Edwards to a meeting with my superior, Superintendent Casey and myself to discuss matters of mutual concern. If you are agreeable, I think it would be best to have that meeting as soon as possible, perhaps even like, this morning.*'

'That is an interesting proposal, Mr James. May I presume that should I agree to this unique event, there will be no other involvement by the Police?'

'*That's correct, Mr Jones. Superintendent Casey and myself will be the only Service representatives present and you are welcome to secure the surrounding area with your people if you wish to be reassured on that point.*'

'May I bring my Lieutenant with me? I will probably do as you suggest and have more of my people in the area, but I'd prefer to have a witness.'

'No problem. May I suggest the Benbow Tavern as the venue and 11:00 this morning as the time? I believe that you and Mr Edwards are familiar with the venue?'

'Very droll, Mr James, and you are well informed. The venue and time are acceptable to me — are they acceptable to Mr Edwards?'

'I haven't had a chance to talk to Mr Edwards yet. Securing your agreement was more important.'

'In that case, allow me to issue that invitation on your behalf. Mr Edwards and I have been talking much more often in recent times.'

'Excellent. I'd be obliged if you would issue that invitation and please call me if there is any problem with either the time or the venue. Otherwise, I'll see you then. Good day Mr Jones.'

'Good day, Inspector.'

ZOMBIE EATERS CLUBHOUSE

'This is Brad.'

'Good Morning Mr Edwards. This is Mr Jones.'

'Gidday Henry. How's it all going? Hey, I saw that there was a bit of a rock & roll party in Maryborough last night. Wasn't that your sister's mob flashing their tits and pussies on national TV?'

'It is indeed and yes, that was my darling sister taking a starring role!'

'Wow! She's a great looking chick, even with all the shit on her! Love the hairdo and I wouldn't mind saying hello one day when she's cleaned up. Can you put in a word for me?'

'I'd be delighted, Mr Edwards. I think you probably deserve each other, but she's in hospital with injuries as a result of that 'party' *you referred to, and may not be in condition to entertain guests for a while.*

However, there is another matter that I called about. I just took a call from Inspector James of the Southport Police, inviting you and me, with lieutenants, to a meeting with him and his boss, Superintendent Casey. The meeting is scheduled for 11:00 this morning at the Benbow Tavern. Are you willing and able to attend? I'm assured that there will only be Inspector James and his boss, Superintendent Casey present. We are invited to post men in the area to look for a trap, but I do believe that this call is genuine and they just want to talk.'

'Hell yes! Tony and I will be there with bells on! Wow, what a hoot! Just us big bad bikie boys having a sit-down social chat with the top Coast coppers! Any idea what it's about?'

'For once, Mr Edwards, I have no further information. We'll just have to wait and see.'

'OK, Henry. We'll see you there and I will have a few of the troops in the area.'

'Likewise, Mr Edwards.'

BENBOW TAVERN

Just before 11:00, a plain white Falcon sedan rolled into the parking lot and found a space right in front of the main doors. A medium height, slim man and a tall, burly man in dark suits climbed out and made their way inside, heading for the Bistro Lounge at the rear. A barman recognised the pair and ducked into the back office to tell the Manager that the two most senior coppers on the Gold Coast were in the Lounge and it didn't look like they were going to have a social pre-lunch drink with their wives.

Two minutes later, almost arriving together, two dark-coloured sedans wheeled into the parking lot and around to the rear, where they stopped close to each other near the rear doors of the Lounge. The four men who climbed out were a study in contrast, from the extremely tall and skinny Henry Jones to the medium height Brad Edwards, who nevertheless was built like a wharf piling and was all muscle. The two Lieutenants were simply tall, wide and tough. As they acknowledged each other with cordial handshakes, a grumbling roar sounded from several directions in the immediate vicinity, causing both leaders to smile grimly as their boys made their presence very obvious as they swept the area for signs of excessive police presence.

Inside the Lounge, they spotted the two senior coppers had snagged a large, round table right at the back, as far from the scattered few pensioner couples who were getting in some early lubrication in preparation for the cheapest lunch special of the day.

The four senior bikies were gratified to see the coppers stand as they approached the table and offer to shake hands — deciding after only a brief hesitation to reciprocate. That set the tone for at least a cordial start to the discussions, although silence prevailed until a nervous young waitress came over on the Manager's instructions to see if the group wanted anything.

Bob Casey looked at Greg James, who said, 'We'd like a couple of schooners of Great Northern please Josie, and whatever these gentlemen would like. And is there any chance of some little snacks from the kitchen? I'll square the bill when we leave if that's OK?'

Josie nervously bobbed her head as the bikies ordered beers as well and they nodded approval at the food suggestion, 'That'll be no problem Inspector. It'll only be a few minutes. Gary has just made a batch of fresh spring rolls and steamed dim-sims.'

Remarkably, the group managed to make small talk for the few minutes it took for beers and several plates of steaming hot food with soy and sweet-chilli sauce to be delivered. Everybody tucked in for a few minutes until it was business time, and also noticeable that most of the early lounge lizards scattered about the large, airy room decided that the Sports Bar would be a better place to have their drinks.

Greg cleared his throat, took another sip of beer and started. Being careful not to reveal or even hint that Harry and crew were undercover, he said, 'We called this meet to discuss the current level of unrest amongst all the Clubs in the SE Queensland area, to share with you some facts you may not be aware of and to hear any constructive opinions you may care to let us in on. We do not intend to cast aspersions or discuss any allegedly illegal activities that may or may not have been conducted by anybody present.

Because of the turmoil happening among all the Clubs at the moment, our purpose here today is to try to avert open warfare on the streets that might inadvertently involve civilians.'

'I think I can speak for Mr Edwards as well, Inspector James, when I say that we sincerely wish to avoid that as well,' Henry Jones stated, the comment receiving a nod from Brad Edwards.

'Excellent. That's a good start so I'll tell you a few things you may or may not know. Firstly, the crew that has been responsible for stirring up the whole mess over the last few weeks has contacted us. They didn't explain who they are or who it is they answer to, so I can't speculate on that, but the message they wanted understood and passed around is that the drugs are gone and permanently off the market!

The money paid to the manufacturer can't or won't be refunded, which to me suggests there might be some level of connection.

The Amazon's were hit hard because they were the ones who pulled that kidnapping stunt on one of their people and that was taken to be amateurs messing with the wrong people.

They want to make it very clear that in fact, the Amazons got off very lightly and if they or anybody else try to pull another stunt like that as payback, and I quote, 'The wrath of God will be mild compared to what will happen next time'.'

'Big words, Inspector.'

Greg shrugged, 'Yes, they are big words, Mr Jones, I quite agree, although please remember that they aren't mine! But can these people back them up? I don't know, but looking at their past form, they're acquitted themselves very well so far. However, all I'm doing at the moment is passing on what they told me. There's no more or less than that and I haven't tried to put any spin on it. It's up to you fellas to make of it what you will.'

He sighed, perhaps a trifle theatrically, 'Look guys. We're laying all our cards on the table, because, like I've said, we don't want a major eruption of inter-Club warfare in public. If the Clubs want to rip the shit out of each other in private, that's your right and your problem, but we'd really appreciate it if civilians were left out of any brew-up.'

Brad Edwards nodded seriously. 'Appreciate your frankness Inspector, but to a large extent, it's out of our hands too. We don't intend to start a war, but if attacked, we will take all reasonable steps to defend ourselves. I mean, we can't speak for the other Clubs but we know they're very upset about these pirates or hijackers or what ever the fuck they are.'

Greg nodded. 'Yep. Obviously, we have no control of anything either, so we understand that, but if we can at least get both your Club's appreciating the situation and not getting unnecessarily excited, that's a good start.'

Henry leaned forward, his stark appearance and extreme height making it's own dramatic statement. 'I hear you Inspector but please understand this, a very grievous injury, embarrassment and insult has been done to my sister and her associates and I can assure you she will *not* be letting bygones be bygones!

And not only don't I blame her for that attitude, but I'm obliged to provide all assistance she needs to track, find and deal with these people. So would you care to share any ideas you might have as to the identity of these pirates? Especially since Etta said they dressed and acted like a specialist military unit.'

Without allowing the slightest trace of guile to show on his face, Greg put on a sorrowful look as he shook his head, 'Mr Jones, there's nothing I'd like more than to have a line on these vigilantes, or pirates if you like, but we've not picked up any indication of who they are yet. We agree that they seem to be some sort of renegade ex-military Special Forces unit, but as to who's behind them, we just don't know. I mean they seem to be very well funded with boats and weapons, so there's a lot of money backing them. There was such an organisation in Melbourne not long ago, but that's been shut down and the owner and organiser is in jail for another 12 years. However, there is obviously another one that's taken its place.'

Henry nodded, a trifle impatiently, 'Yes, yes! We've got that, but have you got any ideas as to who's behind it?'

Greg drew a breath, 'It's worth considering that in our experience, this type of organisation only works on contract. They don't stick their collective necks out unless there's a big profit at the end, so that means someone's hired them. What I can say is that we're looking into the money trail but more importantly, the motive — as in, who's going to gain the most out of this seizure of drugs and money and profit the most by the revolt that's being stirred up amongst the Clubs.'

He chuckled a moment, sounding very forced to Bob Casey, who'd stayed out of things so far, letting his sidekick do his usual excellent job. 'I don't suppose that it could be one of the other Clubs behind it? I mean, you'd probably know about it by now, wouldn't you?'

Henry tried to look impassive, even when Brad Edwards raised his prominent eyebrows and looked across at him to gauge his reaction to the suggestion. Finally, Henry said, 'That is a long stretch of the imagination, Inspector. But to be honest, and we're putting our cards on the table beside yours, the thought had occurred to Mr Edwards and myself as we've been trying to make some sense of this whole mess. But if it is one of the other Clubs, that doesn't bode well for any sort of peace between us!'

Greg nodded thoughtfully, 'If you believe that is a possibility then would the facts suggest that two or more Clubs are amalgamating in order to make a power-play? There are plenty of ex-Special Forces persons around who might be formed into a contract group to do the strong-arm stuff. That scenario would seem to fit the facts better than most others, but you guys would know this better than we would.

At this stage, we're only guessing and tossing out ideas which is why we called this meet in the first place.'

Brad Edwards spoke up, 'As Police Officers, you're taking a very odd role in this, Inspector. You're being surprisingly helpful and that raises a red flag for me. Please try to convince me that you're on the level.'

Bob Casey sat more upright and fielded that shot in his deep, gruff voice, 'Our position Mr Edwards, is very straightforward in fact. Inspector James said we wouldn't discuss the on-going drug issue since our position on that is obvious, but aside from that, we're under a lot of pressure from our superiors in Brisbane as well as the local Council who want to try to present the Gold Coast in the best image possible. Therefore, anything we can do to stop the Clubs fighting in public is on the table.

The dramatic demise of your Mr Wells over at Mariners Cove, in very suspicious circumstances I might add, is an example of what we need to stop happening again. At least in public, although don't take that to mean I'm condoning murder! It plays out like a scene from an American gangster movie — no personal slight intended, Mr Edwards.'

Brad grinned, 'None taken Superintendent and your explanation for this mood of co-operation is plausible, so I'm prepared to accept it at face value for now. What about you, Henry? It sounds like we're almost being asked to work with the Police in tracking down whoever's behind this rogue hit squad.'

'Hmmm! Maybe. However, my previous statement still stands in that Etta has been injured and shamed and wants payback, despite whatever this bunch of mongrels have said. So while we'll be searching for these people, we'll be doing it for ourselves.

However, to continue this current spirit of co-operation with the Police, I'll agree to pass on any information we gain, but only as long as we get first crack at these people.

Provided, Superintendent, that the Police doesn't harass us unduly while we go about our business. We do conduct several legal enterprises, you know.'

Bob Casey nodded, 'Yes, we are aware of those activities and naturally wish that you'd stick to doing just that. But don't expect any leeway with anything we consider illegal. I hope that's understood?'

Both leaders nodded. 'Crystal clear,' Brad said, 'in fact I'd be very suspicious if you did otherwise.'

Greg James looked around the table. 'Well, that's all that was on our agenda, but we're happy to listen to anything you fellas would like to discuss while we're still together.'

Henry spoke up. 'There is something you could do that we'd greatly appreciate. We have a funeral tomorrow for our colleague who died of injuries received recently and would like both Clubs to be allowed to make a mass formation ride through Surfers and Southport on the main highway as a token of respect. Are you able to condone the ride and arrange the traffic aspects for it at short notice?'

Greg looked at Bob who nodded. 'No problem, Mr Jones, we'll do that. Do you have a route planned?'

Henry passed over a map with the route highlighted, which Bob and Greg quickly scanned, noting that it would pass through the CBD of both main centres, before heading for the Southport cemetery. 'Are you willing to maintain a reasonable speed throughout the ride?' Greg asked, 'and how many bikes?'

'How about 40 km/h with the bikes two abreast, the coffin leading, with around 80 bikes. Is that acceptable?'

Greg and Bob nodded, 'That's a long line, but at that speed, it won't cause serious traffic problems. How about if we provide four Patrol bikes leading, with two more bikes plus two Highway patrol cars trailing if you don't mind,' Greg said, 'just to clear the way so there aren't any holdups. And we'll have the traffic lights co-ordinated to avoid stoppages if you can be ready to go from a fixed point at a precise time. Would that work for you?'

Both officers were surprised to see a fleeting glimpse of what could easily have been mistaken for a smile to flash across Henry's face. He nodded his thanks. 'That's very satisfactory gentlemen and we'll make that happen. And I do thank you for being so obliging.'

'No problem. It should make a very impressive sight and sound for the tourists!' Greg said, 'So is there anything else? If not, I think we're done and we'd like to thank all four of you for attending. At least we're on the same page on this and I'll pass any information that may be useful as soon as I receive it.'

Unusually, Henry stood first and gravely shook hands with Bob Casey and Greg James before departing with his 2IC. With a wry grin, Brad Edwards did likewise and followed Henry, leaving Bob and Greg to let out collective breaths.

Bob was the first to speak, 'I don't know about you, Inspector, but that calls for another drink and to hell with the 'on duty' bullshit for once.'

'Bloody great idea, Superintendent. It was an historic meeting if ever there was one.'

Although there normally wasn't table service, when she saw them sit down again, the young waitress hustled over with two more schooners of beer, and with a beaming smile said, 'We were hoping that there wouldn't be any bloodshed. The manager nearly crapped his pants when he saw who was meeting with you fellas.'

'Please thank him and reassure him that all is well, if you wouldn't mind,' Bob said graciously, as she smiled again and left.

CHAPTER 34

Gidday, Greg, how's it all going down there in La-La Land?'
'*Very amusing Harry, but unfortunately accurate. However, I called to let you now that Bob and I have just come from quite an historic meeting with the leaders of the Undertakers and the Zombie Eaters, our local Gold Coast OMC's. As you suggested, we passed on your message and hopefully planted the idea that your group are ex-Special Forces mercenaries contracted by a consortium of two or more bikie Clubs trying to take over the drug distribution network in Queensland.*'

'Wow! Great work mate, if they'll buy that idea. Bob must have been shitting himself!'

Greg chuckled, 'Yeah. He did look a bit white at times, but the bad boys were very well-behaved, except that Henry Jones, who is the brother of the Amazon Queen that got roughed up in that little dust-up in Maryborough the other night, stated that regardless of your dire warning, he's obliged to help her find the persons responsible and exact appropriate revenge.

His sister, the Amazon Queen, Etta Jones, was swearing that as soon as she can get about, she's going on the warpath with her 18 girls and wants the Undertakers and the Zombies to back her up. So that doesn't bode well for you at the moment, Harry, 'cause from what we hear from the hospital guards, Etta now wants Henry and Brad on the job right now and not wait until she's fit, because the Doctors say it'll be weeks before she can use her arm and twice as long before she can take a deep breath without severe pain.'

'Hmmm. Yeah, okay mate. We're about to go offshore for a while to stay out of public view, but that won't last too long. Sooner or later, their network of spies will find us, so that's when there'll be another set-to, I'm afraid. And we're quite well pre-pared for this one.'

'*This isn't supposed to be a warzone, Harry. We can't let you set yourself up as a target again. This time there'll be a sizeable bunch of bad boys heading your way, and they won't be mucking around!*'

'Well, I hate to disagree with you Greg, but it is warzone to these people! But what do you think you could do, officially? The Police can't make a pre-emptive strike, because so far, it's only rhetoric and strong words. Your hands are tied officially, 'cause these darling citizens have rights. We are the un-official strike force, but we can't go pro-active until we get the right opportunity. And it's no good attaching a Special Emergency Response Team to us, 'cause the bad guys will just wait until we're on our own again. We have to wait, be prepared to defend ourselves as best we can by looking innocent and then try to keep the confrontation away from the public.'

'*That doesn't sound like much of a plan to me! Aren't you worried with three bikie gangs chasing you?*'

'Very concerned will have to do, although if we can set them up to come to us on our terms, that'll even things up heaps.'

'*Well, good luck with that one. I'll see if there's anything that we can do to help without scaring the bad guys away and I'll keep you updated via sat-phone.*'

'Thanks, Greg. Amanda says 'Hi'. She and Melissa have done a terrific job so far. They'll need a medal and/or a promotion after this.'

'*Under consideration, mate. Oh. By the way, there's someone here who's been kicking me in the shins and wants to say hello.*'

'*Hi Harry, it's Sandy. How are you?*'

'Sandy? You beautiful, sneaky bugger of a darling girl! Why didn't you say you were coming back?'

'*I didn't know until yesterday. The operation that delayed Charlie was wrapped up suddenly — he wanted to get his station back before I fucked up anything else, so he flew in, we did a quick hand-over, then I was out on the next aircraft.*'

'Fantastic! Hey, I've just thought of something. You gotta put Greg back on.'

She laughed, 'Settle down, big dog! I've already told him I need to take some de-stressing leave, so he and Bob have reluctantly agreed to second me to your little harem on Firebird for the duration of this current dust-up with the bikies. The only question is — where are you and how do I get there?'

'Hang on a second, I'll just pull up a map. Wait one...still there?'

'Yeah Harry, where the hell else would I be, you dick! Of course I'm still here. What've you found?'

'Oh, touchy! Must be pre-nooky syndrome! Sorry, must have had a touch too much sun! Oddly enough, we're at a little beach on Frazer Island called Sandy Point and the closest airport is Bundaberg. By far the quickest way is for you to get the Qantas flight from Brisbane to Bundaberg this afternoon that departs at 16:00 and gets in at 16:55. The closest we can get is a coastal village, southeast of Bundaberg, called Elliot Heads. There's a settlement called Riverview just upriver a short way and it has a boat ramp at the Nature Reserve.

Seeing as how you're officially joining an active operation, Greg and Bob should be able to organise you a couple of rides — to Brisbane Airport, then from Bundaberg Airport to Riverview. We'll be there at the boat ramp with *Firebird* from 17:00 on. It's a very shallow estuary, so we'll leave *Seeker* back at Sandy Point, but the tide will be about half and flooding so *Firebird* shouldn't have any trouble. You know what to pack.'

'OK. We've got that and Greg's nodding about the rides... he's asking about any more weapons or equipment you think we'll need. He filled me in on the bun-fight you've set yourself up for again and is set on playing Grandma Duck.'

'Nah. We're pretty good with most stuff, although a long gun or two with a bit of reach like one of those beaut Remington R4-M rifles would be a good thing. And I've got just the lady here to use it. If he can get one, better have a bunch of 5.56mm NATO ammo for it as well please.'

'OK. Got that. I presume that Dave and Corrine are the only ones on Seeker? And are Amanda and Melissa still there?'

'Yes, Dave and Corrine are on *Seeker*, Amanda and Melissa are still here and your bed in the starboard forward cabin is ready and waiting for your arrival.'

'That's good, 'cause we've got a lot of catching up to do. I know you've been well taken care of by Amanda, and I'm cool with that, but it's been a long time between drinks for me!'

I chuckled. 'Good on you. I'll see you this evening, then I'll take care of all that for you.'

SANDY

As she went back into Greg's office and handed the phone over, Sandy looked at Bob and Greg. 'That seems like a plan. Any problem getting the rides organised?'

Bob shook his head, 'Nope. Already arranged while you were discussing personal issues. A Highway Patrol car will be available at both ends. We've also managed to get a booking for you on the State Government Beechcraft 19:00 aircraft. It's at Brisbane at the moment, waiting to do a job this evening, so they were able to fit in a quick run up to Bundy and back this afternoon. It'll also make it much easier to carry weapons and ammunition aboard. Additionally, Greg and I have come up with an idea to bolster your force without going over the top.'

She raised her eyebrows. 'Mindful of Harry's words about that, sir, what's the idea?'

'There are two Constables that I sent to deliver Harry's latest crazy request to him at Dunwich that he was most impressed with. They're just General Duties Constables but came here with the highest recommendations from their last posting in Cairns.

They've only been involved in the periphery of the case so far, but Harry was very keen to use them if at all possible. They don't know what's going on, but I had them make up the fake drug shipment and deliver it, so there's some involvement already. Anyway, since Harry recommended them to us, it's my intention to send them with you to bolster your force. I gather that there's room for them on that overgrown Italian phallic symbol, *Seeker?*'

'There's room, but these guys aren't exactly Special Emergency Response Team qualified. Or are they?'

Bob smiled, 'As a matter of fact, they are. As you know, there's a squad in Brisbane and one in Cairns, but several additional officers have done the training and been qualified, but as there isn't a posting available at the moment, they were sent back to their previous General Duties.

They are Constable Alf Story and Constable Charles Jakes. I haven't told them yet, so we thought you might like to pass on the news and tell them what to bring.'

'Yes, sir. I'll do that. And do we have the long guns Harry asked for?'

'Yeah, that wasn't a problem. You'll have two of them plus ammunition, plus the standard Glocks your new crew will have.'

Sandy nodded. 'OK, sir. That's sounds pretty good. I'd better call these blokes in and give them the news.'

'Very good Inspector and if I might say, it's very good to have you back. You did an excellent job relieving and I expect no less from this posting.'

'Thank you, sir. I'll get going, if that's all?'

'Yes, Inspector. Keep us informed when you can.'

Five minutes later, a call went out from the Dispatcher to the car containing Constables Story and Jakes that was doing a patrol through the suburbs, 'showing the flag', to return to base ASAP. Slightly mystified, the young officers made their way back, arriving within ten minutes. On arrival, nobody seemed to know who asked for their return, except that it must have been important to interrupt a patrol run. Finally, they found the Radio room and asked the Dispatcher, who pointed them toward Inspector Thomson's office.

They'd never heard of an Inspector Thomson, but when any Inspector calls, mere Constables run! It took a little while to find the right office and when they did, the two men were surprised to see a tall, very attractive, auburn-haired woman wearing delightfully tight jeans and a well-filled vivid-yellow polo shirt standing in front of her desk, holding a Remington R4-M carbine with a disturbing degree of familiarity with another Remington was propped against the wall while sundry equipment covered her desk.

Not knowing whether to salute or not, Alf settled for coming to attention and stating, 'Constables Story and Jakes reporting as requested, ma'am.'

Sandy looked at her watch then blew them away with her stunning, relaxed smile.

'Good job, that was prompt. Please, come in and shut the door. We've got a lot to do and very little time to do it.'

Even more puzzled the two Constables did as she asked, Charlie Jakes closing the door and both wondering if this delightful-looking Inspector was going to send them to the outer boondocks for some infringement of rules.

Sandy smiled at them again, as their nervousness was almost palpable.

'Relax guys. You're not in trouble and we haven't crossed paths before since I've literally just arrived back from relieving duties in Cunnamulla.' She waved a hand down at her civilian clothes by way of explanation.

Alf Story acted as spokesman again, saying, 'Roger that ma'am. Your summons was just a bit unusual and got us a bit concerned that there was trouble.'

'Very perceptive, Constable Story, there is trouble, but we didn't cause it. Although we're probably heading for it.'

They looked worried again so she smiled and said, 'Sorry to be so cryptic. Anyway, I believe that you recently made a peculiar delivery to a Commander Stevens of the ACP at Dunwich Public Boat Ramp?'

Alf Story's face brightened, happy to be able to relate to something he actually knew about, 'Yes, ma'am. He seemed a very nice fella and was very grateful for our help. Do you know him?'

Sandy smiled again, 'Yes. I know the Commander quite well. However, I've called you here to let you know that based on a recommendation from Commander Stevens, you are both, as of now, on temporary transfer to a Multi-Jurisdictional Task Force headed by Commander Stevens. It is an undercover operation to do with the bikie problem you were involved in recently with the work for Commander Stevens and will be a deployment away from base. You are seconded to my command as of this moment and neither of you is to say anything about the transfer or speculate about the job to any other person, in the Service or outside it.

Your boss has been notified, so there's no need to report to him, since I'm your new Reporting Officer.

I don't like to come the heavy, but lives are at risk if the wrong thing is said, so the order is, 'Zip it or else the Service will have gained two brand-new Probationary Constables transferred permanently to Goondiwindi! Got that?'

'Yes, Ma'am. That's crystal clear. What do we have to do?'

'We're travelling as soon as you two can go home and pack a bag for a minimum of three weeks away. As this is an undercover operation, you won't need any uniforms, but take all your Service standard equipment and ID, including your pistol and any additional ammunition you have available. I'll issue you with Tasers when you come here.

A range of smart casual clothing is all that's required, although there may not be any shops handy for a while, so allow for that in your choice of personal supplies. Clear so far?'

'We hear you, ma'am, but not the reasons behind all this.'

'Fair enough. But I'll have to give you a briefing on the run, as we have a plane to catch at Brisbane Airport and a Highway patrol car to take us there just as soon as you two can get back here.'

'Copy that, ma'am. We'll hold the questions for now and get moving. We share a flat not far away, so we won't be long.'

'Excellent gentlemen. Now hustle, but remember you must not tell anybody what you're doing or where you're going!'

The Constables left, exchanging puzzled looks. 'There's no chance we could tell anybody what were doing, since I haven't got a clue,' Alf remarked to Charlie.

'Amen to that, brother. But at least we'll be working with the best-looking Inspector I've ever seen. Love those tight jeans!'

It was just twenty minutes later that the two good-looking young men dressed in casual civilian clothing knocked on Sandy's door again.

'Good work, good timing. We haven't got much time, so I'll quickly go over the gear then I can give you the briefing on the way. I need to point out that as this is an undercover operation, we all have a role to play and the first thing is that once we leave this building, we're just three friends and you're got to act that way. There mustn't be the slightest hint of formality or our official background. Therefore, I'm Sandy and you guys are Alf and Charlie. Don't forget that for a moment.'

Sandy noted their raised eyebrows and went on, 'Slipups aren't allowed, so if either of you don't think you can handle that, say so now and you'll be replaced without any blemish on your record.'

There was no response to that challenge, so she went on. 'Even in private, you're going to have to act that way as well, just in case there's a chance that someone could see or hear us, so you must treat everyone in the crew as a close, personal friend and talk and behave accordingly. Are you both reasonably comfortable with that?'

They both nodded. 'We can adjust,' Alf commented.

Sandy then showed them the two Remington R4-M rifles complete with their protective, padded travel cases, a metal case of 5.56mm NATO ammunition holding 840 rounds. There were also four Police-issue Tasers with spare air cylinders.

'I presume that you're both very familiar with this rifle?'

'Yes ma'am. We are.' Alf replied, but Sandy wagged her finger at him. 'Bad dog Alf. I'm not 'ma'am', just Sandy. Remember?' While he blushed and stammered an apology, she checked her watch again. 'OK. We're out of time, so we'd better get all this stuff out to the carpark, via the back door. We'll have a Highway Patrol car here any moment to take us to Brisbane, so hold the questions for now, please.'

In short order, they carted all the stuff out to the carpark where as indicated, a Highway Patrol car in full dress livery was waiting. The guys helped Sandy load everything in the boot and retrieved their personal gear from Alf's Subaru XV SUV, the guys noting that Sandy just had a small, soft bag only half the size of theirs. She took the front seat, letting Alf and Charlie share the back. The moment they were seated, their car moved away, a female Senior Constable who introduced herself as Tracy Manning doing the driving.

Sandy spoke to her first, 'Senior, while you do your very best to get us to the Brisbane Airport, General Aviation area ASAP and without causing traffic chaos, I'm going to give these officers a briefing concerning an active undercover operation. As of now, you are under a total secrecy order to say absolutely nothing to anybody about your passengers, where you take us, and what you hear about the operation. Lives, including ours, may depend on your silence. If anybody does ask questions, regardless of how senior they might be, you are authorised to refuse to answer and then must report the contact to Superintendent Casey here at Southport immediately. Is that clear?'

The driver refused to take her eyes off the road, but replied crisply, 'Yes, ma'am. Copied that. Total silence it is.'

'Excellent! Now gentlemen, listen up!' Sandy turned sideways in her seat and over the next 30 minutes or so, explained the situation clearly, concluding with, 'Any questions?'

Alf smiled and quipped, 'Only a few hundred, Sandy.'

The Senior Constable driver said promptly, 'Only one from me, ma'am. Can I come too? It sounds far more interesting than stopping speeding drivers.'

That was good for a laugh, but Sandy took a moment to say, 'Thanks for the offer Senior. But not this time, I'm afraid.'

Alf said, 'You mentioned that there are two civilians working with Commander Stevens who is ACP, as well as two QPS Policewomen. What's the Command line for the operation?'

'The ACP Commander is in overall charge, with myself as 2IC and Qld. Police liaison back to Superintendent Casey. The civilians are under his direction and you'll find out more about them when we get there. One in particular is ex-SAS and is very competent with most firearms, unarmed combat and highly talented in both sniping and close-quarters killing. I strongly suggest you don't piss her off!'

Both officers in the back blinked, while the driver grinned broadly and gave a little 'Yee-ha!'

The rest of the trip was filled with a barrage of questions from the back seat and a stream of answers from the front. By the time they arrived at the Airport in near-record time, the Senior Constable driver was ready to do anything to join the party.

Checking in at the General Aviation Terminal, they were met by the pilot, a tall, genial man who projected the air of easy competency that all top-level pilots have, and who quickly organised a trolley for their gear. After checking their ID's carefully, he escorted them over the access road and out onto the tarmac, their driver left behind looking sad and wistful. Ten minutes later they were loaded and seated, doors closed and the first of the two Pratt & Whitney PT6A turboprop engines was being spun over by the starter with a characteristic rising whine.

CHAPTER 35

'Hi Sandy. Where are you? It sounds like you're doing some vacuuming? Aren't you supposed to be heading up here?'

'Jeeze Harry, give it a rest! We **are** on our way up there. The vacuum cleaner you can hear is a pair of aircraft turbine engines. We're running ahead of schedule thanks to Bob organising us a lift, but I'll explain when we get there. What I needed to tell you is that Bob also added two officers to your little task force. They're the young Constables you were impressed with from the fake drug delivery, Alf Story and Charlie Jakes. We also have a few extra toys to play with and we'll be on the ground around 16:30 and should be at the boat ramp by 17:00.'

'That's great news. I'll tell Corrine and Dave that they'll have visitors and we'll be there by 17:00. I'm really looking forward to seeing you again.'

'Me too. I just hope Amanda has left you with enough reserves to look after me properly!'

'Ha, ha. If she hasn't, just remember that you were the one who told me to hook up with her. Otherwise, just have a girl-to-girl talk with her, just like you did with Janice that time. Remember? Anyway Sweetie, I'll see you soon. Bye.'

I called Corrine on the VHF radio to say that she should prepare the twin cabin for the boys, before checking the Chart plotter to confirm that we would be on time.

The Bundaberg Highway Patrol Constable was highly intrigued to see his nondescript, but nevertheless VIP passengers decanted onto the Riverview Public boat ramp at Elliot Heads, where they were greeted rather enthusiastically by a scruffy-looking chap in

326

shorts and bare feet, who'd just dropped a boarding ladder down from the bow of a very large and imposing-looking catamaran that had run it's bows gently up onto the beach.

Sandy and I hugged hard, but for the sake of discipline or some such crap, we kept our emotions in check! I welcomed Alf and Charlie and without messing around, herded everybody on board, stacked their gear on deck and left it to Sandy, Amanda and Melissa to stow everything down below, while I backed *Firebird* off the shore and negotiated the shallow, twisting channels back out to open waters. Jasper had a wonderful reunion with Sandy who in turn introduced Alf and Charlie to Jasper properly so he, Jasper, would know they were good guys. As Dave and Corrine had stayed back at Sandy Point with *Seeker* to save fuel, I soon had all sail raised and *Firebird* scooting along on a fast beam-reach in the brisk Southerly breeze.

Alf and Charlie had remained in the cockpit to watch, and with minimal boating experience, both were very impressed by the results of my line pulling that magically produced such a vast area of fabric from almost nowhere. When that mass of fabric in turn sent us along at up to 20 knots in near-silence, sitting almost flat in the water, leaving almost no wake and without the uncomfortable heeling angles monohulls have to suffer to achieve just half that speed, they were highly impressed.

'I can see why you have a catamaran for a home,' Alf commented. 'This is pretty amazing!'

They were even more impressed when Amanda brewed up tea and coffee for all and delivered it to the cockpit table without spilling it everywhere. Sandy reappeared dressed in boating gear and parked herself close beside me stroking my neck.

The time for the trip back to Sandy Point passed quickly as everyone shared news and caught up on happenings. Alf and Charlie had the most catching up to do and were stunned by what had already happened, now that they could be told everything.

They were also delighted to be part of the team, although nervous by the level of wrath that was about to descend on us with the attention of three bikie gangs.

Amanda had moved the few things she'd left in the Master cabin with good grace, but that didn't stop her from suggesting that the fun and games we'd enjoyed may not be over, by giving me the occasional pat on the bum in passing, much to Sandy's amusement. Once again, I was very grateful for having ladies who didn't get too possessively jealous. I found it interesting to see that Amanda chose to move into the larger port for'rard cabin with Melissa, instead of taking the vacant aft cabin. Knowing that in the past, Sandy had shown that she didn't mind playing footsies with another lady, I looked forward to see how this new domestic arrangement would work out between the three.

On arrival at Sandy Point, Alf and Charlie met Dave and Corrine and I chuckled when I recalled Sandy's story of how she'd warned both Alf and Charlie not to upset Corrine and their reaction to that warning.

The cooks combined their talents and produced a lovely feast to celebrate Sandy's return, so after much wine, beer and NQ teas, we were a happy little band of pissed possums who staggered off to bed much later. Despite the alcohol level in my blood, Sandy and I still managed some glorious celebrations of our own that lasted well into the wee small hours.

FRIDAY

Next morning was a very slow start for everybody, especially for Sandy and me, as she was a bit in the mood for another repeat performance of last night. When we'd arrived back the previous evening, we found that Dave had moved *Seeker* around the corner of the point to the northern side to get away from the choppy little waves that the steady southerly breeze had stirred up and determinedly curled around the point as if anxious to get at any boats trying to hide. Despite the move, as the breeze blew hard all night, both boats tugged fretfully at their anchor chains imparting a jerky motion that made for an uneasy sleep for most.

Therefore it wasn't until around 10:30, that we were all up, dressed and fed and raising anchors. I'd planned to spend a few days at least at Lady Musgrave Island, the second-most southerly little coral cay in the chain of islets stretching up the coast, with Lady Elliot Island as the most southerly. They were classed as the most southerly extension of Australia's Great Barrier Reef and offered crystal-clear water, great diving and excellent fishing.

The only drawback to being at such an idyllic location was that there would be a steady stream of dive boats and fishing charters coming and going every day, but hopefully we could tuck ourselves away from most of the activity.

It was around a 6.5 hour sail to reach Lady Musgrave, although as it was a straight run, I could let George the autopilot do all the steering with the bossy Chart plotter telling him where to go.

It was an uneventful run with only a few other boats sighted in the distance, Dave keeping *Seeker* comfortably off our port quarter, saving a lot of fuel by just idling along on one engine, another advantage of having jet-drives as there was no additional drag from the more usual prop, shaft, skeg and rudder propulsion method. Alf and Charlie elected to stay aboard *Seeker* for the run, although the previous evening, young Charlie had been all over Melissa and probably would have preferred to be in her company for the run, especially when Sandy led the way by stripping naked and heading up for'rard. Amanda and Melissa happily followed suit and it was a pleasure to see them draped most decoratively over the trampolines, soaking up some Vitamin D.

It wasn't long after 16:00 when the low, green smear of Lady Musgrave Island heaved above the horizon, the semi-circular necklace of white surf breaking on the surrounding reef curving out toward us. There were no outlying hard bits to cause us problems on our approach, so as the entrance to the shallow lagoon was on the northern side, we stayed close in as we tracked west about the cay, staying just 200 metres off the deadly, boat-breaking coral. I was happy there were no other boats in sight in the lagoon, my plans to deal with the gathering bikie storm still forming in my mind, despite my casual comments to Greg and Superintendent Bob.

The entrance channel was very narrow, being barely 30 metres at the narrowest point, but was straight and reasonably deep, although once inside, the lagoon was quite shallow with a reasonably good anchor holding of sand over coral. Large coral heads and clusters dotted the shallow lagoon; with the island tucked away in the northwest corner, several permanent moorings and dive platforms were in place close to it to service the dive and fishing charters. We therefore elected to park on the opposite or eastern side, about 1.5 kilometres from the island and an easy run in the RIBs. As usual in sheltered waters, we rafted up to ease the transfer of crew back and forth and that had the added advantage of partly masking the profile of each boat.

FIREBIRD – LADY MUSGRAVE ISLAND – MONDAY

Despite the steady flow of charter boat traffic each day over the weekend, it was a lovely stopover location. The diving was everything that was expected and the fishing re-stocked the fridge and freezer very nicely. Everyone settled in, with Melissa and Amanda apparently getting along very well with sharing a cabin — privacy being in short supply on a boat, but no one cared which made for a happy crew. Melissa also was getting on well with Charlie, although they had few, if any, opportunities to put their relationship on a more intimate footing.

Since Charlie was looking more frustrated each day, I guessed that they hadn't managed to play hide-the-sausage yet, and as

Melissa was getting what sounded like a decent amount of satisfaction from Amanda each night, she didn't seem to be in too much of a hurry to drop her panties for Charlie. Still, I thought that by the way he was behaving; it wouldn't be long before he pushed the issue.

After a late morning tea was cleared away, Sandy and Amanda decided that they wanted to go collect shells on the island that was for once, clear of tourists but I opted out, as I needed to do some maintenance on the water makers. Alf decided to go as well and then Corrine joined in, but as soon as Jasper heard the words shore and beach, he went into a pathetic fit of mewling that was his way of saying, '*can I go too?*' I therefore asked Sandy to take him and little Krazy kitten for a run on the beach.

Charlie and Melissa said they wanted to sunbake on *Firebird's* foredeck, Melissa at last agreeing to spend some semi-private time with Charlie.

We all had a quiet chuckle to see Charlie moving awkwardly with distended shorts as he escorted Melissa, looking very desirable in a brief red bikini, up to the foredeck.

My plan to service the water makers prompted Dave to do the same to *Seeker's* so after the shell-collectors had left with Jasper standing precariously up in the bow of the RIB with Krazy kitten perched on his shoulders, claws dug in for grip, we got stuck in and had the job done in 15 minutes or so, after which, I joined Dave on *Seeker* for a mug of tea in the saloon. That had the unintended consequence of placing us well above the level of *Firebird's* foredeck with an unobstructed view of Charlie and Melissa who maybe thought that we were still below working since they couldn't see us due to the dark-tinted glass windows.

Regardless, Dave happily joined me in perving on our latest shipmate's efforts to convince Melissa to remove her bikini.

He chuckled then said, 'He's been tripping over his dick since he came aboard. Did you hear the girls talking earlier? Melissa was telling them that she's been having a bit of fun with Charlie by winding him up deliberately. And it looks as if she's still doing it.'

It did look like Melissa was playing hard to get, despite Charlie sitting close beside her as she lay on a towel and taking his shorts off. He wore a pair of budgie-smugglers that were totally unable to contain his erection, part of which poked rather comically above the top edge of the garment.

'Bloody hell!' Dave exclaimed in awe, 'Now I really do feel inferior!'

I laughed, 'Yeah. He's a big boy all right! But he looks like one of those anglerfish dangling bait. The question is; will she snap it up?'

Melissa seemed to be eyeing him off, but continued to lie there chatting for a while before she rolled over, sat up and took her top off. Charlie took that as an invitation to move in and smothered her with hugs and kisses. Inevitably, Melissa's pants soon joined her top and Charlie's pants on the deck. Moments later, Charlie was tucked nicely away in Melissa to her obvious satisfaction.

At that point, despite feeling quite stirred by the action, we left them to their pleasure and relocated aft to the cockpit, although we couldn't quite escape the chorus of cries and groans that floated back on the breeze. It did at least demonstrate that Charlie was a stayer, not a 5-second wonder, although I hoped he'd finish soon as lunchtime was fast approaching and the shell party was due back.

Some time later, my wishes were granted and by the time Sandy and crew motored up, the lovebirds were sitting up fairly innocently on the foredeck, cleaned up, clothing mostly in place, including a cheesy grin on Charlie's face. I don't know why they bothered to dress since the other ladies sussed them out immediately with lots of good-natured joshing that gave Charlie a fit of the blushes.

It was a happy day for our last day at Lady Musgrave Island and there was a lot of discussion as to where we should go next, although north was the basic direction. The first discussion point was that while there were a lot of coral cays and pretty little islands to our north, we couldn't visit them all.

The next point was that as the weather was forecast to become a bit unsettled for a few days, we needed to keep in range of offshore shelter, without having to duck across to the mainland. Therefore, we compromised and decided to island and cay hop north, having a quick look at as many as were on our course and only stopping when we found a good anchorage.

<h1 style="text-align:center">CHAPTER 36</h1>

Next morning we were up and away reasonably early to avoid having the charter boats spot the direction we headed out and had just settled into a comfortable 12 knot cruise running before the steady Southeast breeze, when the Sat-phone rang with Greg on the other end.

'Hi Greg, How's it going?'

'Good for me, thanks Harry, but not so good for you. We've just had the word from our contacts that you've been reported as anchored at Lady Musgrave Island, so if you're still there, you'd better move your collective arses, 'cause the boys and girls are on their way.'

'Ah, golly gee! We've been sprung! Damn! It seemed too good to be true that a good, remote spot like this would be truly safe, but I guess with all those charter boats coming and going with fishing and dive parties, it had to happen.'

'That seems a very flippant attitude, Harry, even for you! I don't suppose that your deviant, scheming little mind planned this?'

'Maybe, maybe not,' I replied off-handedly, 'but remember when I said to you once before that I'd like to chose the time and place of the confrontation and that officially your hands are tied? This general area seems to be a good place once we get a bit further north away from the tourist business.'

'Dangerous stuff, Harry. I do hope you know what you're doing. Our informant is getting some of our intelligence second and third hand, but the main thing is that the bad guys know where you are and are making some serious arrangements to get there much sooner rather than later.'

'OK, sooner is better than later for my plan. But I can say that we're on our way as we speak and our destination is Fitzroy Reef — that's the fifth cay up from Lady Musgrove Island. There's no dry land there and we'll be parked up in the lagoon.'

'That sounds suspiciously as though you wouldn't mind if that information was made semi-public in a controlled leak manner?'

'Oh, a controlled leak would be dreadful, Greg. I don't know what I'd do without you!'

'You really are a smart-arse, Harry, but if it'll help, we should be able to leak in a fairly high-up direction, if you get my drift?'

'I got yours and you've got mine.'

'OK, job done, but I can't suggest anything else to help, unfortunately.'

'Well there is one thing that will help. If your Evidence Locker is secure, I'd really like to get rid of these blasted drugs and cash, but only if they can be kept really securely.'

'Now that's one thing I can do, Harry. We have indeed fixed that problem and a whole raft of new security measures have been put in place. The Commissioner has even issued new instructions regarding sensitive and valuable evidence that allows such stuff to be entered without description or being linked to a particular case, so long as it's signed off by the station senior officer.'

'Great Greg. So how can we organise a pickup? With these idiots on our tail, I'd really like to be rid of this stuff ASAP.'

'Yeah, yeah. Copy that Harry. Let me talk to Bob and I'll get back to you soonest. Where will you be later on today, for instance?'

'We're 60 nautical miles east-south-east of Gladstone at the moment. Is that too far to send a Police boat? I wouldn't like to see any civilian agency involved and there are no airfields close by, except back at Lady Elliot Island and that's got a resort full of bored, nosy tourists who'd love to talk to anyone who'll listen about odd goings-on, so that rules that idea out.'

'You've given me an idea, Harry. What's the sea like where you are?'

'Blue, salty and wet, Greg. Same as usual; did you expect something different?'

'*You're being a smart-arse again, Harry. I was going to see if we have any secure contacts with a Charter company that has a seaplane. If so, maybe they could land near you and do the transfer that way.*'

'Yeah, not a bad idea Greg, although I'm a bit over seaplanes at the moment. But like I said before, I don't think it'd be a good idea to involve an outside agency or personnel in something that'll really look like a major drug pickup, despite the Police connection. Better save that stuff for emergencies.'

'*Yeah, I suppose you're right. The only alternative is for you to head for the coast and I'll look at a reasonably remote pickup spot.*'

'OK, mate. As reluctant as I am to delay getting to Fitzroy Reef, I guess we can put up with that to get rid of all this shit, so we'll head that way, if you can make arrangements ASAP and call back.'

'*Will do, Harry.*'

I called Dave and Corrine on the sat-phone, even though they were just 100 metres away, but radio, even if encrypted, was still talking to the world.

'Hi Dave, I just had a call from Greg. He's cleared his Evidence Locker problem and is in the process of setting up a pickup time and place for our stash, so we're going to head for the Mainland to dump all this shit. To save fuel, how about you guys park in Fitzroy Reef; it's the second cay down from Heron Island. The first one south has a small island with houses on it, but the next one south is just coral. There's a narrow entrance and reasonable water inside, so we'll join you later in the day after this drop off.'

'*There was a lengthy pause before he replied, 'Copy that, Harry, but here's a better idea. You'll be all bloody day going to and fro in that cat. Why don't we transfer your goodies to Seeker and we'll do a fast run to wherever it is that Greg finds to make the pickup.*'

'I was thinking about your fuel endurance,' I replied, knowing how those monster V-12 diesels sucked the fuel at speed.

'No problem,' Dave came back, 'when we threw in the turbine booster engine, we sort of nearly doubled the tankage, so we've got heaps to spare. According to my chart-plotter, we've got about 16 nautical miles left to run to Fitzroy Reef. How about we head there together now, transfer your stuff in comfort and leave Firebird anchored with the girls to mind it and we'll make a fast run for the Mainland. We can be there and back in a couple of hours, tops.'

I thought a few moments and then Sandy nodded. 'OK sport. That's a good plan, especially as we're still waiting to hear what Greg's going to come up with. Fitzroy Reef it is.'

For the remainder of the journey, we hauled bags of Super MDMA up from the various hidey-holes where I'd stashed them and stacked them in the cockpit for a quick transfer to *Seeker*. Ninety minutes later, we were threading our way very carefully between sheer coral walls where surf broke on the jagged boat-breaking hard coral close to both sides of us. All navigation sensors were going — forward-looking sonar, digital depth sounder, even radar, although there was nothing showing on that as the cay didn't have any solid ground above water, except at dead low tide.

Our passage was complicated by the outgoing tidal flow, pouring in a raging torrent from the enclosed lagoon and out through the twin narrow channels at six to seven knots, forming massive overfalls and tide boils from the undulating bottom profile that pushed our bows from side to side making the whole boat shudder as if trying to deny us entry and at the same time, feed our fragile hulls to the voracious corals.

I had both engines running nearly flat-out to stem the tide and it was just as well that the channel was quite short, being only a couple of hundred metres before the turbulent flow relaxed its grip on us and we surged forward into a tranquil lagoon dotted with emerging patches and clumps as the tide dropped. As my pulse rate settled, our battle with the tide flow caused another devious detail of my grand plan to click into place.

Away from the entrance on the eastern side of the lagoon, there was plenty of good holding ground to drop anchor on firm sand, although coral growth wasn't far away. I therefore deployed both bow anchors for security and after putting out the stern anchor as well to stop swinging around, decided that this was a good a place as any for the showdown. There was no sign that other boats came here, mainly since there was no dry land, although the diving and fishing promised to be superb.

Dave eased *Seeker* alongside us and rafted up for the time it would take to transfer our cargo. With both crews pitching in, we soon had all the bags of dope stacked on a large drop sheet in *Seeker's* saloon, including the first small delivery from the deceased dickhead Gary and the cash from the deceased bagman.

We'd just finished an early lunch when the sat-phone rang with Greg on the other end.

'Hi Harry. We have a plan for your approval.'

'Hi Greg. Go ahead please.'

'OK. If you can make you way to the Tannum Sands area on the coast out from Gladstone, there's a small inlet just south of the main Tannum Sands inlet called Wild Cattle Creek. It actually separates Wild Cattle Island from the Mainland, but you only need to go about 500 metres in from the entrance Heads to find a boat ramp where the channel swings close to the Mainland shore. The entrance is quite shallow, but you should get through as I'm told the tide is just starting to fall, so if you hustle, you'll be OK.

There will be three Police vehicles from Gladstone and the Inspector in charge of the pickup will be an old mate of mine, Eddie Peters. Only hand the stuff over to him on production of his ID.'

'That sounds good thanks mate. But we have a slight change — my boat will take half the day to get there, so we're going to do a fast run in *Seeker*. Can you let your mate know that we'll be there in less than an hour in a different boat and to be ready for about 250 kilos of stuff, but it's quite bulky so he might need a van or something similar.'

'Fast run alright. OK Harry, I'll pass that on about the volume and the change of boat. A van shouldn't be a problem.'

'OK, thanks Greg. After we get rid of this stuff, we'll be staying at Fitzroy Reef for a while, so let us know any new information you get.'

'Will do, Harry. Take care.'

CHAPTER 37

Forty-five minutes later, Dave was nosing *Seeker's* sleek bow carefully onto the narrow beach close to the boat ramp in Wild Cattle Creek, as the area immediately around the ramp was shallow and rocky. A couple of fishermen launching their tinnie looked on in amazement as the biggest boat that shallow creek had ever seen gently grounded itself on the beach. They were rather more alarmed when a convoy of marked Police vehicles shepherded a plain white Ford Transit van into the parking lot and it was quite comical watching their indecision as to whether to pack up and leave, or keep getting ready to go fishing.

Finally, I took pity and swung down over the bow railings and walked up to them with a friendly, 'Hi guys. Going out to get a few?'

They were still a bit overawed by the Police presence to say much, but hastened their loading and quickly shoved off, roaring off down the creek, as a tall, muscular Inspector in full uniform walked down the side of the ramp to greet me.

He had a bit of a cheeky grin as he took in my shorts, T-shirt and bare feet and said, 'Commander Stevens, I presume?'

I laughed as I stuck my hand out. 'I bet you're been busting to use that line for years, Inspector Peters!'

He laughed back as we exchanged ID cards briefly. 'Eddie will do fine, thanks Harry. Greg has told me enough about you that I don't really need your ID card. Your reputation well and truly precedes you and it's a real pleasure to finally make your acquaintance.'

He was in no hurry to get on with the transfer, so we chatted a while about Greg and the situation while his sizeable entourage of Officers stood back respectfully. To be polite, I asked him if he'd like to have a look at *Seeker*, thinking that he'd decline, but he jumped at the invite and waved his troops to stand easy, before following me the few paces along the hard sand to where Dave had thoughtfully dropped a boarding ladder over the bow. *Seeker* had such a great overhang of the bow that the ladder easily reached the firm dry sand so Eddie didn't get even come close to getting his feet wet.

I let Dave conduct the tour and Eddie was obviously aware of the part *Seeker* and Dave and Corrine had played in the last big operation we'd been involved with down in Victoria, the ramifications of which had been felt in Queensland. He was rather more in awe, however, of the casually stacked mass of drugs and the bag of cash.

'So is this stuff really as potent as Greg claims?' he asked.

'I can vouch for it,' I said. 'I watched one of Greg's Senior Constables, who's on my boat out at sea at the moment, take a 5-milligram dose and it blew her away for several hours. The drop in her inhibition levels was alarming, even for me to witness. She is a very strong-willed girl and had a fair idea what to expect, so the effect on willing but naive civilians would be devastating. I used the description to Greg that if it hit the streets, he'd have, 'strangers fucking in the street in broad daylight until they collapsed from exhaustion or heart failure".

Eddie's eyebrows almost climbed into his hairline. 'So this could be cut by 50% and still be very potent?'

I gave him one of those looks, 'Eddie, this stuff could be cut 90% and still blow someone's mind along with their inhibitions! It really is that potent!'

'Shit!' He looked in awe at the mounding pile of bags at his feet as we stood in the saloon. 'So what was this worth to the bikie boys?'

'About $8 mil, plus another $2 mil for the first sample shipment the backpacker courier brought in.'

'Bloody hell! So this stuff could have netted these guys about $900 mill! That's serious money in anyone's terms. And it was all paid for by most of the SE Queensland Clubs! What a shitstorm! It's a good thing the Clubs don't know where you are, Harry. Your arse would be grass. Ha, ha!'

I smiled back rather grimly, suggesting that if he could call his troops down onto the beach, we could begin the transfer process. He called two Constables to come up on deck to assist carting the stuff to the bow and then it was passed bag by bag down to the waiting group on the beach. Eddie insisted on being down there to supervise the placement of each bag and ticked the numbers off the inventory I'd printed out earlier.

Finally, it was all done, the saloon clear and a considerable weight off my shoulders now I had only one problem to face.

We said our goodbyes and I thanked Eddie for his trouble, suggesting that it wouldn't be a good idea to keep it stashed in the lunchroom for too long. Ha, ha.

He saw the funny side of that and assured me that it would be transferred to Southport that night.

Five minutes later Dave backed us off the beach. We waved to Eddie and his staff then *Seeker* threaded the narrow channel and we growled our way back to open water.

While the return run was exhilarating, I did notice that the breeze had freshened out of the south, the light chop we'd experienced on the way in deepening to a low swell perhaps being the early warning of worse to come. I was much happier that we were in good holding ground in shallow water, even though there was no land to shelter behind, the shallow reef would take care of most of the swells, except at high tide when we could expect our position to become a bit bouncy.

As Dave eased up beside *Firebird*, I helped him set two anchors before we lashed both boats together with every fender we had between us to take up the bump and grind.

For some reason, perhaps just the thought of the impending

confrontation, it was a slightly sombre crew who collected on *Seeker* for our evening meal and where I laid out the foundation of my master plan that wasn't received as enthusiastically as I'd hoped.

Still, they had perhaps a couple more days to warm to my ideas, provided I could convince myself that it was a workable plan. On that depressing note, the *Firebird* crew returned to our boat with Jasper and Krazy for the evening.

UNDERTAKERS OMC CLUBHOUSE
– SOUTHPORT – TUESDAY EVENING

'Undertaker.'

'*Gidday, Henry. It's Brad.*'

'Of course it is Mr Edwards. How may I be of assistance this evening?'

'*I wanted to check on progress on getting a decent size boat to go and take out these pirates or whatever.*'

'Progress is good, Mr Edwards. A Dive Charter company still has one of its older boats available for when bookings are heavy, so we are negotiating to obtain that. Although old, it is particularly suitable since it has accommodation for forty persons. The extra space is necessary since most of Etta's crew want to go along so that's seventeen of the Amazons plus maybe ten from your Club and ten from ours. One of our brother Clubs in Brisbane has a licenced Captain in the ranks and we are trying to get the Charter Company to let us use him instead of one of their own, which obviously wouldn't be acceptable under the circumstances.'

'*That sounds good Henry, but we need to lock that deal up quickly and move out. Would force get things moving or will money work better with them?*'

'Money is being waved under their noses and the greedy little buggers are about ready to take it and turn a blind eye to what happens to their boat. If there are any problems, they'll say the boat was stolen anyway. However, you seem particularly anxious to get going, but we're waiting to find them again after the Lady Musgrave Island sighting.'

'Well, I may be able to help with that, but there's something I've wanted to ask you Henry. Did your Mother really know what she was doing when she named you and Etta? I mean, school must have been made very difficult for you both.'

'Oh, dear. Just when I was starting to appreciate your finer qualities, Mr Edwards, you come out with that bit of utterly unoriginal stupidity. However, to satisfy your mania for trivia and the mundane, I will say that we are twins, though not identical. Mother wanted to name the girl Henrietta, but my appearance prompted her to split the name for some reason never explained.

Now can we move on to the here and now? What did you want to tell me?'

'Wow Henry. I didn't realise big dude. I mean that's really out there! I bet you got back at dear old Mom for doing that?'

'Please Mr Edwards, let's move on. You are becoming tiresome on this subject, so tell me your information or go away.'

'Sorry Henry. I didn't mean to take the piss. I respect you too much for that. I was just curious and I apologise. But what I wanted to say before I side-tracked myself was that one of my boys was in Court today on a possession charge when he overheard two Detectives talking. He was only getting bits and pieces of the conversation, but he heard enough to work out that the wallopers have heard that the pirates have gone to ground at Fitzroy Reef.'

'Thank you for the apology, Mr Edwards, accepted. Now, where might I find Fitzroy Reef?'

'I 'Googled' it, Henry. It's a circular reef enclosing a lagoon and is part of the Bunker group of coral cays off Gladstone. It's just up from Lady Musgrave Island! Apparently they are camping there for a while. That's why I was keen that this boat deal be made as quickly as possible so we can head out ASAP and nail these pricks!'

'That's very interesting information, Mr Edwards. How confident are you that it's genuine?'

'Very confident, Henry. I can't say more than that, but I repeat that I'm 100% certain the info is correct, but we need to move tomorrow if that's possible. I can have ten guys in Gladstone tomorrow morning. My lieutenant, Tony Bradford will be in charge. Can you push this boat deal through and move your troops as well?'

'Indeed I can, Mr Edwards, in the face of such enthusiasm. Although I'm not negotiating directly for the hire of the Dive boat, I will push that as best I'm able as well.'

'Excellent Henry! Would this Dive Company have any of those rigid inflatable boats with the big outboards like the coppers use? If they do, can you get two of them as well?'

'I'm sure that will be possible, Mr Edwards. I'll get on to organising all that and let you know progress as it happens.'

'Thanks Henry. Be talking to ya!'

FIREBIRD - FITZROY REEF - WEDNESDAY AM

'Hi Greg, what's up?'

'It looks like the bad boys have taken the bait. I have it on good authority that an old dive charter boat has been chartered from a company in Gladstone. It has accommodation for forty and they have their own Captain. They also have two RIBs with big motors and seventeen of the Amazons plus ten each from the two Gold Coast Clubs. They know you're at Fitzroy Reef and plan on heading out there late today or this evening. Are you sure you're ready for this, Harry? I'm getting just a little bit concerned, especially since you're putting five of my best people in serious harm's way!'

'Gee Greg. And here I was thinking that you were worried about me. Well, if it's only the girls and boys you're concerned about, everything will be OK. Actually, the timing for arrival of these turkeys is just about perfect. There's a strong wind blowing that's whipped up a decent sea swell and the tide will be just into the ebb.'

'*Sorry Harry. Of course I'm concerned for your welfare too, but forty to eight isn't very good odds. Anyway, how can a strong wind and a swell help you?*'

'Because if it's the one I'm thinking of, that old dive boat has a narrow hull and is horribly top-heavy with all the extra cabins built up like a block of flats. Being a monohull, she rolls her guts out in a heavy dew, let alone a half-gale like this one, so at least half the crew will be sick as mongrel dogs and totally incapable of lifting a finger against us. And being night, the Captain won't take a chance at the narrow passage into the lagoon, so he'll have to stand off all night in rough conditions, which should knock out even more crew. That'll even up the odds considerably.'

'*Even so, Harry, you don't have to take them on head to head like this.*'

'Oh yes we do, Greg. We've been through this before and it's the only way. There'll be too much publicity if you just drop a SERT squad into the mix, since there's no way to keep it quiet. Keep the faith big dog, we need to thin these dudes out a lot and that's what my team and I are best at. Bye now.'

CHAPTER 38

The rough timing of the bikies arrival gave us a full 12 hours or more to prepare a suitable reception so we set to work.

I had Corrine sit down with the Semtex we had liberated during the raid on the Amazon's headquarters. There were six 1-kilogram blocks of the stuff, plus a large tin full of detonators and safety fuse. Although Amanda and Melissa, with wide eyes, tiptoed around her as she sat at the dining table, she knew what she was doing. She cut two of the blocks into 4 pieces, carefully crimped a detonator onto a short length of fuse and poked one into each of the 250-gram blocks.

The other four 1-kilo blocks were left intact, but copped the same treatment with a detonator and short fuse inserted, so that we had eight small bombs and four very large and powerful ones.

Amanda and Melissa had the task of moving and tying both our RIBs under *Firebird* between the hulls where they weren't easily seen, but were instantly available for use. Then with Dave, Alf and Charlie helping, I made some temporary additions to *Seeker's* safety rail system, the mods made easier since the boat was fibreglass, the same as *Firebird*.

The modifications went so well that Dave was keen to keep them as a permanent fixture, so I spent the extra time needed to make the job a more permanent installation. It was fortunate that I had several spare voltage step-up driver units, although so far, *Firebird's* system had been very reliable. Dave and Corrine were delighted with the result, although no one was volunteering to test it, so we had to be satisfied with using a whole baitfish as test dummy with suitably dramatic results.

Interestingly, the mood of the whole crew had lifted dramatically, now that we all knew what we were facing and it seemed that we had an excellent chance of coming out on top over the best efforts of the bad guys so long as we stayed on the attack and one step ahead. The wind was blowing quite hard and unimpeded across the expanse of the lagoon, although the shallow water and short fetch only allowed a small, breaking chop to form and the conditions were rough enough to keep any dive boats away. Also fortunately, no other private boats needed the shelter offered by the lagoon.

We next looked at available clothing, the girls outfitting themselves with black or dark tights and dark, tight-fitting tops. They had a lot of fun trying stuff on to get the best fit and looked very sexy when they popped out of the various cabins to display their choice to the four of us males in the cockpit. I had enough wetsuits for the four males and several sets of wet-suit bootees to suit.

Preparations were complete by early afternoon and by unspoken agreement, everyone decided to rest up for the night's fun and games. Charlie dragged Melissa off to a cabin, even though she was eyeing off Amanda and Sandy, while Dave and Corrine retired to their palatial suite on *Seeker*. Alf ruefully decided to retire to the cabin he normally shared with Charlie but was alone.

Sandy and I headed for our cabin, with Amanda close behind. I don't know about the others, but there was not much messing around as clothes were shed between the saloon and our forward cabin.

I was pushed aside at first as the two girls became rather intimately acquainted, although I didn't really mind as they were delightful to watch and my turn came before too long. As it turned out, there was little chance of rest and even with the girls enjoying each other, my famous recovery powers were tested severely as both demanded my attention and it was late afternoon before we stumbled to the shower together to clean up and revive.

In hindsight, that was sort of a bad move as a lot of water was wasted in the ensuing three-way mess-about, but at least the water-makers were well exercised.

Slowly, the others surfaced, all having had showers and looking refreshed. By mutual agreement, the bar remained closed for the evening as we had a light meal, fed the voracious Jasper and Krazy and settled down to re-examine our plan.

There was still an hour of daylight left and the horizon was still empty when I asked Amanda if the *Dragonfly* could handle the conditions.

'Sure thing,' she replied, 'I've launched it in much worse than this and if we launch off *Seeker's* foredeck, we won't have to mess about with booms and rigging on this boat.'

'How about coming home after dark?'

'No problem for *Dragonfly*,' she said confidently.

'OK. How about you get it ready soon as you can with a full fuel load. And please check that the IR camera is fully functional. I think we need to see where the bad boys and girls are.'

Everyone thought it was a great idea. Dave, Corrine, Alf and Charlie were particularly interested, as they hadn't seen it in operation yet. It didn't take long for the two girls to rig the odd-looking beast, fuel it and set it in place on *Seeker's* expansive foredeck, the homing beacon securely in place clamped to the deck under its skids with a suction cup. The Ground Control Station was set up in *Seeker's* saloon and it was almost magical to hear the device start by remote command, warm-up, then lift smoothly off the deck, climbing steeply into the gusting wind before turning toward the coast on the most likely track a boat would take from Gladstone.

With every eye glued to the screen, Amanda took it up to three thousand feet to get a wider view and make sure we received the live video signal without interruption. At that height, the hills behind the coastline were visible well above the horizon, but it took a few minutes of flight at 100 km/h before a long, slender white boat was spotted, making very heavy going into the wind-whipped swells, sheets of spray being flung high over the towering superstructure.

I chuckled, 'Yep. That's the un-lamented *MV Landfall*. I thought the fool thing sank years ago. It's a relic of the Second World War called a Fairmile. They were sold off after the war cheaply and the usual thing was to add extra decks and cabins so the new owners could cram more bodies aboard and make more profit. They weren't a bad sea boat when new, but with a narrow beam and now made extra top-heavy, they'd roll on wet grass, let alone a decent sea like this.'

'But it looks like they're making fair progress,' Sandy said. 'They should be here in a couple of hours if they keep that up.'

I chuckled again, 'Yes, you're right. The Skipper's driving her hard in these conditions, but that's causing their biggest problem. That motion will be unbearable with the whole boat closed down to stop water coming in, so I reckon my estimate of 70% casualties before a shot's even fired will be pretty close to the mark. They'll be flat out mustering a couple of boarding parties, which is what I'm hoping they'll do as a first move.'

As the *Dragonfly* was nearly overhead the *Landfall*, Amanda dropped height a little and set it into a holding pattern, the gyro-stabilised camera effortlessly tracking the rolling, pitching boatload of seasick misery driving toward Fitzroy Reef. The high resolution of the camera showing two RIBs nested on top of the stern cabins, temporarily strapped down with what looked like ratchet straps.

As darkness closed in hiding the worst of the angry sea, she switched to the Infrared camera, choosing the grayscale view as giving the best definition. On several occasions my guess as to conditions aboard was verified by the view of several persons stumbling out onto the stern deck to hang helplessly over the railing as they paid the traditional tribute to the ocean.

'What's our position on taking prisoners, Harry?' Sandy asked sombrely, thinking back to our previous violent encounters in

Bass Strait waters with persons trying their hardest to harm us and those we were trying to protect.

I considered her excellent question for a few moments, all faces watching me intently. 'I'm inclined to say that we give no quarter. The bikies have declared that they want to wipe us out completely, so it's going to be hard to show mercy without these bastards turning on us. Even those that are still standing and functioning won't hesitate to shoot to kill, but I'm willing to hear what everyone thinks before we make a firm decision.'

'Do you really think that it'll come down to that,' Alf asked, looking a little nervous now that crunch time had arrived.

Corrine spoke up, 'Absolutely! These clowns are here to lay maximum hurt on us and they want us to disappear without trace. That's their aim and is why they've gone to a lot of trouble and expense to come out here with forty angry men and women. You can be rest assured that it's not to have a polite sit-down with us and chat over a few beers!'

Alf looked at his partner Charlie who nodded acceptance. 'OK. So it's gloves off and shoot to kill, although that really goes against the grain of all our Police training.'

Melissa spoke up, 'Yes, it does Alf, but our training also taught us that if a person is coming at us with a gun or a knife, we shoot at centre body mass to put them down fast! These people aren't going to surrender peacefully just because some of them are seasick. Why did they come out here in these conditions with forty people if not to make sure we don't return to shore again?'

Her soft, calm and inoffensive manner carried a lot of weight in the discussion and I could see that Alf was almost convinced that a no-holds-barred attitude was the only thing that might save him being shot or stabbed.

'OK,' I spoke decisively. 'That sounds as close as we're going to get to a resolution. No quarter it is, unless a person is definitely not a threat now or later! But please remember that if you fail to take out someone with a weapon by hesitating, that person may in turn take out you or your friend or partner!'

It was no coincidence that I was looking at Alf when I spoke.

He held his hands up, 'You're right, Harry and I apologise to you all. I can see that there can't be any half-measures. We either do the job properly or we may as well bail out right now!'

'Well said, Alf,' offered Amanda. 'I think we all know now that we're of a like mind on this so we can trust and rely on each other.'

There was a series of head nods and a general firming of resolve, so we got down to sharing out the weapons. For longer distance shooting, we had the two R4-M rifles — middle distance there were several shotguns with rifled slugs — closer in, the two sub-machine guns, the new muffled MP5 and the little Mini-Uzi, plus the shotguns with SG or 00 buckshot and then a variety of pistols ranging from .44 magnum down to .22 magnum.

Then for special use were the blocks of Semtex in various weights, along with our super close-in secret weapon, Jasper.

As there were eight of us, we decided to split forces evenly between both boats and shared the weapons according to personal preference. I wasn't surprised when Corrine took a rifle, a shotgun and her favourite, the MP5. Our first defence was that of subterfuge where we would pretend to be totally unaware of the bikies impending arrival and would seem to all be asleep.

Hopefully, that would suck them into a RIB assault directly on our boats where they would hopefully get a nasty surprise.

CHAPTER 39

The *Dragonfly* was still faithfully orbiting the *Landfall* at a slow loiter speed, with it's GPS readout showing that bad guys had just 3 nautical miles to run, so I asked Amanda to bring the UAV home.

'Why don't we leave it up there?' she suggested. 'It's still got seven hours of fuel remaining and can still feed live IR video so we can see exactly what they're up to.'

I thought a moment then acknowledged the sense in doing so. 'You're right. I forgot that it's in auto-tracking mode, so it'll just stay with the boat, no matter what it does.'

'That's the idea. We can recover it at any time or it will self-recover when the fuel gets critical.'

'OK. But I'll fire up our masthead camera as well. We're about 1500 metres from the outside of the entrance where I think the *Landfall* will either hove to or try to anchor, although I don't fancy their chances of getting a good grip on the bottom in this weather.'

We moved the *Dragonfly's* GCS inside *Seeker's* saloon to set up for the first trap, while we watched the violently rolling *Landfall* arrive off the narrow entrance channels. As expected, the Skipper wisely decided against running the gauntlet in the dark with the strong winds and currents to fight against, so he did a good job by manoeuvring in close to drop an anchor in shallow water, paying out a lot of chain to lie back away from the dangerous shallows.

That position also gave them some shelter from the worst of the swells so the unstable boat lay relatively quietly. The UAV's

IR vision showed that not everybody was seasick as there was activity around the RIBs on the stern deck as they were launched one by one to lie tossing wildly astern.

We stayed watching the screen until six persons boarded each boat then started on their way through the access channels to the lagoon. Then the *Firebird* crew made our way back aboard where we checked the vision from our masthead camera then deployed as arranged, with Sandy on the roof over the cockpit, with the TAC-14 shotgun, her Service Glock and plenty of extra rounds in a bandoleer across her chest. Amanda, Melissa and I turned the camera screen light low and waited in the dark with the cockpit door open and Jasper at our feet. Krazy kitten was locked up for'rard out of harm's way.

The progress of the two small boats across the lagoon toward us was horribly reminiscent of the occasion at Erith Island in Bass Strait as Sandy and I waited the approach of bad guys. I fervently hoped the outcome would be as decisive in our favour as it was then. I leaned down to Jasper and said softly, 'Bad men coming, Jasper. Bad men. Attack when I say so. OK?'

Amanda and Melissa looked on in disbelief when my big, black cat looked up at me with his huge green eyes and mewled softly.

'Aww, c'mon Harry. He didn't understand that, did he?' Melissa scoffed.

I shrugged in the darkness, 'It does seem hard to believe, but he's shown time and again that he does understand what I say and that it's not just repetition in common situations. Anyway, watch and see.'

As they closed on our position, the two RIBs separated, one heading for each stern where they gently nosed against our boarding platform. It appeared that the occupants were trying to synchronise their attacks, an action that fitted well with my plans as three dark-clad figures slowly and quietly climbed the steps. I could see that their counterparts on *Seeker* were doing the same, so I warned Melissa and reminded Amanda what to expect.

As it turned out, the boarding party on *Seeker* must have been over-anxious, since two of them grabbed for the safety railing together, just moments before the first intruder grabbed *Firebird's* railing. The salt spray in the air that had misted the windows all day certainly helped to conduct electricity as two brilliant, blue flashes on *Seeker* were closely followed by one large one just in front of us.

From the size of the figures that showed in that first, brilliant flash, it seemed that *Firebird* was the target of the Amazons, although few of the ladies that we had stripped then tied up a couple of weeks ago at the mall, could be classed as small. I'd set the current level on the controllers on both boats to around lethal level with the other side effect being that muscles went into spasm and hands gripped the railing involuntarily.

The spasms also caused the afflicted person to perform an intricate deadly dance, before collapsing in a heap. In this case, when the lead intruder clamped her hands on the live rail, the one directly behind tried to pull her back and promptly got much of the same treatment. The third one fell back in shock, missed the RIB and went into the water.

That left three in the RIB who didn't seem sure of what had just happened as they passed the opportunity to retrieve their swimming compadre in favour of charging up the steps, tossing caution aside, but unfortunately, the stern gate was still closed and still highly energised with the result that the first charging black-clad form suffered the same fate as the gently smoking lump of ex-humanity at her feet.

The other two panicked, still not sure what was being done to their mates and in their haste to get back to the RIB, one grabbed the rail to save slipping overboard, causing yet another brilliant, blue flash. The final one had a shotgun slung over her shoulder and had the presence of mind to try to use it, but by the time she'd untangled the sling and racked a round, I'd turned off the power and allowed Jasper to launch into attack.

This time Amanda kept her mouth shut as Jasper went about his business with ruthless, but noisy efficiency.

When that carcass was reduced to feeble twitching, I called him off and we ventured out to inspect the carnage using dimmed red torches to preserve our night sight and avoid alerting the *Landfall* crew. Amanda wasn't too keen to get close and personal with the corpses, but Melissa was made of sterner stuff, or maybe her experience of being kidnapped toughened her as we inspected the four zapped bodies that were thoroughly deceased and leaking body fluids on my fibreglass steps.

After we had retrieved six shotguns, five handguns of various makes and calibre, two pair of night-vision goggles, a heap of ammunition in bandoleers and a collection of knives, we briefly discussed disposal. It was a very short discussion and although it may have been environmentally irresponsible, we weren't planning on going swimming in the lagoon, so we just dumped them into the water, allowing the wind and current to carry them toward the entrance channels and the always-waiting grey-suited clean-up squad with their triangular fins and razor-sharp teeth. One Amazon had fallen overboard untouched and could be anywhere, although I doubted that she'd stay too close to the boats and wouldn't last long as there was no dry land, only razor-sharp coral to land on. The one who'd actually tried to bring her shotgun into play had been well chewed by Jasper who was sitting close guard, cleaning his face with tongue and paws to remove the gore and other remnants.

'Hey, Harry. This one's still alive — sort of,' Melissa said, wrinkling her nose at the disgusting array of smells rising from the ripped-apart body at her feet. 'Do you want to try to question her?'

'Hang on a moment,' I replied, 'I'll just see if the *Seeker* crew have any survivors.'

I wandered over to the side where *Seeker* was rafted up.

'Hi there troops. Anybody hurt, apart from the bad guys, I mean?'

Corrine giggled as Alf vomited over the side railing again. 'All good here, thanks Harry. Two bad guys were zapped, one fell overboard and had trouble swimming and two more tried to discharge their firearms in our direction so we shot the buggers!'

'Excellent! Any still alive?'

'Yeah. One's awake, but he's not going to last too long with his guts hanging out. There's a major blood vessel been nicked as well so he'll bleed out first. Do you want to question him? I don't think that there's any need to keep our faces covered.'

'Yeah, good point. I'd better try to get something out of him. We've only got one left that Jasper gnawed on, so she's not in any condition to speak.'

Corrine laughed. 'He's a very efficient pussy. He can just about kill by the shock factor alone.'

I swung over the railings between the boats to the body laid out on the deck, blood pooling under him, but as Corrine had said, he was conscious as I squatted down beside him.

'Hello. I'd like you to answer a couple of questions, then we might try to save your miserable life.'

'Get fucked!' was the weak reply.

'Oh dear. I was afraid you'd feel that way. How about I get my very good friend to come over and help convince you to be nice?'

The big, burly bikie half raised his head with a groan and looked around with wild eyes, 'I don't know what you did to the others, but I'm not afraid of you.'

I smiled, 'Brave words, my friend, but it's not really me you need to be afraid of. Allow me to introduce our group's Enforcer. His name is Jasper, by the way.'

As the crippled man's mouth curled into a sneer, I turned my head and whistled once, causing a lean black shape to materialise beside me, staring down at his latest chew toy with intense interest, showing a display of gleaming white teeth, the effect reinforced by a few shreds of bloody flesh still hanging from his lower jaw. The bikies expression snapped from disdain to horror in half a second flat.

'What the fuck's that?' He demanded, 'You keep it away from me.'

'I will if you tell me how many more are still functional on that piece of shit called a boat over there.'

'Get fucked, you arsehole!' was again the disappointing response so I said to Jasper, 'Start chewing, please boy. Maybe on this hand first,' as I pointed to the man's right hand, still clutching the gaping wound in his side.

The look of horror on the bikies face had just started to fade as Jasper gently picked his hand up in his mouth, but then he shrieked in agony and terror as powerful jaws drove razor-sharp teeth effortlessly down through flesh and bone with a disturbing crunching sound, a fresh spray of blood misting across the deck.

'Shit, steady on there, Harry!' called Corrine. 'You're making a fearsome mess of our beech deck planking.'

I grinned up at her. 'Don't worry dear lady. After the Bass Strait mess, I found a really effective cleaner that lifts blood and shit off everything. We'll have this spotless in a few minutes when we've finished with this worthless piece of dog shit.'

She shrugged, 'Oh, well. That's all right then. Carry on.'

The terrified bikie had stopped screaming long enough to follow our slightly bizarre exchange, staring horrified at his mangled hand still firmly clamped in Jasper's jaws.

'I'll tell you anything you want, mister. Just get that fucking furry monster thing away from me.'

A quick word and Jasper carefully placed the gory, mangled object that used to be a hand back on the bikies chest and stepped back a pace, his unblinking eyes fixed on the bikies rapidly blinking ones.

'OK. We'll start again. How many on your boat are still functional and how many are laid up?'

'Twelve came over here to try to surprise you, 'cause we were the least affected of any of them. There's another fifteen who are crook but can at least walk, and thirteen who can't even walk.'

'Good boy, this is going really well. It's so much easier when you co-operate. Now, what weapons have you got and who's in charge over there?'

'Just shotguns, pistols and knives. Oh, and there's a few baseball bats as well. That rabid, fucking Amazon chick is in charge, although her arm is giving her lots of problems as well as her ribs and she limps 'cause there's something wrong with her leg as well.'

I grinned at him, 'Yeah, I know all about her injuries seeing as I caused them. I didn't expect her to brave the boat trip though. It must have caused her a lot of pain.'

'Yeah, it did. She's pretty spaced out on pain-killing drugs and she's one of the ones who aren't very functional!'

'OK. Thanks for that, but neither she nor any of the others will be functional at all shortly.'

'What does that mean,' he demanded, pain twisting his face and slurring his words.

'I mean that you guys and girls came out here to nail us am I right?'

Reluctantly, he nodded gently. 'Yeah. Etta told us that you all had to disappear on account of that stunt you pulled by tying them naked to those flagpoles at the mall and making them shit themselves. Most of the boys reckon that was a pretty cool thing to do to a bunch of case-hardened bitches.'

'OK. Well, she's failed to do her job so she and the rest of you get to pay the loser's penalty. Who's the Skipper and deckhands?'

'They're three brothers from one of the Brisbane Clubs, 'cause they had to have tickets or licences or some shit like that. But what are you going to do to everyone? I told you that a bunch of them can't even walk they're that crook.'

I looked at him impassively. 'You all came out here to kill us and sink our boats. What do you really expect us to do? Pat you all on the heads and send you home?'

He didn't have an answer to that semi-rhetorical question, so I leaned closer, almost wincing at the smell of death, blood and raw guts that rose in a choking miasma from him. 'I'll tell you the answer, shit-for-brains! I don't fucking well think so!

What you do get is to see is what it's like when we do to you what you'd planned to do to us!'

He was almost too far-gone from blood loss to make a protest, so I left him to just fade away, slowly painting Dave and Corrine's lovely deck a fetching shade of arterial red.

CHAPTER 40

When I returned to Amanda and Melissa, I found that the ravaged Amazon had died and the girls had shoved her overboard. They had thoughtfully started to clean up the mess while I'd been questioning the bikie, although thankfully, *Firebird's* fibreglass deck with urethane-sealed cork covering was easy to clean.

After the remaining body had been dumped over from *Seeker*, I called a conference.

'I believe that we need to stay on the front foot so our next move should be to take the fight to the *Landfall*. The ones left aboard who are reasonably alert will be expecting their boats back anytime soon, since all they've seen so far is what could be mistaken for gunshot flashes. Did anybody come across any radios?'

Heads shook all around. 'All right. That means they don't expect any communication before their two attack squads come back. How about we all dress roughly the same as the ones we've topped and go visit. But instead of boarding, I suggest that we pull up to the stern and start tossing Semtex charges aboard. One charge at the nearest stern door, wait until it blows, then we toss a few more through the open hole.

That should blow the arse out of the rotten old thing and it'll go down without us having to get into a protracted fire-fight. We've taken zero casualties so far — let's keep it that way. Thoughts?'

After what we'd all just been through, I really didn't expect any serious opposition to my simple plan, especially after the large pile of weapons that we'd retrieved from the deceased boarding parties. Amanda and Melissa looked grim but determined — Charlie was the same, while Alf looked a bit sick, but rallied gamely to give a thumbs-up to the plan.

It was Corrine who suggested, 'Why bother changing, Harry. We'll be hard to see anyway and I'll bet the dickheads aren't running internal red lights, so their night vision will be cactus. It's not as though we're trying to sneak aboard. Once we toss the first Semtex charge, it's all over anyway.'

I smiled at her, 'I must be getting old, 'cause you're quite right. Staying as we are will be fine.'

Accordingly, we dug out the Semtex charges that Corrine had made up earlier, taking the whole lot; although I hoped not to have to use the one kilogram blocks and we armed ourselves with two rifles, both sub-machine guns and our own shotguns. It was only habit that made me take the time to stow all the captured weapons in one of the capacious stern lockers on *Firebird*.

Then leaving Jasper in charge and releasing little Krazy kitten from her security locker in the bow, we loaded into both captured RIBs and motored carefully toward the entrance channel, the captured night-vision goggles making it easy to pick our way past coral heads and down the channel.

The UAV still orbiting the anchored *Landfall* had given us her exact location, so we knew where to head to find her. It was no surprise when dim lights shining from multiple portholes announced our target's location. Swinging wide, we approached from astern, hoping to achieve total surprise, but that hope was dashed when an alert lookout called out from the stern.

'Jackie? Is that you? About bloody time! How'd it go?'

I didn't want to risk stirring even the capable bikies into life, but Corrine was way ahead of me and used the well-muffled MP5-SD6 to place a three-round burst into the centre body mass of the lookout. A startled grunt, followed by a heavy splash suggested that she was as accurate as ever with her favourite gun and

I knew I was going to have a battle to get it back off her when all this rattle was over.

That cleared the stern momentarily, so we eased both boats up to the stern, leaving the motors idling in forward gear to hold the RIBs in place. I was about to call for Corrine to toss the first small charge, when I saw her small figure slip quietly up the boarding ladder onto the small rear deck.

She opened a tall hatch set into the rear of the aft cabin block, took a quick look inside then flicked an arc lighter against the short length of fuse protruding from one of the large, one kilo block charges. A fine stream of blue smoke proved that it was lit, so she darted inside the hatch briefly, reappearing in a big hurry, pulling the door closed before she scampered back aboard, waving frantically for both boats to back off.

I threw the motor in my boat into reverse and twisted the throttle hard, taking heavy water over the stern, but as it was an RIB, it wasn't about to sink although it was a bit uncomfortable. Once clear of the stern, I selected forward gear and spun it around, trying to make more distance from the *Landfall*, the other RIB with Dave in charge doing the same.

We both made about 100 metres before the dark of the night was momentarily banished by a huge sheet of violet orange flame and a thunderous roar as the entire stern of the old boat simply disappeared, although a variety of odd-shaped bits and pieces were flung skywards to a great height, before splashing back down!

When my night-vision goggles functioned again after their temporary sensory overload, I saw that at least ten or fifteen feet of the rear of the boat was gone, looking as though a giant set of shears had simply cut the stern section cleanly off. Under the aft set of cabins, the engine room stretched well forward like a long, dark cave and was filled with water in seconds. Several panicking people ran down the central corridor toward the stern, but became confused when there wasn't a hatchway there anymore and simply ran out into the water that was already starting to pour into the corridor.

Dave steered his boat alongside so Corrine could call out, 'How about we zip up the bow and toss another charge or two onto the foredeck? That should blow a hole right down to the bottom and might sink the blasted thing faster!'

'OK, but be careful and watch for shooters!'

'Yes Dad,' came the cheeky answer as Dave twisted the throttle again and they shot forward arrowing straight for the bow of the old boat. I didn't see Corrine light the fuses, but I did see their boat suddenly shoot away from the side and head back toward us.

They hadn't quite reached us when there was a massive explosion that blew the bow clean off the *Landfall* and appeared to shatter every external window in the boat.

The bow section, weighted down with the anchor chain and windlass, quickly sank.

Overall, the desired effect was achieved as the rate of sinking increased dramatically and helped the old boat settle in a level attitude.

We couldn't see any survivors, so we turned both boats toward the entrance channel and carefully made our way back to our boats where a surprise awaited us on *Firebird*.

As we tied up to the stern, Sandy was asking me what we were going to do with the spare RIBs, and I'd just suggested that we sink them in deep water as we left in the morning, when I noticed that Jasper hadn't come to the stern to greet us, something he has always done and nor was Krazy kitten in sight. I signalled for Amanda and Melissa to get back in the RIB, while I quietly checked the magazine on the Mini-Uzi and worked the charging handle to set the open bolt. Its selector was set on semi-auto, as I didn't want to chew a hole in my boat.

Slowly I moved up the steps until my eyes just cleared the seat backs, scanning the cockpit for any bad guys, but all appeared clear, until I noticed that Jasper was standing over a bundle of something on the deck that was jammed under the cockpit table. The bundle didn't appear to be moving, so I cautiously advanced to the light switches by the door and flicked the red lighting on.

The dim red light didn't help much at all, except to show that Jasper wasn't going to look or move away from whatever it was on the deck, although he did give a soft growl. I retreated to the switches again and selected normal white and turned the lights on. There was a gasp from Jasper's bundle, another growl from Jasper, followed by a feminine whimper from the bundle.

'OK, Jasper. Stand back please and let her up. OK you. C'mon out from under the table, very slowly get up and tell me who you are.'

The bundle slowly and painfully unfolded to reveal a small female, aged somewhere in her twenties, clad in the remnants of a black skivvy-type top that had been partly shredded by something very sharp and wasn't doing much to cover her from the waist up. From the waist down, she was bare, her legs and feet were heavily scored by a multitude of cuts and scrapes that slowly oozed blood.

'Turn around, slowly!' I commanded.

With a glance at Jasper, she complied, showing, along with a nice little bum, that she didn't have any sort of weapon and that she was just as heavily scratched and scraped on that side as well. Given a choice, I decided that I'd rather look at her front side, so I had her turn around again.

She seemed too far away from reality through pain, shock and maybe blood loss to argue, resist or be embarrassed about standing mostly naked in front of a stranger.

Something about her injuries rang a bell; then I remembered where I'd seen them before, put 2 and 2 and 4 together and came up with — 'You're the Amazon who fell overboard during the raid on us! We didn't see where you went and presumed that either the sharks took you or you just drowned. It looks like you got washed up on a coral bommie, is that right?'

For the first time she spoke, her words hesitant and jerky as though she was having trouble speaking, her voice soft and husky.

'I must have banged my head ... when I fell overboard and had trouble staying afloat. That's when I ... got rid of my boots and pants ... they were dragging me down. Anyway, the wind and a current were slowly pushing me away from the boats and I could barely stay afloat, until I washed up against a huge rock or something covered in coral. I didn't realise how sharp that fuckin' stuff is until it slashed my legs and bum to ribbons! But I wasn't about to let go!'

'Yeah. That would've been stag horn coral. Your cuts will have to be disinfected very thoroughly or the infection could kill you. The coral and most of the water in these lagoons is a real biological soup! Every organism possible is in it! So how did you get back here?'

'Great, thanks for the good news! Anyway, although the waves kept shoving me against the coral, I moved around the coral mound until I found a smooth area where I wasn't getting cut up and I could actually rest. I could see your boats were less than a hundred metres away, so after you all left in our RIBs, and when I'd regained some of my strength, I pushed off and swam here, but that knocked me around even more. I found that pull-down swim ladder thingy, but could hardly climb out of the water! Then suddenly that bloody cat-thing of yours grabbed me by one arm, half-dragged me up those steps, bailed me up under the table and wouldn't let me move! Good thing I didn't need to piss.'

'You'd be cleaning it up, just like you're going to clean up all that blood you've leaked onto the deck,' I said without a trace of compassion, remembering that this one had a shotgun as she charged up the steps, dropping it when her mates got zapped and she fell back.

'Well, how about some clothes at least?' she asked, fingering the tattered remnants of her top that had barely enough material to hold it together, let alone cover her tits.

I shook my head. 'Nope! We need to decide what to do with you before we go wasting good clothing on a slag like you.'

She started to burr up, but I held up a hand, pointed at Jasper and went back over to the top of the stern steps to re-assure the girls that all was OK and call them aboard. I gave them a quick rundown on the situation.

'We need to decide what to do with this bitch. Do we give her first aid for the coral cuts and scrapes? Do we even let her live? She's the last one left from the boat group, so it's not like she'll be missed! Although she's seen us and Jasper.'

I was happy to have the conference later, but the girls wanted to resolve it now. As usual, it was Sandy who took the moderate line, saying, 'Let's do the first-aid thing first, then decide what to do from there. I suspect that being washed in Dettol will be rather painful process and if we take the long view, there may be some good information Corrine could get from her using her special stuff.'

I considered her remarks before saying, 'You may be right. I'd forgotten about Corrine's stuff. That seemed to help those girls in Lakes Entrance forget about a lot of things. OK. We'll do as you suggest and do the first aid bit, then see where it goes from there. First up though, we need to clean up everything and retrieve the *Dragonfly*. I'd hate to have to explain to that eccentric genius of yours that we'd left his precious UAV orbiting an empty patch of ocean off Fitzroy Reef until the fuel ran out!'

Amanda laughed, easing the tension that we all felt. 'I'll go and do that now. Ian would never forgive me either and I have to take it back to the old busted-arse pilot sometime or other.'

'Thanks for that. In the morning, I'd like to leave early in case a charter boat wanders by, so we'll sink the RIBs on our way out.'

We decided that Sandy and I would look after the prisoner, while Amanda and Melissa cleaned up the various messes. It took a while to round up a litre of Dettol, but then we took the fairly compliant girl, Marie we learned her name was, into the big master shower cubicle. It had crossed my mind that the painful cleansing process might be another opportunity to learn a bit more about the bikie clubs and their key players.

While Sandy cut the remaining rags of her top off the pain-wracked girl and stood her under the shower to get off the worst of the blood, I eyed her lean, trim body with automatic, but detached interest, before asking, 'Who were the others on the boat with you?'

Although whimpering with pain as the hot water stung all the open cuts and abrasions, she answered without hesitation. 'Pretty well the best of the Zombies, the Undertakers and nearly all the Amazons, I reckon. Certainly all their senior people except for the Presidents, although our leader, Etta was on the boat. Where are they, by the way and how are you keeping them under control? I'd be very careful — they're a dangerous lot. Even the other Amazons scared the shit outa me! And Etta is a real psycho bitch!'

I looked at Sandy with raised eyebrows, and she gave a slight nod.

'Well, I've got good news and bad news, depending on how much the other Amazons really did scare you. You won't have to worry about Etta or those Amazons who were on the boat with you. They're all gone!'

'What'd you mean, gone? Where'd they go? Did they just sail away 'cause you guys did a number on some of us?'

I shook my head, 'No. They didn't just sail away. We blew that festering boat up with Semtex and they went straight down! As far as we can tell, none survived.'

Sandy turned the shower off and wiped her as gently as possible, but the thought pictures I'd planted in her mind distracted Marie.

'What are you saying? They're all dead? Bullshit! You couldn't have done that!'

I shrugged, 'Sorry, but we have and none of us even got a scratch! I don't know how to convince you, although there may be some video of their demise, but when you get down to it, I don't really give a fuck whether you believe us of not. They're dead — carked it — done and dusted — finito — shark food — gone for good, and you're the only one left who knows what went on. The sharks have cleaned up the bodies, so there won't even be any remains for the Forensics people to pore over.'

I gave her an evil grin. 'As an unfriendly word of warning, I wouldn't try jumping over the side for the next twelve hours, if I were you. The sharks in the lagoon are so thick at the moment; you could walk halfway to the entrance on their backs if you had a mind to be suicidal! Ha, ha.'

She had a stricken look on her admittedly pretty face, 'So you really are serious that everyone's gone and I'm the only one left?'

'Yep. You're it, unless we decide that guarding you or putting up with more of your crap isn't worth the trouble, in which case the sharks get dessert.'

She gave such a dramatic shudder at the thought of all those razor-sharp teeth finishing the job of ripping her apart; that I momentarily felt sorry for her, but it was only a very fleeting sentiment and I promised myself it wouldn't happen again.

'Can't I promise to be really good and not try to escape?'

I shook my head, a sad expression on my face. 'Nope, sorry. Can't trust ex-bikies. Especially those who come gunning for us in the night with shotguns in hand and a belt full of knives!'

Her shoulders slumped and she shut up, submitting to Sandy's ministrations, that brought a stream of tears to her eyes and a series of moans of pain as Sandy swabbed each and every cut, scratch and scrape deeply with the powerful antiseptic solution that had looked after the cuts and scrapes of millions of Aussie kids over the years.

I tried for one last piece of information. 'So you reckon that the guts have been ripped out of at least three Clubs?'

She glared at me with a flash of spirit that I couldn't help admiring, her naked body having absolutely nothing to do with it. 'I said that didn't I? And don't forget the three brothers who ran the boat. Their family is going to want revenge in the biggest possible way!'

'What Club were they with?' I asked casually.

'The Billy-Jacks,' she replied 'and let me tell you, they're a truly psycho mob if ever there was one! They make the Amazons look like a Convent!'

At that point, I left Sandy to finish up cleansing her lesions, grabbed my oldest T-shirt with the most holes in it, tore a few new ones and asked Amanda to donate an old, tattered pair of panties. But while I was returning to the bathroom, I remembered my last encounter with a female captive and the value of keeping female prisoners naked to knock the defiance out of them. Therefore, I tossed the two items of clothing back into my cabin and waited for Sandy to lead our captive back up to the cockpit.

I pointed at a plastic cockpit chair that would be easily washed, since despite Sandy applying a box load of adhesive dressings, her multitude of slashes and gashes still leaked. 'Sit there and keep your mouth shut. The slightest complaint out of you and you'll be over the side. You'll wear handcuffs at all times and we'll make up a set of ankle cuffs as well, just in case you reckon I'm bullshitting about the sharks!'

The best she could manage was a shake of the head as Sandy slapped the 'cuffs on her, clamping her wrists together in front. We had to improvise with a pair of large nylon cable ties for her ankles, but unfortunately for Marie, they were just as effective as the metal ones.

Sandy got my attention and indicated she wanted to talk, so we adjourned into the saloon out of earshot, Amanda and Melissa just finishing the clean up, came and joined us.

'Are we going to put some clothes on her? She's in shock already and that'll probably get worse over the next few hours.'

I shook my head. 'No. She's still showing a few flashes of

defiance, so we need to break her of that. Remember what the two girls did to that woman who came to kidnap them at Erin Island? That worked a treat!'

Sandy had to giggle at the memory, 'How could I forget! But you're right it did the trick. OK, we'll leave her naked; it's not cold, although if she gets wet the wind chill will knock her around badly in her current state.'

I nodded, 'Yep. Point taken. Just keep an eye on her condition, but keep in mind that she and her mates came here to kill all of us.'

Sandy nodded soberly then helped me make the point to Marie about the futility of trying to escape, by helping her hobble to the side railing. I turned on the pretty blue underwater LED's around both sterns and was somewhat shocked myself to see what was swimming beneath us. Sharks of every size and description were darting thither and yon, hoping to find a morsel of flesh left over from the unexpected feast that had been dumped in their laps.

Right on cue, as if to make my point, the smaller sharks cleared the way for the grandmother of all Tiger sharks to lazily glide past, rolling slightly so she could eye off the tasty humans still topside and available for a feed if she could get at them. *Firebird* was 8.6 metres or 28 feet wide and she looked like she spanned three quarters of that distance, her huge head taking up a good third of her body length. She arrogantly stuck her curved, sickle-shaped dorsal fin clear out of the water, making it look like the sail on a small dinghy and like a smart-arse teenager, dragged that massive fin under the two captured RIBs still trailing astern, nearly upsetting both.

I heard a strangled gasp from our female captive, before she threw up, thankfully over the side. With a flicker of brownish-grey and a giant swirl of water, the monster Tiger whipped around to investigate the splashing, gulping savagely at it as she glided through the murky mess, before snapping the tail off a small reef shark that had imprudently ventured too close.

I hauled Marie back from the side rails and commented to the others, 'I guess we'll not be disposing the RIBs tonight while our big friend is hanging about, although I'll bet she's had a good feed outside the reef already!'

There were more than a few grim expressions on the faces of both crews as 'Tiggie' kept cruising around, occasionally bumping either the RIBs or the boat hulls.

The huge Tiger also inadvertently solved the problem of how to guard our pain-wracked captive for the rest of the night. By applying a variation of a cunning plan I'd learned from a very smart 18-year old girl in Bass Strait, by locking Marie's wrists to the handrail on *Firebird's* stern boarding platform where she had almost a fish's eye view of the giant predator who delighted in cruising past the stern every few minutes, now that she saw what was must have seemed like a sacrificial virgin offering.

No words were or needed to be exchanged; she got the message about behaving herself, although there were a few shrieks when the Tiger tried to push her fat head up onto the stern to get at her, causing the whole boat to lurch. After the second such attempt, we had to move Marie up one step, although that didn't stop the Tiger trying, so we had to suffer the bumping and lurching every time she leant her nearly one tonne mass on the stern. I left Jasper sitting safely at the top of the steps to keep watch at the top side, dividing Marie's terrified attention between the Tiger literally snapping at her feet and Jasper glaring at her from just above with unblinking eyes.

Before we parted to go to our respective beds, I said, deliberately in her hearing, 'We'll decide tomorrow what to do with her. It may be useful to take her back to face a string of charges, up to and including conspiracy to commit murder and attempted assault with a deadly weapon. Maybe that'll send a message! But we also need to consider that she's seen our faces, so that could be a problem. Anyway, that's for the morning, but we need to be moving out of here as soon as there's enough light to see the coral heads.'

'Where are we heading, Harry,' Corrine asked. 'Are we to consider this all over and head for home?'

I shook my head, 'No. Afraid not Mouse. Until we have Greg check out the situation with the bikie clubs, we're going to stay low profile. I think we'll continue heading north as per the original plan.'

CHAPTER 41

Despite my desire for an early start, both crews were so tired from the events of last night that sunrise came and went without so much as a sleeping body stirring. Even our captive was quiet, staying curled up in a softly whimpering little foetal ball to try to retain a little bit of body warmth, or maybe it was just the effect of Jasper's oppressive personality toward those he disliked that kept her silent.

Finally, I awoke and stood up in bed with my upper body out of the overhead hatch to survey the surroundings. I noticed that the wind had dropped at sometime through the night, although a heavy swell boomed on the half-exposed reef to our south, smaller swells making their way across the shallows toward us. The sky was clear and it looked like being a lovely day to exchange one paradise that had turned to hell, for another one that might just stay unblemished.

My appreciation for the wonders of nature was rudely interrupted by Sandy yanking on my extended ripcord, but for once she didn't want to fool around, but was in the process of dressing and had found an amusing new way to get my attention. Once dressed myself, I started both engines and as I waited for them to warm up, went to see how prisoner Marie was doing. Jasper greeted me effusively, what passes for a big grin plastered across his be-whiskered face. Marie was barely capable of speaking, as she was very stiff — in considerable pain from the cuts, scrapes and other wounds — and very cold, despite the relatively warm evening and hungry.

There was one strange, fresh wound in the form of a long

slice along the inside of her right foot, and although the bleeding had stopped at some stage, it looked like it would need a heap of stitching to help it heal and would be very painful.

When I looked around after hosing off her pee residue and some small patches of blood, the cause of that wound may have been explained when I found, to my disgust, that the big Tiger had left her mark on *Firebird* in the form of a long, deep score mark, a good 750 millimetres long, in the outer edge of the fibre-glass boarding platform. She at least had the decency to leave me a decent souvenir in the form of one massive, intact tooth, itself about 90 millimetres long, the razor-sharp tip still embedded in the 'glass work at the end of the score mark.

It belatedly occurred to me that if the fresh gash in Marie's foot had been caused by the Tiger shoving her way up unto the stern platform to have a piece of her, it was no wonder that she was semi-comatose this morning! It was fear and terror, not exposure that was to blame. Still, I had few regrets about her condition, figuring that she'd brought it all on herself and her mates by coming out here in the first place trying to kill us and destroy our boats.

At least she hadn't made too much of a mess on the steps or herself and both were easily washed off with the fresh-water hose, so with Jasper's whiskers tickling her bum, I had to half-carry her limp body up to the cockpit where Sandy took over, binding up the fresh gash to her foot, before trying to revive her from a near comatose state with some ammonia cleaner. I exchanged greetings with Dave who had just started both *Seeker's* engines ready to take on the narrow channel back out to open waters and asked him to get Corrine to bring her little interroga-tion kit over as soon as she could.

'We'll get going as soon as Corrine can hit Marie with a shot of that sleepy stuff that induces amnesia,' I told him. 'Hopefully, that will take care of most of her bad memories, including those about us. Then I'd like us to head for Hummocky Island, closer to the coast. It's about 56 nautical miles, so with these lighter breezes, we'll probably take five or six hours to get there.'

Dave grinned and shrugged. 'No problem for us. A slow, quiet day will go down very nicely right now.'

'Good oh, thanks mate. Watch the channel on the way out, as just to make life interesting, that tide's running in really hard.' I looked around, seeing Sandy had been only partly successful in getting Marie awake, the girl lying half-sprawled forlornly in a plastic cockpit chair, looking out over the lagoon entrance to where all her friends had perished.

'I guess there's not much point getting the girls to feed our newest and un-loved crewie,' I commented to myself as Corrine appeared, her little leather satchel clasped in her hand.

'Good morning Harry, how's your captive this lovely morning?'

'Good morning, dear lady. She was comatose when I got up, but Sandy's been waving a bottle of ammonia under her nose, so she's partly awake. If you can give her a shot of that sleepy stuff, maybe she'll forget some of the stuff that's happened over the last few days. We'll keep her with us for the run over to Hummocky Island, but then we might stick her in that old crew space up for'rard on *Seeker* if that's OK?'

Corrine nodded. 'Sure, no problem. We took out one bunk some time back and just use it for extra storage space, but it's still liveable for one, and the hatch is still lockable from outside.'

I grinned at her, 'Yes, I do remember that feature, but I'd forgotten about it last night. My bad, she might have had a better sleep with a bunk to lie on and wouldn't have been terrorised by Grandma Tiger!'

Dave looked curious. 'Is that why she's so dopey this morning? By the look of those coral cuts and scrapes, she's in a lot of pain.'

I laughed, 'Yeah! What a shame, but pain's only part of it. I reckon that fighting off the big Tiger last night caused most of her problems. She's gone a bit mental over that and there's a gash on her foot that was probably caused by the whole tooth I found stuck in the stern platform, so no wonder she's out of her tree and running around wondering how to get back up it! And why she's still in shock this morning!

Anyway, that's what we get when we try to look after her and keep her alive. Probably should have just tossed her overboard like someone suggested at the time and it would've been all over in seconds! But it was my fault for trying to be civilised to people who didn't know the meaning of the word!'

'It's called being humane, Harry,' Corrine pointed out, 'we all get an attack of it sometimes.'

'Yeah! Maybe we should just bomb her out and off-load her on Hummocky, then tell the Gladstone coppers who's stranded there in case they're inclined to go get her. I'm inclined to think that's the best option. I'm sick and tired of trying to look after these idiots who seem hell-bent on trying to kill us all the time. I'm a bit over that scene!'

'That seems a good plan. Harry. Let's be shot of her ASAP.'

So as soon as Corrine had administered Marie a shot of her strange sleeping compound that also brought on an unknown degree of amnesia, we parked her on a towel on the stern daybed where we could keep an eye on her, before untying the connecting lines and fenders, and hauling up both anchors. There was no sign of the shark population from last night, nor any sign of human remains on the shallow bottom around us for that matter, as the grey-suited scavengers had done their job to perfection! Passing through the narrow channel was the usual nerve-wracking experience fighting the sudden swirls and surges of current in three dimensions. While we were getting tossed around by the swift-flowing, incoming mass of water, I risked a quick glance at the reef either side and thought I saw what could have been two bodies on the coral, but it would've been very dangerous and difficult, even if we were so inclined, to go check if they were alive or not.

Even if still alive, a day of exposure followed by the next high tide would take care of them.

Therefore, it was with swiftly lifting spirits that we left the cay of horrors to slowly settle back into its normal existence where life and death was a normal, daily on-going occurrence and it neither wanted nor needed the clumsy, destructive and intrusive hand of man to mess with the balance.

Once we'd gained a bit of distance to the north, I was able to lay a direct course to Hummocky Island, although we would pass close enough to a submerged reef that would need watching carefully, as well as passing just north of Masthead Island. It looked a pretty spot, but we were over pretty coral cays for now, and looked forward to a real island with rocks, grass and trees for a change. In fact, I couldn't think of anything better than to sit on a hill on real, green grass with some trees around and not be worried about where the next attack was coming from.

After we'd settled on course, with the light breeze coming over our left quarter pushing us along at about ten knots, I fired up the Sat-phone and called Greg.

'Hi ya, Harry, how're things?'

'Gidday, Greg. They're pretty good now, but we had a few dramas last night.'

'Aww, bugger-it Harry! I'm starting to realise that anytime you admit to having a 'few dramas', that usually means that I need to send in a clean-up squad! I presume your comment means that you met up with the boatload of bad boys and girls?'

'Yeah, you could put it that way. They came at us, but thankfully we were prepared. I'll give you the gory details at another time, but for now we have one live body with us and there's another couple that look to be deceased washed up on the edge of the reef here, but I reckon that the next high tide and the Noah Arks should clean them up.'

'Holy crap, Harry! What happened? There were supposed to be 38 or 40 bikies on that fuckin' dive boat; don't tell me they bailed out?'

'They've carked it, Greg, to be blunt. Except for the couple that made it onto the reef edge, but they looked like they were dead when we put to sea twenty minutes ago, they've all gone. Then there's the one that crawled back aboard *Firebird* for a second time last night, although she was badly banged up by coral and while she was terrorised and slashed by a giant Tiger shark through the night, she should survive. I thought that you might like to question her about the Amazons, but if you don't need to, we'll chuck her over the side. She won't last long in these waters at the moment.'

'*Shit Harry! That's rather cold-blooded, even for you, old mate, so keep her reasonably healthy for me, please. I would really like to have a chat with her, even though it sounds like the whole Club has been wiped out. Fuckin' hell, Harry. Henry, of Undertaker infamy, is going to be very, very pissed off if you've killed his sister!*'

'I thought you wanted us to make a big dent in both the Undertakers and the Zombies?'

'*Ha, ha. That's funny, Harry. A dent is one thing, mate, but wiping out 35 or 40 bikies is more accurately called a mass slaughter! So, yes, you have made a fuckin' huge dent in their ranks, no doubt about that. And stringing Henry's sister up naked and covered in her own shit is one thing, but drowning her or whatever you did to them is something else again! Henry is going to be very upset!*'

'Actually, Greg, and very briefly for the record if you want to keep track, we zapped five or six or them, shot several more, then blew the rest up while they were on that old piece of crap boat they chartered.'

'*Oh bugger me! You don't exactly fuck around when you get going, now do you? So is there much evidence of this mass mayhem for the public to stumble over?*'

'Nope, the boat sank in three pieces in deep water and the bodies were cleaned-up by sharks. There were a shitload of the big, grey buggers around last night, but they've all gone now. Amanda and Melissa are just cutting the flotation chambers on the two RIB's the boys and girls used last night to come calling without an invitation, so they'll be gone in the next few minutes and that pretty well cleans it all up, except for those bodies on the reef edge near the lagoon entrance, but like I said, I don't expect them to even be there past tonight!'

'*They might be a problem, mate, is there any way you can check on that? Apparently dive boats do go there fairly regularly, but the strong winds lately made them cancel the trips for the past few days, so we'd really hate to have even dead bodies being found by a charter boat, let alone a live one babbling about massacres!*'

I thought a few moments then replied in a weary tone that I couldn't be bothered suppressing, 'Yeah, OK mate. The only reason we didn't check this morning is that they're on the edge of a fringing reef that's just underwater at high tide and there's no safe landing place, but since we're not far away yet, I'll have Amanda and Melissa launch that beaut UAV and send it back to have a close look. Will that do?'

'*Yeah, that'd be great Harry. Bob and I will feel a lot better if there aren't any remains draped over the pristine coral to muck up the public's fun day out!*'

'OK, Greg. We'll get on it and I'll report back shortly.'
Thanks Harry. Cheers.'

CHAPTER 42

I cursed and ranted for a minute then called Dave on the phone and asked him to come alongside so we could transfer the girls and the UAV, as *Seeker's* deck was much easier to launch and retrieve from. Twenty minutes later, the aircraft lifted smoothly aloft from *Seeker's* broad foredeck and sped back the short distance to the reef edge beside the channel.

We were clustered around the screen when *Dragonfly* came in over the reef and at first it looked like I must have been mistaken about seeing bodies on the semi-exposed coral, but then we saw a number of sharks at two locations close to the very edge where small waves were breaking against the coral as the tide rose and encroached on the reef.

'Take it down, please Amanda and slow down all you can; all those small sharks clustering together are after something tasty. These might be the bodies.'

The view closed in as the *Dragonfly* descended smoothly to enter a slow orbit over the two locations. They were both bodies all right, although one clearly qualified as a corpse, with one leg and both arms missing, the head torn off and neatly impaled on a stalk of stag horn coral, the eyeless sockets locked in a forever gaze across the jagged coral and careless, heaving ocean. It was a male torso and was well snagged on some jagged arms of coral, the rising tide already causing small waves to break over the remains.

The other body looked different, so I had Amanda bring *Dragonfly* to a high hover until we saw what was different. It was a mostly naked female, with all limbs still attached, but covered in thousands of cuts and slashes. It was curled up on the large, corrugated dome of a giant mushroom coral and looked dead, but something didn't seem right, until the penny dropped and I exclaimed, 'She's still bleeding! She must be alive!'

Amanda carefully directed *Dragonfly* into a low hover just a metre away from the body and sure enough, the myriad cuts and abrasions, similar to what Marie had, were still slowly seeping a slight trickle of blood into the water. No wonder the sharks were going ape-shit!

'OK. Whoever it is, we have to go back. Even by my standards, that's a shit of a way to die — having a bunch of hungry sharks and fish chew off a bit at a time as the tide comes in!'

In a couple of minutes, we had reversed course and with my sails furled, made the best speed of *Firebird* with both engines flat-out, nearly 16 knots. The woman was on the very edge of the reef less than a hundred metres or so along from the entrance channel, with the rising tide bringing the water level closer by the minute. How she survived the night was anyone's guess! Fortunately, the winds had dropped so that here in the lee of the cay it was relatively calm with only small waves breaking gently against the broken, jagged shoreline, but the rising water level brought the voracious pack of small reef sharks ever closer.

I put Sandy on the wheel with instructions to jockey the throttles to keep *Firebird* more or less in the same position, just twenty metres away from the coral. On the radio I told Dave what I planned and he turned *Seeker* over to Corrine to do the same as I dropped the RIB back in the water.

'How are you going to reach that lump of coral she's on?' Sandy asked, worried for the four of us as the rescue team, as much as for the survivor on the reef.

'We'll use the bow boarding ladders off both boats,' I replied, seeing Dave, Alf and Charlie feeding his into his RIB. I fetched *Firebird*'s and awkwardly stowed it in the RIB as Dave pulled alongside to transfer Alf, keeping Charlie with him. Within a couple of minutes, we were set and making our way very carefully in amongst the submerged, treacherous, fingers of coral to where we would have a shot of making a bridge of sorts from RIB to more stable coral near the woman. There was no chance of walking over that tangled mess of coral without being slashed to pieces, so we had to get as close as possible.

The sharks were in a frenzy of hunger with the faint taste of blood in the water to spur them on, to the extent that the larger ones were ramming the RIBs trying to get at us. It was unnerving to say the least.

As we jammed the bow of the RIB into a small gap not far from the woman's precarious perch, I was thankful that the rigid part of the boat's hull was aluminium and not fibreglass, which would have been torn to shreds already since it was continually grinding against coral stalks. Dave drove in behind me, effectively wedging my RIB in place and holding it steady against the small waves and the more anxious of the small sharks trying for an early dinner. I awkwardly slid my boarding ladder across as far as I could onto the coral, but it didn't quite make it to the body, so Dave passed his ladder forward to me, Alf leaving our outboard tilted since we were held in position by the other boat's bow. To place the second ladder, I had to precariously venture onto the first one, holding the end of the second ladder while Alf fed the length to me. Finally, with only a few slips and some gashes to shins and ankles, I got the far end of the second ladder onto the edge of the domed lump of coral supporting our victim.

With Alf edging his way along the creaking unstable ladders behind me, I shuffled about until I had a firm foothold on the woman's perch, effectively straddling her and waited for Alf to reach me. There was no way I'd lift her just by myself since I'd identified our victim as none other than the giant-sized Amazon Queen, her Royal Lowness herself, Etta Jones.

As I waited, the thought crossed my mind that Henry might actually be pleased we were at least trying to save his demented sister, although he'd probably blame me for her being here in the first place! As I waited for Alf to get in position to help lift the very tall, very well built Amazon, I took a closer look at her injuries so we didn't make her condition worse, if that was possible!

Oddly, most of her clothing had been ripped off, perhaps by the blast of one of the bombs with just an incongruous scrap of shirt collar around her neck, the top button still neatly done up, but nothing attached to it, not even a ragged edge. Likewise, the waistband of a pair of jeans still clung stubbornly to her narrow waist, but only a few shreds of denim hung off it to show what it had supported. The thin band of elastic below that could have been her panties, but that was the only trace remaining. There were the expected plethora of cuts, scrapes and bruises, but her lower right arm was still encased in a rigid, lightweight fibreglass cast, and a mottled collection of colours still adorned her ribcage on the right side. Her pulse was so weak, I though we were too late, although the slow weep of blood said otherwise, so it was just as well she was unconscious, as we had to be quite rough to get her off the coral and onto the ladders, Alf holding her by her arms while I held her ankles. She was too heavy and our balance way to precarious to completely lift clear, so we had to half-drag her slowly bouncing her pre-lacerated bare bum from rung to rung toward the dubious security of the RIB. Undoubtedly, we inflicted a few more coral slashes before we gained the more stable platform of the RIB.

By the time we finally got her propped up on the gunnel and retrieved the boarding ladders, both her former perch and the ladders were almost submerged by the rising tide and the sharks were poking their snouts all around us, several nearly stranding themselves in their frantic blood-lust desire to get their promised meal that seemed to be getting away. Finally, with Charlie braving shark bite by leaning over the bow of Dave's RIB to hold onto the prop of my tilted outboard motor, Dave reversed the motor on his RIB and dragged us out of the gap we'd been wedged into.

Once clear, I lowered our motor, fired it up and we got the hell out of there, leaving the sharks to attack each other in frustration at the escape of their meal. In deference to Greg's concerns about upsetting the tourists, I detoured to quickly check the corpse and saw that it was nearly submerged, with a frenzy of small reef sharks already snapping at bits of it. Confident the remains would be removed before long, we resumed our return to the safety of *Firebird* and *Seeker*.

Back aboard *Firebird*, we managed with difficulty to get Etta's still shapely, bloody bulk up to the cockpit where Amanda and Sandy could start to administer first aid. The girls had thought ahead and laid out a big piece of soft plastic drop sheet on the stern daybed so we hoisted her bulk up there, the sun doing the job of warming her as the night on the reef had dropped her core temperature dangerously low.

Luckily, the boat's very well equipped first-aid kit had such luxuries as a saline drip setup, so doing something about that was the first order of business as her blood pressure was very low and her pulse very fast, thready and erratic. We weren't in a position to attempt to perform a transfusion without cross-matching blood types, but I recalled reading of recent experiments that showed that a hypertonic saline solution of up to 7.5% salt was very beneficial in replacing blood in the absence of plasma or whole blood.

Accordingly, while the standard saline solution dripped into her arm at the highest rate we could set, and the girls cleaned and taped up the hundreds of cuts, scratches and scrapes that adorned most parts of her body, I boiled some water then tipped a litre into a clean glass container, before adding several heaped tablespoons of salt to it. Plus a few more for luck! Very un-scientific, but it was an emergency, as the consensus was that she wouldn't last much longer without immediate help, so we'd do our best, particularly as we'd gone to so much trouble to retrieve the psycho bitch after we'd thought she was already giving a shark indigestion!

Once the new brew cooled slightly, we added the hot fresh solution to the drip-bag that was being used and sat back to continually monitor her blood pressure and pulse, while the girls continued cleaning and taping up her wounds.

Despite the damage she'd sustained from the coral, she was in very good general condition and must have had a strong will to survive, since after about 15 minutes, her blood pressure started slowly rising to where it could actually be detected by our machine and her pulse felt stronger.

'That's looking better,' Sandy said, pressing the button for the blood pressure and pulse machine again. 'But we can't leave her out here all day and she's too big to carry down below, so what's the plan, Harry?'

'I think we'll drop the dining table in the saloon, put a long seat cushion from out here in the cockpit and use this plastic as a carry sling to put her on that until we see if she's going to come around. If she doesn't pull through, we slip her overboard and leave it at that, but if she keeps improving like she has been, we'll call in the paramedics to take her to proper care once we get to Hummocky Island.'

'If we do that, we need to be careful who we involve in the pickup,' Sandy suggested, 'We still can't go public until everything has settled down with the bikies.'

'Yeah, you're right. It'd be best if the Water Police can bring a couple of paramedics out to us. I'd prefer not to have to just leave her on a deserted beach, but that's probably what we're going to have to do. We can leave the other one, Marie, there as well so they both get treatment and the Gladstone coppers can look after them from there.

If we don't show our faces, then the paramedics can't blab anything to others if they don't see us. Anyway, we'll see if she keeps showing signs of recovery while we head for Hummocky Island. Now it's time I get to bother Greg again.'

'How come you're smiling when you say that?' Sandy asked

with a laugh, 'we should feel sorry for the poor man getting all these problems dumped in his lap.'

'Pig's arse!' I said laughing back, 'we're out here getting shot at while we do all his dirty work for him, cleaning up his major problems!'

'Hello again, Harry. What's the story?'

'Two bodies, mate, hung up on the reef, one missing several vital parts and positively deceased — the sharks are at it already and should get the rest shortly when the tide rises enough. The other one was alive and remarkably, given her condition and our lack of medical skill, still is. She's badly knocked around and has lost a lot of blood, although her vital signs are slightly better since we shoved a few litres of concentrated saline solution into her, so if she doesn't slip back in the next hour, she might just survive, although she'll need urgent hospital treatment immediately.'

'OK, that's something we can look at. I don't suppose you know who she is?'

I laughed, 'With no clothes on and covered in abrasions, I'd be hard-pressed to recognise you under the same circumstances, but in this case, I do recognise her as Etta Jones, dear Henry's sister.'

'Bloody hell, Harry. That's a really good thing, cause Henry doesn't know that the whole mob got taken out, so if he can at least get his sister back, it might defuse him slightly! And of course, while she's recovering, we just might suck some good intel out of her. So assuming she improves, where do we find you?'

'We're going low profile again, since I reckon that a bunch of crazy bikies are going to be even more determined to be looking for our blood for a while, so we don't want paramedics eyeballing us, even from a distance. What's the chance of getting a Police boat out from Gladstone to Hummocky Island ASAP with a couple of paramedics aboard?'

'That shouldn't be too hard. They've got a new toy to play with, an 11.5 metre RIB with way too much Suzuki horsepower, but I'll make some calls and see what we can do.'

'That'd be great, thanks Greg. We're heading there now, although we won't be there until this afternoon. We plan on leaving them on the beach, once we're sure the paramedics are close, so let me know how you get on and we'll co-ordinate things from there.'

'*Will do. And try very hard to keep Miss Jones alive in the meantime, will you please?*'

'Yes, Dad. I promise!'

'*Smart arse!*'

I looked around at my crew, as Dave and his lot were back on *Seeker*, both boats headed for Hummocky Island at *Firebird's* best speed. 'OK. We have a plan. Keep psycho bitch alive until we get the paramedics to come out to retrieve her and Marie from Hummocky Island.'

'How do we handle the anonymity bit when they lob on the scene?' Amanda asked.

'I think the best thing will be if we land them both on the beach just before they get there. Hopefully, the beach will be deserted at the time, so we can hang around a mile or so away. There's a pair of very rocky little islets to the south east of Hummocky Island and I thought we might just hold position there while the pickup's made, so if you launched the *Dragonfly*, we could keep an eye on what's happening and even talk to the retrieve crew by radio or phone. I'll get a number off Greg when he calls back.'

Amanda smiled, 'That sounds a good plan — we're getting really good value out of *Dragonfly*.'

We were still two hours out from Hummocky Island when Greg called back to say that it'd taken some very high-up pressure to cut the Police RIB loose from whatever job they were currently on, but the mention of bikie gangs, a badly injured Gang leader and another damaged Amazon to take into custody did the trick. '*They'll be on their way within an hour, or so I've been assured, with two Paramedics aboard with a heap of gear to treat severe blood loss, exposure and shock. Is there anything else I need to tell them?*'

'Yes. Both patients will be left on the beach, under whatever cover we can find or improvise. If you get me a mobile, Sat-phone number or radio frequency for them, we'll be in touch to guide them straight to them and can tell them what treatment they've both had so far.'

'*How are you going to do that if you're not there?*' he asked.

'Easy. The UAV! And we won't be there so the paras won't see us.'

'*OK, fair enough. But I assume that you won't be far away?*'

'Nope. Just far enough that we won't be obvious, but once they've gone, we may stick around for a day or two before heading off again. Our loose plan is to let the dust settle following this bit of a dust up, by staying out of sight as much as possible. If you get the chance, you might like to let at least the two Gold Coast Clubs know that we were just defending ourselves from attack from an armed force of overwhelming numbers and that we didn't have to risk our necks to save dear Henry's little sister from both the reef and the Noah's Arks!'

'*Yeah, got that Harry. I'll do what I can, but there are some Brisbane Clubs involved as well, since the boat's skipper and crew were brothers and part of another Maryborough Club, I'm told. That family is considered psycho and are going to be very upset when they hear about all this.*'

'Understood, mate. But you might like to remind anyone who'll stand still and listen, that we didn't start this rattle, the bloody Amazons did by snatching one of ours, or yours to be precise. Then half the bikie tribes in South East Queensland decided to have some fun by going on the warpath, but it backfired on them. Remind the cock-heads about that!'

'*OK, Harry. Settle Petal, please. I'll tell them all if I can get the message out. Naturally, it'll really help if Henry's sister pulls through.*'

'Yeah, yeah. Just do what you can, please Greg. We're totally over these clowns constantly trying to knock us off! Anyway, call me later after the pickup and let me know how she's getting on, if you would. We went to a lot of trouble and risk to retrieve her.'

'Ok. Will do. Cheers for now.'

HUMMOCKY ISLAND, FRIDAY

As we approached Hummocky Island, I asked Amanda to get the *Dragonfly* ready again. She'd left it and all it's support gear on *Seeker* after supporting the retrieval of Etta Jones from the reef, so I called Dave and had him stop long enough for Amanda and Melissa to transfer across and for Alf to come onto *Firebird*. Once back on course, it only took fifteen minutes or so before I saw the now-familiar shape that looked like a Patriarchal Cross, ascend smoothly from the *Seeker's* foredeck and climb to 1500 feet altitude.

Amanda was still working on setting up a system whereby both boats could receive the *Dragonfly's* video telemetry simultaneously, but hadn't got that working yet, so we had to be content with a suitably cryptic UHF short-range radio calls.

'Target area clear of traffic,' she reported shortly after the UAV reached Hummocky Island, *'and the western approaches are clear at the moment.'*

'Copy that. Remain on primary station and report any fast in-bound traffic.'

'Copy. Will do.'

With Dave keeping *Seeker* a little way back from us, and Amanda feeding information about other boats, we went directly to the main bay on the North side of the Island. It was a pretty spot and very sheltered from southerly winds, but wide open to northerlies. Two hills gave the Island its name, the western one being the most prominent, while the steep, rocky slopes were thickly covered in grass and light scrub.

The sandy part of the beach was barely 200 metres long,

but there were only a few rocks in the shallows and the bottom offered very good holding for the anchor in sand.

With our aerial observation platform keeping watch, we nosed in close and anchored on a short scope — *Seeker* keeping a moving patrol a kilometre further north. We used the bottom boards from the dinghy once again to improvise a stretcher to support Etta Jones for the transfer to shore and I slung a line off the tip of the main boom, using it as a crane to lift the stretcher and lower it into the dinghy. Marie had been given another dose of Corrine's cocktail of amnesia-inducing drugs and was barely able to walk, but it was better than carrying her!

It was a very short trip to shore, but the real struggle for the three of us was to manhandle Etta's 6 foot 4 inch, frame out of the RIB and up the beach to the shade of a small patch of scrub at the end of the main gully between the two peaks. Fortunately, she was still well out of it and didn't feel a thing.

We laid her out on an old beach towel as we needed the bottom boards for the RIB, draped another one over her as she still had no clothes, and hung a fresh bag of my concocted hypertonic saline solution from a branch above with several sheets of paper taped to it detailing how she'd been injured and what first aid we'd given to stabilise her and left her. Marie was seated beside her but promptly keeled over and started snoring softly.

Ten minutes later we were hauling the anchor, ready to move out when Amanda reported that the *Dragonfly's* camera had picked up a fast-moving boat heading east from the North Eastern tip of Curtis Island.

'*Only eight to ten minutes to target,*' she warned.

'Copy that. Moving now,' I radioed back, 'Proceed to the holding point.'

'*Will do,*' was her brief reply before I saw *Seeker* power up and almost launch out of the water, as the power of the two huge V-12 diesels was unleashed. They departed the Bay at high speed propelled by a pair of huge white rooster tails of jet wash arching up ten metres high behind the transom as Dave cut loose and blew some carbon out of the turbochargers after days of idling along keeping pace with *Firebird*.

We followed at a more sedate pace around the east tip of the Island, initially heading for the tiny islet of Fairway Rock Reef just 1.5 nautical miles away. Moments later, I re-thought our move and decided to stay close inshore on the east side of Hummocky Island where *Firebird* would be shielded from sight of the Police boat, until they anchored and it was safe to move out to the islet.

Accordingly, I radioed Dave to hold his position down at the little Islet and wait. I asked Amanda to advise when the Police boat had anchored and let me know what was happening. I moved *Firebird* around to a rocky cove on the south east side and held position against the breeze and currents until Amanda advised that the Police RIB had nosed up on the beach and that the paramedics had found Etta Jones and Marie as per my earlier instructions phoned through and were working on Etta. At the end of that call, I powered up and rather more slowly than Dave, headed for the rocky little islets lying south east of Hummocky Island.

At anytime other than fairly calm weather, the waters in and around the little reef would be very dangerous. The main portion was only about one hundred metres long, with a smaller ridge laying a hundred metres away on the east side with several much smaller outcroppings ready to catch unwary boaties. There was no place to land and even anchoring would be difficult and inadvisable, if not impossible. Still, as a temporary place to hide from view from the north and west, it was ideal and we only had to jockey throttles to hold position against the swirling currents that prevailed even in these calm conditions. I shuddered to imagine what conditions would be like in rough seas or a storm.

After about 30 minutes, Amanda radioed through that the primary subject appeared stabilised and both were being moved to the transport. Minutes later, she reported the RIB moving at high speed back toward the northern tip of Curtis Island and the start of the inland channel down to Gladstone that would give the big Police RIB smooth, fast running.

Happily, I pushed the throttles up and drove out of that dangerous place with its contrary currents and starkly inhospitable walls of rock and headed back to Hummocky Island. Dave came on the radio to say that they were going to stay there a while longer as Corrine and Melissa had found that the fishing was brilliant, so I suggested that Amanda could retrieve the *Dragonfly* at her convenience then we happily left them to it and were soon anchored close in to the beach.

Sandy and I decided to take Jasper and Krazy kitten for a run on the beach, leaving Alf to mind the radio in case *Seeker* had a problem. We carried a small hand-held UHF radio in case he needed us. Feeling adventurous, we climbed the steep, scrub covered main hill to be rewarded for our efforts with a spectacular view of the mainland, Curtis Island as well as a great view almost looking straight down on *Seeker* as she hovered effortlessly between the rocky walls of Fairway Rock Reef. Surprisingly, little Krazy kitten made it most of the way to the top, only climbing up on Jasper's back for the last stretch, both pussies loving the exercise and the feel of the coarse grass under their little feet.

I'd brought the Sat-phone with me as well in case Greg called, but as we sat on a convenient rock to recover, with the two cats lying at our feet, I decided to call him.

'Hi Harry. Has it all gone well?'

'Yep. No problem and we kept our faces and the boats out of the picture, so all they know is that an anonymous phone call alerted them to one critically injured woman and one less injured woman, on a remote beach on a remote island where there was a written note detailing the treatment given.'

He chuckled, 'Very devious, Harry, and quite up to your usual excellent standard.'

'Thanks Greg, but have you had a chance to contact the local bikie Club dudes yet?

'Yeah, I'm just about to. In fact I'm looking forward to telling them what happened. I don't think that either Henry or Brad know what's happened yet, so I'm going to love to see their faces when I bring them up to date.'

'That's evil, Greg, but I really like it.'

'No problem, sport. I'll get back to you when I know more. In the meantime, relax a bit and enjoy. The pressure is off a little bit for now.'

'Yeah, maybe. Bye for now.'

CHAPTER 44

'Undertaker.'

'*Good afternoon Mr Jones. This is Inspector James of South-port Police. I trust you are keeping well?*'

'Good afternoon, Inspector. Very well, thank you. How may I be of assistance to the Police this day?'

'*For a change, it is I who can be of assistance to you and to Mr Edwards too, in this instance. I wish to have another meeting with you both as soon as possible. I can assure you that it is very much in your interest to hear what I have to say.*'

'Once again you intrigue me Inspector, and I must say that the information we gained at our last little get-together was most useful and beneficial, so I'm inclined to say 'yes', although I cannot speak for Mr Edwards, but he usually goes along with strange requests like this one.'

'*Excellent, Mr Jones. Shall we say the Benbow Tavern again? In one hour if that would suit. I'll call ahead and have a table reserved outside. As it's Friday afternoon, they will be rather busy, I should imagine.*'

'One hour is acceptable, Inspector. I shall endeavour to have Mr Edwards attend as well, although I won't have my Lieutenant with me as he's out of town at the moment, but that shouldn't matter, as I believe that a certain level of mutual trust now exists between us. Would you agree with and confirm that sentiment?'

'*Indeed I would, Mr Jones, and very good of you to point that out. In one hour then.*'

BENBOW TAVERN – SOUTHPORT

As was his habit, Greg arrived first with Bob Casey in tow, to find that his phone call alerting the staff had worked, as a large outside table, well separated from the early, 'POETS day' crowd, had been reserved, although a big crowd was building already, and the bars and lounge area were crowded.

The manager, a nervous little man who sweated easily, rushed over as they walked in and went to the bar.

'Will that be OK, Inspector?' he asked, almost wringing his hands with worry, 'and there won't be any trouble, will there?'

Greg looked at him dispassionately. 'No Jean-Claude, but should the unthinkable happen, just call the Police!'

Jean-Claude swung his eyes from one to the other, but was met with stony faces.

'But you.... Ah,' he said, 'Ha, ha! You're joking, I can tell. Very funny! I get it — you *are* the Police.'

Greg clapped him on the back. 'There's just no getting around your lightning-fast mind, is there Jean-Claude? I wouldn't dare to try to fool you.'

Jean-Claude got a funny look on his face as if he wasn't sure if Greg was taking the piss or not, but settled for a quick nod, before scuttling back into his garlic-impregnated cave behind the bar that masqueraded as an office.

Shaking their heads in wonder, Greg and Bob bought a schooner each then wandered back out to their reserved table, where several half-pissed Tradies in fluoro safety shirts had set up shop in defiance of the reserved sign.

'Hop it, lads,' Greg said, pointing at the 'Reserved' sign, 'we're having a business meeting.'

One loudmouth with a red, beefy face, a shirt-straining beer-gut and attitude and alcohol leaking in equal proportions out of every greasy pore, spoke up, 'What bloody meeting? There are only two of you! That's not a meeting — that's what a couple of poofs do! Ha, ha!'

Beside him, Greg could feel Bob starting to bristle, but as he looked over the Tradie's shoulder, he smiled and said politely, 'Look sport. Please don't be a bother. We don't want to spoil your afternoon and you *really* don't want to spoil ours!'

The half-pissed Tradie sneered, thinking his mates were right behind him as back up, 'Or what, little man?'

He yelped as a hand nearly twice the size of his grabbed him lightly by the back of his neck and started squeezing slowly while a calm, deep voice said, 'Or I will pick you up by the neck and throw you into the canal. Now please do as the nice Police Inspector has politely asked and go somewhere else.'

He let go, so the Tradie could plop back into his seat, before squirming around to see what seemed like a monstrous apparition standing behind him. At 6' 7" tall, gaunt in the face, slim of build, with broad shoulders, huge hands and dressed in a black suit with white shirt, Henry Jones, aka the Undertaker was the stuff of children's nightmares.

The effect on the half-pissed Tradie was almost comical as he spilled most of his beer hurriedly vacating the chair he was parked in, when he realised that his 'mates' had quietly faded away out of sight when Henry the Undertaker and Brad Edwards, the equally frightening Zombie Eaters leader had pulled up together in an immaculate dark-green HSV GTS Commodore and were the rest of the 'business meeting'.

White of face, his eyes spinning as he realised his mistake the Tradie stammered an apology to all four, before beating a hasty retreat.

Henry inclined his head to the two officers, 'Good afternoon, Superintendent and Inspector. I trust I acted in an appropriate manner?'

Greg smiled easily at him, 'Perfectly, thank you Mr Jones and very gentlemanly of you. Good afternoon Mr Edwards. Thank you both for coming at short notice, but please sit down and I'll get some drinks.'

Both men sat, but declined drinks, so Greg and Bob sat as well, amused by the clear space that had miraculously opened up around their table when the identity of the two notorious bikie leaders was circulated.

'Before you share the information you said concerns the two of us, I wish to thank you, Inspector, for your co-operation in organising the traffic flow for our Brother's funeral parade recently,' Henry opened with.

Greg inclined his head politely, 'My pleasure, Mr Jones, and thank you for the way your men conducted themselves. My Officers complimented your men on their excellent behaviour.

Now, to get straight to business, this discussion concerns the boat called the *MV Landfall* that was chartered by a large group of men and women possibly known to you, and sailed from Gladstone to Fitzroy Reef yesterday for the express purpose of attacking two boats belonging to the so-called 'pirate' group that has been causing various levels of mayhem lately.'

The usually imperturbable Henry, raised his groomed eyebrows at this revelation and said, 'Go on,' while Brad Edwards lost his usual jocular demeanour and became stony-faced and as still as a marble statue.

With a tight little smile on his face, Greg did so. 'We have been contacted by the leader of the pirate group you have all been hunting, with some very disturbing news.'

The two bikie chiefs continued to sit motionless, their full attention on Greg who was trying very hard not to chuckle with glee at their obvious discomfort.

'I've been advised,' he went on, delivering the coup-de-grace, 'that virtually the whole primary raiding party has been eliminated, with just one survivor, a young female who has relatively minor injuries. The chartered boat, the *Landfall* has been totally destroyed and sunk with just one survivor from it, a female who is in very poor condition.'

Brad Edwards lost even more colour from his face and

suddenly developed a pronounced tic in his right eye, while Henry slowly closed his eyes briefly, a spasm of pain transforming his normally placid features.

'Have...' he stopped to clear his throat, 'have the two survivors been identified?'

Greg made a big production out of searching through his pockets until he found a folded sheet of paper that he unfolded, scanned carefully, then said, 'Hmmm. Yes. They're both female. The one in reasonable condition, with many minor cuts, abrasions and scrapes from encounters with coral and a large shark, is named as Marie.

The other is not so fortunate. She experienced much worse injuries from being tossed around on coral by waves and apparently escaping a pack of sharks and has suffered severe blood loss, plus a night and half a day's exposure on the reef. At least she managed to mostly avoid the ravenous packs of sharks that were swarming the area feasting on fresh food. Her name is Etta Jones — your sister, I'm led to believe.'

Henry made a small sound and slumped back in his seat, closing his eyes and giving in to his emotions for once. Greg gave him a moment or two to digest the news, then continued, 'Apart from giving you this good news — bad news, I have been asked by the group that were attacked to pass on further information.'

Both Henry and Brad looked up, sat up and showed a bit more interest.

'Both survivors were given comprehensive first aid, and in the case of Miss Jones, it may very well have saved her life, although that is not guaranteed yet. The 'pirate group' went to extraordinary lengths to rescue Miss Jones from her precarious perch on the reef, fighting off a mass shark attack, rough surf and razor-sharp coral to save her.

They also applied some radical and revolutionary first-aid treatment that apparently made a big difference, as without that treatment, it is believed that she would not have survived at all. She was very nearly dead when rescued, with very little blood pressure and barely a pulse. Some degree of brain damage due to oxygen starvation hasn't been ruled out.

Under the circumstances, they were naturally under no obligation to do anything to save her, since she would appear to be the main instigator of this whole attack enterprise. Should she survive with her faculties intact, we will be having some long talks with Miss Jones.'

'W...where is she now?' Henry asked in a stricken voice, so unlike his usual sardonic drawl that Brad glanced at him to see if he was all right.

'After being brought in from the outer reef and treated by the 'pirates', the two ladies were handed across to a paramedic team who arrived in a fast Police boat which was summoned by and met the rescuers part way. They are still on the water as we speak, but should be almost back in Gladstone.'

Greg paused to sip his beer, his throat dry from the tension.

'The initial report from the paramedics praises the work done by the rescuers and say that Miss Jones would definitely be dead hours ago without the treatment she was given. Needless to say, both ladies are, and will remain in Police custody, as there are a number of complaints that are pending against both of them for their part in the raid. There will be multiple charges to face and you can expect a major enquiry into the reasons behind this whole affair. As a friendly warning and in the spirit of mutual co-operation, I can advise you that the enquiry will leave no stone left unturned by the time it has finished, so if you need to put your house in order, do so quickly. Senior persons are screaming for heads to roll, so if you're quick, you may survive.'

Henry looked at Greg and Bob. 'You will both have to forgive my emotional lapses. This has been quite a shock with so many friends and Club members lost, and with my dear, misguided sister in such a critical condition. We have always been very close since our parents died in a plane crash when we were very young. Will I be able to see her?'

Greg looked suitably solemn. 'Yes. We can arrange that, but I hope you understand that you will have to be accompanied by a Police Officer all the time you are with her.'

Henry nodded, 'I understand and thank you for your consideration. It's not what I've come to expect from the Police and is causing me to re-think our relationship.'

That caused Brad Edwards to look sharply at the tall man again to see if he was delusional or some other way affected by all these revelations, despite having difficulties himself coming to grips with the fact that he'd lost ten of his best men, including his Lieutenant and close friend overnight and with no bodies to show for it.

Greg and Bob nodded sagely at Henry's words, before Greg added, 'In addition, I've been asked by the so-called 'pirates' to pass on some thoughts in the aftermath of this whole affair, so to virtually quote the leader — 'If you get the chance, you might like to let at least the two Gold Coast Clubs know that we were just defending ourselves from surprise attack by overwhelming numbers of a heavily armed force. We also didn't have to take the extreme risks that we did, to save dear Henry's little sister and that other female from the reef and the Noah's Arks, nor to spend so much time patching them up, treating Etta's severe blood loss and getting her and Marie to paramedics ASAP!'

'In addition, you might like to remind anyone who'll stand still and listen, that we didn't start this rattle, the bloody Amazons did by kidnapping one of my people. Then half the bikie tribes in South East Queensland decided to have some fun by going on the warpath, just because I dared to retaliate, but it backfired on them. Remind them about my last lot of comments I had you pass on!'

In case that reference has slipped your minds, it was, 'the wrath of God will be mild compared to what will happen next time!'

As Henry seemed to be intently contemplating the pattern on the table in front of him, Brad spoke up. 'I do recall that statement, Inspector, and at the time I believe Mr Jones responded by saying that they were 'big words'. However, events seem to have proved the truth of that prophesy, so I think I can speak for Mr and Miss Jones when I say that there will not be any more attempts by our three Clubs to indulge in any retaliation against these 'pirates', whoever they are.'

Greg and Bob exchanged significant looks before reaching over to shake hands with both Leaders. 'Thank you gentlemen for your time and the accord we seem to have reached. I realise that there are all the other Clubs in Brisbane and the surrounding areas that feel they have suffered in this debacle, but if you have any contact with them, please let them know what's happened and the outcome.'

Brad nodded, 'We will Inspector, and thanks for your time and your considerate attitude also.'

'I'd like to visit my sister as soon as I can get up to Gladstone,' Henry said, 'are you able to clear the way for that to happen?'

Greg nodded, 'I'll call the local coppers from the office as soon as we get back to say to expect you and that you're to be allowed unlimited access, depending on medical opinion, but under escort at all times. Will that do?'

Henry nodded gravely, 'That will be quite acceptable, thank you Inspector. We'll bid you farewell.'

With that, the two Leaders went to the dark green HSV GTS and quietly drove away.

SOUTHPORT POLICE STATION – FRIDAY EVENING

Back at the Station, Greg called his contact at Gladstone Police and asked for co-operation for Henry Jones to visit his sister, but emphasised that he must be accompanied at all times by an officer.

'*That's standard procedure Inspector, anytime we have a suspect in custody in hospital. She'll have two Officers on duty 24/7 — one in the room and one outside. Only approved visitors such as her brother.*'

'OK, thanks for that,' Greg replied, 'but be very careful with both of them, especially her brother. He's the leader of one of the

OMC's that started all this fuss and a very astute and intimidating man in his own right, but he should be OK and I'm expecting and hoping that he'll play by the rules.'

'OK. *Thanks for the heads-up, Inspector. If anything of interest comes out of the visits, we'll call you immediately.*'

FIREBIRD - FRIDAY EVENING

'Hi Greg, How did your meeting go?'

'Good thanks Harry. I didn't think it was possible to shake old Henry up with anything, but this fairly flattened him! I guess losing ten men and nearly losing his sister is a shock to anybody! Anyway, I passed on your information and messages and they appeared to be well received, with the boys promising to pass the story on to the Brisbane Clubs.

It might take a while for that info to filter through all the Clubs involved, but after that I'm hopeful that the hunt will be called off for good.'

'I'd like to think so too, mate, but we might stay low profile for another couple of weeks if you don't mind monitoring the word on the streets for us?'

'That'll be a pleasure, Harry. The Commissioner is absolutely delighted with the outcome so far. A massive haul of drugs, cash seized, and three Clubs decimated without any direct Police involvement! Quite an achievement! He's making noises about making your team an Official Special Strike Force within the Service, so watch this space, as the saying goes.'

'That would be funny, but none of us will be sorry to hear that the bikies have backed off hunting us and have gone back to warring with each other again.'

'Yeah, copy that. Needless to say, keep everyone together for now, but depending on what the Commissioner decides to do, the boys and girls may have to go back to General Duties.'

I laughed, 'That won't go down very well. I think the blood lust has been stirred up in them now that they've had a taste of real action. Nothing focuses the mind like having some one shooting at you!'

'Understood. Go relax and I'll be in touch.'

FIREBIRD & SEEKER – HUMMOCKY ISLAND AND PLACES NORTH

For the next few days, we hung around the pretty little bay, swimming, fishing and chatting with the crew on the occasional visiting boat until a gusty northerly sprang up one morning heralding an approaching cold front. That turned the anchorage very uncomfortable very quickly, so we got under way and bashed our way north to the Keppel Islands, sheltering in a snug anchorage at Clam Bay on the south eastern corner of Great Keppel Island for two days while the hot north wind whistled and moaned through the rigging. The warm winds did make for very pleasant swimming conditions and lots of beach walks with Jasper and Krazy who took maximum advantage of the extra company and affection as we all slowly unwound. There were an increasing number of instances of out-of-character behaviour from most of the team, something that Corrine and I had seen many times in the Middle East after a hot fire engagement, but nothing that wasn't resolved by a drunken party or some old-fashioned, energetic bonking, with the girls looking for tension release as much as the guys.

Just before the front hit with cold, gusty southerly winds, we moved the short distance around to the delightfully named Butterfish Bay on the north side of Great Keppel. For a pair of shallow-draft boats that were able to avoid the rocks scattered around the anchorage and get close in to the small beach, it offered excellent shelter from the blustery south wind. When those winds abated, we sampled the delights of Middle Island where few boats came to disturb the peace.

And it was peace that we all wanted, with everyone continuing to unwind in his or her own way. Even the tension we all felt afresh when a strange boat joined us in an anchorage slowly abated until we enjoyed interacting with other boaties again.

There were also the usual withdrawal symptoms felt by not to have to be constantly planning fresh strategies to keep us out of the clutches of the bad guys, or gird our collective loins for an attack upon the unwashed and ungodly few that were hell-bent on making our lives a misery.

Corrine and I, experiencing similar letdowns following the end of each action in the desert, had learned to expect it and cope with it, and that it was mainly time spent getting back to a more leisurely routine that was the necessary healing agent.

Therefore, those days and nights spent in frivolous pursuits like playing and cheating at Scrabble and Monopoly, and taking long beach walks with the two kitties were a very necessary part of the process.

CHAPTER 46, FIREBIRD & SEEKER, TUESDAY

As usual, all good things come to an end and we were finally summoned back to base. We didn't rush too much, so it was several days later, late in the afternoon before we motored in through the Southport Seaway in close company. Phone calls ahead had secured a prime berth for *Seeker* at the Yacht Club, while I picked up my old mooring nearby.

We all spent a last night aboard the boats, dining together on *Seeker* and having just a little bit too much to drink. Amanda, Melissa, Alf and Charlie slept aboard for the last time.

The following morning, we all were required to report to base, but it was a tearful Amanda and Melissa and a reluctant Alf and Charlie who had to pack their bags. I took them all over to the Water Police base in the RIB, where Melissa was going to run

Alf and Charlie over to the Southport Station where Alf had left his vehicle, then take Amanda back to their unit. There were lots of hugs, kisses and handshakes, but as we were all going to be in Southport Station later that day, it wasn't like a permanent parting.

Sandy stayed aboard as she had moved in before her relieving posting came up, so the boat wasn't empty, although Jasper and Krazy kitten missed the extra bodies to play with and were more demanding of our attention. Perhaps it was the more familiar surroundings, but the violent events and tension-filled days suddenly seemed part of another time, one that was more easily tucked away in the more remote areas of the mind.

I reported in to my Controller and was advised that I had been highly commended yet again by my Superiors for the excellent outcome to the operation that I'd stumbled into by happenstance. They were also delighted with the way that I'd worked seamlessly with the Officers of a State Police Service, although that shouldn't have been a surprise after the last operation where I'd worked very co-operatively with both the Queensland and Victorian State Police.

My reward was to have my funding boosted again and to be allowed to slip back into my cover as a self-indulgent playboy boatie with too much time and money and always with a lovely lady or two hanging around. The fact that the cover was nearly completely true was beside the point. Especially about the ladies!

WEDNESDAY AM.

Next morning, the full eight-person crew of both boats attended Southport Police Station where we found the place in a state of quiet chaos, as the Police Commissioner had made a rare and generally unannounced appearance, along with several self-important, but utterly useless aides and with the Deputy

Commissioner in tow for good measure. In a surprisingly relaxed ceremony in the largest meeting room, several awards were made:

Sandy, Amanda, Melissa, Alf and Charlie were presented with the 'Commissioner's Certificate for Bravery' with appropriate entries in their records.

Corrine and Dave were presented with a special 'Commissioner's Certificate of Meritorious Service to the Queensland Police Service', citing 'Bravery under Fire and Extreme Hazard' as the reason for the award.

Constables Alf Story and Charlie Jakes were both promoted to Senior Constable.

Senior Constable Amanda Burke promoted to Sergeant

During the fully catered morning tea, the Commissioner spent a lot of time in a corner chatting with Corrine, Dave and me, continually waving away the approaches by his aides. He was very excited about the way Corrine and Dave had fitted in with the operation and he quizzed Corrine at length about her military career, her frank replies to his queries raising his eyebrows on several occasions. Several proposals were put forward and rejected as unworkable for one reason or another, but finally an agreement was reached. Then, once the food had been eaten and the dead mugs cleared away, the Commissioner announced to the small and very select group that included Greg James and Bob Casey, that with the co-operation of, and partly financed by the ACP, his concept of an undercover 'Special Marine Strike Force' would become reality immediately with the six Service Officers and two civilian contractors present as the core, along with their boats. Remuneration, expense and compensation details for the Contractors would be handled by the Police legal branch and jointly co-ordinated by the Deputy Commissioner and Bob Casey.

As there were no operations pending that would require the services of our new unit, Amanda, Melissa, Alf and Charlie were required to return to their normal duties immediately, with three of them having to learn how to handle the increased responsibilities that promotion brings, while Sandy was given three weeks leave since she hadn't taken a work break once her relieving duties were completed and still had normal holidays accrued.

One week later, life on *Firebird* had settled down to a pleasant routine, with Sandy going shopping on several days, usually with Corrine, leaving me to play boat husband with the kitties, catch up on the extensive list of maintenance items or take the RIB over to chat with or go for a run on the surf beach with Dave. When they were just on normal street patrol, Alf and Charlie would often drop in to *Seeker* for a coffee and a chat.

I also had the daily trips to the nearest exposed sandbank or deserted patch of beach to let the kitties have a run around and poop and pee somewhere they could re-learn the arcane art of how to dig and bury it.

One afternoon, Sandy came home quite excited from a shopping trip and could hardly wait to tell me why. 'I was looking in the window of a small jewellery store today,' she announced, after she'd changed into boat-casual attire that varied depending on the weather and her mood. Today, it was very skimpy, consisting of just a shrunken T-shirt, which suggested that she'd appreciate a round or two of romping on the bed before we went to have tea at the pub, but for once, she had to explain her excitement first.

'There were some interesting and unusual jewellery pieces in the window and it was conspicuously missing the usual racks of low-end watches, necklaces and rings, so I went in and got talking to the Jeweller. He's a lovely old Jewish fella, so I asked some questions about diamonds, since he had quite a few displayed inside the shop. Anyway, it turns out that he specialises in diamonds and making special settings for precious stones, but more exactly, deals in coloured diamonds. So I happened to mention that we had a couple of blue ones and would they be any good?'

We had two very deep-blue diamonds, square-cut in what

seemed to me to be an old-fashioned design with rounded corners, that had been given to us by Dave and Corrine as a 'thank you' for not sending them to prison for kidnapping. They had once been part of the stash of a very shifty criminal type they'd had worked for in Victoria and who was currently detained at the Government's pleasure for many crimes and for many years to come.

The diamonds were very pretty and quite big, but I'd heard somewhere that coloured diamonds were valued a lot less than white ones, so I didn't hold out much hope that Sandy would get a good return on her gift if she wanted to sell it.

I butted in, anxious to speed up the story and get her onto the bed and me into her, as the sight of an excited Sandy bouncing around clad just in a brief T-shirt is a very stirring sight at any time. 'Let me guess that the first thing he said was, 'I'll have to see them first before I can say what they're worth'.'

She pouted then smacked me on the arm, 'Smart-arse bastard! Yes, that's exactly what he said, so tomorrow, can we take them in to see him? Please? I asked around and the other jewellers say that he's probably the best diamond guy in Australia. He was a big man in the diamond business in Tel Aviv years ago, but retired here to be with his daughter, then got bored and opened a small shop, but he only deals in precious stones. He still makes most of his own jewellery settings to suit the stones he sells.'

I readily agreed, having nothing more exciting planned for tomorrow than another oil and filter change on the port diesel and that made her very happy and even more excited, if that was possible.

All that excitement translated into a truly memorable romp on the bed that almost made us late for the 20:30 kitchen closing time at the Marina Tavern. Ellie the bar manager and my pre-Sandy very casual bedmate, laughed aloud when she saw us hustling into the bar from the waterside deck where I'd hastily tied up our RIB. We'd remained great friends and she and Sandy got along extremely well.

The next day found us at the jewellers at 10:00. I had the stones in a small, black velvet bag and it felt disconcertingly empty, so I'd tucked it casually into the top pocket of one of my old boat shirts that was at least clean, but had the built-in stains of past oil changes and paint touch-ups adorning the front portion and one sleeve. The shop was very small, just off the main street in Southport and not far from the Police Station. Mr Jacobs proved to be the typical Jewish jeweller, but was a very nice, gentlemanly old bloke as well. He pretended to ignore my lack of decent clothing and as I'd already copped an earful from Sandy for not, 'dressing properly in public' that I'd ignored as usual.

He remembered Sandy, (like who wouldn't), then swung his gaze expectantly from one to the other, waiting for the goods to be produced.

Belatedly, I dug in my pocket, having trouble finding the little bag at first, but then handing it over.

Mr Jacobs carefully laid out a white velvet cloth on the counter where a shaft of sunlight came through a skylight positioned directly overhead, before opening the drawstring on the little bag and gently decanting the contents onto the white cloth. It'd been many weeks since Dave and Corrine had presented them to us, so I'd forgotten how beautiful the blue colour was as the two little rocks tumbled out, gleaming with a deep, rich, royal blue hue onto the white cloth. They lay there, winking and glowing in the sunlight as though happy to be free of the eternal darkness of their confinement. The carefully cut facets threw dozens of tiny shafts of beautiful, pure blue light back at us and over the ceiling and walls as though they were alive, instead of being inert lumps of carbon, moulded by unimaginable forces and temperatures so deep beneath the Earth's crust.

The first sign that there might be something different about them came when Mr Jacobs sucked in a sharp breath, grabbed his loupe, screwed it into his eye, grabbed a pair of stone grippers and picked up one stone to peer into it's flashing depths from many angles. After a minute, he placed it reverently down and subjected the other to the same treatment.

Finally, he placed it down and looked at us.

'Do you know where these came from?' he asked.

I replied honestly, 'Not originally, but they were a gift to us from the legitimate owners for services rendered. What's wrong?'

He shook his head in wonder. 'Never, in all my years in the industry, have I seen such stones! They go way beyond magnificent! The depth and purity of colour is unprecedented. To the best of my knowledge, and I might add, humbly, that with my experience, I know of these things, there are no stones the equal to these anywhere in the known world!'

I must have looked sceptical, so he went to the back room where we heard the 'clank' of a big safe door being opened, before he returned with a very small tray of white velvet that he placed on the counter beside our 'rocks' With a casual wave of his hand, he invited us to make a comparison between the stones on his tray and our two pebbles.

It didn't need one to be an expert to see the difference. They ranged in shade from barely coloured to mid-blue, with the best-looking stone of his stock being a sky-blue stone that was almost lifeless by comparison to the two deep-blue beauties beside it.

I coughed, 'We can see what you mean, Mr Jacobs, but I hate to say that I know of at least four others. Three belong to the persons who gave these to us, and one went to a dear friend of ours. I posted it to her just last week.'

His eyebrows climbed up toward his receding hairline, 'Four more! Really? Are they just like these?'

I shrugged, 'I don't know. I haven't seen them. Our friends just gave us the three and I posted one on to our dear friend.'

'But how could you just post one? Oh my goodness! Just in the normal mail?'

I gave him a puzzled look, 'Sure. I wrapped it in a piece of Kleenex tissue, shoved it in a small postbag and sent it. What's wrong with that? I mean, they're a pretty colour, but that's all surely? I've read that a coloured diamond is only worth a fraction of a white one.'

Without saying any more, he reached under the edge of the counter and pressed a button, whereupon several electric dead-bolts engaged on the front door with loud 'clacks' and the 'Open' sign blinked to a defiant 'Closed'. Sandy was amused rather than alarmed by these actions, but kept her mouth closed when I touched her on the arm. He groped behind him for a stool and sat his slight frame carefully on it, before pulling out a spotless white handkerchief to pat his brow. Removing an array of testing equipment, both old-fashioned and new ultra-high tech from a deep drawer under the counter, he then subjected both stones to a variety of tests, making notes on a pad in a cramped, spidery scrawl that he referred back to frequently.

Finally, he sat up to ease his back, invited us to pull up two stools to perch on as well and said, 'First, some information on diamonds, if you will kindly indulge me, since you need to understand what you have here. While your earlier statement about the usually depressed value of coloured diamonds compared to white was correct, in recent times, the rarity of coloured diamonds has taken over from white or colourless ones on the desirability scale, pushing the price up from the relatively low point that you, Sir, had heard about. But that was quite some time ago and now, they are worth more — sometimes very much more than whites, since well-coloured diamonds are much more rare than whites. That's why pink Argyle diamonds from Western Australia, which is set to close in a few years time, are currently 11.5 times the value of their finest white diamond cousins!

The absolute rarest diamonds, and I mean that only a few come onto the market every five years or so, are the red shades, which transition from the very deepest pinks through to the deep reds or even purple. There are only twenty to thirty genuine red diamonds in the whole world and only a few of those are over 2 carats!

The best ones can look like a very good ruby, but the deep colour blues are only just second in rarity. The pinks, then the greens come next in value — and all of them many times the value that of the purest white provided the colour is reasonably deep.'

He took a deep breath then went on to explain his extreme excitement. 'The most important thing to remember with coloured diamonds is that it is the depth of colour that is the mark of the rarest stones and it is that that has pushed up the value. The two you have here are probably the best blues that have ever been seen in public, because of their deep, intensely pure blue with no other shades to detract from the colour. Even the famous Hope blue diamond was classed as a steel-blue or grey-blue, although at 45.52 carats it was rather more dramatic than these!' He laughed at his weak joke, so Sandy and I dutifully joined in.

He went on, 'Blue diamonds are produced very deep below the Earth's surface, much deeper than white diamonds, which also contributes to their rarity since they literally don't surface very often. I am 99.9% certain that these stones are genuine, naturally coloured diamonds, very nicely cut and weighing 3.2 and 3.3 carats respectively. I would conservatively value them at $1.3 and $1.45 million each, although if two stones of such size and depth of colour were to be presented together at auction, I feel that they would almost certainly fetch more than that!'

Sandy slumped on her stool and grasped feebly at my arm for support as, in a tremulous voice, she asked, 'Who would buy these stones for that sort of money?'

Mr Jacobs smiled gently, 'Certainly not me, my child, although I'd love to be given the chance to mount them properly to show off their stunning colour, but there are many who would buy them unmounted without hesitation. Not only do they have the money to indulge their passion, but also it is a prestige thing in the world of a collector. To pick up three of them, as an almost matched trio, many will happily pay a hefty premium to become known as the person who found, bought and possessed such magnificent gems. However, the real coup in the gem collector circles would be if the whole six were to be presented for sale together.

I should add that the valuation I have just given you is based on a sort of 'book' value and may not reflect the price you could be offered on the open market, say at auction.'

Sandy had been having some trouble following his discourse; her mind obviously spinning with large numbers, so her face fell a bit at his last statement. 'I'm a bit confused by all that, but you're saying that at auction we could get a lot less than those figures you quoted.' She looked at me and gave a shaky little laugh, 'still that would be a lot more than what we have now. To me, they're just very pretty stones that may not be worth selling, although I'm not sure I could even afford to have mine mounted in a ring or necklace at the moment, considering the balance of my bank account.'

Mr Jacobs leant forward over the counter and reached for her hands in a very old worldly, courtly gesture. 'My dear lady. I fear that I've expressed myself very badly and given you the wrong impression. I'll blame old age for my lapse, if I may try to explain more clearly to clear your confusion.'

Sandy nodded and indicated that he should go on.

'There could be four prices for your stones; the first price is for a private sale and would be roughly what I've quoted. There are a few collectors of my acquaintance who are always on the lookout for special pieces.

The second price is what you would receive if you allowed me to spread the word through the collector circles worldwide, that these stones are available. This would create a form of unofficial auction and an offer would certainly be made that should be quite comfortably over the base or 'book' price.

The third price is what you would make at open auction for one, two or even three of the stones, should your friend wish to put her stone in with your two. This price should be above what a private collector would offer.

The fourth price, and this will depend upon your friends who hold the remaining three stones co-operating, is to auction all six together as a package. I believe that there might be extremely strong interest generated in such an offering of six perfect coloured blue diamonds, especially as I have a sneaking suspicion, even without seeing the other four, that they all came from one very large parent stone.'

He paused to take a sip of water from a glass under the counter, before resuming.

'The cut is a very old style, known as an 'Old Mine Cushion cut', so the history will be shrouded in mystery and if the advertising is handled carefully, this can help push the price up to quite interesting levels!

As a manufacturing jeweller, I would find it an interesting challenge to design a piece to display all six to their best advantage. the piece would be simply stunning and would eclipse anything yet seen!'

Both Sandy and I were silent, rocked by this revelation and even I started feeling excited about the prospect.

'Would your friends be willing to part with their stones?' Mr Jacobs asked gently, 'it would be a shame if the gem world was deprived of the chance to see all six stones united again, if my theory is correct. What do you think?'

Sandy seemed speechless, so I spoke, 'It would seem, Mr Jacobs, that we need to speak to our friends as soon as we can. May we get back to you on this?'

'Of course, Sir. I'm here to serve you with the best of my knowledge, but I would dearly like to be involved in the marketing of these stones. It would be, as is said, 'a major feather in the cap of a small businessman'! Should you and your friends decide to proceed with my plan, I would need to have all six stones available for independent testing and verification.'

Sandy looked a bit dubious about that idea, but he hastened to assure her that the highest level of security would be maintained at all times.

'What sort of costs would we be up for in doing this?' she asked, obviously still reluctant to part with her pretty rock.

'Nothing up front, dear lady,' he said, 'I will cover all costs associated with the inspection, verification and security of the items; those costs will come off my fee which will be 1% of the net return of whatever you receive.'

I raised my eyebrows, 'Do you expect to make sufficient out of the deal at just 1%?'

'Indeed, sir. If things go as I hope, that will be quite sufficient for me. My main gain will be the glory of being the one to present the gem world with what I hope to be a coup of stunning proportions!'

He gave a depreciating smile, 'However, I must curb my enthusiasm until we proceed, and I test the waters to see what reception our beautiful little pebbles might generate.'

He carefully picked the two glittering rocks off the white velvet cloth and placed them almost reverently back in their little bag, handing it to me with obvious reluctance.

'Do take care of them, please sir,' he asked, wincing as I stuffed the little bag casually back in the top pocket of my paint-stained shirt.

'She'll be right, Mr Jacob,' I replied flippantly, with a grin. 'We'll be in contact shortly with a decision.'

'Yes, yes. Please do so quickly. There is an excellent gemstone auction being held by one of the smaller houses next month that would be perfect for this enterprise. They would be delighted to score such a coup over their much larger rivals. If you proceed, it will take some time for the testing and advertising, so I would really like to hear from you as soon as you can.'

By now he was almost pleading, so we took his proffered business card and left the small but elegant store, needing the dose of fresh air outside after the slightly stunning news we'd received.

CHAPTER 45

Sandy was silent for a while as we made our way back to her car, but then said, 'It's all a bit hard to believe, don't you think?'

'No, not really. We just didn't appreciate what we were given and obviously nor did Corrine and Dave. I mean, they had plenty and wanted to thank us for getting them off the hook. Don't forget, if charges had been pressed, they would still be locked up for kidnapping.'

'Yes, I know, but it still seems a bit bizarre. I mean I really should have declared the gift to my boss. You know we've not supposed to accept any gifts, especially from someone we should have arrested! But I guess that's too late now.'

She suddenly gave me a stricken look, clutching at my arm, 'Oh shit! What if they want them back when they find out?'

I laughed, 'I thought that you knew Corrine better than that by now. There's no way she or Dave would renege on their deal. A gift is a gift and besides, if it works out like Mr Jacobs expects, there should be a good share of money for everyone.'

Sandy settled down, letting go of the crushing grip she had of my arm. 'I'm still having trouble coming to grips with the idea that I might suddenly become reasonably wealthy. What do I do?'

I laughed again, 'It depends on what we get, if we get it! If it should happen to be substantial, then you must do nothing different for at least six months. Don't resign your job that you've worked so hard for and don't rush out and buy stuff just because you can. Invest your money while you get used to the idea of having money. They're the first rules. Once you've done that, you'll be much more comfortable with the concept. But don't worry about it yet. We may not get too much out of this at all!'

She nodded ruefully, 'Yeah, you're right again Harry. I'll just cool it until we see what happens. But it's OK to dream, isn't it?'

Back at the marina, we found Dave and Corrine kicked back in lounge chairs chatting with the crew of a neighbouring boat. While Corrine put the kettle on, we chatted politely as we waited for the others to leave then told our friends of our experiences that morning.

Corrine looked at Dave as she passed around teas and coffee and shrugged. 'I don't mind selling them — we'll just invest the money. They're just three pretty blue rocks at the moment, sitting in a safe deposit box with all the others in a Southport bank vault, 'cause we brought our whole stash with us.

Oh, yeah. Don't forget, there are the red ones as well, although personally I prefer the emeralds. If I were going to get some jewellery made, I'd want them, not the coloured diamonds. That jeweller I went to said that the red ones were worth a lot. I wonder if this Mr Jacobs would be interested in those as well?'

I shrugged, 'We can only ask him. The main thing we wanted to check on for now was to see if you guys wanted to sell your three blue ones, then we have to see if Janice wants to move hers.'

'I'll give her a call now,' Sandy offered, 'It's been a while since we spoke.'

She did so on the spot, catching her at her new home near her dear friends Hilary and Debbie. Following an exchange of how-are-you and what's-going-on-up-there, Sandy got down to business, explaining the situation very concisely.

'Sure, I don't mind,' Janice came back with, 'I mean I've got a reasonable amount of money tucked away, but a few grand more wouldn't hurt and if there's no cost apart from a 1% commission at the end, that'll do me. I've never been one for jewellery.'

I could see that Sandy was about to try to explain the possible return, but I held my hand up and mimed zipping my lips. After exchanging some more news, mostly about the girls, she signed off with Janice promising to send the rock by Express Post almost straight away, care of the Yacht Club Secretary whom I'd given authority to sign for my mail.

'I'll go to the Bank this arvo and pick up all the rocks,' Corrine said, 'there's a bit of other shopping I want to do elsewhere.'

'I'll come with you,' Sandy promptly said in a stern manner, 'you can't go wandering around the Gold Coast with all those diamonds in your pocket.'

Corrine laughed at the thought of her friend acting as bodyguard, but agreed willingly enough, although I made a mental note to tell Sandy before they went not to act as though she was guarding something!

The girls came back safely in the late afternoon and Corrine passed over two small drawstring bags similar to the one I had. Tipping the contents of the larger one out on a hand towel spread out on the cockpit table, I found another three blue diamonds that to my untutored eye, looked exactly the same size and colour as our two.

But it was the contents of the smaller bag that I was keen to see and was stunned by the brilliance and beauty of the two red stones that spilled out, their facets catching and reflecting the sunlight in a mass of red fire. They were a beautiful oval cut, unlike the three blues that were a nearly square cushion cut.

The reds were a deep, glorious, living hue that was nothing like the washed-out pale colours I'd seen when I'd researched on-line. They looked to be a similar size, or maybe a bit larger than the three blues in the other bag.

'There are six white diamonds as well as the four emeralds, but we decided to leave them in the Bank for now. I didn't realise how big the emeralds were. I hadn't looked at them for a while.' Corrine added.

Sandy chipped in, excited by seeing such beautiful and

hideously expensive stones, 'The emeralds are huge and abso-lutely beautiful, but they're all way too big for a ring, so a necklace or pendant would be the best thing to have made, when you feel the urge to show them off. I'm sure that Mr Jacob would be delighted to make something special for you.'

Corrine poked a face then laughed, 'C'mon Sandy, get a grip. Can you really see me in a ball gown and four bloody great emer-alds on a chain hanging down between my tits?'

Sandy grinned ruefully back, 'No, that's a difficult scene to picture at the moment, seeing you in boat gear, but it could still happen.'

I carefully dropped the two reds in their little bag and the three blues in theirs, pulled the drawstrings and tucked the smaller red's bag into the larger bag holding the blues, before tucking them the top pocket of the old shirt I was still wearing, belatedly realising that I still had our two rocks there as well, but there was plenty of room so I left all three bags together as a good omen. The bags were different colours, so there would be no confusion tomorrow.

Next morning, Sandy could hardly wait to get up town to see Mr Jacobs again and I had to forcibly detain her with personal activities until it was at least mid morning when the Express Post from Melbourne came in. Once we got started, however, she seemed quite delighted with my detaining process and we were running late to pick up the small Express Post bag from the Secretary's office. As it was still wrapped in the Kleenex tissue I'd sent it in, I kept Janice's stone separate from the others until we found out what it weighed.

'Good morning Sir and Madam,' Mr Jacob called out, bustling through from the rear of the shop with an excited air about him, 'I'm very happy to see you again.'

'Good morning Mr Jacob,' I replied. 'And good to see you too. We have news for you.'

'Good news, I hope?' he asked with a twinkle in his eye.

'We think so,' I said with a warm smile, placing the scrunched-up ball of tissue on the counter.

He tut tutted over my irreverent handling of such precious items, then he activated the door locks again before laying out his square of white velvet and peeling open the tissue to reveal Janice's stone. He pulled out all his examination equipment again and carefully went through the process, noting the details on the same pad as yesterday. '3.2 carats, same cut as your two and certainly cut from the same parent stone. He carefully placed it aside as I dug in my top pocket again, making sure I found the right bag holding the three blues.

He almost almost pounced on it in his haste, before carefully tipping it up onto the square of white velvet, except that this time, three sparkling blue gems tumbled out, flashing their amazing radiance all around, the same as our two had.

He sucked in a long breath, nodded then reached for his measuring and checking instruments. Checking each one thoroughly took fifteen minutes, so Sandy and I parked on the stools again and patiently sat back to watch and wait.

When he finished with Corrine and Dave's three blues, I passed over our two that he'd already measured and he lined them up in order. Finally, he sat back and rubbed his aching back.

'Unbelievable!' was his first response, 'I had hoped, as one does, but never dared to fully believe that all six would come together like this. I have done some research overnight and believe that perhaps I've found the origin of our beautiful pebbles, if you will excuse my slightly possessive expression.'

I raised my eyebrows. 'Well done and quick work. So you were right that they have come from a single large stone?'

'Indeed. It appears that in the 16th century, a very large pure blue diamond of some 93 carats, was found in India, and quickly made its way to the collection of a Maharaja. Although largely left uncut, some time after that it had a few basic facets ground onto it to pretty it up. It was not properly cut until the 18th century, after parties unknown stole it from the Maharaja. It re-appeared in the possession of a Dutch trader, who had acquired the stone under very dubious circumstances — and presumably to conceal the origin of the resulting diamonds, had commissioned the cutting. He had the large stone cut into six smaller stones of just over three carats each, and one larger one of 42 carats. None of the stones have ever been sighted in public since that time, until now. Of course, the 42-carat stone is still missing.'

He raised his eyebrows, 'Unless of course...?'

I laughed and shook my head, 'Sorry. We don't have that one, as nice as it would be. But how can you be sure that these are the same ones described in the records from so long ago?'

'Gem cutting records, even back that far, are much more detailed than anything else, so there is quite a lot of evidence that points toward these as being the same ones cut from that single, very large, stolen stone. It was too much to hope for that you had the main stone as well, but I must not be greedy. These six smaller ones will be more than enough and their weights are all just over 3 carats, although I've recorded them individually in the paperwork as Lots 1, 2 and 3. So, are your friends all happy for me to proceed as I explained yesterday?'

I nodded, 'Yep. No problem. I presume that there are some papers for us to sign to cover all this?'

'Yes. I'll just get the folder from the back room.'

As he made his way out back, I called out, 'By the way, our friends have two more stones from their collection they'd like you to look at and maybe try to sell.'

'One moment, young man. I'll just get these papers organised then I'll look at whatever it is that you have.'

I winked at Sandy, suspecting and hoping, that Mr Jacob was about to get another shock, as he came shuffling back, a new folder in his hand and began placing forms on the counter in front of us. Ten minutes later, we'd signed everything and received copies in a folder of our own, the six blues wrapped in order, placed in a new white glove-leather bag and locked in his modern, very high-tech safe.

'Excellent,' he beamed. 'I always like to get the paperwork correct. Saves a lot of time and bother later. Now, you said there was something else for me to look at?'

I casually dug the second small bag out of my shirt pocket and laid it on the counter.

'When I told our friends about the auction, they weren't sure if these could be included, or perhaps you could find a buyer from among your collector acquaintances.'

He untied the drawstring and tipped the contents out onto the white cloth. Instantly, the area was lit with deep red fire, flashes and beams bouncing off every surface like a disco-laser display. Mr Jacobs sat stunned for long moments, until he drew a wavering breath.

'You young people seem to have the uncanny knack of springing the most amazing surprises upon me. It's almost unfair for an old man to receive shocks like this, but I'll not complain too much in this case. Where did these come from?'

'No knowledge on the background, Mr Jacobs. Our friends acquired them along with the blues, some sundry whites and four large emeralds in a business deal. A man was under a lot of financial pressure to liquidate his holdings very quickly. They decided that they would hang onto the white diamonds and emeralds for now — our lady friend likes the look of the emeralds, but she may be in touch with you later about them.'

It was the cover story we'd come up with over drinks last night to allay suspicion that they were stolen.

Mr Jacobs couldn't take his eyes off the stunning red stones, still patiently, endlessly flashing their brilliant beauty as if secure in the knowledge that they were the rarest of the rare and as such, were utterly incomparable.

Several times, he reached out almost dreamily, and pushed at them with a stainless steel four-pronged picker, turning them so the flashing light display moved. Finally, he roused himself and weighed, examined, held high-tech probes against their impervious surfaces and carefully recorded all results onto the forms.

'They weigh 3.8 and 4.2 carats and like I said yesterday about the blues, I am completely overwhelmed by these stones. They share only one thing in common — their shade actually requires a new classification.'

Sandy looked puzzled, 'What do you mean by that?'

He smiled apologetically, 'I'm sorry. Once again I do not explain myself well. I said yesterday that the deeper the colour, the more the value rose. Well, there is a grading system to classify the shading of coloured stones and it ranges from Faint to Fancy Deep and Fancy Vivid.

Both the blues here, and now these reds, surpass any other stones before them in the saturation of colour that will not just create a new price point, but it's the classification that I believe will have to change just because of these eight stones.

I'm going to propose that they be classified as Intense Deep Vivid which, I believe, better describes the incredible intensity of colour. For these reds, I wouldn't even hazard a guess at what price they would fetch.

They will be the star of the auction, with the six blues as a very close second!'

We were all silent for a time after that information, so while Mr Jacob fetched more forms, we just looked at the amazing pair of beautiful red stones lying on their pure white bed.

Soon after, papers signed and copies in our folder, we were about to bid goodbye to Mr Jacobs, when he asked, 'If these are received as well as I expect, it is customary to assign them a name for identification purposes. Do you have such names in mind?'

I looked at Sandy, mentally communed for a moment, then said,' Oh let's call the Blues the *Firebird Blues*' and the Reds the '*Red Seekers*'! Will that do?'

He beamed happily. 'That will do extremely well and thank

you Sir and Madam for gracing my humble establishment. I am more excited and alive than I have been for a long time, and I feel great things will come from this most fruitful meeting!'

He then promised to keep us informed of every step in the process of placing the eight stones into auction.

It was only ten days later that Mr Jacobs contacted us to say that the photographs of the *Red Seekers* and *Firebird Blues*, that he'd sent to the prestigious Auction House had been received so enthusiastically that they had immediately decided to reprint the whole fifty-page full-colour glossy catalogue that had been ready for world-wide distribution, so that the new entries, along with a skilfully-written piece on both sets of stones could take the prominent first few pages.

Local representatives had already been to visit him, view the stones and take a series of high-resolution photographs for the brochure, then had taken the stones for exhaustive checks, which they passed perfectly. The representatives were beside themselves over the new entries, anticipating that record prices would be set in two weeks time.

The auction was scheduled to be held in London and while I expressed concern about the security for the stones when they were transported, Mr Jacobs and the Auction House representative assured me that it was a routine operation, happening several times every week without incident and that much more expensive shipments were commonplace.

On the day before the auction, the local branch of the Auction House invited the six of us to view proceedings on TV at their Sydney branch offices. I had to hastily arrange for Ellie, the Tavern manager and ex-girlfriend who knew the boat and Jasper very well, to feed the beasts and take them for a run on a sandbank each day we were away. I left *Firebird's* RIB tied up at the small boat landing beside the Tavern to make it easy for her to get out to them.

With all our travel and accommodation costs and

arrangements taken care of by the Auction House, we were flown First Class to Sydney and met up with Janice at the Airport, who brought her new man along. He was called Steve and of all things, was a Financial Advisor!

I was crass enough to pull her aside and ask if it was safe letting him in on her new fortune, but she assured me that he was wealthy in his own right and that she kept a tight rein on her money.

'But anyway, dearest Harry, I really don't know what you mean by a fortune and really, isn't this flying in just to watch an Auction on TV an awful lot of fuss over not much? I mean, it was lovely of Dave and Corrine to give us a diamond each, but it's only a little thing and isn't mounted in anything, although if we *can* sell it, the few extra thousand will be very welcome. I used to think that the girls' school fees were high, but that University! It's like a big black hole that is sucking in my bank account!'

I gave her one of my looks. 'You did actually look at the rock, didn't you?'

She looked abashed, 'Well no, as a matter of fact, I didn't. You'd told me it was coming, but I could hardly feel it in the padded bag, so put it aside to open later, but then something came up and I forgot about it until Sandy called. I did wonder why she sounded so excited, but I still didn't get around to opening the bag and taking a look, so after she called, I just stuck another address label on the bag and stuck it in an Express Post bag.'

Slightly exasperated with the dear lady, I patted her arm and said, 'Well. Let's just say that the colour makes it very rare and therefore rather more valuable than most.'

She beamed, 'Oh good! If it'll cover the next two Semesters fees, that really will be great! And as a bonus, I get to see all of you again!'

I gave up trying to get through to her at that point and decided to let events take their course.

We were all cossetted in a huge stretch limousine with

chauffer and put up at the best hotel in Darling Harbour. It was noted by some dry wit that with the fees the Auction House would make from the buyers of our two items alone, they could easily afford it.

I watched Steve as the talk between bonded friends who've shared life-threatening adversity washed around him, but either he was genuine or a very good actor, as he didn't even show a single wrong expression when talk of money was exchanged.

On auction day, we were escorted by a charming and beautiful hostess in a black cocktail dress, into a large very comfortable looking room with ten or twelve other customers who had major items in the sale. Endless supplies of the very best food and drink were ferried about by several pretty young ladies wearing extremely fetching German costumes with very short skirts, which together made the occasion akin to being at a Melbourne Cup party. There were small groups of large armchairs facing a matrix of TV screens that covered the entire end wall of the room, yet was still in full 4K resolution. A series of smaller inset screens showed the crowd assembled in the Auction rooms in London, most holding their numbered paddles, as well as several employees manning the computer screens for on-line bidding and others manning a bank of telephones for the phone-in's.

The items expected to sell for the least money were up first, with the major ticket items like ours, held until last. That gave everybody a chance to get quite pissy on someone else's booze.

A large, florid-faced gentleman, was attracted to Sandy who wore very tight jeans and displayed her delightfully bra-less boobs contained more or less inside one of my checked shirts that looked heaps better on her than it ever did on me, with the shirt tails tied across her tight, tanned midriff. She'd artfully left it unbuttoned most of the way to the lower tie, a cunning move that distracted most of the males in the room, so they forgave her casual dressing style.

When he could tear his eyes off her, our large new friend

casually informed us that he'd entered several paintings, including two Picasso's, a van Gogh and a Monet. He had a wonderful time peering at her lovely boobs, one or the other of which was usually displayed in its beautifully-shaped entirety through the gaping front of her shirt, while I summoned a steady supply of drinks from the serving wenches and chatted with the picture man's delightful and much younger wife who soon showed that she was the brains of the outfit and had most of the money as well.

We refrained from saying what our items were and it was apparently considered very poor taste to ask.

We were all somewhat pissed little possums by the time the auction got around to our new best friend's paintings and when the dust settled, he was reasonably pleased by the final bids. *'And so he should be, I thought, considering the final figure with its whacking great string of zero's'.*

Then came the set of blue diamonds, announced as the *'Firebird Blues'* and the tension rose among our group, with even Sandy's friend working out that these were ours. The auctioneer made a great job of talking the likely provenance up and bidding opened briskly. Apart from Janice who was still thinking a couple of thousand per stone, the rest of us knew that the base value was around the seven million mark for all six, so when the bids sailed past that figure without even slowing down, Sandy gave a soft, almost orgasmic moan and gripped my arm very tightly with a trembling hand. I had Janice on my other side, and her reaction, even to the opening call by the auctioneer, was almost comical.

I thought she was going to faint when bidding slowed briefly at fifteen million as several previously keen bidders dropped out, shaking their heads in disappointment, before advancing more sedately, but steadily, with two phone bidders fighting it out to top the bidding at a record twenty-one million, five hundred thousand.

Conscious of our surroundings, I settled for giving Sandy, Janice and Corrine a hug and shaking Dave's hand. Sandy and Janice had to sit down hugging each other, crying and looking very flushed and a little disoriented.

Then came the *Red Seekers* and although there was no provenance to even speculate upon, the auctioneer made much of their incredible colour, the new colour classification they required as proposed by Mr Jacobs, and which was immediately adopted by diamond organisations worldwide and of course, their rarity. He claimed that these were the first new reds to be found for a hundred years!

The bidding was started at five million and with only four bidders, moved smartly up through ten million where it slowed as two dropped out, the anonymous phone bidder pushing the lone bidder actually present hard, until bids stalled at twelve million for a short time, but just as the auctioneer called all done for the last time, a paddle was raised to lock the final bid in at 15 million, five hundred thousand for the pair.

Corrine and Dave let out big breaths each and got silly grins on their faces as we all congratulated each other. Back in the limousine, Sandy said quietly as the champagne cork popped and bubbly spilled, 'So what did I make out of that?'

'Well, my lovely, sexy millionairess, less the 1% that Mr Jacob takes, your share assuming that we split things evenly which would be sensible, comes to around three million, five hundred and forty-seven thousand, one hundred and seventy dollars. Welcome to the Millionaires Club!'

She gave a shriek of delight and gave me an awkward hug and a very passionate kiss, before quietly passing that news onto Janice who was back under control and tending to ignore Steve for the moment.

Looking over at Dave and Corrine, she said, 'I can't thank you both enough for this! This is one hell of a gift!'

Dave waved her thanks aside, 'Avoiding 20 years in prison was a pretty big gift to us, so we reckon that we're square, Anyway, we just picked up twenty-six and a quarter mill ourselves, so on top of what we already have, we're not going to be hurting for funds in the foreseeable future!'

That started a round of hilarious laughter that had the chauffer looking back with a grin on his face, probably used to some happy customers leaving the auction house post-sale.

EPILOGUE

1 ... Sandy took Harry's advice and used his smart, young beach-shirt wearing accountant, to invest her money and kept quiet about the outcome of the Sydney trip. She stayed with her job and lived happily with Harry, Jasper and Krazy on *Firebird*.

2 ... Janice sent Steve back to Melbourne by himself straight after the auction, and stayed on *Firebird* for a week during which she renewed her relationship with both Harry and Sandy. After returning home, she and Sandy talked on the phone most days. When Steve tried to push Janice into allowing him access to her funds so, 'he could invest them more effectively', Janice politely but firmly told him that their relationship was permanently over.

3 ... One week after the 'Battle of Fitzroy Reef', the first boatload of happy snorkel-suckers and scuba divers arrived at the reef on a day trip. As the Skipper negotiated the narrow entrance to the lagoon against the last of the swirling, boiling, ebbing tide stream, screams erupted from the upper deck where a group had armed themselves with binoculars and cameras with telephoto lenses, hoping to see something interesting.

When deckhands hurriedly climbed up to see what the fuss was about, they saw that the tourists had certainly got what they wanted! Barely 20 metres west of the channel, on the outer edge of the reef, a stark white human skull was speared by an up-thrusting forked branch of stag-horn coral, with both tips of the fork poking out of holes punched through either side of the skull top, giving it the appearance of having grown horns! Equally bizarrely, the lower jaw, complete with teeth, was still in place, held securely, but in a slightly open position by another stalk of the beautiful, but razor-sharp coral, giving the whole skull the appearance of delivering a grinning, mocking warning to those humans who had the temerity to venture to this place of violent death.

The usually powerful attraction of the warm, gin-clear water and abundant marine life was additionally marred by the unusual presence of an enormous female Tiger shark who closely followed the boat into the lagoon and slowly circled it, even after they secured the boat to a permanent mooring buoy. Despite the marvellous photo opportunities offered by the 'Grey Lady's' close-up presence, the unprecedented event put such a dampener on all diving activities that the Skipper and Tour Director hastily decided to get the flock outta there and head for One Tree Island, 6 nautical miles north, in the hope that enough diving could take place to avoid a mass refund.

The huge Tiger escorted the boat out through the narrow entrance, turning back only when she saw that they were leaving the vicinity. Such are legends born!

While dive tours to Fitzroy reef remained depressingly unpopular and seats unsold, one enterprising Tour Company promoted the 'Devil Skull and Tiger Shark Tour' and found that it couldn't keep up with demand, mainly from Chinese and other Asian tourists who returned to their homelands telling tales of a race of crazy Aussies who lived in a country where almost everything that crawled, walked, flew or swam was (a) lethal and (b) actively looking for new humans to overwhelm.

Several official attempts were made to retrieve the skull for forensic testing, but after the third case of severe lacerations that included an excessively friendly and very close visit from the 'Grey Lady of Fitzroy Reef', all official attempts to retrieve the skull were abandoned, to the relief of the 'Devil Skull and Tiger Shark Tour Company' with their brand-new, three million-dollar catamaran.

4 ... Etta Jones was kept in an induced coma for a week while her system was brought back to something approaching normal. Henry Jones stayed in Gladstone the whole time and was present when she regained consciousness. He was made to remain 2 metres away from the bed and was under the close scrutiny of a Police officer at all times. Henry commented to his minder that Etta seemed to be still rather 'out of it'.

Several days later, the Doctors gave approval for him to tell her about the demise of all her Club, apart from Marie, and the elimination of the boat and all the other bikies. He was heard to tell her that both the Undertakers and the Zombies were badly affected by the losses as well and he had commenced talks with Brad Edwards about the possibility of amalgamating the two groups.

As he spoke openly to Etta, he was also an excellent source of information to the Police on the activities of the Brisbane Clubs and their attitude to the loss of the drug shipment. That attitude had changed considerably since the near-total destruction of the raiding force, with most of the individual members openly saying that they weren't keen to go and head-butt a small, well-trained and equipped group that could inflict so much damage on other humans.

5 ... The only exception to the quickly spreading feeling of 'leave them alone and maybe we'll survive' was the Gladstone-based family of the three bikies who had run the boat and were all brothers. Their large, extended family, who lived mostly on the proceeds of various criminal enterprises, with many other brothers, sisters, cousins, etc. were still incensed about the elimination of their kin and demanded vengeance of the harshest kind.

However, the more they screamed for blood, the more support for them dropped until they were virtually on their own in wanting to strike back.

Despite the strict ban on strike-back imposed by their Club

President, three of the biggest, dumbest and most vocal of the bunch of dysfunctional relatives were determined to achieve payback and were heard to announce that the next morning they were heading to the Gold Coast to track down and eliminate the small group that had killed three of their family.

The matter was resolved in a rather final way when, next morning shortly after dawn, two fishermen at a Tannum Sands beach at the mouth of the Boyne River were casting into the outgoing tide flow hoping to pick up a big barramundi hovering around the mouth of the river on the edge of the discoloured water.

Noticing ripples of disturbed water around what looked like a small bundle of weed floating down the river toward the entrance just on the surface, one of the men cast his lure close to the disturbance, but the hooks snagged on something just under the surface. Trying to reel in, the man felt extreme drag, although there wasn't the expected wriggling of a hooked fish.

Slowly he managed to drag the mass closer to the shore where they were shocked to find three bodies joined at wrists and ankles with nylon cable-ties, in a strange, three-pointed star arrangement. The three males, who were liberally covered with tattoos which aided identification, had suffered extreme blunt trauma to the heads and a single, small calibre gunshot wound to the back of the head of each had ensured death.

6 ... Dave and Corrine on *Seeker* decided to stay on the Gold Coast for the winter, much to Harry and Sandy's delight who for a week, were joined by two delightful young ladies from Victoria that they'd come to know so well, and who took time off from their Uni studies to enjoy the Queensland sun. During that time, the two boats moved down to Moreton bay, spending time around Horseshoe Bay and Myora, fishing, swimming and generally lazing around.

Dave and Corrine had no fixed timetable and admitted that

the recent caper was, 'very exciting' and 'beat the hell out of pandering to the stupid demands of overpaid, stuck-up wannabe boating fuck-wits!' There was even talk of basing themselves permanently on the Coast, 'just in case anything exciting happens that requires the services of the Special Marine Task Force'.

7 ... After a great deal of discussion at several meetings, Brad Edwards and the remaining fifteen members of the Zombie Eaters OMC, decided to join forces with the equally depleted Undertakers OMC. There was a great deal of very spirited discussion as to who should be in overall charge, but in the end, Brad graciously conceded that Henry was indeed the Undertaker with a much more imposing and intimidating profile, although they agreed to share decision making. As both leaders had lost their best men and Lieutenants, there was a lot of re-shuffling of positions but in general the two groups merged remarkably peacefully and got on with their various moneymaking enterprises, most of which were actually legal.

Relations with the Southport Police and Inspector Greg James remained reasonably amicable, despite the few illegal enterprises still carried out by the OMC, a happy situation that increased considerably once Brad Edwards was helping with the decision-making process.

As Greg had earned the grudging respect of Brad and Henry through his fair and reasonable handling of the various problems that arose during the events, meetings at the Benbow Tavern became quite regular. He took the opportunity to pass on the information that the 'vigilante' or 'pirate' group had come out into the open and been given official status by the Queensland Police by forming them into the 'Special Marine Strike Force', making the subtle hint that any more payback attacks would not only be hitting directly at an operational Police unit, but would probably suffer the same fate as all the other attempts. Despite the relatively cordial relations and regular meetings, Greg continued to get anonymous but very helpful phone calls from a person with an electronically disguised voice, passing on detailed information on the more private doings within the local Club and within the other OMC's in Southern Queensland.

8 ... When Etta Jones had recovered sufficiently to stand trial, she was charged with a range of offences to do with possession of drugs, weapons and explosives. However, due to what seemed to be a permanently debilitated state, she received a greatly reduced sentence at a minimum-security prison. That ruling was conditional that she was never again an active member of an OMC.

On her release 12-months later, she moved to the Gold Coast to live with her brother, Henry. Word filtered through from the prison system that she had never fully recovered her mental acuity and had a degree of amnesia for the period leading up to the disastrous boat venture.

Although it was possible to fake the symptoms, psychiatrists pronounced her amnesia genuine, which went a long way to reassuring everyone involved that she wasn't going to do anything stupid, like start another vendetta anytime soon. Her general demeanour changed from the 'psycho bitch' persona to that of a far more pleasant and relaxed person who was actually pleasant to have around.

Because of the amalgamation of the two bikie Clubs, Brad Edwards visited the Undertakers HQ quite frequently and partly due to her changed personality, began seeing more of Etta. The interest he'd once expressed in her had never waned and it wasn't long before, much to Henry's disgust, Brad and Etta were a regular couple.

9 ... Henry Jones's burning hatred of the 'pirate group' and their leader, who had been responsible for so much carnage amongst the ranks of his and Brad's bikie Clubs, took a long time to settle. His reconsideration process was accelerated; firstly by having his sister, to whom he was very deeply attached and absolutely adored, back with him, complete with an obviously improved personality. The second part of the process were the reports he finally received from Marie, the only other survivor of the disastrous raid at Fitzroy Reef, and the only one who retained a full and vivid memory of those dreadful few days and nights. She made a full recovery from her encounters with the coral and the large female Tiger shark, and while she harboured some resentment for being kept handcuffed and naked for so long, she admitted to Henry that the 'pirate group' had in fact saved Etta's life with their prompt and radical first aid treatment. That treatment had even greatly reduced the level of scarring both girls now displayed, although the marks were fading quite quickly now they were back on proper diets.

The penultimate end to the protracted hate spell came at one of the semi-regular meetings with the Police at the Benbow Tavern when Henry requested that he and Etta be allowed to meet with the leader of the 'pirate group'. That historic meeting took place a few days later under heavy supervision, and since Brad Edwards and Etta were almost inseparable, he was there as well when Greg James introduced them to an impassive Harry Stevens who had little to say, but was at least not hostile.

Henry and Brad had to work to control their emotions, but Henry finally thanked Harry very sincerely for his efforts to save his sister's life. It was obvious that they'd never be friends, although Etta bore no grudge and also thanked Harry politely and shook his hand.

10 ... Marie returned to a quiet life in Maryborough, getting a 9-to-5 job like anybody else, happy to sink back into obscurity, once the admittedly lucrative offers of nude photo shoots, adult films and 'celebrity' TV appearances slowly diminished.

11 ... The turmoil within the other SE Queensland bikie Clubs also slowly subsided, although the level of mistrust that had been created between the Clubs when the drug shipment was stolen persisted undiminished.

12 ... Dave and Corrine finally decided to make the Gold Coast their home base, although they held off on the purchase of any real estate, as had been suggested. Like Harry, they were happy and comfortable with their boating lifestyle and while they could easily afford the outrageous berthing fees charged by the Yacht Club, they made the Club an offer it couldn't refuse and bought their berth. They mentioned their idea to Harry about upgrading *Seeker* to a larger boat, as in *Seeker II*, but were still thinking about it.

They even allowed one of the Coast's main helicopter operators to talk them into the occasional high-priced day charter to Moreton bay, seeing as they could do the run in around 40 minutes each way. Nothing on the Gold Coast, apart from a few race boats, were as fast and this allowed them to be very choosey as to what work they did take on.

They had some trouble containing the enthusiasm of the charismatic owner of the Tour Company, but Corrine managed it without raising a sweat!

When the working members of the 'Special Marine Strike Force' had days off at the same time, both boats made the trip to Moreton Bay to catch up with their Naturist Club friends and re-visit some of the more tranquil areas, gaining a greater appreciation for this beautiful area of the Queensland coast.

13 ... At an Interstate conference on Outlaw Motorcycle Clubs, Greg James and Bob Casey were invited to deliver the opening address and were quizzed on the role the 'Special Marine Strike Force' had played in the spectacular success of the recent operation that had become part of the various Police Academy teachings. Details of the previous operation in Victorian and

Tasmanian waters were still shrouded in mystery, but enough had leaked to ensure that the members of the 'Strike Force' were held in the highest regard.

When asked if the 'Strike Force' could be made available to assist with marine-related problems in other States, Bob Casey indicated that although no decision had been made in that regard, any request would probably be met with a favourable reply.